to be a FAE QUEEN

to be a FAE QUEEN

TRICIA COPELAND

to be a FAE QUEEN

by Tricia Copeland

Edited by Jo Michaels
Proofread by Jennifer Oberth
Interior Formatting by Jo Michaels
all of Indie Books Gone Wild

Cover by Shower of Schmidt Designs
Published by True Bird Publishing LLC, Superior, CO

Borean
Elita
N
NW
NE
W
E
SW
SE
S

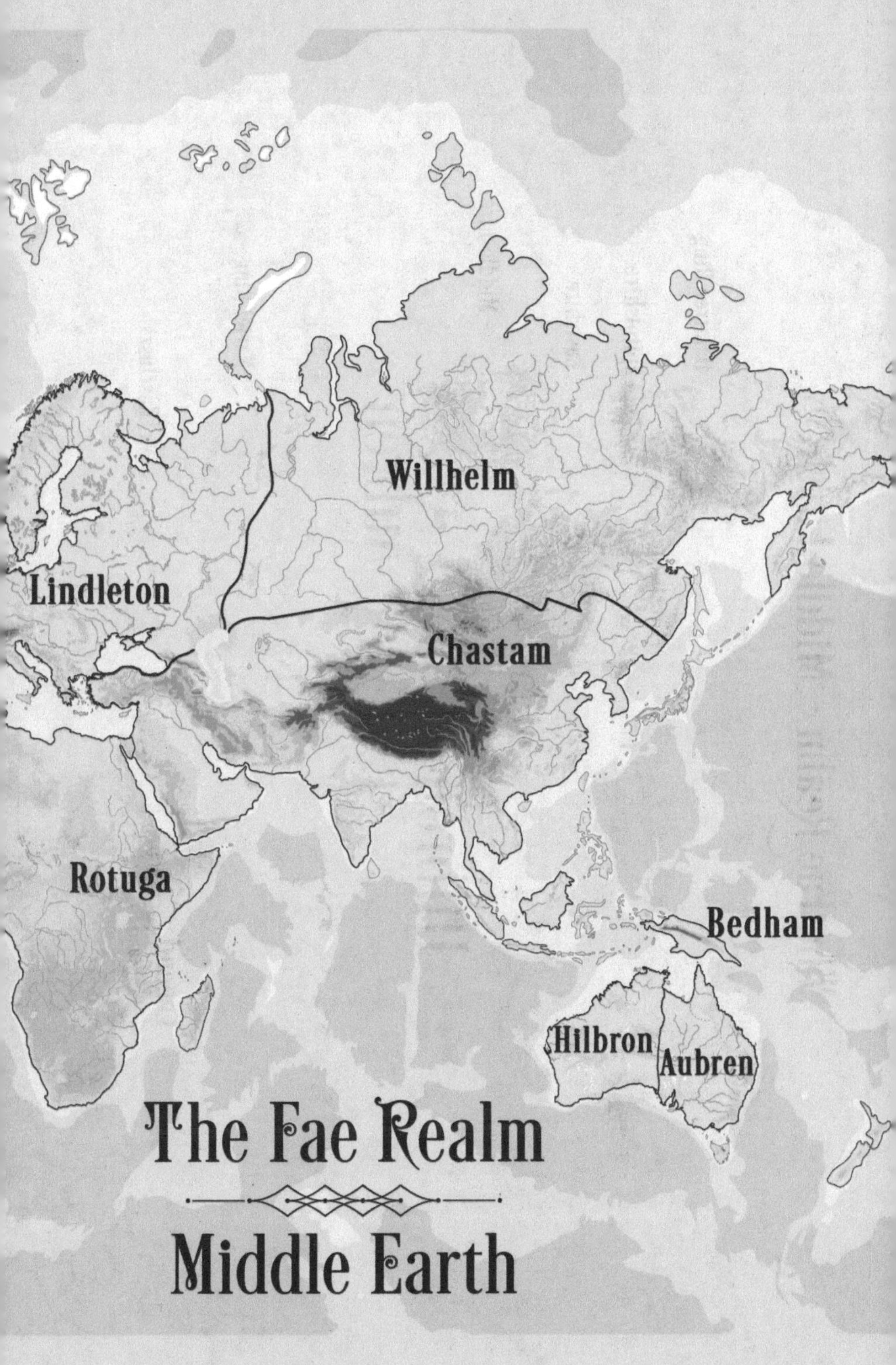

Willhelm
Lindleton
Chastam
Rotuga
Bedham
Hilbron
Aubren
The Fae Realm
Middle Earth

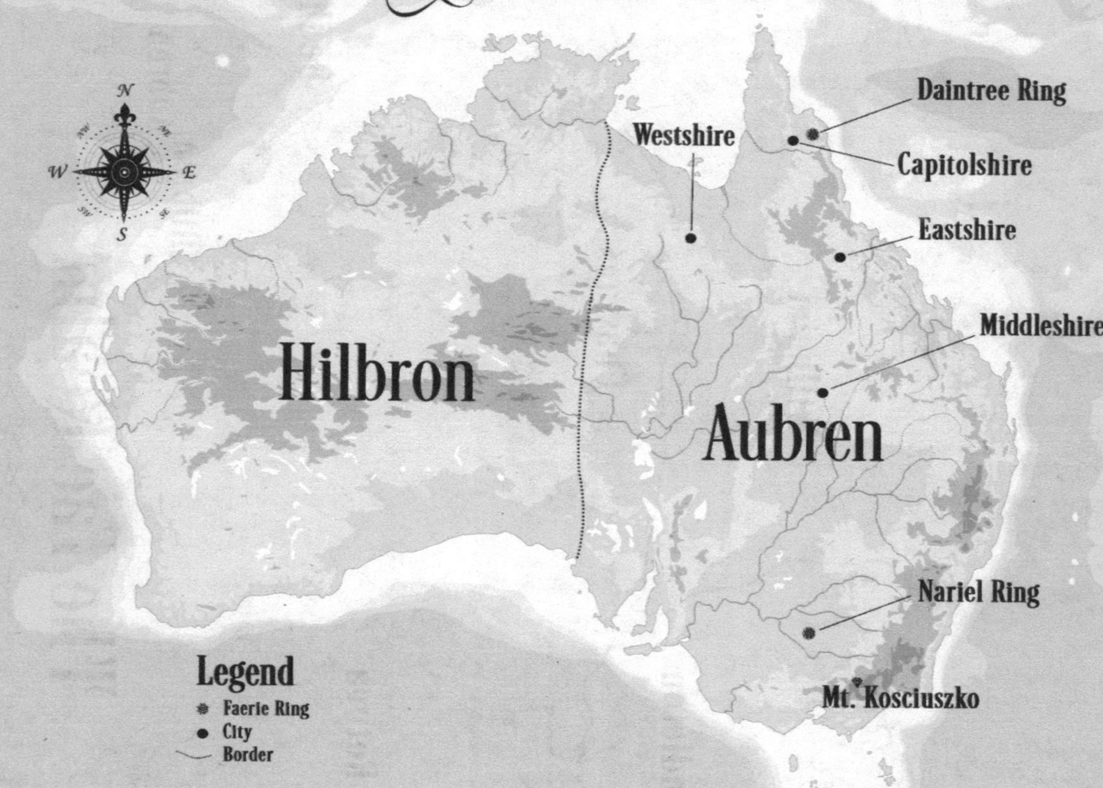

The Fae Realm ~ Middle Earth
Daintree Ring
Westshire
Capitolshire
Eastshire
Middleshire
Hilbron
Aubren
Nariel Ring
Mt. Kosciuszko
N
NW
NE
W
E
SW
SE
S
Legend
Faerie Ring
City
Border

Heaven
Upper Earth
Faerie Ring
The Fae Realm ~ Middle Earth
Passage Between Realms
Lower Earth - Sheol

Chapter 1

I GLANCE UP AT MY CRYSTALS AS the last rays of the setting sun cause splotches of amber to dot the stone walls and ceiling. It is my favorite, yet saddest, time of day. I dread and cherish my next task in equal measure and linger at the window to relish the last bit of sun on the meadow.

Forcing myself to turn from the scene, I raise my wings. Light from the window shines through them, causing the room to glow with a slight green tinge.

Crossing to my doors and opening them wide, I scan my ceiling to savor the dimming light illuminating my prisms. I close and open my wings, rising into the air and exiting my room. Flying through the castle to my parents' chambers, as I do every night, I alight in their study.

Mother sits in front of the fire, harp on her right, Father on her left. Seeing his chin dip, I approach Mother.

I kiss her cheek. "Mother, will you play for us, or shall I?"

She blinks, and I think I see the edges of her mouth turn up just a hair. Sitting on the hearth before her, I await a reply. *Had I imagined a slight smile, or was it wishful thinking?* Her gaze shifts to her lap.

"Perhaps you could play, Titania. Your mother loves hearing you." Father stands and wraps his hands around her shoulders.

Mother's eyes stay trained on the flames in front of her while I slide the stool to the harp and begin a tune. After years of lessons, I play well, but nothing like Mother used to. She could draw tears from a crowd with one pluck of a string. Father retakes his seat, and I note his furrowed brow. Laying a hand across the strings, I halt my song.

"Father, is something wrong? Surely, Mother will…" I swallow before uttering the same hope-filled words I repeat every night. *She will be better when her mourning is over. One year per lost child seems appropriate.* Several years have passed since my four brothers were slaughtered while fighting the kobold army. Three years since we have heard her voice or gotten more than a blink of her eyes in response to kisses; hugs; condolences; pleas; and sometimes, on my part, tear-filled rage at her inability to see I not only lost my brothers but my mother as well.

I thought one of her sisters would stay after the official mourning period. I loved having my cousins here, but each of the aunts crumbled under the duress of Mother's catatonic state. Father offered their husbands prominent positions in the army, but after the prior massacre, even the promise of wealth and admiration would not sway them to stay in our kingdom, and they sailed north, over the sea, to their home in Bedham. As much as I wanted to, I could not place blame. Each kingdom faced their share of foe, but none proved more dangerous than the kobold.

"Many thoughts weigh on my mind." Father's voice brings me out of my self-pity.

"Please, tell me."

"Finish your tunes first. They bring me joy."

Not knowing how else to help, I begin a new song.

He works hard touring the countryside with his guards, hearing grievances of our people, and keeping the accounts balanced for the kingdom. I worry he is lonely with only his advisors to converse with.

Once the ballad ends, I spin my stool to face him. Taking a deep breath, I wait for him to speak. He smooths his beard and begins the story of the kobold. How they live in caves and hollows between our realm and Lower Earth.

"Father, I know the histories. I am not a child anymore. Please, just tell me what troubles you."

I guess that he may not wish to dwell on all we lost either, especially as we try to keep our nights together happy and carefree. With my brothers gone and my mother's condition, he and I only have each other. His two brothers and their sons were killed in the battle as well, leaving us the last remaining royals of Aubren, me the only heir to the throne.

Seeing Father raise his hand to his beard brings me back to the worries at hand.

He spins a lock of the curly hair between his fingers. "You will be Queen one day. I guess I cannot shield you forever. I just know the anxiety the memories cause you."

Remembering the purple wings and gnarled claws of the beast that tried to kill me, my heart rate rises. "The kobold have returned?"

Staring at the flames, he rubs his hand down his pant leg. "Several anchor crystals that support our Faerie Ring have disappeared. We believe a mutant kobold took them. Soldiers found footprints near a cave in the wood on the eastern side of the kingdom."

My heart thuds and mind reels with the implications of the missing crystals. The Faerie Rings create portals between our realm, known as Middle Earth, and Upper Earth. If the anchors cannot be replaced, the ring dies, the portal closes, and we will be cut off from all that is above: sun, rain, and winds to clear our air. With no light or water, our plants will die and our animals will starve, and with no access to Upper Earth, we will die with them.

"Mutant kobold? Why do you call them that? Do we not have multiples of the crystals? Why not replace them?"

"We found footprints in the wood, but the Ring Keeper was not alerted to the kobolds' presence. Somehow, they stole the anchors without being detected. We believe either they have bred with a magickal being or were aided by magick. And yes, you are correct. There is one additional set of crystals set aside for each ring. But we cannot risk these being taken as well."

"So, gather a group of soldiers to investigate. Surely the kobold did not just disappear."

"I cannot send my fae into the caverns below. It is too dangerous. Too many evil beings lurk about. I have posted guards at the cave entrance where we saw the footprints. If they come again, we will be ready."

My heart races, and sweat beads on my forehead. I sense the first warning signs of one of my episodes. I picture my crystals hanging from my ceiling and take a slow, deep breath. *Crystals. If there is anyone better at finding crystals than I, I doubt it.*

"I am good at finding crystals. I could learn which we need and search the streams for new anchors. The water brings them down from the mountains."

Father shakes his head. "It is too dangerous. I do not have enough warriors to guard you, guard the Faerie Ring, and watch for the kobold."

"There are far too many fae for the kobold to overtake the whole realm. What do they hope to gain?"

Father paces to the hearth. "A foothold perhaps? They have attempted it before. It is not unprecedented. Perhaps their numbers have grown too vast for the caves. They seem to be getting desperate. Either that, or there is a darker force at work here."

"Do you really believe they have developed magickal abilities?"

A chime sounds from the clock on the mantle. My eyes cut to Mother, wondering if she registers our conversation, holds opinions, or even cares her daughter and her husband need her.

"I have kept you too long. You need your rest for your studies and training." Father crosses to me. He leans over and kisses my forehead as he does every night, but his smile does not reach his eyes.

"I want to help. If there is anything I could do—"

"I have my generals and advisors. You need not worry."

"Okay, goodnight, Father." I wrap my arms around him and squeeze his shoulders.

Approaching Mother, I bend over and take her hand. "Goodnight, Mother. I love you."

Her stare does not move from the fireplace. Still, I pull her to me and kiss her cheek. Fighting the water pooling in my eyelids, I beat my wings and take to the air. I fly out the door, maneuvering through the halls to my room. I click my door shut and press my back to the soft wood. Heart pounding and breaths becoming jagged, I imagine the worst. *What if these kobold and their new magick steal all the anchors? What if they overcome our troops?* I slide to the floor and stare at my crystals, trying to control my breathing. The cool stone beneath me calms my nerves. *Father will figure this out. He always has in the past. We lost many in the last battle but were victorious in the end.*

Rising, I cross to my dressing table, brush my hair, and dress for bed. Carrying my candle to my bedside, I slip under the blankets. I pull them up tight around my neck and study my crystals overhead. The faerie crosses are not the most popular because they are mud brown. Some of them form diagonals, but I keep only the most perfect, right-angled versions. I polish each face so they reflect the light. The candlelight bounces off those above me. They protect their owner from bad luck and connect the spiritual planes. My brothers helped me start the collection and it helps me feel connected to them. Beginning my ritual of counting each crystal, I pray, as I do each night, to grow strong and wise enough to make Father proud. I shall be seventeen in just over a year and ready to take a position on Father's council if they will have me. If not, I plan to find a way to prove myself.

I bite my lip as my pulse quickens. *How am I, an anxiety-ridden girl, to rule a nation? Do I even want to follow in Father's footsteps? Have the weight of a kingdom on my shoulders? Perhaps I should focus on searching for a distant relative, someone untouched by memories of past battles. There are more pressing issues,* I admonish my thoughts. *The Faerie Ring* must *be preserved.* That should be my focus.

Sleep evades me as I toss over ideas for helping Father. Giving up, I slide from my covers and slip on a robe. I take to the air and weave through the halls to the library. There, I search for texts on the Faerie Ring. Arms loaded, I make my way back to my room, dropping the books on the bed. I read through each one, making notes on descriptions of the anchor crystals. Studying the texts until deep in the night, I fall asleep and dream of the stones, guards, and mutant kobold.

⸺◈◈◈⸺

I WAKE TO THE SOUND OF BIRDS calling, not the normal chirps of morning but ominous tones of premonition. Sitting up, I note the time and wonder why my curtains are not open. No breakfast tray sits on my table. I have slept well past mealtime, nearly till mid-morning, yet little sunlight reaches through the slits in the drapes. Throwing off my covers, I race to each window and sweep the fabric back. Muted light greets me, and I peer out over the orchard, noting the dull green of the leaves and somber, grey sky. My breath catches in my lungs, and I bolt to the door. Flinging open one panel, I stop short.

Alfreda stands, one hand balancing my breakfast platter and the other over her heart. "Blessed be! You scared the life out of me."

"Has another crystal been taken from the Ring?"

"Well, good morning to you, too. But that is not for you to worry your pretty head about. Your father does not want to alarm you. He ordered me not to draw your curtains."

"Did he think I would not notice? I am not a child. Were more crystals taken by the kobold?" I put my hands on my hips and glower at her, astonished they thought something like this could be kept from me.

"Nasty creatures." She skirts around me to the table, setting the tray down. "Goodness, what is going on? Where did all these books come from?"

I flit to my bed and gather the texts. "I thought I could help Father by studying the crystals of the Faerie Ring."

"Eat your breakfast. Your father ordered that you stay within the castle walls."

"What about my walk in the wood with Mother?"

Alfreda cups her hand on my cheek. "I know your pleasures are few and far between. With the threat from the mutant kobold, your father's fae are spread thin. He does not have enough soldiers to watch for the kobold *and* guard you."

"I am not a child. I can take my bow."

"Dear"—Alfreda shakes her head as she backs to the door—"do as you are told. Your father has enough worries without thinking of you being in harm's way."

Inhaling, I dig my fingers into my palms, hardening my resolve. I hate being coddled. I am fifteen, almost sixteen, not a youngling who needs to be protected. Slumping in my chair, I pull the breakfast tray to me. While I chew, I count my crystals. My eyes trace the pattern on the ceiling, starting with the outermost circle and following the concentric rings to the center. One thousand. A smile spreads across my face, and I release my breath. Saying a silent prayer to the goddesses, I snatch the last berry from my plate.

I slip on a top and some walking pants and take wing in the direction of Mother's chambers. She sits in front of a mirror, a lady brushing the long strands. The handmaid hands me the brush, and I rake it through Mother's soft locks. Muted rays from the window cause her straw-colored hair to glow.

"Your hair shines like the sun today, Mother. We will be walking in the garden and orchard instead of the wood. The apples are ripening, and we may find a tasty one."

Studying our images in the mirror, I remember how she used to braid my hair and wind it atop my head. We look so different, and I think it odd how we contrast each other—her with blue eyes and light hair, and me with golden eyes and dark mahogany hair like Father's. Thornton favored Father as well, but my brother kept his hair and beard so short it did not seem a prominent feature. Garrison's and Bryce's coloring matched hers. I picture their light beards in my mind and how Garrison doted on me, teaching me to hunt in the woods. Hair the color of strawberries graced Rigel's head, and I almost laugh thinking of how our older brothers teased him. Seeing Mother's stoic eyes in the glass, I refocus on the task.

I lift her arm, tucking it in mine, and lead her to the garden. My bare feet savor the feel of the smooth, cool pebbles, but the dim light above me causes me grief. The mutant kobold must be stopped. Still, I force myself to walk every trail with Mother and wind to the orchard. Mother's arm twitches, and her torso shivers.

I wrap my arm around her back. "I will take you to your room. I do not want you to catch cold."

Leaving her with a lady, I take wing back to the apple trees. No noise from the castle reaches the glen, and I land between the branches. Even with the threat of the kobold, I relish the soft grass under my feet. I hear a crackling sound behind me and jump into the air.

A limb rustles, and I project my voice. "Who is there?"

A soldier emerges from behind the branches. "Forgive me, Princess. I am Foster."

"What are you doing here?"

"They sent me to watch over you."

"Why are you not guarding the crystals or watching the caves for the kobold? And why were you hiding?"

His strawberry-blond lashes flutter as he blinks, and red-tinged bangs swish over his forehead as he shakes his head. "They sent me to guard you, but I was not to be seen."

"Well, you have not done a very good job. Are you even old enough to be a soldier?" I try to ignore his large green eyes, squared chin, and muscled chest.

He broadens his shoulders, and his wings, white with umber streaks, spread out. "I am seventeen."

"How long have you been in the army?"

"Three months." He lowers his wings, and I note the gold-tinged edges, wondering if they shimmer in the sun.

I roll my eyes. "I guess that means they do not believe me to be in any real danger." *If Father sent Foster with the hope I may be distracted by a handsome boy, Father will be disappointed.*

He holds up his bow. "I have this."

Shaking my head, I spin away from him. "Throw it to me if you spot something dangerous. I never miss. Do not call me Princess or Your Highness. My name is Titania. And stay at the border between the garden and the orchard. I prefer to be alone."

"But—"

Before he can utter another word, I charge him, snatching the bow from his hand and quiver from his back. I cock an arrow and release it. Some hundred feet away, it lands in the dead center of an apple, ripping it from its branch and projecting the fruit to the ground beyond.

When I meet his gaze, his spring-green eyes lock on mine. "Yes, Your High… Umm, Titania."

He speeds away, and I secure the bow and quiver on my back. It is much bigger than mine, and the weight of the weapon feels odd, but I decide I like it. Adjusting the two shoulder straps, I realize they hold the bag in place better than my sling. I shall ask Alfreda to have someone fashion a similar pack for myself.

With the knowledge that Foster watches me, I cannot relax but still pace through each row, pondering how I may help Father. There seems to be little I can do from the confines of the castle walls. I circle back to the orchard's exit, retrieve the fallen apple, and take a bite of its flesh.

"Here." I toss the quiver and bow to Foster as I cross into the garden. "Thank you."

Weaving through the bushes, I sense Foster trailing me. I pledge to ignore him and make my way to my first class, history. With Foster by the door and my worry for the Faerie Ring, it is hard to concentrate. The school master reprimands me but sends me along for my fencing and music lessons.

Foster's presence feels smothering, and while it fuels me to swing my blade harder, the harp strings and our ears fare worse. Returning to my room to dress for the evening meal, I draw a bath. I catch sight of my bow in the corner and wonder if I may be of some use to Father as a soldier. Perhaps I could dress in their armor, and no one would be the wiser. Father retains hundreds of warriors. *What is one more archer? But you probably know the woods and stream better than anyone else.*

The evening passes, as most of them do, with dinner in the small hall with Alfreda and Father's Army General, Kane, dining with us, and my session with Mother and Father.

⋙⋘

WHEN MY EYES OPEN THE next morning, I sense a chill, a darkness that pierces my bones, and my shoulders shudder. The air smells odd, as though full of dank, moist dirt.

I scan my room. The curtains have been drawn back, and muted sunlight produces a slight glow. My tray of nuts, berries, and fruit sits next to my bed.

Shrugging off the unsettling feeling, I sit up and transfer the plate to my lap. As I place a berry in my mouth, I lift my eyes to the crystals. *One, two, three.* Halfway round the first ring, I freeze. *One is gone.* My breath catches. *This cannot be. Are others missing?* I continue tracing around the circles. Two-thirds in, another is absent. When I get to the center, I spring up to the ceiling. My favorite crystal, the one Garrison and I found on the bank of the river when I was eleven, is gone.

Shooting to the exit, I throw open my doors and run smack into Foster. "How long have you been here?"

"I took over watch at sunrise."

"Well, whoever guarded last night failed." I cringe at the thought that one of those huge, dirty kobolds was in my room. "Three of my crystals are missing."

I speed down the hall with Foster close behind. Swinging open the doors to my parents' quarters, I find them seated at the breakfast table.

"Three of my crystals have been taken. Someone, *something* stole them in the night."

Father drops his fork, and it clinks on his charger as he stands. "What?"

My eyes dart to Mother, hoping for some reaction to the scene. Her blank stare holds to her plate.

"Are you sure? I mean, you have a lot of crystals. I do not see how you would notice three missing." Father bends to retrieve his napkin.

I zip to him, hating that he would question me and that I may have to admit to my odd routine in front of Foster. "The center one, the crystal I found with Garrison, is gone. Plus"—I cut my eyes to Foster—"I count them twice a day. A thousand. There were a thousand when I went to sleep last night. There are only nine hundred ninety-seven now. The center one and two others are missing. I could tell something was off the moment I woke up. The air smelled foul. It was one of those mutant kobold. I know it."

Foster steps towards us. "A guard was at your door all night. I replaced him. Were your windows locked?"

My rage erupts anew. "Yes! I checked them. Perhaps the guard fell asleep."

Father rubs his beard. "Did you see footprints? Anything out of place?"

I shake my head.

"I will have a team come to your room to investigate."

The thought of huge guards rifling around my private sanctuary makes my stomach turn. "No. I will not have soldiers stomping through my room. I will figure out what happened to the crystals myself."

I dart from my parents' chamber and race through the halls back to my room. Sweat beads form on my cold forehead, and my breathing becomes jagged. *A kobold entered my room, flew over my bed while I slept, and it took three of my crystals?* I lower my head to my knees and take in a slow, deep breath. Part of me knows it is juvenile to place such importance on stones, but Rigel and I found my first faerie cross when I was four. Collecting them with my brothers was what I did.

"Are you okay? How are you going to find the kobold who took your crystals?" Foster's voice interrupts my internal struggle.

"What are you doing in here? Get out."

Chasing him into the hall, I slam the doors. I circle my chamber, embarrassed that he witnessed the exchange with Mother and Father and my fit of anxiety. I continue circling my room, my breath evening out with each pass. After several rounds, my eyes land on my arrows. A plan forms in my mind, and I snatch my quiver and bow.

Bolting out of the doorway, I halt in front of Foster. "How many arrows can you get?"

"What do you mean?"

"Do you think you can amass hundreds?"

He shakes his head. "All the supplies are allocated to the warriors. The ammunition closets are empty."

"We will have to ask Father then."

I force my wings to beat as fast as they can, propelling me through the corridors to Father's chamber. Not finding him there, I speed to the throne room. "I need arrows, lots of arrows."

"What is this? What do you mean?" Father glances from me to Foster.

"You say no one saw a kobold, only footprints, that magick may be aiding them, making them invisible. I am the best archer in the land. I can launch arrows for hours without missing my mark. If I fly arrows across the cave opening, I will eventually hit something, even if it is cloaked."

Father stands and paces. His eyes cut around the room to his advisors and back to me. "It may work. I will get my warriors on it."

I meet his stare. "I am your best marksman. No one can beat my range, precision, or stamina. It is the best plan. You know that."

"Titania, it is a good idea, and I commend you. But it is dangerous in the wood. You are to stay in the castle."

No matter what Alfreda or Foster say, I stew all day. *How can Father not let me help? I am more than capable of defending myself. And something, probably a kobold, took my crystals. It was not enough that they killed my brothers, now they are stealing my link to them as well.* I stare at my ceiling, counting my crystals. Tears roll down my cheeks as my gaze lands on the missing centerpiece of my design. That night, it takes a long time for sleep to come, but well past midnight, it does.

⊰⊱

IN THE MORNING, I NOTE THE dimmed light from the sky and count my crystals again.

Making my way to the throne room, I approach Father. "Is there news? Did the warriors find a kobold?"

"I am guessing not. General Kane has not reported in yet, but I instructed him to alert me if they found anything."

"And you positioned them so their arrows flew across the opening every ten seconds all night?"

"Well, I am not sure of the details, but I ordered that they attempt your strategy."

A soldier enters and bows, and a hush falls over the room. "King Oberon. I have your morning update, sir. Additional anchors were stolen from the gem room, and the Keeper of the Ring reports that three toadstools from the Faerie Ring withered during the night."

"And the archers were positioned at the cave as I asked?" Father inquires.

"Yes. They hit nothing."

The silence begins to wane as whispers break out between those gathered.

Father stands. "Double your fae at the cave. Sound the alarm if you sense anything strange."

"Father, I know the wood like the back of my hand, perhaps there is another—"

"Titania, that is all." Father motions for the soldier to approach.

If I could shoot fire from my eyes at Father, I would. Tears pool on my lower lids. I rush from the room, zipping through the halls to the garden. Foster trails me, keeping his distance, as I enter the orchard. With heaving lungs, I descend to the grass, the coolness of the blades calming my mood. In the next breath, new fears erupt. *What if the circle dies, and we are cut off from Upper Earth?* With no sunlight or water, our people will be left eating the creatures of the dirt. I examine the grass under my feet, imagining chewing an earthworm or centipede, and my stomach turns. *And who will guard the humans from the creatures of Lower Earth? Is that not our sole purpose?* My chest seizes.

"Do you really think you can find the kobold? Bring one down?" Foster's voice breaks through my spiral.

Blocking out the image of the looming beast above me, I spin to face him. "You saw the crystals in my room. I found every one of them in the eastern woods. I know every hollow and thicket. Plus, I do not miss my mark, ever. No matter how long I shoot for. Where are you from?"

"Westshire."

"May I?" When I hold out my hand, Foster places his bow and an arrow in my palm. I shake my head. "The whole quiver."

He relinquishes the bag, and I fit it on my back. Traipsing to the last row of trees, I point to the end tree a hundred feet away. I cock an arrow and launch it, then another, and another, until all twelve shafts are away.

Foster squints. I motion to the tree, and we dart to it. Twelve arrows, each one an inch apart, form a line up the trunk.

"How are you so good at this?"

"I know not." I shrug. "Skill borne of hours of boredom, I guess."

"I know of your brothers. I am sorry for your loss."

I do not want to feel sad. "Do they speak of my odd habits in Westshire as well? Or perhaps the guards poke fun at my peculiarities."

Foster's eyes widen. "No, never. No one should have to endure such loss."

"I am sorry. I should not berate you. Your sentiment is kind. I am just frustrated. No one will ever take me seriously unless I can prove myself."

Holding my gaze for a second, Foster scans the trees. "So, what would you do if allowed to aid in the hunt for the kobold?"

"Search the wood. Make sure there are no other openings for the kobold. Then, I will keep shooting arrows across the entrance to their hideout until I hit something."

"How long can you keep it up?"

"Last time I started, Father made me stop after thirteen hours."

"When was this?"

"Last week." Face flaming, I direct my attention to the ground. Sometimes, when nothing else calms my nerves, shooting is the only thing that works. The repetitive motion and counting the shots helps ease my tension, frustration over my mother's state, and worry for my future.

Chapter 2

THAT NIGHT, WHEN I FINISH playing for Mother and Father, I suggest again that I may be of some help with tracking the kobold. Father repeats his order that I am to stay within the castle walls. Frustrated and angry, I dig my nails into my palms but nod in acquiescence. I take my leave and race back towards my room.

"Do you always fly so fast?" Foster asks as he trails me.

"Only when I am angry."

"What is wrong?"

"Father will not let me leave the castle walls."

His wide-eyed concern sends me over the edge.

I do not need his pity. I slam the door in his face. I rest my back against the wood and try to catch my breath.

There is a rap on the door. "Are you okay?"

An idea forms in my mind. If I am not watched, I could slip out my window unseen. "I am fine, Foster. It is dark. Go home. I am sure the night guard will be along soon."

"Can I come in? Perhaps I can help you."

"Why would you help me?" I do not have friends. Father keeps me sequestered in the castle most of the time—I guess for fear that I, too, will be taken from him. My emotions rage out of control from fear to over-confidence. I cannot continue to act this way. A princess should appear regal. I open the door. "Forgive me. It is late and I am tired."

"It seems as though you could use someone to talk to." His emerald eyes reflect the candlelight.

"Thank you, but I am fine."

Reaching in a pocket, he hands me a whistle. "Let me know if you need anything."

"Thank you. Goodnight." I click the door closed.

My mind races with the events of the day. Frustrated, I begin to count my crystals. I count, skipping the missing pieces, and my anger rises. I take a deep breath and start to think of a way around Father's orders. If seen outside the walls, I will be dragged back to the castle and watched around the clock.

Still, I can guard my own crystals at the very least. Dragging a pillow, blanket, textbook, and hourglass to the window, I start my vigil. My eyes grow heavy after an hour of reading. I jump up and fly around the room to rouse myself. Resting back on the sill, I count the crystals again to stay awake. Exhaustion still takes me.

⸺◈⸺

I STARTLE AT THE SOUND OF Alfreda's voice.

"What are you doing up there, child? Come down." Alfreda motions to the floor.

"I am not a child. I was trying to keep watch. I guess I fell asleep. What time is it?"

"Seven. Time for breakfast."

My eyes cut to the window. "Why is it still so dark?"

Alfreda wrings her hands and shifts weight between her feet. "I am sure everything will be fine. Your father will take care of it."

"Alfreda, tell me now. That is an order."

"More crystals were taken in the night. The ring is dying."

I peer overhead, seeking solace from my crystals, only to find over half of them are gone. "My crystals! How did this happen? I lay on the windowsill all night."

"Those horrid creatures." Alfreda's hand pops to her gaping mouth. "Just eat your breakfast. Foster is waiting to escort you on your walk. I will let your father know what happened."

"Are you mad? Something needs to be done. I cannot just go for a walk like every other day. Our world is falling apart."

"Titania"—Alfreda rubs her hands down my arms—"that is what your Father wants you to do. He and his generals are holding meetings now. They will think of something."

"Fine, leave me." I flit over to my breakfast.

Once she is gone, I dress and pull on my boots, planning to listen in as Father confers with his fae. At the door, I hesitate. My crystals call to me. *You cannot leave without counting your crystals*, the internal voice beckons. *No.* I retaliate against the thought. Garrison, Bryce, Thornton, and Rigel are gone, counting the crystals will not bring them back. I must think of some way to help my people.

As I open the door, Foster greets me. "Are we walking through the garden and orchard today?"

"No, we are spying."

"I am under strict—"

I raise my palm. "I care not."

Grabbing his arm, I drag him to the back of the castle and into my secret passageway. I press my ear to the stone abutting Father's study.

"We are spread too thin. Perhaps we could work with the neighboring kingdoms."

"The kobolds must be aided by someone."

The pitch of the voices rise and fall. I hear it, sense it: fear, dread. Sweat forms on my forehead, and my heart begins to race. Recognizing the signs of an imminent anxiety episode, I take a deep breath.

I turn to Foster. "We should take that walk now."

His forehead wrinkles. "You do not want to hear more?"

"No, I want to walk. *Now.*"

Before he can say anything else, I dash through the narrow tunnel. I weave through the hedge, the garden colors diluted as if they are sun-faded water paintings. Birds call from the tops of the trees in the orchard, and the eerie, half-lit scene leaves me more anxious about losing our opening to Upper Earth. I head back towards the castle after one pass of the outer circle.

"Perhaps we can practice fencing or archery," Foster says.

"What of my studies?"

"Alfreda said none for today. All minds are focused on figuring out the how to save the ring." He motions to the sky.

"Yes, of course." I draw in a breath.

We pass the day fencing, shooting arrows, and playing games. I hate that I have been left out of the discussions. No one calls me for dinner, and Foster and I take supper in my room. Even this chamber, usually my favorite place, offers me no solace. As the last bit of light leaves the sky, he and I make a pact to spend the night on my windowsill, waiting for the kobold.

WE ARE AWAKENED BY ALFREDA'S screams the next morning. "What, dear children, do you think you are doing?"

I zip into the air. "We are not children. Foster is a soldier. We were waiting for the kobold. What time is it?"

"Seven, as always." Her eyes land on Foster. "You should go to your quarters."

"Yes, ma'am." He bows and backs to door. "Your Highness."

"I guess it is good you have a friend." Alfreda's eyes cut to the sky as she draws the curtain on the other window.

"Where is the sun?" I race to the opening.

"This is all, dear."

"What happened?"

"Your father is going to the neighboring kingdoms to ask for assistance. He believes the kobold will target them next. They will aid us. You and Foster should pass the time together again today."

"How can I do that when our kingdom is crumbling?"

Alfreda sighs. "Dear, please, just listen to your father."

"Fine. Go, then. I will summon Foster later." I grab my breakfast tray and plop onto my bed.

Looking at the ceiling, I realize only a few hundred of my crystals remain. My heart thuds in my chest. *This cannot be happening.* I grab my bow and quiver and jump to the window.

I blow into the whistle Foster gave me, and he appears within seconds. "What do you need?"

"We must do something."

A smile spreads across his face and he bows low. "Whatever, you wish, High—"

Swinging my legs over the sill, I hop to the ground. "We need arrows. Lots of arrows."

He leads me to the ammunition stores, but the rooms are empty, and my mood plummets. Between us, there are only twenty-four arrows.

"The troops are sleeping after the long night. We may be able can sneak some away." Foster tugs my sleeve, motioning for me to follow him.

We fly to the barracks where the troops lay resting and flit between their beds, swiping several arrows from each quiver, and soon, our arms are full. Making our way to the garden, we wind through the maze to the orchard. We jump into the air, flying high over the wall, over the farmers' fields, and to the eastern side of the kingdom. Descending into the forest, I adjust my vision. A small group of warriors flank the cave. They shoot arrows across the entrance every minute or so.

I turn to Foster. "Something is not right. This is where they saw the footprints?"

"Yes, I believe so."

"What if it is a diversion?" My mind spins, remembering several openings I knew along the banks of the river. "Come on."

Following the stream, we inspect each hollow, but cannot find evidence of kobold in the forest. We head south, following the waterway to the ocean. A darkness, blacker than any night I can remember, descends, and we circle back to the castle. As with the prior night, Foster and I sleep on the windowsill, this time taking turns keeping watch. When my clock strikes seven, I sit up and inspect the grounds. No light glistens in the sky, not even on the edges.

Foster rouses, rubbing his eyes. "How are we going to find anything in this darkness?"

"We will need lanterns and fuel. But first, we must find out if there are any crystals left in the Faerie Ring or if the kobold have absconded with all of them. If there are not any left, I doubt they will return. They will probably move on to the next kingdom."

Flitting from my window, we make for the home of the Keeper of the Ring. He is the oldest fae in Aubren and has watched over our Ring since the age of seventeen. I have seen him in the castle but only spoken to him a couple of times. *What will I tell him? Why would he give us information?* An idea forms in my mind.

As we land in front of his cottage, I whisper to Foster, "Let me speak with him."

"I was hoping you would say that. The Keeper does not seem like one to be trifled with."

I knock on the door, and a bent gentleman with long white hair and a beard greets me. His thin, holey wings hang slack from his back, seeming as if they may crumble at any second.

Straightening my shoulders, I lift my chin. "King Oberon sent me to get a report. Are any functional anchors left in the ring?"

"That is very interesting, Princess Titania, because I just spoke with his First Advisor, Gunther, moments ago." The Keeper holds my stare.

I swallow and take a second to devise another strategy. "So, you know who I am. Good. Then you know how important it is that the royal family be apprised at all times. I am on a mission for my father."

"One anchor stands. You could pass to Upper Earth, but if we lose this one, you would be stuck with no way of return. Perhaps that is what your father intends? To safeguard his only daughter until he can secure the realm? I would allow this. His majesty must know that. Will your mother be accompanying you?"

"No, I mean, thank you, good day, and blessings." I back from the door, taking to the air.

"Do you think that is what your father means to do? Have you secured away?" Foster's words echo my fears.

"I know not. But I cannot let that happen."

"If your father wants you to go to Upper Earth, I do not see how you will avoid it."

"I will not go back to the castle then. You can get all the supplies and meet me at the bend in the stream." I land outside the castle wall.

We think of all we may need, including a map, lanterns, food, and additional arrows. Foster agrees to meet me in the wood and jumps into the air.

"What if I am seen and they ask where you are?" Foster hovers above me, ready to take his leave.

"Tell them I am napping, at the library, fencing, in the garden, or roaming the orchard. It does not matter, just be quick."

Pulling my wrap around my body, I start towards the forest. I think of Alfreda coming to my room to find me gone. *Perhaps I should have told Foster to make some excuse to her.* But our kingdom sits on the brink of disaster, we have not time for such things. When I enter the trees, the darkness envelops me, and I spring into the air. Enough light filters to the middle of the canopy for me to stay hidden yet avoid a run in with a branch. I find the stream and wind to our meeting spot.

I sit atop a stump to wait. I hate the dark, and every crackle and tick causes me to jump. Thinking of what may lay ahead, I say prayers to the gods and goddesses. An image of the kobold looming over me flits through my mind. I extend my hand and envision light springing from my fingers. Nothing. I close my eyes and focus on my core, picturing a ball of light emanating from my chest, spreading down my arm, and leaping from my hand. I lift my eyelids to blackness. *How are you, a fifteen-year-old, sheltered princess, going to make a difference?*

Standing, I slide my quiver from my back. I can but try to help. Doing something will be better than nothing.

I launch arrows into the soft bark of a tree opposite me. When my arms tire, I pace the small clearing wondering why Foster is not here yet. Was he detained or assigned another duty? What if he does not come at all? What shall I do then? Just as I decide to give up, I hear the rustling of wings overhead. I hide beneath a bush until I see his red hair.

"What took you so long?"

"The kitchen staff thought it sweet I wanted to pack a picnic to entertain you in the orchard. They felt the need to make sure the biscuits were warm and cream cold."

"A picnic? They will think you are courting me." I lift a bag of arrows from his shoulder.

"I thought it smart of me."

We study the map, marking off areas already searched, then we take to the air, searching each hectare. By what would have been nightfall, we have only one corner of the kingdom to rule out: a small strip of land on the southern tip.

"The map says the earth slopes up to a volcanic cone. I cannot imagine there would be anywhere to hide there." Foster pops a piece of bread in his mouth as we rest on a rock.

"Except a huge mountain with plenty of space for underground caves and tunnels?"

"The map does not indicate any caves in Mt. Kosciuszko. It is an active volcano, and it could erupt at any moment."

"A perfect hiding place, I should say. One no fae would dare enter."

After finishing our snack, we shoulder our packs and take flight, rising as the mountain does below us. The air cools, and I wish I wore my winter coat. We zigzag over the surface, making sure to survey each parcel. Higher up, no trees grow, and with thinning air, we land, hiking back and forth to the top. At the summit, I behold the countryside stretching to the next kingdom and watch the light from their rings fade with the sun above. I imagine what the view may be when the full sun blesses the whole realm and wonder why I have never ventured to this spot before.

The ground beneath me shakes and, gripping a nearby rock, I steady myself. "What was that?"

Foster holds out his hand. "Something is not right. We have to go."

"We have come this far. We are close. I know it."

"If anything happens to you, I will be blamed."

"You are my subject, and I ordered you to follow me."

"You know that is not how your father will see it."

"Then we must hurry." I jump into the air and head down the mountainside.

Seeing a steep rock face and ledge hidden behind a row of trees, I land, Foster quick at my side. I hold the lantern up to visualize the space, and wind back to the cliff around the curve of the mountain. An opening, five feet wide and twenty feet high, looms in front of me, hidden from view of the valley by a copse of trees.

I raise my light and step inside. "What do you think?"

"It is worth inspection." Lighting another lantern, Foster inches to me.

We tiptoe into the passageway, dodging rocks jutting out from the walls. We tread five, ten, twenty, fifty feet into the cavern. Bone-chilling air hits my face, and a rancid smell, the scent of a kobold—I will never forget that smell as long as I live—surrounds me. *How did I confuse the smell in my room with this one? It has been three years. Similar, yes. Both foul, but not the same. The one in my room smelled more of oil and musk rather than fermenting meat.* I tuck that thought away for later.

"This must be it."

"It is definitely some type of passageway." Foster lifts the lantern between us and kneels. "Are these footprints?"

"If you can call them feet." I recognize the claw marks of a kobold. "We should go back. We would be no match for one kobold, much less an army, and also whatever magick creature is aiding them."

Jumping up into the air, we race back out of the opening and to the trees. I extinguish my lantern. "Do you think they will know we are here?"

Foster snuffs out his light. "We have no idea how long that tunnel is or if they will even come out."

"But it is worth trying. We searched every parcel. I feel it in my bones. This is where they are hiding. Give me an arrow." I raise my bow.

Foster hooks his quiver on a branch. "Do you not think we should call for backup? These things are strong flyers. And they can be invisible. What other powers might they have? If something happens to you—"

I snatch an arrow from his bag. "What about my guilt if something happens to you? Did you ever think of that?"

"But I am a no one. Only my family cares if I come back."

The mountain rumbles, and our tree shakes. I grip the trunk. "We are not going to have families to go back to if we do not find the kobold and the anchors. Do not sound an alarm until we see a kobold. That is an order. Father will just lug me back to the castle."

I cock my bow and release the arrow, sending it speeding across the opening. I count to thirty and repeat—then again, and again. Foster flies to the other side, retrieving the arrows to keep them replenished. I pull my arm back and release repeatedly. Adrenaline shoots through my veins as I repeat the motion.

With the darkness, I lose track of time. Foster shakes my shoulders, breaking my concentration. "You have to eat something. Let me take over."

After snacking, I resume my post but begin to doubt the kobold will come. The arrows make little sound, but perhaps the beasts have detected the motion. *Thirty*, I finish counting and let the next arrow fly, and the next—one after another.

"It is the witching hour," Foster whispers.

"What? We have been here eight hours?"

"Yes, Your High… Titania."

"Okay, focus. This could be the most important hour." I study my target.

"They could figure out your system. Maybe you should just shoot them at random times."

I bite my lip. "I do not think the kobold are that smart."

"Maybe." He shrugs. "Does not hurt to try."

Shooting after ten seconds and then twenty, thirty, back to twenty, and ten again, I vary the time. After letting the tenth arrow loose, a screeching sound cuts through the night. My eyes dart to the opening, and I see a huge, lumbering kobold, holding his side where my arrow entered. I cock the bow again and release, hitting another beast. Foster launches an arrow at the opening, hitting an at-first-invisible target that morphs into kobold. We fire arrow after arrow, and more kobold fall.

I nudge Foster. "I think we should sound an alarm. Call for the warriors."

"Your father is not going to be happy with me."

"The armies are far away, and we do not have many more arrows. If we miss, we are in trouble. Plus, we are the heroes here. The only thing my father is going to do is give you commendation and a promotion."

"I pray you are right." He puts the horn to his lips and blows the high-pitched signal only faeries can hear.

I refocus on the cave opening and launching arrows but do not hit any more kobold after shooting another ten. Not wanting to risk retrieving them, and with only four more between us, we halt our attack.

"What do you think? They gave up? Retreated back inside?" I whisper.

"Or are coming with a bigger army, different weapons, or going out another way?"

I peer into the darkness. "Where is Father's army?"

"I think we wait."

The moments drag, and cold envelopes my skin. Shivering, I rub my arms, trying to keep warm.

"Highness, huddle in my jacket." Foster opens his coat.

My teeth chatter as I slide to his side. The heat from his chest warms me, and my muscles relax. I note his scent, like that of hay and fresh-cut grass. After a few minutes, the flapping of wings catches my attention. Slipping from his side, I stand on the branch to see Father and a legion of faeries descend. Jumping into the air to join him, I hold my breath, waiting for his reprimand.

"Titania, how are you here? Who sounded the signal?"

"We did." I motion to Foster as he approaches.

"Foster, you were to—"

"Father, the kobold. We have found their entry point." I point to the crevice in the rock and the fallen kobold.

Father directs his troops to give us additional arrows and leads his warriors into the cave. Foster and I continue our assault on the cave entrance, hoping to stop any kobold that escape the army. Ten more kobold fall from hits with our arrows. I lower my weapon as four arrows land on the rock ledge.

"I think that is all of them."

Foster squeezes my hand. "You saved us from the kobold."

"*We* bested them." I smile at him. Jumping into the air, I head to the opening. "Now to help Father."

"I do not think he would want—"

"Whatever magick creature is aiding them could be hiding inside. The army needs all the soldiers it can get."

Flying over the kobold corpses, I divert my eyes to the dark opening ahead. As we descend into the mountain, the passage grows dark, the air heavy and cold. A light in the distance grows brighter, and as we round a bend, I stop short. Soldiers hunch over a form.

I push through the rows of fae to the center. My father lies motionless on the dirt.

"What happened?" I kneel beside his body, running my hands over his legs, arms, and torso, searching for a wound. "Father, wake up!"

Removing his helmet, I test his neck for a pulse. I feel a slight erratic vibration under my fingers. His chest rises, and he coughs up blood. My mind reels. *I cannot lose my father.* Sensing the fae behind me, I stand.

"Where is the rest of the army?"

"Highness, come away." One of the fae pulls me towards the exit.

I shake my head. "Did we find the anchors? Where are the other soldiers?"

General Kane steps forward. "The others are chasing the kobold farther into the cave, searching for the anchors."

"Have four of your fae take the King back to the castle and call for the Healer. The rest of us should aid the army. We need all the soldiers we can get." I hold my palm out to Foster, and he sets my bow in it.

Taking wing, we charge deeper into the tunnel, finding the others fighting hundreds of the kobold—half-sprite-half-reptilian-like creatures. I thought them bigger but realize most are not much taller than the male fae. Without my sword, I am no match for them in direct combat, so I cock my arrow, bring down one, and motion for the others to do the same. We pick off the ones we can from the air while the warriors aid their comrades on the ground.

Scanning the cave, I see an orange glow at one end. I approach the opening and find it leads to a smaller cavern. With the kobold army locked in battle behind me, I slip inside. Huge chests litter the floor. Beyond, hot pools of lava bubble and fester. I drop to the ground and lift the lid of one of the chests.

Foster lands beside me.

"Guard the exit."

He opens the box to my right. "I stay with you. We do not know what lies beyond those lava fields."

"I would guess whatever evil being is aiding them." I dart to the other crates, searching for the anchor crystals.

Opening yet another wooden box, I find it full of crystals, including some faerie crosses, and wonder if they are from my chambers. I drop one in my quiver and move to the next chest. Blinding white light sears my eyes.

"These have to be the anchors. Give me your bag." I fill Foster's pack and then mine, taking all the crystals. As we fit the quivers over our shoulders, the ground shakes. A fissure opens between us.

"What was that?" Foster offers his hand.

I fit mine in his as the lava bubbles higher. The rock rumbles beneath us. Red magma shoots from the cracks and splatters the cavern ceiling. A column of rock topples to the ground, and we jump into the air. Shooting for the exit, I yell for Foster to sound the retreat.

Foster blows into his horn as we pass into the large hollow. With a boom, rocks fall from the cave ceiling, blocking the entrance to the inner cavern behind us. One by one, our soldiers take to the air, leaving the remaining kobold wide-eyed. I hover near the ceiling as the passage grows tight with our warriors. The rock around me shifts, and I press my back to the wall behind me.

"Titania, you have to come now. We need to get the anchors to the Keeper before they are lost forever. The cave is going to be buried." Foster tugs at my arm.

"I will be the last." I slide the pack from my back, hand it to him, and then push him into the wave of flying soldiers.

One stops in front of me. "Titania, you must come."

"I will see the last of the army out safely."

"No, you will come now. The fae of this kingdom need you." He grabs my hand and drags me into the sea of flying fae.

We weave through the tunnels, rubble pelting our bodies. I dodge falling rocks and shifting walls. Landing outside, I wait on the ledge for our last warrior, instructing the soldiers to rendezvous in the valley. Some carry injured or limp bodies, and I steel my emotions against the tears threatening to form. *How many will we lose?*

In the dark meadow below, we light torches and take count, finding all soldiers but two—whose comrades report the kobold overtook the men. Of those gathered, seven no longer draw breath, and fifteen are injured such that they cannot fly on their own. *Nine dead*, I summarize in my head, pushing away the thought that my father could make ten.

I approach General Kane. "How many troops did you bring?"

"Three hundred, Highness."

"We lost many tonight."

"It would have been much worse if not for your fast thinking and archery skills. You saved our kingdom, maybe even our realm."

"Let us hope the anchors to the Faerie Ring are with the crystals we found."

I instruct the fae to make stretchers of branches, and when these are finished, we take to the sky. Seeing the first light of the sun glowing above the trees, I guess Foster delivered the anchors to the Keeper. I glance back at the mountain, and my breath catches in my throat. Kobold stream around the ledge.

"General." I point back at the peak.

He sounds the alarm, ordering the injured to be returned to the castle and all others to follow us. We charge up the mountain, arrows and swords held ready. We pelt the kobold with arrows, and other troops meet them on the ground.

I yell to Kane, "If their numbers grow much more, we will not be able to hold them off. There must be some way to stop them from entering this realm."

Realizing the kobold must be fleeing because the mountain is unstable, I wonder if there is a way to collapse the opening. I fly above the cave entrance and see there is just enough room for one kobold to exit at a time. Lava seeps from several fissures beside the passage.

I gather ten of our biggest soldiers, and we cut down five trees. Stripping the branches, we form battering rams and carry them to the peak. The warriors ram them against the side of the mountain. Each blow causes rock to fall over the entrance until it is sealed. We join the forces below, making sure every kobold is brought down.

The mountain trembles, and the top explodes with gushing lava. Racing away, I round up the soldiers on the other side of the meadow under cover of the trees. Kane instructs a small battalion to keep watch, and the rest of us take flight, bound for the castle.

Even from a distance, I can see the sun shining off the white stone of the structure. Drawing near, I descend to the meadow beside my home. Funeral pyres line the space, and I steel my emotions against my impending loss. One of these may be my father. I stop at each, picking flowers and laying them atop the fallen fae. My chest tightens as I reach the last body. Realizing it is not my father, my guilt matches my elation, for this fae is most likely *someone's* father.

Your brothers' pyres were set up in the courtyard. My brain tries to block the memory. Exiting the meadow, I walk through the orchard and into the garden. Each fae I pass drops to one knee as I approach. Even though I fight them, tears stain my cheeks. *My father is dead, and I am Queen.*

I arrive at the edge of the courtyard, but it is empty save soldiers milling about. Dropping to a knee, they clear a path for me. Tears cloud my vision. *There has not been enough time to prepare his body. You must be strong, Titania. Every fae watches you.* Knowing I must now bear the torch for my family, for my kingdom, I square my shoulders and raise my chin.

As I near the entrance, I see a red-headed soldier approaching. I blink, and Foster's face becomes clear. He drops to one knee in front of me.

"Stand up. You deserve as much honor as I."

As he rises, he takes my hand and kisses it. "I am so glad to see you safe, Highness."

My face flushes as his eyes lock on mine. His wide-eyed stare does little to give me hope, and I ball my hands into fists. *You cannot be a girl with a faint heart anymore. You must show strength and courage.* "Where is my father?"

"He is in the hall. He asks that you be presented at once."

"He is alive? But I thought…" Relief washing over me, I release my breath. I skim the faces of those gathered. Their stares trained on me, I am bewildered as to why the soldiers have taken a knee. "I do not understand."

Foster's eyes stay fixed on my face.

"What are you staring at?"

"Sorry, Highness. It is your face."

Cheeks flaming anew, I wipe my cheeks. With the tears and dirt, I must look horrid.

Fingers pull at my wrists, and Foster's hands wrap around mine. "Do not hide."

I take in his emerald eyes and full, red lips, inches from mine. "Hide what?"

He traces a line across my cheek. "Your markings. They grew darker."

"Highness." I recognize Kane's voice. "Your father waits for you in the grand hall."

Father. Following Kane, I cross the corridor into the great hall. Father sits at the far end in a wheeled chair to the left of the King's throne. Bandages wrap his torso, but he retains good color. It takes every bit of self-control to walk across the room instead of racing to his side and flinging my arms around his neck. I remember who and where I am and nod as each of those lining the walls bow to me.

"Father." I curtsey. "I am glad to see you are well."

"The doctors say I have a collapsed lung and two broken ribs, but they will heal."

"That is good."

"You have a report for me?"

"General Kane?" I spin to face him.

Kane smiles. "I believe you can give the King the information he needs."

Raising my chin, I look at Father. "As you can see"—I motion to the window—"the anchors have been returned to the Keeper. They were hidden deep inside Mt. Kosciuszko at the southern side of our kingdom. We killed all those that escaped, sealed the rest inside the mountain, and left twenty soldiers to ensure there are no stray kobold roaming about."

Father pushes on the arms of his chair, hoisting himself to a standing position "And you and Foster left the castle to find the kobold all by yourselves?"

"Yes, but it was my idea. Foster was only obeying my orders. If you need to blame someone for disobeying you, it is I."

A smile spreads across his face. "I underestimated you. Even at your young age, you have proven yourself more than worthy of the throne I now relinquish."

"Relinquish your throne? But why? You are still fit to rule. The doctor said you would heal."

"I am an old man. Perhaps you do not see that. But you have shown me that you could save this kingdom when I, or any of my generals or advisors, could not. You should be ruling Aubren as Queen."

"All hail Queen Titania!" General Kane drops to one knee.

Shouts ring out through the hall, and those gathered in the courtyard crowd into the throne room. The voices deafen me, and my head swims. *Is this real? Surely I am dreaming. Am I prepared for this?* Father draws his sword, and I focus on the bright blade. *This is your destiny. You will be worthy of this post.* I bow before him.

"I hereby relinquish the rule of Aubren to my daughter, Titania, the only heir to the throne. Long live Queen Titania."

"Long live Queen Titania," the crowd echoes.

My heart thumps in my chest as I rise. I take Father's hand as he leads me up to his throne, my throne. I sit down on the weathered, soft wood and run my hands down the arms, barely breathing. Raising my chin, I scan the crowd.

"We are victorious today because of the bravery of many, including Foster"—I raise my hand and motion to him—"our generals, and all the soldiers who fought bravely in service to this kingdom. Let us honor those lost in this battle."

I lead the others outside to the meadow. Families gather around each pyre, and in turn, General Kane, Father, and I greet each and offer our condolences and thanks for their loved one's service. Upon seeing the first pyre set ablaze, memories of my brothers flood my mind. I picture their faces and say a prayer, vowing to do everything in my power to spare others these fates.

We watch until the last pyre burns to embers and proceed back to the castle. Servers have brought wine and food, and I declare we honor the soldiers and celebrate our victory with an evening feast, music, and dancing.

Father places his hand atop mine. "Well done, daughter."

I bend down and wrap my arms around him. Tears fill my eyes. "When they took a knee, I thought you were gone."

"No one can keep a secret around here. You would do well to remember that." He pats my back.

Releasing him, I spin to accept congratulations from all the generals, advisors, soldiers, and castle faeries. Sundown approaches as I greet the last of the well-wishers. I search the room for Foster, wondering where he may have gone.

"Princess—I am sorry—*Queen* Titania." Alfreda lays her hand on my back. "Would you like to retire to your chambers to clean and dress for the celebration?"

Looking down at my leather pants and vest, I realize I am covered in dirt and blood. "If Mother were well, she would have a switch ready to whip me."

Water pools in Alfreda's eyes. "I wish she were here to witness this."

"No tears." Ignoring the tick in my side, I squeeze her shoulders. "Only food, music, and dancing tonight. I will check on Mother once I have cleaned up."

I take the back passageways to my chambers and find Foster waiting at my door. "There you are. I was wondering where you went."

"I am not much for crowds."

"Well, I hope you are not opposed to being seated next to me at the feast."

His face flushes red. "Of course not, Queen."

I slap his arm. "Do not call me that. You and I make a good team. I hope we can be friends."

"I thought we already were."

"Well, of course, but you know what I mean." My cheeks warm. "You do not have to call me queen, or bow, or anything."

"I hope to be bowing in front of you for a long time." He takes my hand, drops to one knee, and kisses my fingers.

My face flames anew. "I need to clean up and dress."

"May I have a dance tonight?"

"Of course. At least, I think." I bite my lip, trying to remember protocol for queens and dancing.

Foster rises. "I think there may be a line of eligible courters waiting to dance with you."

"I am not of age to marry, so there will be no such thing. Tonight is about celebrating our victory."

"As you say, my Queen." He bows again.

My head spins with the weight of the word *Queen*. "Stop calling me that. And go! I have to dress."

Jumping into the air, I enter my room and click the panels shut. I slump to the floor and press my back against the cool, soft wood. *How am I supposed to do this alone? Know who to dance with and how many dances? You have, Father,* I remind myself. *But I need my mother.*

"Dearie"— Alfreda appears from my dressing chambers—"I have your bath ready. You must be exhausted."

"I suppose I am." I rise.

"I laid out a dress. Your father wanted you to join him in the study when you are ready."

"Thank you." I eye the light-green silk gown she laid out on my bed, complete with sash, white, elbow-length gloves, and an emerald necklace with a stone bigger than my thumb.

Crossing to the outfit, I lift the necklace. "Where did you get this?"

Alfreda wraps an arm around my shoulders. "It is your mother's. She wore it the day your father was coronated. We thought she would want you to have it."

"We?"

"Child." Her eyes large, I recognize the look of her pity. I have seen it a thousand times. "Your father told her what happened, how you lead the army, defeated the kobold. He begged for her council, and still, she sat there, just staring at the fire like she always does. I do not think she is ever coming back to you. Your father wanted you to wear this."

"I will not." I shove it in her palm. "I will wear my own jewel."

Scanning my room, I find my quiver and dump it. The one faerie cross I retrieved from the cave clinks across the stone floor. Retrieving it, I hold it up to her. "Have one of the jewelers set this. I have no clue which brother I found it with, but I will wear it in their memory. I slayed the kobold—not only for our kingdom, but for them."

Alfreda holds my stare and lifts her finger to touch my cheek. "Your face is different."

My face flames with heat. "Foster said my markings were darker."

"I thought it was the dirt. But it is not."

"What is happening to me?"

Her eyes drop. "We have never known a female ruler."

My head swims. But I cannot think of that now. It is too much. "I should clean up. Have the jeweler set the stone.

"As you wish, madam."

"Alfreda."

"Yes?" She lifts her chin.

"Thank you for not calling me queen."

"You will always be my Titania."

Chapter

3

I watch her walk out and close the door. Leaning over my dresser, I study my face in the mirror. Where slight red freckles graced the skin around my eyes, now rests solid green dots. Lines like tiger stripes flair our from my nose and eyes. I wipe the dust from my cheeks and touch the marks. The skin feels smooth and soft, just as before. *How many kobold did I slay?* I would not have thought myself a killer. *But you knew you were.*

Turning from my reflection, I strip my muddy jacket and pants. I step into the tub and lower myself into the warm water. The smell of lavender surrounds me, calming my thoughts. The heat soothes my searing muscles, and I shut my eyes. *It is finished. We are safe.* I wash, clean my hair, and recline my neck on my soft wings.

"Madam." A voice wakes me. "Alfreda sent us to help with your hair. She said you need something special."

"Yes." I stand, towel off, and slip into a robe.

I sit for an hour at my mirror while they dry then curl my mahogany locks, pinning them atop my head and weaving sprigs of ivy throughout. They admire their work, noting how the golden highlights match my eyes. I thank them and study my face. My markings, spots and dots on my cheeks and forehead and long, sweeping lines from my eyes, appear more prominent now that my face is clean. They bring out green highlights in my eyes I never noticed. *They make me look angry, perhaps scary to a small child,* I think. I soften them with light powder, brush rouge of rose petals on my cheeks, and highlight my lashes with dark cream from coffee beans. For a finishing touch, I dust green powder, made from ground, dried beans, on my eyelids. Crossing to the plush green dress laying on my bed, I slide in one foot then the other and pull the garment over my hips. It is nothing like I have worn before, and I run my hand down the soft velvet. It clings to my body like a second skin, the color bringing out the soft greens in my wings.

Staring at my reflection, I wonder what Mother would say to me now, if she thinks of me at all, or whether there are any sentiments left within her. I turn from the mirror and slide my legs in the suede leather boots, lacing them up over my knees. *A queen should never be without protection.* I fit my short blade from the top drawer of my dresser between the soft leather and my calf.

A knock on the door startles me, and Alfreda pokes her head inside. "Are you ready, madam?"

"Madam? Seriously, Alfreda, just yesterday you were calling me dear, and darling, and child. And since when have you knocked to enter my chambers?"

"You look stunning."

"Thank you."

"But this morning I came to find you gone"—her hands tremble and tears form in her eyes—"and your father almost died. I feared I would never see you again. I can hardly fathom you fighting those, those hideous kobolds deep in the caves, and they are saying you led the charge." Her shoulders shudder, she swallows, and she meets my gaze. "But now you are Queen. There are rules and protocols to be followed. Forgive me."

I wrap my hands around hers and squeeze tightly. "No, Alfreda, forgive me. You will always be my friend. I betrayed you. I am sorry I left that way. But it is over, our kingdom is safe, we no longer need fear the kobold."

She slides her hand from mine to wipe the tears from her face.

Squeezing her arm, I kiss her cheek. "I cannot have you crying. This is a celebration."

"They are happy tears, Mad… Your father asked you to meet him in his study… Miss?" She cocks one eyebrow up.

"I guess that will do."

I choose the back passageways to wind to Father's private quarters, and I find it feels odd to walk the halls on my feet. But my hair cannot be risked, and the breeze from flying would surely loosen the pins. Clunking of my heels on the stone echoes through the tunnel. I enter the private study to find Father seated in a rolling chair in front of the fire, opposite Mother. Seeing the bandages on his face, him wince as he leans forward, and white streaks in his dark beard, my hearts skips at how close we came, *I came*, to losing him, the only real family I have left. My eyes cut to my mother's blank stare as I approach. *Does she register that the kobold will never threaten our realm again?* My mind ticks with worry. Of course, we cannot know that for certain. Hearing father cough, I refocus on him and a box on his lap.

I kneel at his side and grip his arm. "How are you feeling?"

"The doctors say I must remain still for a bit, a week or so is all, but I have not summoned you to talk about me." His lips form a smile. He lifts the box. "Stand, dear child."

Rising, I open the lid to find his crown resting on purple velvet. "Father, I cannot wear this."

"You can and you will. I have already had it altered. See"—he spins it around—"you cannot even tell where they soldered it. Kneel."

I rest one knee on the stone in front of him. He lowers the crown to my head. The metal headband sinks into my curls and rests on my skull, a perfect fit. I keep my eyes trained on his face, noting the wrinkles and ridges that are so familiar to me. *How many nights have we sat in this room, him reading, me playing, Mother staring at the fire?* I pray it will be many more. Father grips the hilt of his sword and raises his blade, touching my left shoulder, then my right.

Resting the weapon on his palms, he holds it out. "Rise, Queen Titania, and claim your birthright."

My mind spins but I obey. Taking the sword, I rise. As his youngest, we both know this was not my birthright. Also, our realm has never had a lone female ruler.

Mind grappling with the enormity of my charge, I suck in a breath. *I have studied and trained three years for this moment. With his help, you can do this.* "I shall strive to make you proud, to wear this crown and wield this sword as you and your fathers before you have."

"I hope you will find your own new ways of ruling as well. You have shown in the past days that is much needed." He kisses my left cheek and then the right. "We will hold an official coronation once it can be planned. Now, it is time to celebrate the victory with your countrymen."

I force my worries away and flash a wide smile. "A joyous celebration it shall be now that our Faerie Ring is restored, and we are safe from those creatures of the deep."

Standing, I spin to face Mother and grasp her hand. "Mother, will you join us?"

"We will have Alfreda walk her to the celebration." Father wraps his hand around mine and directs me to the door.

"I am not sure I know how to do this. There are so many things I would want to ask—who to dance with, how many dances. Foster said courters would be lining up to dance with me. And what of the advisors, and generals, an—"

Father chuckles. "Titania, let us leave the 'morrow for the morning. Tonight, we are celebrating a victory. As for Foster, I would guess him to be one of your courters as well?"

My face flushes. "He may be, but I shall have none of that tonight. We shall only dance jigs."

"I agree. Jigs it shall be." Father wheels his chair backwards. "You will not be sixteen for a month, and I will not approve a marriage until at least seventeen. You only need to enjoy the celebration."

I lean down to whisper in his ear as I open the door. "Alfreda said you talked to Mother."

"I hoped, with justice for your brothers, the kobold defeated, you rising, she would say something. And to have you avenge them…" He shakes his head and looks back at her.

I plant a kiss on Father's cheek. "I will speak with her."

Watching him roll away, I straighten my back, cross to the hearth, kneel, and take her hands. "Mother, did Father tell you? We have defeated the kobold. Our realm is safe from them again, and it was me who led the charge. Father made me Queen." Tears spring to my eyes, and I squeeze her fingers. "I need you. Please, come back to us."

She blinks, and water pools in her eyes.

My heart soars at her show of emotion. I hug her to me, daring to hope she heals. "Everything is going to be fine. I promise." Releasing my grip, I clasp her hands. "There is a celebration. Will you come? Sit beside me?"

Wriggling her fingers from mine, she touches my cheek. She opens her mouth, and I hold my breath, waiting for her to speak. But her lips press together. Lifting her hand from my face, she shakes her head. Her eyes cut to the fire, and the familiar glaze returns.

"This is but the beginning." Her words are but a whisper above the crackle.

"The beginning of what?"

Mother's eyes cut to me and back to the flames.

"Never mind her." Father's voice startles me.

Standing, I spin to face him. "Those are the first words I have heard her utter in years, and she tells me this is the beginning."

"We will talk of this tomorrow. Everyone is waiting."

"Is there something you are not telling me?" I loom over him, and with my mind on alert, my wings rise.

"It is nothing, dear. Come." He turns his chair around.

"I will not stand for secrets between us. You have led me to believe that she has not uttered a word in three years, but now you act as if this is a common occurrence."

His shoulders slack, and he lifts his face. "She says things once in a while. Rarely, really. At first, I thought they were nonsense, but two weeks ago, she uttered, *'They are coming.'* Then, just seven days ago, she spoke of a darkness."

My stomach lurches. *Mother foretold the kobold stealing the anchors? Causing a darkness? She is gifted?* "Are you saying she is a seer now?"

"Or always was." He holds my stare.

My emotions turn from disbelief to anger. *What else did she say? How could he keep this from me? Of course, if I shared my secret, perhaps he would have as well.* "Father, how often does she speak?"

Alfreda flits into the room and lands in front of me. "Miss, I have your stone."

I glare at Father and take a deep breath. "Thank you, Alfreda."

Winding behind me, she clasps the necklace on my neck. "You look beautiful."

"We should go." Father's eyes brim with tears.

"I am ready." I hug Alfreda. "Will you see to Mother?"

"I will. You go." She kisses my cheek.

I look down at Father then back to Mother. I am the only one left to carry on the line of the House of Alpheaus. It is my duty. Still, I am but fifteen. I step into the narrow corridor and see the bright torches and fae gathered ahead. Even though I spoke the words, assuredness for my readiness wains. *Am I ready for a state dinner, a celebration where I am the host of honor, when my father has just passed his crown to me, the first female fae to be given a monarchy? Much less running a kingdom?* But there is no turning back. Thoughts jumble my mind.

Father squeezes my arm.

I lift my wings as we enter the main passage, crowded with fae, two and three deep. Torches fixed above their heads light the corridor. A chandelier made of hundreds of crystals adorns the stone walls with swatches of light. I think of the faerie crosses that once made a beautiful patchwork of light on my ceiling, picture my brothers' faces, and harken their spirits. Taking a deep breath, I focus on my path.

The two women who weaved my hair stand to my right, and they curtsey as I approach.

I squeeze their hands and take the embroidered handkerchiefs they offer. Girls throw flowers in my path, women reach out to take my hand, and men drop to one knee, an arm crossed over their chests, as I pass. My worries fade into the background as I accept hugs and kisses to my cheek, warm wishes, and congratulations. As we near the great hall, soldiers line the passage and lift their weapons and voices in celebration. Seeing Foster, my smile widens, and I fight the urge to wink at him. Soldiers pack the ballroom, and as we enter, someone clunks their mug on a wood table. Others follow, and the sound rumbles in my ears.

As I approach the front, the chanting wanes. I slow my pace and stop to speak to the advisors seated at a long wooden table to the right of the head. Each tips his chin and offers congratulations on our victory: Terrence, Jesper, Cedric, Bran, Angus... I stop. *Where is Gunther? He is First Advisor. He should be here. I have never known him to miss a gathering.*

"Sir Angus, what of Gunther? Is he not well?"

Angus's eyes cut down the line of advisors and then to my face. He lowers his eyes briefly and looks back at me. "One of his sons was injured. I believe he will join us later."

"I will say prayers for his quick healing then."

"Yes"—he pauses—"Miss Titania."

I force a smile. *Miss?* At the very least, he should have addressed me as Madam.

"Titania." Father takes my hand and motions to the other side of the room.

Lifting my chin, I march across the stone floor to the generals' table. "Generals." I smile at each, letting my focus land on the Head General, Kane. "Congratulations on the victory. Our kingdom owes you and your men much."

Kane steps around the table. He lifts his goblet and draws his sword, holding it high above his head. "I believe it is you who deserves our commendation. To Queen Titania."

The sound of clanking metal fills the room as shouts ring out. "To Queen Titania."

General Kane bows and offers me his drink. I take a swig of the red liquid, steeling my reaction to the strong wine that coats my mouth and throat. Walking to the center of the space, I lift the goblet. "To all those who fought bravely." My eyes land on Foster and I smile. "Victory is ours. The kingdom is safe once more. Long live Aubren."

"To Aubren." Cheers echo through the hall.

I toast the generals, advisors, and the soldiers. All gathered taking a swig of wine with each commendation. My head swims, and I pass the chalice to Kane. "Now, enjoy the celebration."

Behind me, the quartet of fiddlers begins a brisk tune, and servers enter, carrying large plates of meats, breads, vegetables, and fruits. I snake between the advisors' tables and ours, noting Gunther's still-vacant seat. Father sits to the left of the throne. Fighting the anxiety flitting just below my air of self-confidence, I wind behind the large wooden chair. I gather the folds of my gown and lower myself into the seat. Back straight, face forward, toes pressed to the floor to still my shaking legs, I smile. I belong here. This is my birthright now. Not only has this position passed to me through my bloodline, I am worthy of it, all the studying and training, this is what I have worked for all my life.

A maiden lays saucers of commons in front of me, and Father and I thank her. Looking up, I catch sight of Foster. He cups his hand, raising it to his mouth again and again. I cut my eyes to the others gathered. Everyone sits, staring at me. *Ack! I forgot.* I lift my plate and recite the traditional blessing. "Blessed be the fae."

"Blessed be." The crowd replies.

"Well, that was interesting." Father lifts his goblet. "Otherwise, well done, daughter."

Thanking him, I reach for my chalice but think again. My head already swims with wine. It is probably best to eat something first. I tear my bread and dip the piece in the meat juices.

The music, the crowd, the torches, and the voices of the men mesmerize me. Men… I search for another female, but with Mother absent, as usual, the only others I can see from here are those serving. Alfreda said all the halls were being filled with tables. I imagine the castle staff, most of which are maidens, and families of women and children squeezed into the tight passageways, like the warriors who pack this room, but not. Warriors, men, not women or maidens like myself. *How I am to get on in this position? You have never been like other maidens. Be yourself. You will figure it out.* I force my thoughts to my surroundings and find Foster. He converses with his battalion and does not notice my attention. I focus on the generals who sport red cheeks from the spirits, and the advisors, who whisper, tight-lipped, amongst themselves.

"Eat more, child. You will starve. You need your energy for dancing." Father squeezes my arm.

I glance behind me, catching the eye of our server to ask for water. Butterflies churn in my stomach, but I force another few bites of broth-covered bread in my mouth. Seeing others pushing their plates aside, I motion to the attendants to start clearing trays. Pages wind through the tables with pitchers, filling goblets. General Kane rises and places his sword on his table. He spins his finger in the air, and the quartet begins a jig.

Offering his hand, he bows in front of me. Dipping my chin, I gather my skirt and join him. He dips his head, and I curtsey, beginning a traditional fae jig. I focus on my posture and my footing, knowing all eyes are on me. Seeing the advisors with their arms crossed over their chests, I check Father's reaction. He eyes them, shrugs, and winks. Taking him to mean all to be well, I refocus on the dance. I lift my hands into the air, motioning for the advisors, generals, and others to join us. Wood scrapes across rock as the soldiers vacate their chairs and lug tables to the walls.

The advisors stand and join us, followed by the other generals. Father claps in unison with the beat, and the hall echoes with the sound of boots against the stone floor. A huge circle forms as others join the jig. Kane winds his large arm around my waist, and we spin. I hook my arm through his as the Chain of Fae starts. Then, I weave from dancer to dancer. It seems like there are at least fifty soldiers I congratulate before finding a familiar face.

Foster's cheeks shine red.

"Are you enjoying our victory?"

"I am." He places his hand over his chest, and I note the medal hanging there.

"Queen?" A soldier steps between us, arm out.

"Soldier." My cheeks flush as I am spun away from Foster.

I watch him wind farther and farther away, wondering what will come of our friendship. Kane stands in front of me as the Chain of Fae completes. He bows low, his red wings spread high above his head. As he steps to my right, the Archer General appears before me. Another tune starts, and we begin a new dance. I dance with the Cavalry General, the Militia General, and advisors Terrence and Jesper, stealing sips of my water between breaks.

As Advisor Bran approaches, I note the sudden absence of thumping heels and see the crowd parting. Fae in front of me move to the walls, and the sounds of thudding boots replace the banter and laughter.

Gunther, dressed in full battle armor, weapons in both hands, and bright purple wings stretched out high, marches towards me. His eldest son, Ethan, on the left, and three other sons following on the right.

I fight the blood rushing to my wings and take a deep breath, squaring my shoulders and raising my chin. If I read this right, Gunther had not come to offer me congratulations. I will not give him the satisfaction of thinking me scared or insecure. I will fake calm, confident, and regal. I lift my wings in a slow, controlled fashion then pop them to full wingspan at the last second.

"First Advisor Gunther, I am glad you and your sons could join us. I trust all wounds are healing quickly?" I smile as he stops just two feet from me. I am tall for a female fae, but he looms more than a head above me, his broad chest sporting the crest of his family, thick arms covered in chainmail, one fist around a sword, and the other clutching a blade.

"I am not late to this party because of wounds." He holds my stare for a second then shifts his eyes to Father. "You cannot make her our queen, Oberon. You have been marred by the loss of your sons and are not fit to make such a decision."

Father rolls his chair towards us, stopping inches from Gunther's steel boot.

Still, Gunther does not move.

Father grips the arms, pushing himself to a stand. I want to help him, wish I could support his weight as he grimaces, but I know he must do it alone. He needs to show strength, and I will do the same.

"Titania is the only heir. My family ruled Aubren since the beginning. Our line has been entrusted with this kingdom's prosperity, and we have delivered. Just today, Titania led the army in defeat of the kobold when my generals, and even you advisors, could not see a way."

Gunther's lip edges up on one side. He studies me. "She was lucky. A shoddy victory earned from desperation. Just because the mountain is sealed does not mean the kobold are defeated."

I ball my fists. "I am not ignorant or naïve. I know a threat still exists. But our ring is restored, and this is a problem for the 'morrow. I have trained for this position all my life. I am a strong warrior, know the histories of our people, and with Father and the advisors and generals at my side, will ensure continued prosperity of our kingdom, the realm, and Upper Earth."

"A female is not fit to rule. You were coached in protocol, dancing, and party tricks, raised to be a princess, to be married off to some other kingdom where you will be a king's queen. It is because of your brothers' passing that you even lifted a weapon." He spins to face the crowd. "A female has never ruled Aubren or any other kingdom in the Fae Realm. My line is second in succession to the throne. My sons fought in this battle, led many men with valor and skill. Who does this girl lead?"

Motion catches my eye, and I see Foster slide my quiver onto the table behind me. I am grateful for the gesture, and even as my fingers and muscles twitch, craving the feel of the smooth arrow between my fingers, drawing my bowstring back tight, and the release, I hold my ground.

"I found where the kobold were hiding, directed the army into the cave where we retrieved the ring stones. I made sure our fae were safe and sealed the kobold inside the mountain." My fingernails dig deep into my palms as I stave off my shaking legs.

Kane appears beside me. "She speaks true. And no one will dispute her archery skills."

At least Kane, the man who has supped with us day after day, is true. I wish that much could be said for Gunther, the fae Father looked to as his second.

"Archery?" Gunther chuckles. "You are going to kill the evil spirit aiding the kobold with an *arrow*? We all know it to be true. A large evil lurks underneath our ground."

Anger grows in my chest. "Why are you here? What do you propose? Do you mean to take my crown by force?"

Gunther spins to face the crowd. "Who among you believes this girl to be worthy of leading our kingdom? Of facing our enemies, keeping peace with beings of Upper Earth, making treaties with the other kings? A girl who must count crystals on the ceiling before she leaves her room, is plagued with breathing fits, enjoys no siblings nor friends, stays locked in this castle, and knows nothing of our faes' lives. Or may I ask a better question?" Turning towards the advisors' table, he raises an eyebrow. "Who among you believe we need to decide the succession to the throne by other means?"

My side ticks, and I force a slow breath out through my nose. *I must show strength and reason, but how?* I look to the generals then the advisors. "Sir Gunther"—I will not refer to him as First Advisor. I cannot believe he forsakes Father this way, and Gunther will never be *my* First Advisor—"raises a valid point." I stride towards the generals' table. "I *am* almost sixteen. But your King Oberon, who ruled for over thirty years after his father's death, provided me every tool I need to become ruler of Aubren. Since I was a small child, I have studied histories, learned science and math, grown strong, and have learned to use weapons: bows, arrows, swords, blades." I bend down, lift my skirt, and pull the knife from my boot, holding it high above my head. "I will do everything in my power, use every fae and resource our kingdom has to ensure the prosperity of our people and Upper Earth, as is my duty.

But"—I lower the blade to my side—"I will not assume to know I am the best person for this kingdom. The will of the people must be heard."

Gunther spreads his arms. "You have heard Titania. Choose my line or hers."

Boots scrape the rock floor, whispers spread through the chamber, and eyes cut to those near.

Drawing a sword, Kane steps to my side, followed by the Cavalry and Militia Generals.

Chin high, the Archer General, Raymond, crosses to stand in front of Gunther. Advisors Angus and Cedric follow Raymond.

I hold my breath, waiting for Bran, Terrence, and Jesper. With a nod towards Father, they cross to stand beside me. There are three advisors on each side. Although the king, or queen in this instance, is ultimately responsible for Aubren, most decisions are made with input from the advisors. There are six of them for a reason. Six advisors plus the monarch ensures there should never be a tie, but in this case, I cannot vote.

"I believe we are at a stalemate, gentlemen." Gunther paces in front of me.

I am certain I can best Gunther in most any test, the bulging, aging fae that he is, so I straighten my back. "The law of the land decrees a trial, three tests to decide who should rule if no decision can be made."

"Then it shall be." Gunther wraps an arm around his firstborn's shoulder. "*Ethan* and Titania should be tested to see who is most fit to rule. That is, if a woman can even be allowed to rule. Is the Keeper of the Ring present?

Surely, he will be able to advise on this issue. What sayeth the High Council on female rulers?"

Ethan? How could Gunther? I never liked the First Advisor, and now, he shows his true colors. I glance at my would-be opponent, Ethan, who stands even taller than his father, wearing a captain's insignia. Ethan's bare arms ripple with muscles, and his dark eyes meet mine, his jaw hard. One eyebrow twitches, but I will not be intimidated.

Gunther must know there is no position on female rulers. *Does he mean to undermine my rule while waiting for the High Council to weigh the issue? How dare he stage such theatrics.* I greeted the Keeper of the Ring, Aleem, in the passageway, and I scan the crowd, finding him seated at the end of one table.

Aleem reaches for the cane behind him and steadies himself with the tabletop as he stands. "The Fae Disciplines are silent on female monarchs. If you wish to challenge, you would need to take the issue to the High Council."

Rolling his lips over his teeth to form a half-sided smile, Gunther tips his chin in my direction. "As First Advisor, I will be happy to take the responsibility of ruling Aubren until the line of succession is confirmed."

My blood boils and head swims. A chill passes over me, and I grip my knife in my sweating palm. *This rule will not be taken from me.* I step forward. "The line of succession is intact. You are the challenger. Until there is a decree by the High Council that females cannot rule, I am sovereign monarch of Aubren. If you try to take my crown, you will be charged and tried for treason, and no one in your family will be allowed to rule our kingdom."

His cheeks rise, forming wrinkles around his eyes and he charges me. I lift my left arm in defense and hold the blade in, as trained. Time freezes.

Gunther's hot breath on my face smells of dank, moist dirt. *Just like the stench in my room?* I bend my knees and stare into his eyes, waiting.

Swoop.

Kane's blade passes between us. "Queen Titania is right. Her line are the true monarchs of Aubren. Anyone wishing to challenge must go to the High Council if there is not support enough within the kingdom. There may be a trial, but until my dying moment, I will defend Queen Titania and King Oberon of the house of Alpheaus, the first line of rulers of the Fae, from which all lines were created."

I release my breath, heart soaring at Kane's defense of me, my family, my reign. I drop my blade, straighten my legs, and step back, waiting, hoping, praying, others will follow his lead.

"Here, here!" the Cavalry and Militia Generals call from behind Kane.

He sheaths his sword. "It is late, gentlemen. Let us leave this discussion for tomorrow and finish the celebration."

Gunther inches backwards. "So be it."

Clunking his heels together, he spins and marches towards the exit, Ethan and his three brothers, as well as Advisors Angus and Cedric, and General Raymond, following. Watching them stride away, I hold my chin high.

Ethan stops in the doorway, extends his wings, and spins to face the soldiers. "All of those who wish to right the wrongs of this day and follow the future King of Aubren, join us now."

Chapter 4

I glare at Ethan. How dare he ask my army to choose his side. Future king? Over my dead body! I want to see the soldiers' reactions, gauge their leanings, but will not give Ethan the satisfaction of thinking I am concerned about his threats, so I keep my eyes fixed on him. "All those siding with Ethan and his father tonight, hear this: You will not be welcome in this castle, nor will you hold post, again."

A small group of men, about twenty, maybe those from his battalion, join him. Snapping his wings together, he spins and leads them out the door.

My hand quivers, and I take a step towards our table. Laying the knife on the table, I steady myself with one hand and raise my goblet with the other. "Please, enjoy another round of wine and more dancing."

I force a smile and turn to those gathered beside me. "General Kane, thank you for defending my reign. I am happy to have you at my side. And you as well, Generals Milo and Walter, Advisors Terrence, Jesper, and Bran. There is much to discuss, but for now, let us enjoy the rest of the celebration."

Warm fingers wrap around my left hand, and I turn my head to find Father smiling up at me. "I could not be prouder of you right now."

I take a sip of my wine. "Let us just get through this party."

After a few dances, families from the passageways start filing in to say their goodbyes. As this crowd wanes, the soldiers make a line to bid us goodnight. I greet them all with a smile and thank them for their valiant efforts, receiving many kisses to my hand and cheeks. When Foster appears in front of me, my face warms.

"Queen." He bows. "A lovely celebration. Thank you."

And then he is gone, just like that, as if he were every other soldier. I plaster a smile on my face for the next fae in line. How I wish to be sitting on my floor, knee to knee with Foster, discussing the events of the day. I wonder if that is even possible anymore. *Can I be alone with him?* I know the answer. It cannot be. As a maiden of title, I probably should not have been alone with him ever, but a country at war and a castle under duress bends the rules. A public stroll in the garden… Even that would be frowned upon because he is a soldier and I am a queen. *Will I never know true friendship again?*

The hall clears, and the servers flit about, clearing goblets, tumblers, cleaning tables, extinguishing candles. I turn to Kane and the two generals and advisors beside me, instructing them to meet me in the King's study. Seeing the physician with Father, I approach them.

"Your father should retire to his chambers. He needs plenty of rest to help his wounds heal." The doctor wheels Father backwards.

"Yes, of course. I will take him to his chambers."

I hoped to speak to Father alone, but the physician and four guards trail us. Knowing Father must need help dressing and climbing into his bed, I lean down and kiss his cheek. "I will come in the morning."

"Yes, we will talk then."

Questions spin in my head as I pat his hand. I wish we could talk before my meeting with the generals and advisors. *Did Father suspect Gunther would try to take the crown? Was it him who took my crystals? Can I trust Kane, his generals, and the other advisors?* As it is, I only have my instinct to go on. Kane has always been a friend to my family. He seemed genuine in his defense of my line.

I am tired of walking and the sound of boots echoing through the passageway and take to the air. Behind me, the four guards do as well. Even with their presence, the feel of the cool night air on my face calms me. Four guards stand outside the King's study, and I hear voices inside. Part of me wishes I thought to use the back passage to spy on them, ensure they were on my side, but that would not be very queenly. Perhaps I would hire a page, or several pages, to be my eyes and ears in the castle.

"Do we ask for a trial straightaway or go the council first?" I hear Terrence ask as I enter the chamber.

I take a deep breath and summon my queen spirit. Taking the head seat, I motion for the others to sit. I listen as the men debate strategies. I long to be counseled by Father, to talk to Alfreda about what she may know, to bounce ideas off Foster, but I listen to each suggestion, trying to make sense of how we should proceed.

When there is a lull in the discussion, I offer an idea. "What if we do nothing?" Standing, I circle the table. "We have made our point clear. It is Gunther's place to go to the Council or call for a trial. Let us shore up our arguments, plan for each scenario, and wait until he makes a move."

"What if he seeks to draw out the process? He could gain support and lead a coup." Kane counters.

I had not thought of that. "So, we should be proactive, have this settled as quickly as possible?"

"I would say yes. But, Titania, this will not be pretty for you. Gunther will try to expose your every weakness, paint you as delicate, unstable, inadequate to rule." Kane follows me as I circle the group.

"The Council will decide if a female should be able to rule, not me specifically. I say we press for the trial as soon as possible." I make a mental note to find the rules of the trial.

Cavalry General Milo turns to face me. "Pardon me, Your Highness, but how do you think you can win? The tests were designed with the assumption two men would be taking part. As they are written now, there is almost no way a woman half Ethan's size could win."

"The trial will have to be modified then." I take my seat. "We will need a nonpartisan board to decide how they can be fair."

"That cannot exist." Terrence rubs his forehead.

"Well, a board made up of an equal number of representatives from each side then?"

"And there will be a stalemate." Kane lays his palms on the tabletop.

"What if Aleem was the deciding vote? He is the oldest member of our community, well respected by everyone, a man of science, and as Keeper of the Ring, he is to have no political affiliation."

"There are not supposed to be any politics at all. That is the purpose of the monarchy, a ruler for the people, all the people." Bran shakes his head. "Gunther is making a mockery of this kingdom. He should be tried and hung for treason against all fae."

"Bran, you spearhead the effort to draw up arguments in support of female rulers. Kane, make a list of people you believe should be called to decide how to alter the trials. I would like the trial terms agreed to in one week and a date set. You must inquire as to whether Aleem is willing to serve as arbiter of that board, also. Call Gunther and Ethan to the castle to meet with us at ten. No, just Ethan. If he is to be ruler, *he* should be negotiating, not his father. Gunther, nor his followers, are allowed in this castle unless called by me." I rise. "Now, gentlemen, it is late. Let us all get some rest. We will need it for the coming days."

All rise. Bran, Terrence, Milo, and Walter bid me goodnight. Kane and Terrence remain.

"Gentlemen, is there more?"

Terrence eyes Kane then focuses on me. "We need to make sure you are safe. Kane, do you have men you know you can trust?"

"Yes, the King's Guard is loyal. We will double security."

"I will rest easier." Terrence bows and backs from the room.

"Madam." Kane places a hand on my arm. I take a step back and he dips his chin. "Apologies, my Queen, but I have known you your whole life, have seen the effects of your brothers' deaths on this family, on you. You acted well tonight. Showed strength yet fairness. But are you sure this is what you want? I am not suggesting you should hand your crown to Gunther's line, but maybe your father could be swayed to retake his crown, or maybe there is a distant relative?"

Could I let all this pass to another? Or put off ruling until I am older? I am too tired to even think straight at the moment. "I have not spoken with Father about his reasons for the timing of naming me ruler of Aubren. There has not been a chance. I have many questions for him."

"Gunther will try to paint you in the worst light possible. He is probably already spreading rumors. You must be more careful than ever. I know you befriended Foster. He is a smart, good soldier and already asked to be reassigned to the kingdom's western boundary so there will be no question of a relationship."

Foster is gone? My heart sinks but I raise my chin. "Foster is a hero to this realm. He served my family well. And thank you for your counsel. I will consider all these matters. You should get to your family. The morning will come quickly."

"Yes, madam." He dips his chin and backs away.

I circle the table and sit at the head. Placing my hands on the soft wood, I imagine all my ancestors who sat here before me.

Why did father crown me so young? Am I ready to rule Aubren? I have not even ever kissed a boy, and I will be asked to decide fates of men? Who will go to battle? What family may lose their father, son, husband? Is there another who should be in this place?

"Madam?" Alfreda's face appears in the doorway.

"Alfreda? Madam?"

"Sorry. Miss. It is the crown."

"It is okay. What do you need?"

"It is late. I thought you may want to turn in. I could help with your hair."

Such a motherly thing to offer. It was as if she knew exactly what I needed: To be with someone I trust completely. I fight tears threatening to form, knowing every action of mine is watched. "That would be nice."

We walk, side by side, back to my chambers, followed by four guards. Four guards stand at my door, and as Alfreda latches my shutters, I see guards are posted at either side of each window.

"I feel like a caged bird. How shall I ever sleep again?" I whisper to Alfreda as I sit before my mirror.

"Maybe a hot bath will help." She lifts the crown from my head.

I take the headdress from her and place it in front of me, staring at the crystals. "Did you hear everything that happened tonight?"

"I cannot believe that snake Gunther. I never liked him, and to weasel his son into position? A spineless worm is what he is." She slides a pin from my hair, and a strand cascades down my back.

"Did you know of Mother's gift? She spoke to me tonight. Said this was just the beginning. Do you think she saw what Gunther would do?"

As she regards my reflection, tears form in her eyes. Laying her hand on my back, she sits beside me. "Maybe he should have told you, or I should have told you, long ago. She always possessed the gift. That is why she reacted so badly to your brothers' deaths. She saw it, and they tried their best to prevent it, but it happened anyway. I think she blames herself."

Tears spring to my eyes. "But that makes no sense. It was not her fault."

Alfreda lifts another pin from my curls. "We cannot convince her."

Images of the winged kobold looming over Rigel and I flash through my mind. "Did she see me die?"

"She did." Alfreda pulls several pins from my tresses. "Thank goodness you were spared."

"A twelve-year-old with a bow and arrow does not pose that much of a threat, I guess. Mother's reaction makes more sense now. Thank you for telling me. Do you know what other predictions she made? Father said she warned him about the kobold."

"Your mother never speaks to me."

I wrap my arms around Alfreda. "Thank you for sharing all of this. For taking care of me."

She squeezes me to her. "How about I draw you a hot bath?"

Releasing her, I stand. "Perhaps some tea and extra blankets. And ask that they bring the texts about the trials to me at once."

"Those can wait for the 'morrow. You need rest."

"What I need is to know what to be prepared for."

I wrap a blanket around me and sit at my table, sipping the tea and reading about the trials. Although they have never been held in Aubren, there are several instances recorded, the most recent some hundred years ago in Elita, the fae kingdom under the continent of South America. The ruling family bore but one son who was not favored by some. The challenger won the trials, and his line usurped the throne and have remained the ruling family since. It does not mention what became of the son who lost the trial or his family. I skim the other examples, finding no information as to what happened to the other losers. At the back of the book, I find the rules of the trials. Three tests make up the trials: one of knowledge, one of strength and skill, and a battle. I sit up, and my wings spread flat. For the battle, competitors choose a single weapon, and the contestants are put in an arena to fight until one cannot continue. The only rule being you are not allowed to take flight.

This must be what Milo meant. If flying were an option, I could envision wearing an opponent out. If I chose my bow and arrows, I may be able to best even a male opponent. *But could I launch an arrow at another fae? A countryman? And what if I used all my arrows?* Then, perhaps I would choose a long sword or spear, something to keep my opponent at bay. But a strong opponent could have me disarmed in a matter of minutes.

My thoughts swim. I lay the text on the tabletop. Alfreda was right, I should have left the reading for the 'morrow. But the battle rules will be renegotiated. I have the best tutors in the land, have been studying histories since I could read. I think I can win a test of knowledge, but as for the strength and skill test, I will need to train, become stronger. *But what of the battle?* Maybe Kane speaks with wisdom. If I found a distant cousin to reign in my stead, at least the monarchy would be maintained by our family line. Or if Father took back the crown for perhaps two more years, until I am eighteen. Maybe his injury caused him to overreact. Perhaps he decided in haste.

I slide under my covers and pull the blanket to my chin. I stare at my blank ceiling. That chapter of my life is over. I am no longer the girl who lost her brothers. They helped me start the collection of crystals, and now my brothers and crystals are lost, along with my childhood. My mind jumps to the memory of Rigel's death and my secret. Holding my hand up, I spread my fingers. Nothing. Perhaps I understand Mother a bit better now, her guilt, but I cannot go down that rabbit hole tonight, or I will never get to sleep.

I think of my family. Father lost his brothers and their sons in the war with the kobold. Mother's line came from Bedham, a kingdom north of Aubren. I have not seen my uncles, aunts, or cousins since my brothers' funerals three years ago. Their absence from our court made more sense knowing of Mother's vision. *Why would they want to stay in a castle marked for death?* My confinement seems better justified given she saw me die as well. Still, three years with only Alfreda, tutors, trainers, and Father as company left me with few I could take advice from. I look at my quiver and think of Foster. I roll my eyes. *How can you miss someone you have known for five days?*

And what do I really know of him anyway? His family, even he himself, may side with Gunther and Ethan. *Is that why he fled?* No, I would not think that way. Kane said Foster to be true, good. This train of thought did not help either. *What could Foster ever be to me?* If I retain my position, we could hardly be friends. Thinking he could ever be more serves no purpose. He holds a guard's position nowhere near officer status. I would need to marry a prince from another kingdom. *But if I am queen, can I not choose who I wish to marry?* These thoughts presume I can best Ethan and that I should continue as queen.

I know I need rest and attempt to clear my mind. Picturing them on my ceiling as they used to be, I count crystals in my head backwards, one thousand, nine-hundred ninety-nine, nine-hundred ninety-eight, nine-hundred ninety-seven…

⸺◈⸺

I WAKE TO BIRDS CHIRPING, and I sit up, spreading my arms and wings high. I jump from my bed and flit to the window, face to the rising sun. For those few moments, I push away thoughts of Gunther and Ethan and enjoy the warmth on my face. Our rings hold strong, the kobold defeated, Father recovering. The green leaves of the forest call to me, but there is no time for such things as strolls under the vast green limbs anymore. I dash to my closet and pick out a long suede riding skirt, fit on tights to go underneath, and slip on a white shirt and dark leather vest. I lace my boots up over my knees and slide my blade in the top of the soft leather. Traipsing to the mirror, I see I have achieved my goal. It is feminine enough yet shows I mean to work. I will not cover my marks with powder this day.

Crossing to the doors, I swing them open wide to find Alfreda holding a breakfast tray. "Is Father awake yet?"

"Well, good morning to you, Miss."

I take the food from her. "I am going to eat breakfast with Father."

With a leap, I sail into the air and zip into the back passageway. I hear the hum of guards' wings beating behind me and recount last evening's events and my goals for the day: Figure out why Father handed his crown over now, seek counsel on whether I should pass this crown to another, learn of all Mother's predictions—I pray he wrote them down, and assemble a taskforce to draft acceptable trial stipulations. Alighting before Father's chamber doors, I add training for the trials to my list.

A guard steps in front of me. "Highness, your father still sleeps. The doctor said he needs much rest."

"Please, call me Miss. Okay, well, I will be in the study. If someone could alert me as soon as he is awake?" Seeing Alfreda behind my guards, I hand her my breakfast tray and proceed to the study to find it empty. "Where is everyone? Has anyone seen Kane? Do we know if Ethan will meet with us?"

"Miss"—the guard nearest me starts—"court business does not usually start until nine. And it is just after seven."

"Then we shall ride and begin training. What are your names? Can you ride horses?" I inspect the four guards in front of me.

"Of course, Miss." A soldier with bright blue wings and bright white hair bows. "I am Grant, and this is Nicholas, Adam, and Timothy."

Nicholas, Adam, and Timothy dip their chins in turn. I realize they all rival Ethan in size and height and commit their names to memory. Nicholas stands a bit short and is fair with light wings of barely any color. Adam, with dark hair and beard, sports wings of the slightest purple hue. Timothy's wings of dark green remind me of Father's when he was younger. I realize I missed signs of his aging—graying beard, wrinkles in his face, hunching shoulders—over the past three years.

Shaking a memory of my last supper with my brothers away, I focus on the men in front of me. "And you are to be my day guards?"

"Yes, Miss, weekdays," Grant answers, and I assume he is the lead.

"Then it is good we are acquainted." I pick up my skirt. "Let us take an hour to exercise."

Maybe I do not have friends, but my new guards can at least be company. *Who better to train with than soldiers?* Grant flanks me as I proceed through the castle and outside, advising me that the stable boys should be notified in advance if I want to ride. Reaching the barn, I spin to face my companions.

"I have perhaps only five days, maybe less, to be ready to face Ethan, a man at least two-thirds bigger than I, in a trial of strength, skill, and combat. Do you think you can help me or not? You know how to saddle a horse and ride, correct?"

"Yes, Mad"—Adam dips his head and opens the barn door—"Miss."

I go straight to my favorite horse, Ginger, a tan mare who stands just taller than me. When I spin around, Adam holds a saddle out. "No, no coddling me. I will get my own saddle."

Rolling his eyes, he backs away with the load. I slip a lead rope over Ginger's head and guide her out of the stall, securing her to a post outside. Heading back into the barn, I pick up the leather bundle, complete with saddle blanket, stirrups, and girth strap dangling below. My muscles twitch with the effort, but I cross to Ginger and heave the tack onto her back. After securing the girth strap, I find the reins. I release Ginger from the post, and putting one leg in the stirrup, swing the other over the saddle. I tap my foot to her belly.

The four guards follow me as I run Ginger across fields, ford fences, and bound across streams. I love the feel of the wind in my face, having to think about nothing except her footfalls. I watch the sky and stop a half hour later. Legs tight from the effort, I dismount and hand her reins to Grant. "Take her. I am flying back."

"But—"

"No buts." I jump into the air.

"Adam, Nicholas, Timothy, follow her." Grant's voice trails off.

I push myself to fly at full speed, and by the time I land in the orchard, I am panting from the effort. I double over to catch my breath and pace in a circle.

"What are you trying to do? Kill us?" Adam lands beside me.

"So, that was fast, you think?"

"I say." Nicholas's feet touch down beside Adam.

I fan my face. "I am going to clean up and change before breakfast."

Lumbering off, I realize the three follow me. *Ugh! Will this ever stop?* "I can walk to my room myself."

"Our orders—" Adam starts, but I raise my hand to silence him.

In my chamber, I shed my sweaty clothes, stand in the tub, and rinse. I find another pair of riding pants and skirt and lace a green vest over a fresh white blouse. Grabbing the text on the trials, I exit my quarters and fly to Father's chamber. I find the doors open and Father and Mother at their table. Kissing them both, I take my seat.

"I hear that you were already out riding?" Father comments.

"Yes. I need to train for the trials."

"You should take some extra meat." He points at the sausages in front of me.

"Same for you. You need to heal." Dipping my bread in broth, I realize I am famished.

While eating, I look between him and Mother. There is so much to ask but little time before court opens. Plus, with all the ears just outside the door, I do not dare discuss Mother's gift or his reasons for handing over his crown. I decide to wait for the evening. Perhaps then, when I usually play my harp for him, we can talk. It is odd to think of how, just two days ago, he and Alfreda planned my schedule, dictated my activities, but now, I am ruler of a kingdom, beholden to no one. I decide if I shall ride or fly, walk or run, eat or dance, read or play. *Or is it quite the opposite?* I am bound by everyone, in service to all those I lead. I swallow and replace my bread on the plate.

Noting it is quarter till nine, I rise and kiss Father's cheek. "Will you come to the study when you are done? I could use your counsel if you are willing to give it."

He chuckles. "Thank you for not commanding me as I did you for so many years."

Kissing Mother, I tell her she and Alfreda will walk in the wood, and I take flight through the halls to find Advisors Bran, Jesper, and Terrance seated in the study. "Excuse me, gentlemen, I hoped to arrive before you. Is there news? Has Kane contacted Ethan?"

They rise, only taking their chairs when I am seated. There is no news save that Aleem is willing to join the trial board. They propose the advisors could make up the board with Aleem serving as tiebreaker. Opening the text with the rules of the trials, we discuss how they may be altered. The knowledge test could stand as is. Same with the skill test. The strength section seems problematic, and we hope it can be done away with altogether. That leaves the combat test. I propose that we take away the rule about flying, which would even the playing field for me. In addition, I wonder if we might be allowed a certain number of weapons, and the one to lose all his or her weapons first becomes the loser. Bran proposes a fencing match with points scored for making hits, and it sounds far less barbaric than my idea.

As we wait for word from Kane, the men slide in closer and speak in whispers, questioning my sincerity in undergoing the trial and repeating the General's question from the night afore: Did Father crown me too early, and would there be another member of my family willing to take the crown? Under the table, my knee bobs. *Even they, my would-be supporters, Father's faithful advisors, question whether I should be ruling. How can I not?*

I have a good chance of winning the knowledge test and the skills section, and I have been fencing since the age of three. I must only win two of the three tests. But Gunther and Ethan, as well as the other advisors, would know I have these skills and may sway the tests to their benefit. *And what of the High Council? Would they decide a woman not fit to rule?* Fae edicts state a ruler must be fourteen, from the lines of the monarchy, and have support of the advisors and kingdom. *What if Gunther can smear my name, turn our fae against me?*

Bran lays a hand on my arm. "Do not fear in this. We have respected your father for years. The last few days, with the war against the kobold, your father's injury, and your victory, have been a whirlwind, and we look forward to hearing his counsel on these matters as well."

I force a smile. "He said he would be here. There is one question that does not seem to be in any of the histories: What happens to the faerie who loses the trial?"

Their eyes cut to the table and then to me.

Bran stands and crosses to the back of the room. "The contenders decide the fate of the loser. Most times, the loser's wings are clipped, and they are banished."

My wings pop out. Clipped wings for a faerie means never flying again. "Those are high stakes. I am surprised Gunther would put Ethan up for the trial. I would rather die than live without my wings."

"I am sure there is no doubt in Gunther's mind that Ethan will win." Bran turns to face me. "Are you sure there is no one to take your place?"

My thoughts bumble around. Mother saw me die at the hands of an enemy. *A kobold or another enemy?* And what of her new prediction: *This is but the beginning. The beginning of what? My reign, my end?*

Chapter 5

THE DOORS SWING OPEN, AND Father and the three generals, Kane, Milo, and Walter, enter. My anger flares, thinking perhaps they sought his counsel before coming to see me. Two things I will not tolerate are secrets and side conversations. I have been left in the dark about so much in my life, I will not abide it any further.

I stand. "Father, gentlemen, welcome."

Father rolls towards me, stopping his chair on my right. I bend to kiss his cheek. The advisors circle the table to my left, allowing the generals seats beside Father.

Sitting, I study the generals. "Kane, generals, have you been in the castle long?"

Taking a seat, Kane grips the table with both hands and leans forward. "Madam, we have just come from Gunther's and Aleem's."

Now, I like that he addresses me as Madam. If I am to rule, I will have no insubordination, no question as to who is in charge. Yes, I will take fair counsel, but as Bran stated well the previous night, this is a monarchy, and at the moment, I am the Monarch.

Looking at the others seated around the table, Kane refocuses on me. "Aleem agreed to be the arbiter of a board to decide the rules of the trial, but—"

"Kane, out with it. What news is there?"

"He is off to serve on the High Council. Gunther sent messengers to ride through the night. The High Council is convening in Hilbron on the 'morrow. We did not think to follow everyone coming from his compound."

"It is well within his right. He did nothing wrong." I swallow and smooth my vest to my stomach. We share our western border with Hilbron, but others must travel from all over the world. One ambassador, usually the elder Keeper of the Ring, from each of the nine kingdoms serve on the High Council. "Well, we could still begin discussions on the trial. I cannot imagine the High Council will decide against female rulers. That would be incomprehensible because there is no such law. I hope they will be quick with their decision. Bran, what say you on creating a board for deciding the trials?"

Bran clears his throat. "The most obvious choices are the advisors. They are already well respected. We are equally divided into your camp and Gunther's, and if Aleem serves as arbiter, I cannot see why Gunther would object."

"So, the only question left is what we will propose. There is no use quibbling about the knowledge or skills tests. The question is the combat test." Out of the corner of my eye, I catch Father's wince but push on. "We should push for a fencing match, or joust, any contest with points based on quality of hits. I have already started my training and will train to grow stronger leading up to the trial."

"Miss—" Milo starts, and I fix my attention on him. "Madam, if I may. How are you to win? Should we be thinking of a substitute?" His eyes pan to Father. "Or is this the right time to turn over the crown? Excuse me for being blunt but desperate times. Gunther has never been a friend to the crown. He is arrogant and self-centered and saw a weakness he could take advantage of."

I sweep my eyes to Father, wondering how he will react. He shifts in the chair, and his face contorts. I remember the fear of thinking he was gone not twenty-four hours ago.

"Friends"—Father starts, his labored voice no louder than a whisper—"my reasons for crowning Titania are many. You have witnessed her skill with weapons; riding; and most recently, leading our army to defeat the kobold when no other could find them. She bears the spirit of a monarch. If you question my timing, I would answer that I am growing old. Could I rule for a few more years? Yes, but with her victory, support for her reign will never be higher. I raised her to rule this kingdom, and rule this kingdom, I believe she will."

My heart thuds in my chest. *Was Father giving me no out? What if I lost the trial?* I would be banished and destined to a life of *walking* this realm forever. *But did Mother see a different fate?*

Father's gaze lands on me. "If I may have a few moments with my daughter."

"Of course." Kane rises, and the rest follow him out.

As the door clicks shut, I lean towards Father. "I came to your chamber early this morning to discuss all of this with you. I need your counsel. Do you think I should search for another to rule in my stead?" I scoot in closer. "Has Mother said anything about my reign?"

He lays a hand on my arm. "No. I know you have many questions about her, but now is not the time. I cannot decide this for you. I believe you can win the trial if you put your mind to it. But I do not wish to see you live a life that would not make you happy. You have borne enough sorrow for several lifetimes. Being a ruler is a hard job, but it is also rewarding and enriching. Study your heart and your mind. You will know the right thing to do. But keep this question to yourself. Until the decision is made, there must be no show of wavering. We will appear weak if there is any hint that you are thinking to relinquish the crown."

"Did you know Gunther would do this?"

"Gunther is a smart man. I knew he wanted more and that he probably meant to seize any opportunity."

"Why did you keep him as First Advisor then?"

"He is powerful and respected. His line served as advisors for many generations. And it is better to keep people like him close at hand."

"Hold your friends close and enemies closer?"

He chuckles and winces.

"What of the others? You have to tell me who I can trust and who to be wary of."

He fiddles with his fingers. "You can trust Kane and Aleem without question. Aleem will remain impartial, but he will also be true to whoever is in rule and the laws of the High Council."

"What of Milo and Walter, Advisors Bran, Jesper, and Terrence?"

"Milo and Walter will follow Kane. But Bran, Jesper, and Terrence will be more apt to seek favor with those who seem to have the upper hand. Right now, you have the law on your side. They will follow the rule of the law… As long as sways the way of the victor, that is."

"And what happens if the Council rules against female monarchs?"

Father cups his hand on my cheek. "Then you, Mother, and I shall retire to a cottage in the woods, and you shall find a nice husband to love you, and you will be the happiest woman alive."

I picture that. A small cabin with a garden, a cow, some goats, berries growing at the edge of the trees, the sound of a brook babbling over rocks in the wood. Father reading to Mother on the porch, me sewing a leather jacket for my husband. An image of Foster's face flits through my mind. I could walk away. *But what of the feeling in my gut?* The same one that made me so sure I could find the kobold… *Will I also be plagued with doubt, fear that I will let my people down, that somehow my fate is tied to the survival of our realm?*

Taking Father's hand, I kiss his palm. "I will think about this for a day and come to you with my decision."

He nods. "I should rest. You tend to all of this. I will be in my chambers if you need me."

"Can we talk more tonight after dinner?"

"Yes."

Rising, I wheel him to the door. Voices outside sound panicked, and I take a deep breath. Opening the panels, I find Kane in a discussion with a page.

"What is going on?"

Kane straightens his back and dips his chin. He takes a deep breath and reveals that Ethan refuses to talk until the Council votes. Further, he sees no reason the trial should be amended. If the Council is to allow a female ruler, the trial should remain the same. The only question in their mind is that of the fate of the loser, and they contend that the loser be given position as First Advisor.

I pace away and back as Kane speaks. Gunther and Ethan stall on purpose, seek to scare me, hoping to play on weaknesses, I guess. Well, they will find none.

Not in *this* queen.

I gather my skirt in one hand and instruct Kane and Generals Milo and Walter to build a course to practice strength and skill and to have the advisors ask the historians to draw up a list of questions that may be asked in the history portion of the test. As they disperse, I realize Father is still there, and deep in thought, I wheel him back to his chambers.

As we reach his door, he takes my hand. "Do not let your hard-headedness get the best of you. I know you like to win, and you like to be right, but this may not be your fight."

"You told me, you told the others, you thought I could win."

"Stubbornness and arrogance are traits that run thick in our family. Our line always held the monarchy of

Aubren, and it is difficult for me to see it any other way. But it is a real possibility that you could lose the trial, especially if the tests are not amended."

Anger wells up in my middle. My thoughts spin with confusion. "So, you do not want me to stand against Ethan? But you said…?"

He pats my hand. "I want you to do what is right for you."

I open his chamber door and wheel him in, and seeing Mother sitting by the fire, a tinge of guilt catches in my middle. It has been our habit to walk in the morning for years. I leave Father to his helpers, cross to her, and kneel.

"Mother, have you been out yet? Would you like to walk in the garden or the orchard for a bit? It should not be too hot under the trees."

Her eyes cut to my face and back to the flames. The handmaid explains they have not been out, that Father instructed her to wait for me. I wrap my hands around Mother's and give them a slight tug. She rises as she always does at my coaxing. I wrap my arm around her waist and guide her out into the passageway.

As my four guards fall into position, her shoulders shudder. I assure her we are safe and lead her through the garden to the orchard. Sticking to light subjects, I describe my morning ride. I pick a flower for her hair and an apple from a tree. She clutches these in her arms as a child would a doll. When I run out of topics, and she shows no response, my patience grows thin. Her lady approaches to say that Mother's lunch is served, and I relinquish her hand to the maiden, grateful for the reprieve.

Thinking I must be the most horrid daughter, I turn to my guards. "We should train more. How about a fencing match?"

They protest, saying they are not fencers but are trained in sword fighting, an altogether different sport. Intrigued to learn something new, I insist they show me, and we head to the soldier training area. The men halt their activities as we enter and dip their chins as we pass. Grant and Nicholas take up wooden training swords and begin to spar with Adam, commenting on their moves. It is not much different than fencing, but the moves are more exaggerated, sparring quicker with greater intensity.

Poking the sword to Nicholas's rib, Grant tosses the weapon my way. I catch the hilt, surprised at its weight. Adam instructs me on stance, keeping my center of balance low and weight distributed. Then they teach me jabs and lunges, cross swings, upper cuts, and the top down. After practicing those, I learn defensive moves using my arms and legs as well as spinning to avoid the blade. I coerce Adam into a mock battle. I know he holds back, but my muscles sear with strain from wielding the heavy wood weapon. Even with the pain, my nerves twitch with excitement, adrenaline courses through my body, egging me on.

"You need meat, more muscle on your bones. If we were up above, I would get you one of those protein shakes." Adam takes my sword.

"Well, I shall have to settle for chicken or steak."

"Your wish is our command." Timothy holds a tray of meat and cheese.

We find an empty spot at the end of a row of soldiers' tables and take a seat. I sense eyes on me and catch glances in my direction. I guess it is not often a female monarch, especially one of fifteen, sits with soldiers to eat. Still, I am determined to learn as much as I can, gain every advantage. Drink is passed, and I pour the liquid into a mug placed in front of me.

Adam snatches it from my grasp as I lift it to my lips. "Easy there. This is not for you."

He instructs Timothy to bring me water, and I roll my eyes. I guess it will not do to have a lushy queen—at midday no less. I listen to the banter around me, watch the activity, realizing this is what I missed: comradery, peers, if I could call them that. *What would my life have been if I were allowed to remain in school and attend normal functions?* I may continue this, have this as queen, or be forever the First Advisor to Ethan, puppet of his father, Gunther. Or I could relinquish my crown to some distant cousin. I make a mental note to find one who may be worthy. Not an easy task when one is being watched every second.

Finished with my meal, I traipse back to my quarters for a bath. Waiting for me are books with histories I am to study and ledgers of High Council votes. I wash and change, eager to learn more about the Council. The older kingdoms, ours being Aubren, under eastern Australia; then Hilbron, under western Australia; and Bedham to our north, lying under Southern Asia; Chastam being under China; Rotuga, under Africa; Willhelm, under Russia; and Lindleton, under Europe, seem to vote more conservatively. Elita, being under South America, and Borean, lying under North America, lean more towards progressive ideas. Two votes to seven, I think.

I note that I saw no female soldiers in the camp today, but muscle is muscle. I study my arm. I have little brawn compared to Ethan. *Why am I even thinking of being a ruler? How can I even imagine that I am strong enough?* My psyche battles back. *Look at what you have accomplished. This is in your blood.* My pulse races, and I slam the text closed. I long for a nap, but with my head swimming and so much to study, I open the next text.

—◆◆◆—

AN HOUR LATER, I CANNOT SIT still any longer and, wishing for a respite from my studies, exit my room. I intend to have one more workout in my day, and then dinner and talks with Father. My four guards fall in behind me as I take to the air. Weaving through the passages towards the courtyard, I note eyes cut my way then to the floor. Whispers fill the halls. Still, I press on. There has been much to discuss the past few days: the battle, my crowning, Gunther's challenge… *How could my people not be on edge?*

Instead of going straight to the courtyard, I cut across the building to the King's study. I find Kane, Bran, and Jesper there. They dip their chins as I enter. Alighting at the head of the table, I ask for updates as to the timing of the Council vote. Kane's eyes cut between the other two.

"Is something wrong?" I study his stoic face. "Just tell me, what is it?"

"There are rumors in the village." He shifts in the chair.

"Yes?"

"They are saying you mislead your father, set him up to fail in the forest, knew where the kobold were hiding all along, ensnared Foster to act with you so you could take the crown, and that you sent him away so he could not tell anyone."

I bolt out of my seat. "That is ludicrous! Why would I do such a thing? Father was almost killed."

"They are saying you hated being kept in the castle like a prisoner, wanted out from under your father's control."

I look between the men. "You know this is crazy, right? I would *never*. I love my father to the ends of the earth and never would betray him or our kingdom in this fashion. Any would testify to that. Bring Foster back. He and Alfreda, my instructors, will speak in my defense."

Kane stands. "We sent for Foster, but rumors are rumors. We cannot know how far Gunther will take this."

"What do you mean? He could not press charges. There is not any evidence. Right?"

"Evidence can be bought. Are you *sure* there is no one else to bring in? A distant cousin? A male of appropriate age and skill?"

Sweat forms on my forehead. "Even you, Kane? I thought *you* would be the one to defend my reign, back me up!"

"They mean to ruin your reputation and smear your family name. And how can you win the trial? You cannot best Ethan in combat. He is one of our strongest soldiers."

Balling my fists, I cross to the shelves. Histories of our kingdom and the realm line the wall. Jumping into the air, I find the text of our family tree. We are of the line of the first rulers of all Middle Earth, and from this first family, all rulers have been bred. I open the book to the last written page. Seeing my brothers' names, Rigel, Bryce, Garrison, and Thornton, beside mine causes my side to twitch, and I bite my lip to stave off tears. I follow the lines up to my father and his brothers and their sons, also lost in the Kobold War three years ago. Many were lost, but still I think it odd my whole family was wiped out. It could not be a coincidence. That was a question for Father, and I press on, following the line up to his parents and my grandfather's siblings.

It notes they settled in Bedham, the kingdom to the north, and I follow the lines to their children and their children's children, my cousins, who are such distant kin I have only met them once when I was very young. They are Faye, Bernice, Adria, and Quinn, the only male.

I calculate Quinn's age and land on seventeen. He would be acceptable. *But how can I even know?* There is no way to spy on him, not with Gunther's men surely watching my every move. Any attempt to send an investigation team would be seen as a sign of weakness. *And how could I just hand my kingdom over to a stranger? But what if he could beat Ethan? Is Quinn a true and upstanding fae? Would it not be better than Ethan's rule and me sitting around this table as First Advisor under him? I would rather have my wings clipped than serve as helper to that family.*

I slam the book shut. "I will think on this. And if this discussion goes beyond these walls, each of you can be assured I will have your heads. We will have dinner in two hours. I expect Terrence to join us as well as the historians, Generals Milo and Walter, and your wives if they can. Also, bring Foster back to the castle. And gather all the information you have on Ethan. We need to know of his strengths and weaknesses."

Standing, I force myself to take slow steps to the door, trying to appear dignified rather than being the rebellious teen my innards wish me to be. *How could Gunther betray my family in this way? Paint me as a vengeful usurper? He is the only betrayer here. And how could Kane ask me to hand my reign over to a stranger?* I jump into the air, letting my anger fuel my speed. In the orchard, I picture that brute Gunther and his hulk son and sprint from one end to the other until my muscles seize from exhaustion. I ask for the guard's bow and arrows and practice my aim, imagining the tip landing in Gunther's bloated gut. When the sun dips below the horizon, I retreat to my chambers to wash and dress for dinner.

I aim for the affair to be a light social evening and greet the advisors, generals, and their wives, repeating their names in my head to commit them to memory. Mother and Father sit near the head of the table, and I kiss their cheeks and take my seat. It feels odd to sit at the head, Father to my right and Kane to my left. At affairs such as these I used to be given a chair between Mother and one of the wives and would converse about sewing, which I detest, and music. But tonight, I find myself speaking of hunting, harvests, and wine—all very adult things.

Even with these pleasantries, the issues of the day hover in my thoughts. What to do about the rumors, what of Mother's visions, and how to decide whether I should stand against Ethan. I keep the meal short so Father will not be so fatigued and bid goodbye to our guests in under two hours. Mother's arm hooked around mine, I wheel Father back to their chambers. He asks me to play the harp, and I oblige him one song. I roll the harp away when I am done and wait for him to speak.

He rubs his beard and takes a long, slow breath. "You have studied histories and heard of gifts sometimes bestowed on fae?"

I nod and fold my hands in my lap as if to hide the gift bestowed on me that fateful day. Fae herald from The Creator and were made to protect the children of Upper Earth. Our powers, as a general rule, only manifest in that realm. We hear not only spoken language but thoughts of others, are blessed with strength and speed, enhanced senses, and the gift of magick. Only a few of our kind retain some of those abilities in our own realm.

"Capabilities seem to run in your mother's line." He takes her hand. "She sensed things before, gut feelings, but never a vision until four years ago."

"When she saw us die? Please, you must tell me of all her visions."

His hand trembles around hers. "They only started again a couple of weeks ago. She knew the kobold would come."

"They did, and we defeated them. What else has she predicted? She told me this was but the beginning."

Biting his lip, he diverts his gaze to the fire.

I stand. "Father, you *must* tell me."

"They want you."

Chapter 6

"Want me? What do you mean? Alive or dead? Who? The kobold? Why? They were in my chamber, took my stones, but left me unharmed. That does not make *any* sense. They did not even try to kidnap me. Has Mother told you what this is the beginning of?"

He shifts in his chair. "No, I do not know. All she said to me is that they were coming for you and then said this is the beginning."

"So, what? I should run, hide, far away where they cannot find me? Do I endanger all by being on this plane?" I spin to face Mother and grip her arms. "Is there more? Can you tell us more? I need to know what to do. How to protect our fae, our realm."

She blinks as if I am invisible. I want to yell, scream. Taking a deep breath, I release her arms and slump to the hearth. "This is not helping me."

"You thought there would be something that would tell you what you should do. If you should face Ethan or enlist another." Father nods as he speaks and strokes his beard.

I rise and pace in front of the fire. "Gunther's line *cannot* be allowed to win the monarchy. That is my only goal."

Father extends his leg into my path. "And I trust you will find a way. Retire to your chamber, take a bath, count your—"

"My crystals are gone."

"Well then, replenish them. Go to the stream tomorrow and start collecting again. Let your brothers speak to you in the wood. Clear your mind, and the answers will come."

Patting my chest where my one faerie cross hangs, I nod. I lean down and kiss Father's cheek. "Thank you. I believe you are right. I shall rise early and walk in the woods to harken the spirits of my siblings."

Walking to my room, I hold my necklace, letting the cool stone calm my nerves. Gunther has yet to press charges. I cannot be sure whether that is good or bad, but I count it as a win. Foster will come and clear my name, testify as to my motives. Still, I will not be able to speak with him or it will raise suspicion. I wish I could go back to how things were before. But tomorrow, I shall walk in the wood and hunt for crystals as I did when my brothers were alive, and I will think of a way to stop Gunther and Ethan from taking this kingdom and my family's reputation.

⋆

I AM WOKEN BY MOVEMENT IN my room and open my eyes to find Alfreda drawing the drapes. *Sunlight.* I smile. *Something normal.* Breakfast sits at my table. I thank Alfreda and flit over to snatch a pastry. I fly around my room in a circle, picking at the soft bread.

"You seem happy."

101

"I have a plan. It involves walking in the wood until I figure out what to do."

"Never one to walk the middle of the path, are you?"

I land in front of Alfreda. "What would you have me do?"

"You know I am not your mother, but I am as close to a mother as you will get. If you were my child, I would tell you to find someone else to fight that brute Ethan and fly far, far away where you can meet a nice fae boy and be happy for the rest of your life. You endured enough worry and strife to last a lifetime. What happiness will you find even if you can best Ethan? You will have him to contend with as First Advisor forever. Where will you find a husband to love you? You will need one that can help you secure your reign. Because Ethan will always be lurking. And there will always be men fae thinking you are not fit to rule. So, no, I do not think you should keep the crown."

Poking out my bottom lip, I plant my hands on my hips. "Why would Father pass it to me then?"

"Because he is a man and a king. He cannot imagine his legacy just being gone, poofed to nothing."

"I have trained for this all my life."

"No, dearie"—she cups her hand to my cheek—"you have trained for this since your brothers died three years ago because you felt you must bear the family's burden, but you do not. Choose to be happy."

"I thank you for your thoughts and honesty." Crossing the room, I slide my quiver on my back and, wrapping breakfast in a napkin, fit it inside.

"You are going to the wood in your nightgown?"

I smack my forehead with my palm, set down my pack, and head for my dressing area. After donning appropriate attire, I take up my bag and head to the door. When I open the panel, I hear the clank of metal boots on stone and peer down the passageway to find a hoard of guards approaching. They are led by a purple-winged fae—Gunther. My guards, Grant and Adam, step in front of me, and Nicholas and Timothy flank me.

Gunther stops in front of Adam and opens a scroll. "Queen Titania, you are hereby charged with treason against your king and are ordered to relinquish your crown and be held in the dungeon until trial."

"Trial? This is ludicrous. I have not committed treason against my father."

"The court says otherwise. We have enough witnesses for the charge. You purposely sent the King's soldiers on a wild goose chase in the woods and then put the King's life in danger by sending him and his men into the mountain to fight the kobold. You are charged with treason and attempted murder, all for the purpose of taking the monarchy yourself. These guards will escort you to your cell."

Flapping wings alert me to incoming fae, and I spot Kane, followed by Milo, Walter, and a dozen guards flying towards us. Landing beside Gunther, Kane authenticates the seal.

He focuses on me. "Sorry, Highness. It is true."

My guards back away, and Gunther takes my bag and bow and throws them on the floor. The guards shackle my wrists and ankles.

As I am led away, me taking quick steps to keep up with the parade of stomping feet, I hear Alfreda's high-pitched voice over the commotion. "She did not have breakfast! At least give her this."

I imagine her forcing my wrapped meal on a soldier. A haze glazes my eyes, and time almost stands still as we weave through the castle, disrupting workers. They stand, backs to the stone walls, some with round eyes and open mouths, others with hard stares, but all watching as I am paraded by like a prized sow off to slaughter. My heartbeats sound in my ears. First racing, then an errant thump, and then racing again. *Could they really find me guilty?* We wind down a narrow staircase, and the tunnel grows dank. Even with the flame held above me, I squint to make out each step, determined to maintain my footing.

We reach the bottom, and when I hear metal sliding against the stone floor, I raise my chin. I will *not* let Gunther see my fear. I have never been to the dungeon. It remains empty much of the time. As beings of The Creator, fae seldom engage in subterfuge. I guess not so rare an endeavor in Gunther's case.

Tugging on my wrist chains, they lead me into a small grotto lined with metal-barred cells. As a torch is raised, I catch sight of red hair on a fae leaning against the cave wall. *Foster? They have imprisoned Foster as well?*

"What is he doing here? He is innocent. I am innocent. We have done nothing wrong." I tug at my bindings.

Gunther spins to face me. "That will be for the judge to decide. Put her beside the soldier."

The door of the cell next to Foster's slides open, and I am pushed inside. I stumble and fight to find my footing. Circling to face them, I lift my head. The breakfast pouch hits my face, and the contents spill to the dirt. Even though I fear I will have to fight the rats for the meal, I will not give anyone the satisfaction of scrabbling for the food.

"I should have council, as should Foster, as is the law."

"You each get one visitor. Choose wisely. Who say you?"

My thoughts whirl with the decision. *Kane? Father? Who else can I trust?*

"Kane. I select General Kane." Foster, now on his feet, stands with his back straight, facing Gunther.

"And you, Princess?"

"I am your *queen*." I raise my chin a notch. "I call my father, King Oberon."

"You will not be Queen for long." Gunther snarls.

His men chuckle as they lumber out of the cavern. Two stay behind, one posted in front of my cell, and the other beside Foster's. I note that two more guards stop on the other side of the outer door.

Kane enters the small cavern and approaches my cell. "They said you would like to see your father. I will have him brought to you. Do not worry. This will all be sorted out."

I trudge to the bars. "Who would speak against me in this way?"

"We will have the witness list soon. You should think of those who can speak *for* you. As should you." Kane side-steps to Foster's cell.

They cross to the far wall and speak in hushed tones, and with the echo, I cannot make out a word. There is little physical evidence of treason. *Perhaps the arrows we stole from the barracks and the map I used to mark off the hectares?* The map lies in my desk drawer. Foster would testify that we crossed off the squares together. Alfreda could witness to my character, my love for Father. *Who would speak against me?* Especially being that Gunther fabricated this story days after the battle.

I back away from the bars and spin to assess my surroundings. Tripping over a pastry, I dip to retrieve it then crawl across the rock to gather the apple and cheese chunk. I down the pastry in two bites and, picking up the handkerchief, wrap the cheese for later. Looking up, I note a hole in one corner and water pump in the other. Aleem, who would serve as judge, will not be home till the Council decides the question of a female ruler. That could be a few days or a week.

The whispers cease, and Kane appears before me. "I shall have your father brought down at once."

Stumbling to the door, I clutch the bars. "What reason would I have for overthrowing Father?"

"They are saying you went crazy. Hated being watched and protected every moment, that you wanted your freedom."

"That is ludicrous."

"Miss"—the guard opposite me steps forward—"is Kane to be your counsel?"

Kane backs away. "I will get your father."

"Thank you."

I cannot even look at Foster, knowing he is here because of me. *Why does this keep happening?* Rigel died defending me, my father was nearly killed fighting the kobold I led him to, and now *this*? *What karma brought me here? Alfreda is right.* I should go far, far away so I do not hurt anyone else.

Leaning against the wall, I slide down to my butt. The stone is cold and wet. Gunther would probably as soon see me die here. Then our line would end, and he could take the throne. My breaths become jagged, and sweat beads form on my skin. Pulse racing, I fight for air.

"Titania? Are you okay?" Foster's voice halts my spiral.

I focus on his face. His wide eyes catch the little light that enters the cavern. *Concentrate on him. Fight for Foster if not yourself. He is an innocent in all of this. Think. There must be a way out.*

I recall the days leading up to the battle. I did as Father said: tending to my studies, practicing fencing, and passing my time with Foster. We fell asleep on my windowsill, and the guard at my door would testify to that, or at least to the fact that Foster spent the night in my room—which raises more issues than just plotting to overthrow Father. I wonder if they will paint us as forbidden lovers. I bury my face in my hands. *How can things have gone so wrong?*

⊶⊷

S ITTING AND STARING AT THE guard in front of me does no good, and I decide pushups, sit ups, and planks will be good training for me. I wish my arms and legs were not bound so I could practice some punches, jabs, and kicks.

"What are you doing?" Foster asks.

Guilt twists my stomach, but I dare not say anything that could be used against me. "Training for the trial. I saw the soldiers doing these in the yard."

"Ha, like you could be stronger than Ethan," the guard in front of me exclaims.

"He is right," Foster whispers. "Ethan is one of the strongest soldiers in the army. He usually wins the wrestling matches."

I do not know what to do with that information, so I shuffle away. Wrestling. My mind pings. *Pressure points, choke holds.* I have watched matches between the soldiers. You need not be bigger than your opponent. *If you are found guilty it will not matter. You will be banished.* I lift my arms, wishing I could punch the rock face in front of me. Tugging at my shackles, an idea forms. A chain could be a weapon. It could be used to hit an opponent or pulled tightly around a neck to suffocate the life from them. I drop my wrists, rebuking the dark thought. I may not even last seconds against Ethan anyway. *No, it would be better to let the rule pass to another, right?* Perhaps the Council will not allow a female ruler anyway. All my deliberation could be for naught.

I work my muscles until they refuse to move. Then I hobble from one side of my cell to the other, fanning myself with my wings and stretching my limbs. *Am I really to be in this space for days?*

I size up the cell. The ceiling is not as high as in my room, but it *is* high enough that I could hover to keep my wings strong.

I lift my hands and shake the shackles connecting them. "Is this really necessary? I am locked in a cell. I do not think I need my hands and feet bound as well."

The guard approaches. "There is no telling what powers you have. Those are not just any bands. They are carved of lodestones. Keeps you from using your magick powers to escape."

Too shocked to speak, my mind reels. *Could they really know? No, it is impossible. It just happened that once.* I narrow my eyes. "They think I can do magick? I am a faerie, just like you, like every other faerie in this land."

"We have witnesses that say they have heard your mother is a seer. Magick runs in your veins. It is probably how you bewitched that poor soldier into helping you." He motions to Foster.

Foster jumps to his feet. "There was no bewitching. We did nothing wrong."

"That is for the judge to decide. Do not waste your energy on me." The guard shakes his head and retreats to the far wall.

Additional lights flicker in the passageway, and I hear footsteps. Father's chair lands on the bottom step. Guards roll him into the dungeon and to my cell. I press my nails into my palms for fear I will cry. Noting his pale face, my heart aches. *And now he must worry over me being locked in this cell and possibly banished.*

"Father, thank you for coming. Can you believe what Gunther is accusing me of?"

"Gunther must be scared to be going to these lengths." Father's eyes cut to the guard and back to me.

"And they have these shackles on me because they think I can do magick."

"I am not surprised by anything Gunther does now." Father turns his head to Foster. "How are you holding up?"

"I have been better, sir."

"We all know the truth, and the judge will recognize Gunther's antics for what they are." Rubbing that gray beard, Father looks at me. "Should I send for our family in Bedham?"

Quinn. He speaks of Quinn, my distant cousin that could take the throne. I study the stone ceiling above and bite my tongue to keep the tears from springing to my eyes. I can tell Father to send for Quinn, have him fight for our family, succeed Father, and all this will end. I could get a cottage in the wood with Mother and Father, and we could live happily forever.

Or Ethan will best Quinn and become the next ruler of Aubren. Would he give Quinn the same offer of First Advisor, or would he send him back to Bedham? It would certainly be more advantageous for Quinn if he returned home. I guess he knows little of our kingdom. *Why would he want to stay?* But then Aubren would be ruled by a treasonous liar. I cannot leave this to another. I must ensure our kingdom is ruled by a true and just monarch, no matter the cost.

I lower my chin and hold Father's gaze. My heart pounds in my chest. "No. I *will* be found innocent of these charges, and then I will stand trial against Ethan. I will fight to keep my kingdom and reign."

A smile spreads across Father's face. "Spoken like a true Alpheaus. I am proud of you, daughter. I pray you do this out of loyalty to our kingdom and not stubbornness."

"This is not me being obstinate or rash. Aubren deserves a just ruler. One that will put it first. I shall make you even prouder still when I best Ethan."

"Umm." The guard behind Father chuckles.

Father reaches through the bars and takes my hand. "I will do my best to make sure you are treated fairly. Alfreda frets for your health."

"And Mother?"

Tears form in his eyes, and he blinks them away. "I thought I saw something, just for a second."

"We see what we want. I have been noting those glimmers for years. But you should go. It is too cold and damp down here for your healing lungs."

I call out to his guards and clutch the bars as they wheel him out, praying I have made the right decision for our people.

Foster sidesteps to the bars separating our cells. "How are you to best Ethan? Is not one of the tests a combat?"

"I only have to win two of the three tests." I do not wish to say too much with the guard just feet away and lower myself to the floor.

I ask Foster to show me more exercises. He gives me some examples but begs me to wait until we know how they will be feeding us. I hate it, but agree. If I am to build muscle, I need meat. With no windows, it is impossible to tell time, and I plod from one side of my cell to the other—first, because I am anxious to know if we will get a midday meal and second, to stave off the cold. I dressed in leather pants, skirt, and jacket at least, but it was meant as a flying and riding outfit, and I need another layer for warmth.

At least Foster wears a warm jacket. He must have been travelling when they arrested him. He offers me the sheepskin with thick pile, but I refuse. I can stay heated enough with movement. I hear footsteps in the stairwell, and lights from lanterns bounce off the walls.

Second Advisor Angus steps into view. He holds the light over his head and steps into the cavern. "I have news and sustenance."

Arms piled with blankets and baskets, Alfreda stands beside him. "Heavens, it is ghastly down here. How could you hold them in this place?"

"It is the dungeon. Where else would we keep them?" the guard responds.

I fix my eyes on Angus. "What are you doing here?"

He raises his chin. "With Gunther involved in your trial, rule of the kingdom falls to me."

"How can you betray Father this way? Side with that usurper?"

His face contorts. "You are not fit to rule. Even if the High Council allows a female monarch, Ethan will best you. It is what is right for this Kingdom."

"To have liars on the throne?"

"Your father should have found another to groom, someone untouched by the tragedy that befell your family. You are not stable or mature enough to lead this country."

"I saved our kingdom from the kobold. My actions speak for themselves. You would do well to think about your choice. When I win, you will not hold post in this kingdom again."

"At best, a serendipitous discovery of the kobold's location, or at worst, a deception aimed at getting your father killed. You are one to speak of treachery."

My blood boils. I draw in a deep breath, trying to maintain a calm head. What I need is information. It will do me no good to argue with him.

"I will be acquitted of these charges. What news do you have from the High Council? Have they started the deliberations?"

He apprises us that they have indeed begun the discussion but there is no way to know when a vote will be called. My trial will commence once Aleem is home from Hilbron. We will be held in the dungeon cells throughout the trial. Alfreda waits beside him, transferring weight from one leg to the other under the strain of her bundle. Finally, Angus motions to her, directing her to deliver the supplies.

I am surprised they allow her to visit me. I would think Gunther would detain and question her as well, being she has been my caretaker for so long. Wondering if they brought her here on purpose, to trick me into admitting something to her, I am wary of discussing the matter of my charges.

"Thank you, Alfreda." I kneel at the bars as she slides a bundle of food and blankets between the metal rods.

"This is just ghastly. I cannot believe it. How someone would think you would do such a thing. Completely preposterous, and I have told them such."

"I know. But all will be well. Can you make sure Father and Mother are cared for? That Mother gets her walks?"

"Of course, dear." Tears fill her eyes.

"I will be fine. Do not fret for me."

She nods and sidesteps to Foster's cell, transferring a bundle of food and two blankets to him. He thanks her.

"Okay, woman, you have seen they are unharmed and being cared for. Will you stop your incessant pestering now?"

Alfreda stands and spreads her wings. "I will come three times a day to bring them food and supplies. Only then will I let you have peace."

Angus huffs. "Fine. It is agreed."

She spins and curtsies to me. "I will come again tonight, madam."

"You take care as well. You need not stress yourself. There are many here who will aid us."

She lays a hand on her heart. "You are like my child, dear. To not lay eyes on you, know that you are okay, would bereave me more."

"See? Everyone is happy now. Come, woman. I have other matters to attend to."

Alfreda struts past him into the stairwell. "No one required your presence."

Angus nudges the guard and cuts his eyes to me. "Women. Always thinking they are so important. They shall know it is not so soon enough."

Rage seething in my chest, I glare at him. I will not give him the satisfaction of a reply. He is the one who shall be enlightened when I beat Ethan in the trials. I wait until I can no longer hear his footsteps on the stairs to relax my stance and plod to the back of the chamber. *How could Father have such hateful men on his council? Did he not realize his advisors plotted against him? Did they take him for a fool?* I am guessing so, which furthers my fury. I raise and lower my wrists as I tramp from one end of the space to the other.

"You should eat. Then we can continue training. Have my meat as well." Foster holds his sausage out to me. "You need it more than I."

"That is a kind offer, but I cannot starve you."

"Well, at least take most of it." He breaks the link, tossing me the larger portion.

The piece falls into my lap. *How can he be so charitable to me? After I have gotten him imprisoned here, jeopardized his position, nae even his family's livelihood?* I study his face, the square chin, high cheeks, and light eyes.

"What are you thinking?" I watch his perfect lips move barely caring what the words are.

"I do not deserve your friendship but am grateful for it."

Chapter I

I EAT THEN TRAIN UNTIL I can push my muscles no more. Refueling, I rest, using the time to recite histories. I am quite sure Foster could not care less about the succession of monarchs in Aubren, but he spurs me on none the less, asking me of battles, the Keepers of the Ring, quizzing me on the important crystals that anchor our Faerie Ring. I list all the kingdoms and locations of their rings.

We go on this way through the afternoon until Alfreda brings supper. Eating a bit, I exercise again doing sit-ups, planks, push-ups, and leg and arm lifts, my shackles serving as weights, and fly around my compartment like the caged faerie I am. I try to think of anything but being locked in this cell. There is nothing I can do about it. I must make my body as strong as possible and recite as much information as I can to use this time well.

If I were free, this would be how I spend the time anyway, plus riding, fencing, knife and sword practice, *wrestling*. I remember my earlier idea. Alighting on the cold stone, I implore Foster to teach me wrestling moves and strategy. He claims it is not his strong suit but reviews what he learned by watching the soldiers in the yard. I push him to remember how they evade being pinned, thinking this is where I will shine. Ethan may be bigger and stronger, but I am sure I am faster. If I can hold him off, tire him out, I can gain the upper hand.

"You should not focus on the combat test. You are more likely to win the histories and skills tests," Foster says as I sip water from my cupped hands.

Swallowing, I shake my head. "The history perhaps. But not the skills test. I have to win two of the three tests. I am sure Ethan is quite accomplished at many skills."

"But with your archery skills, you can win that portion, and the fight is the last test, only entered if the opponents are tied."

"But that is where I am weakest and need the most practice."

"It will not come to that. You will win."

"You think I will win because you want me to win. That does not mean it will be so."

He hangs his head. "I cannot watch you fight that brute."

I like that he seems to care for me, wants to protect me. *As would any of your soldiers, right? You must not harbor feelings for him.* "Or"—standing, I dry my hands on my skirt—"the High Council will not allow a female ruler, and I will not have to stand trial at all. Father will call for Quinn to fight in my stead."

He asks about Quinn, and I admit to knowing nothing about him save he is a distant cousin from Bedham. Exhausted, I lean on the rough wall and slide my butt to the rock floor. Our guards switch out, and I guess it must be nearing time for sleep. I roll out the blankets Alfreda brought me for a bed. They do not make a very soft mat, but at least they offer insulation from the cold stone.

I spin on my side and stare across the chamber at Foster, his light skin reflecting the glow of the torch. It is not good that I think of his smooth skin or broad shoulders and muscled arms. I favor him too much for any good to come of it. Even if he felt the same way, I would only bring him pain. "Thank you. I do not know what I would do if you were not here."

"Another soldier may be of more use to you."

"No, he could not."

His cheeks turn rose colored.

My face warms as well. Looking at the stone floor, I close my eyes. Every inch of my body hurts, but it is a good pain, one earned from work and progress. Worries swirl at the edge of my consciousness, but I am exhausted and drift to sleep. I dream of kobold stealing my faerie crosses in the night, dark wings hovering above me, Father's face, Mother's face, Gunther, Ethan.

⸺◈⸺

My eyes pop open to find bright torch lights above me. Four guards stand outside my cell. I shut my eyes and pretend to sleep, hoping to hear something of use. As I suspected, they have listened closely to all my conversations with Foster, and the night guards share the information with the others. I wait for them to finish their discussion, and for the night guards to leave, before rousing. Seeing Foster's eyes closed, I use the latrine in the far corner and pump to draw water for my face. I have no clue where the sun sits in the sky, but by the time he wakes, I have already gotten in one workout and pace my rock floor, letting my breath settle.

"Why did not you wake me?" He approaches the bars. "I need to be pulling my weight."

"Yeah, because we can achieve so much stuck in these ten by tens?"

"Is someone hungry?"

"Beyond."

He crosses to his bed and picks up a knapsack. "I saved this for you."

"You cannot go hungry because of me. No wonder you slept so long. You have got to keep your strength up as well."

"We will not be in here that long. I will be fine." He squishes the pack between the bars.

As I take the pack, my hand grazes his. The warmth of his fingers surprises me, and I raise my eyes to his face. His light skin turns pink. He blinks, and his blue eyes transfix me. Light green, they seem odd ringed by his red lashes.

"What are you thinking?"

His voice startles me, and I press the sack to my stomach. "Sorry, your eyes are odd."

Chuckling he steps back. "I do not think anyone called me odd before."

"Sorry, I mean they are so light and your hair so red."

"Surely you have met people with red hair before."

"Rigel had red hair, but lighter, like strawberries, not a cherry red as yours is."

He leans against the bars. "And what do you call your hair?"

I lift a ringlet. "It only possesses a few red highlights. Mostly it is dull brown."

"I would not say anything about you is dull," he whispers.

My face flushes.

"What is this? No whispering here." A guard approaches with his torch.

I move back to my blankets. Taking a seat, I glance at Foster again. I marvel at how I came to trust him so easily. We have only known each other… *Ten days.* I count in my head. Really, he is my only friend save Alfreda. Who is more like a mother to me than anything.

Opening the pack, I find a piece each of cheese and bread. I ask him to tell me of his family and home as I eat. He describes a sister who always picks on him, a mother who always is working, and a father who tends to their land and animals.

Foster holds my gaze. "I am glad they do not know I am here. They would be so worried."

"Did your family like you becoming a soldier?"

"I think Father understood that I needed to do something of my own."

"Do you think you will go back and farm once you have served in the army?"

"Right now, I would give just about anything to be turning the fields."

I want to say I am sorry, let him know how horrible I feel that he is in this mess because of me. But with the guards listening, I cannot be sure they would not twist my words, use them as an admission of guilt. I cut my eyes to the guards and back to Foster's, hoping he understands.

"Well, you rested and ate. Back to work." He stands.

"Yes." Setting the pack on my bed, I bounce into the air.

My wings, arm, and leg muscles feel tight from the prior day. Still, I press on, and we spend the day like the last, working on my strength and testing my knowledge. Alfreda brings food and additional clothes and blankets but reports no news from the High Council, Father, or Kane. She says they are busy gathering witnesses on our behalf, and we should not worry.

As I eat the final meal of the day, I think again of what evidence Gunther could use against me. The arrows we stole from the soldiers are the only physical evidence. Beyond that, I guess testimony will be my word against his. I work through how it might be contrived that I tricked Father, told him the wrong location for the kobold, then used Foster to help me call the army to the right place, making me the hero. Me sending Father into the tunnel, putting him in grave danger to take his throne. *How is someone to judge my true intentions? Could Foster even know for sure my actions were not based on trickery?*

"Where are you?" Foster's voice brings me out of my spiral.

I peek at the guards. "I am just tired."

"We should rest." He reclines on his blankets.

Tugging a piece from my loaf, I pitch it at him. "You have been resting all day."

"Hey!" He retrieves it from the stone and tosses it at my head. "I exercised with you."

"Some." Retrieving the dough from my curls, I throw it back to him.

"It would be good if we had cards or maybe a fire."

"Music would be nice."

Foster starts to whistle a tune I have never heard, but it contains sweet notes that remind me of the wood, walking under the trees, and green pastures. I imagine what his farm may look like: a small stone cottage with a thatched roof; flowers in the windowsills; the smell of hay all around; a horse grazing in a field; blue sky overhead; and soft, warm dirt underfoot. Water forms in my eyes as I realize I may have taken him from that forever, and further yet, that I would never have such a simple life as that. The music stops, and I open my eyes, realizing tears wet my cheeks. I swipe them away.

"It is meant to be happy."

There is an odd gust, and my wings fold out. A light grows in the stairwell, and I hear footsteps. Just one set, I believe. Standing, I cross to the bars, waiting to find out who our visitor may be. Aleem, bent and with white hair down to his waist, a lantern in one hand and staff in the other, appears in the entry.

"A fine mess this is. I am away not three days, and all goes south for the lot of you. I hoped to get a good day's rest, but I see there are more urgent matters." His voice is low and sure as if it harkens from his chest—so out of place with his wrinkled face and wiry frame.

"Did the High Council make a decision on female monarchs?" My stomach twists with worry because I am not sure what I hope for, to be relieved of this burden or to have a victory for equality.

"They did, and what do you think they decided?"

"They voted that it does not matter." Foster's voice is strong and clear. "To not rule that way would go against all that fae believe."

Aleem's eyes cut to Foster and back to me. "This is the soldier who trailed you in the days leading up to the battle? That is why he is detained with you?"

I glance down and back up to Aleem's face. "Yes."

"He is a smart one. Yes, they have concluded that our laws do not prohibit female rulers, and further, that female fae should never be banned from ascending to the monarchy."

My middle feels as if the whole of my torso contorts inside. Now, I must face Ethan. I berate my reaction. This is what I wanted, what should be, for me to be allowed to follow my destiny. *But will I prove worthy?*

Gathering my breath, I raise my chin. "This is good news indeed. I mean not to rush you. I know you are weary from travel, but we tire of being held here. When can you set our trial?"

"I do not wish you to be detained further. Your trial will begin in the morning."

Thanking him, I bid him farewell and a good sleep. I cannot settle and decide another short workout is in order. Foster begs me to go easy, but my mind needs distraction. After I tire, I have him quiz me on geography, history, and science. My eyelids grow heavy, but still, my brain turns with worry. *How will this court decide who is telling the truth? Surely Gunther's theories cannot stand, right?* I pray Father and Kane have come up with good witnesses.

Seeing Foster yawning, I feel bad for keeping him awake and bid him goodnight. I lay down on my blankets, and he starts to whistle a tune. The notes are low and soothing. When I ask what it is, he says his mother sang it to him at night. I huddle under my blankets and listen to the melody until exhaustion takes me.

⸻

"Heavens, it is freezing down here." Alfreda's voice wakes me.

She holds a basket, and I flit to the bars to retrieve the goods. After eating a small roll, I do not dare eat more for fear my stomach will betray me, I convince the guards to let me remove the shackles binding my wrists and ankles just long enough to change into the dress Alfreda brought. With white lace around the collar and a green, lace-up bodice, it seems too frilly for a legal battle, but I trust she picked the outfit for a reason. The guards lead us, shackled and chained, up the stairs, giving us just enough slack between our ankles to climb the steps. As they swing the door open into the upper passageway, light blinds me.

I raise my hands over my head to shield my eyes from the rays streaming through the windows. As they lead us into the courtyard, my skin welcomes the warmth of the sun, but the brightness overwhelms my senses. Through the blur, I make out body after body of fae gathered. I am guessing to witness either my demise or victory, or perhaps to gawk at the circus my reign resembles. The space is oddly silent however, with only the sounds of the trees rustling in the wind and birds calling from the skies.

Blinking, my eyes become accustomed to the light, and by the time we reach the table where the judge sits, I am able to make out a form. A dark-headed fae sits in the middle seat at the judge's table, and I scan the rows for Aleem. He sits behind the accuser's table, where Gunther and Ethan sit. *Argh!* I recall visiting Aleem to inquire about the Faerie Ring the night of the battle. *Now he is to be a witness as well? What evidence can they glean from me asking as to the status of the ring?*

There is no way to know my mind except to ask me. *But I could lie? Correct?* Fortunately, or unfortunately for Gunther, the First Judge is a seer like Mother. Instead of predicting the future, he knows what is. My breaths come quick as I jump to the next thought. *How much will he know of me? Could my secret be revealed?*

We are led to the defendant's table where Father and Kane sit. At least the general still sides with my family. I hug Father and take a seat behind him. The dark-headed judge asks that court be in session, and the two other judges affirm.

Gunther is called to lay out the charges and make his case. He claims I created the distraction in the wood, knowing the kobold lay in Mt. Kosciuszko waiting to attack, and led Father to a sure death to end my restrictive life and take control of the realm so no man may confine me again.

They call their first witness, Alfreda. *Alfreda!* Her hands shake as she sits in the witness seat. I hate this trial for so many reasons. They ask her what I said in the days leading up to the battle, and she admits I seemed agitated and frustrated that Father would not let me help stop the kobold in the wood. But on questioning by General Kane, she testifies that she never heard me utter a negative word against Father.

They bring Foster up for questioning. He was closest to me leading up to, and during, the battle. Gunther paints Foster as a lovesick, brainwashed, naïve pawn in my plan to win the monarchy. He must admit that it was I who suggested the kobold could be hiding in the mountain caves.

And this is how all the witnesses, including Father, answer. Yes, I could have cooked up the scenario to mislead my father and king, put him in harm's way, and skew things so it appeared I won the battle for our soldiers. Finally, it is our turn to call witnesses, and Kane calls me to the stand. I tell the story of how I thought up the idea to find the kobold because I knew the forest so well, having seen caves in the high banks of the river. I explained how I woke to find the stones missing from my ceiling, how I asked Foster to help steal arrows, and how we searched the kingdom for the kobold because the army could not find the beasts.

"I love my father. I would never wish him harm. All have testified how upset I was at the thought he may be dead." I finish my testimony.

Gunther paces in front of me. "But you knew your father was injured, and still, you stayed with the army to ensure the last of the kobold were killed, waited until the battle was finished to see to his health? Do you not think the generals and soldiers were capable of finishing the job?"

My heart races. "I thought we needed as many warriors as possible to stop the kobold. I thought I was more aid in the battle."

"Yet you knew your father could be dying, and you did not go to him. Is this correct?" He stops in front of me.

"Yes, but—"

"And was it not you who suggested the kobold were in the mountain caves in the first place? And you did not allow the soldiers to search your room for evidence of the kobold when you reported the stones missing. I think you hid your own stones in the cave. Or maybe tracked the kobold there, discovered their whereabouts, and cooked up a plan to paint yourself the hero."

"That is ludicrous. Why would I? I wish nothing but goodwill and health, have nothing but love for Father and our fae."

"To paint yourself the victim." Gunther's hot, rotting breath accosts my nose as he leans towards me.

The smell sparks a memory of my room the morning I discovered my crosses missing. It makes complete sense. It was not the kobold that took my stones, it was Gunther, trying to incite me to go over the edge, trigger my anxiety to make me out to be a crazed, incompetent princess. *But how can I prove it?* I found lots of faerie crosses in the cave hoarded with the rest of the ring stones. *Were those mine or just random collections?* If I accuse him, it may make me appear as crazy as he proposes I am.

I hold his stare. "How would I have gotten the crystals to the cave? How would I have gone to the cave before? I was being watched night and day."

He points his log of a finger at my face. "Because I know your other secret. You possess the power of magick. You could become invisible and fly them there yourself or transport them with your magick spells. Maybe you even entranced the kobold to steal the ring stones in the first place. Or maybe you stole the ring stones and put them in the kobold cave."

My mind explodes. *This man is mad. How could he propose such a theory?* I want to scream that he is a ludicrous, traitorous fae. I stare at him, wide-eyed, trying to comprehend how anyone listening could entertain that he speaks the truth.

Wagging his finger at me, he approaches the First Judge. "Take the shackles off, know the truth for yourself, and judge her for her evil witchcraft against this realm."

There is but one way out of this trial. I must let the judge read me even if it means revealing my secret. He will know that I did not conspire against Father. I will be cleared of these charges and Gunther exposed as a liar. All those backing Gunther and Ethan will see them for what they are: liars and power-hungry usurpers. Everyone will drop their support for the monarchy trial, and my reign will be secured. Gunther does not realize how wrong he was to bring these charges. He has lost everything.

I stand. "Read me. I have nothing to hide."

Aleem stands. "We only use this gift in rare circumstances where there is no other way. I beseech you to consider your options. Let the judges state their opinions."

Spinning to face the judges, I swallow. The three judges rise, the First Judge directing the others to give their opinion. The one to his right shifts his gaze from me to Gunther and states no decision can be made. The other consents as does the First Judge.

I approach the judges' table and hold up my shackled wrists. The First Judge asks Gunther to remove my bindings. I hold my nose while he struggles with the small key. Taking a deep breath, I relax my shoulders and pray to Mother Nature that whatever this fae sees will not damn me further. The judge holds out his palm, and I lay mine in it. A zing of electricity shoots up my arm.

He closes his eyes. "She loves her father and mother, wishes them nothing but health and happiness. She did not know where the kobold were hiding. She found them with her soldier friend, Foster. Everything she did was for the good of the kingdom and was just and right. She did not deceive this court in any way." His eyebrows shoot up, and I hold my breath. "She thinks Gunther may have stolen her crystals to paint her as a weak, crazed girl."

"This is preposterous!" Gunther seizes the judge's arm. "You are in league with her. What has she promised you?"

Aleem approaches us. "Kane, take Gunther to the dungeon and send some guards to search their property. We will get to the bottom of this."

"I have done nothing wrong. This girl and her judge are crazed lunatics." Gunther struggles as two guards attempt to fit chains around his wrists.

The crowd behind me descends into pandemonium. Fae push into the aisle to gawk as the guards drag Gunther away.

I jump to the tabletop. "Please, let us have peace. Transitions are hard for everyone. We had a great scare with the kobold and nearly losing our fairy ring. The battle took a toll on all of us. But we need to come together to support each other and ensure each fae flourishes for the good of the kingdom and the realm."

"Long live Queen Titania." I hear a shout from the crowd.

A form casts a shadow on my face, and I look up to find Ethan descending from above. "This does not mean that you are fit to rule us. My challenge still stands."

I want to laugh in his face. He cannot believe that after what his father did they will have support for a trial. "You must have backing to call for a trial."

"I am not my father. I am a captain in the army and next in line to serve as First Advisor. You are still but a fifteen-year-old girl." Ethan raises his fist. "Who here will support my case?"

A hush falls over the courtyard and then whispers rise. I note a group of fae weaving through the crowd. As they break through the front line, I realize his alliances have grown. Advisors Angus and Cedric are backed by Generals Raymond and Walter. *Walter? Walter has switched sides?* Why *would he?*

Ethan posts his hands on his hips. "I believe I have enough support to challenge your reign, *Miss* Titania."

Miss Titania? At the very least, it is still *Princess* Titania. My blood boils, and I want to spit in his face. Fists tight, I expand my wings and spin to face him. "You will call me Queen until you have won the trial. And if you do not win, I will not have you grace our kingdom. You will be banished, and you and yours will never hold office here again."

One of his eyebrows shoots up. "I assume that you are willing to be condemned to the same fate upon your loss."

"I am, but you will not take my crown. I am ready to be tested. Are you? If so, we start the first test tomorrow at sunrise."

A gasp echoes through the crowd. Ethan cuts his eyes to the advisors and generals flanking him and back to me. "And so it shall be."

Chapter 8

Wings still spread high, I jump to the ground. General Kane and Foster join me; Advisor Bran wheels Father to me; and Jesper, Terrence, and Milo follow behind. Feeling everyone's stare, I fight the impulse to fly into the castle. I will not flee this scene. All will see me with my backers, appearing as if I can prevail.

"Long live Queen Titania! Long live House of Alpheaus," Kane shouts, walking in front of me to make a path through the multitudes gathered.

Several echo his call, and the crowd divides, forming one mass in front of me and a second around Ethan. I glance back to find him glaring at me, his wings high and tight at attention. Holding my wings out wide, I greet my supporters. We meander through the fae gathered at a slow pace, and I force myself to take long, deep breaths. How foolish I was to think Ethan would back down or those supporting him would falter. For I am but a girl, not even sixteen, and him, a man of twenty, a captain in the army, from a family next in line for my throne. Still, it is *my* throne. I hold my chin high and smile at the faces we pass. In front of me, someone swings open the hall doors and our party marches inside.

As soon as the doors shut, Alfreda accosts me. "Dear child, what have you done?"

I squeeze Alfreda's shoulders and pull her from my chest. "I am ready. All will be well. You will see. Have them bring breakfast to the study."

Father wheels his chair into my path. "You need to visit your mother. She has not seen you for two days."

I hold his stare. "Is she not well?"

"She misses you."

As if he could tell? I wonder if she made another prediction. There is no way to ask now, and his countenance gives nothing away. "There is still much to attend to. I will walk with her after our meeting." I spin to face the group huddled around me. "Advisors, generals, Foster"—seeing him in the light of day brings a smile to my face—"let us convene in the study in half an hour."

Realizing I must look and smell as dingy as Foster does, I whisk to my quarters and pump water for a bath, not even caring that it is cold, then scrub and redress. My guards, Grant, Nicholas, Adam, and Timothy, flank me as I whiz to the study.

"Queen, if I may? How are you to best Ethan? He is one of the strongest soldiers in the army." Grant holds the door open for me.

"I need you to train me in wrestling. After I meet with my advisors and Mother, we will begin."

Entering the room, I close the doors behind me. The others stand around the table, speaking in hushed tones. Seeing Foster, clean face and clothes, my heart warms that he is here. He believes in me, and I need that positive energy.

"Gentlemen, Alfreda, let us eat, and then you can give me council." I motion to the long table.

Father sits to my left with Alfreda to his left, and Kane to my right followed by Foster. The soft, warm pastries taste sweeter than they ever have before, and I fill my goblet with cold cream. I fork a long sausage onto my plate, remembering that I need much protein.

"If I may?" Kane says as he pats his lips with a napkin. "We do not have much time. You need to prepare for the tests."

"Yes, I am aware. I will be learning wrestling with my guards this afternoon."

"But the histories test is first, so you should study," Bran says.

"I have been testing her for two days. She needs fighting skills and practice." Foster motions to me.

"What of the skills section? You should prepare for that as well. It is the second test. If you win both the histories and skills test, then you will not need to fight Ethan. It is the best strategy." Bran nods as though affirming his own words.

"Her archery abilities are beyond any other in the kingdom." Father beams.

"She knows her potions forwards and backwards." Alfreda winks at me.

"What of fencing, riding, and hunting?" Kane asks.

"She is good at fencing." Foster points out.

"There are five skills. I need only win three of them. I shall have fencing practice as well, today and tomorrow."

"But fencing is the last event. You could be weary. I think you should at least be given pointers on riding and hunting." Bran suggests.

"Okay, I will add those to my list. Find me the best teachers for each. But now"—I stand—"I must attend to Mother. Father, will you walk with me?"

The others rise, bowing as I step away from the table. I insist they should finish their meals at their leisure. Taking hold of Father's chair, I wheel him from the room. Guards follow as we make our way to his chambers. I am happy to see his color return, and him appear stronger. I ask about his healing, and he says his lungs feel stronger and ribs less sore. We enter his quarters and close the doors behind us.

Finally alone, I kneel before him. "What of Mother? Have you told her everything? Has she had a vision?"

He takes my hands. "What of you? Why would you risk banishment? This is your home, all you have ever known."

"Does it matter? What do I have here? You, Mother, Alfreda? If I lose, I hope that you would come with me. And we could live a simple, happy life."

"It is my fault, locking you away as we did. I only meant to protect you, and now it leads you here. If I let you lead a normal life, go to school as you did before, be surrounded by friends, know your people, things would be different."

I squeeze his fingers. "You cannot know that. It was not all you. I am just as traumatized by losing my brothers as you and Mother are. And I have support: Kane, Foster, Bran, Jesper, Terrence, my instructors. I assume they have stayed in the castle. Even my guards have pledged to help."

"But you could just let this pass to Ethan or negotiate, make a deal with him, perhaps even an alliance, maybe a marriage. Kane says he is not like his father. You could rule together."

My stomach turns when I think of wedding anyone, much less a son of Gunther, with his bright purple wings. I know why I do not like his physique and coloring. It cannot be untangled from his father or the similarity to the kobold. I know it is not fair. I do not know him at all. *But marriage at fifteen? To a stranger?* Perhaps Father has gone mad.

"Why would I do that? You do not think I can win? It does not matter. It is too late. If I ask to speak with him, I will appear weak, scared. That is not how I want to start my reign. Is this about Mother? You must tell me what she said."

"It is vague. I am not even sure what her words mean. Cannot know if she does. That is why I want you to talk to her. See if she will say anything else."

"Just tell me what she said."

"She kept repeating, 'It is but the beginning.'"

"Do we know of what? My reign, problems with the kobold?"

"I have no idea." He rubs his beard. "But this morning, she uttered something new. She whispered, '*The fate stands.*'"

Rising, I pace away. "What does that mean? That I will be killed by a kobold? Or in a battle? Ethan would be locked away if he killed me. The kingdom would fall into turmoil. He would not risk that. All of us die at some point. I would as soon be killed in battle as pass in my sleep, wrinkled and wasting away."

"You are young, too young to even know what pleasures life has to offer, what even matters."

I pivot to face him. "That is not true. I lost my brothers. I hold you and Mother more dear than any. But you are right. I am young. I am just beginning my life. *My life*. Why are you still trying to dissuade me? I thought you were proud of me, wanted me to carry on your name, our family's legacy? I do not understand you. All I know is I feel it deep inside, that this is my destiny, what I should be doing, that I can help this kingdom. I weighed my choices. I think I can best Ethan and believe this is my path, whatever the cost. I cannot spend any more time debating this. I will walk with Mother now."

Twisting on my heel, I start towards Mother's sitting room.

"Would it not be better if you were present in our kingdom in some capacity rather than none at all? If you feel it is your destiny to serve our kingdom, then why not serve as a monarch's wife? Promise me, if you lose one of the first tests, you will consider it. Our line, our blood, should run through the monarchy of this kingdom for eons to come."

I stop and take a deep breath. *Is that what he cares about? Our bloodline staying in the monarchy? How can he even ask this of me?* I cannot look at him. "Do you not have any faith in me at all?"

"I see it, too, how this kingdom runs in your veins. How could you forsake it? You were rash, acted out of anger in the courtyard. You should have offered Ethan First Advisor. Then you could have served as the same."

For as much as I love my father, I wish to pummel his chest. Balling my fists, I swing to face him. "He called me *Miss* Titania. Did not even recognize my place. You, as King, gave me the crown. Did you just do it to attract a husband for me? I have worked for this for three years. All my effort cannot have been for nothing. I will honor my brothers by retaining the monarchy of Aubren."

He raises his palms. "I surrender. I pushed you because I wanted to know your true heart, that you felt it in your bones, could think of no other future for yourself. I just pray you are doing this because it is what you want, not because it is what has been fated to you."

Approaching him, I take his hand. "We cannot change the past. I am on the path I wish to be on. I beg you, let me do this, and let us not speak of it again."

"Then go child, face your destiny, and I will be happy for you."

"Thank you." Lifting his hand, I kiss it. "I will attend to Mother now."

I find her sitting in front of the flames, as she often does, take her hand and guide her out the door, through the halls, and to the garden. Our habit would be to walk the woods, but with little time, I opt to stay close. I tell her all, as I always have: about Gunther's accusation, the dungeon, the trial. She serves as my personal diary of sorts, though I have not gotten a response in the three years since my brothers died.

Turning to face her as we loop back to the castle, I take both her hands. "I will be training and in the trial, perhaps the next three days, so I will not have time to walk with you. I shall miss our talks."

My mind pings with guilt as I realize I may not miss them. Our strolls through the forest used to bring comfort. Maybe they were more about being in the wood than being with her. Perhaps I have outgrown the need for her company. *You have just been handed a monarchy that you must defend.* I settle in my mind that there are more pressing tasks, and things may return to how they were before once things settle.

Leaving her in the study, I find Kane, Milo, and the advisors gathered with my instructors. They have laid out a schedule for the day, suggesting I focus on skills until dinner then histories after dark. We skip archery, as there are few who can best me with a bow and arrow, and move straight to fencing practice. They bring in three guards who are gifted at the sport. I focus and try to commit their suggestions to memory. I note Foster in the background, watching, and it brings me comfort to see his smile when I catch his eye. By midafternoon, the matches stand with a few better than fifty-percent wins in my column.

We break for sustenance and head to the stables. Cavalry General Milo assesses my skills and offers suggestions for improvement. I work with several different horses to get a feel for different personality types and how they may be guided. At dinner, the men press me to discuss hunting, and when I also take up the topic of potions, the history instructor begins questioning me. As we move to the study, I insist we make it a game to include everyone. After Father and the instructor, I take third place. I count this as a win, praying that I can recall the new information when needed.

When the clock strikes nine, Kane insists we should retire for the night so I can get a good rest.

Foster hangs back and is the last to bid me goodnight. He motions me away from the door, and my eyes cut to Kane who nods just a nudge. Seeing his approval, I cross to the fireplace and spin on my heel.

Foster follows and takes my hands. "How do you feel?"

"I am a bit anxious but not nervous, if that makes sense."

"You know your histories. I believe you can best Ethan tomorrow." Ducking, he holds my gaze. "You exhibited good form in fencing today. And you handled the horses well."

His smile is contagious, and I lift my chin. "Thank you. Right now, believing in myself is the most important thing I can do. It is a mental game at this point."

"You are ready. You can win." He squeezes my fingers.

Peering into his eyes, I wish we could sleep on my windowsill as we did the night before the battle with the kobold. How I would like to pass the time with him, hearing more of his family farm, sister, and goats.

Hmm, hmm. Walking towards us, Kane holds his fist to his lips.

I wriggle my hands from Foster's grip and clasp them at my waist. "Thank you. Your presence and support means much."

Foster's eyes cut from mine to Kane as he approaches. Smiling at me, Foster bows, backs a few steps, turns, and exits the room.

"Now that the charges have been dismissed, I should send him back to his post." Kane stops in front of me.

I steel my face against my emotion. "If you must."

Kane's lips form a smile. "But you do not wish me to?"

"I have very few friends. Actually, no friends my own age."

"But he is not your age. He is a man, a soldier in your army."

"He is not much older than I. What friends shall I have? Alfreda? Father and Mother? You?"

"Do you trust me?"

"I do."

"I will make him a guard at the trial then."

My heart brightens, but I know I cannot be selfish. "It should be his choice."

"You are a wise girl."

"I pray you are right."

"You can win these tests, but it will take more than knowledge and skill. They are also tests of strategy. You need to be smart as well as intelligent. Ethan knows the personalities of his men and can bring out the best in them. I would guess the worst as well. He may use your temperament against you."

I fold my arms over my middle. "And what temperament would that be?"

One of his eyebrows shoots up. "Just this. You are hot-headed, impulsive, proud, and perhaps a bit entitled."

His words sting, and I take a minute to digest them.

"Do you not believe you should reign just because your line always held the monarchy?"

"Yes, but I know I can be a good ruler as well."

"And after today, madam, I believe that even more. You take advisement well, and this impresses me." He lifts a hand to the mantle and stares at the flames. "Your compassion. He will try to play on that, too. Perhaps cast himself as a victim of his father's plots or use his other charms."

"I find no charm in Ethan. His purple wings alone make my stomach turn."

"You have something against purple?"

"A kobold killed my brother right before me."

"Purple wings… It makes sense. But you are young, so you perhaps do not understand things yet."

I move one hand to my hip. "I live in a castle with tons of soldiers and maidens. I see many things. I am not naïve. What have you heard of Ethan? I must know everything: his history in the army, his family, his upbringing."

Motioning to a set of chairs, he allows me to walk ahead of him. I learn many things: As first born, Ethan has established himself as a leader since boyhood, organizing hunts and outings. He entered the military at seventeen, moving up the ranks quickly to earn captain. He treats his men fairly but with a firm hand.

I lean towards Kane. "So he is not his father. You think him an honest man?"

"I have found nothing to make me question his integrity, but he will not want to lose. He also values what is thought of him, his position, and his rank. He may not have thought he wanted the monarchy at the outset, but you saw him in the hall and in the courtyard today. He wants it now because it could be his for the taking, and losing means disgrace. His training will help him keep a calm head. Do not expect any mercy because you are female. Do not let him play on your guilt, and do not be distracted by smiles or praise. Do not be his friend. This is war."

I stare into the fire, letting his words sink into my core. I cannot feel compassion or kinship for my foe, or I will lose. I must believe I am the best ruler for Aubren. That is how I defeat Ethan. *How could he play on my compassion? Appear weak, show poorly in the beginning, such that I would pity him?* I picture his face, his body, as if his wings were bronze as Foster's. The color does not sit with Ethan's dark coloring, and I imagine them to be blue or red. I could guess a maiden may find him attractive, the blue eyes and dark hair. I think of Father, my brothers, my crystals, and all Ethan's family took from mine, to be embroiled in this drama, me accused of treason. Even if it was not him, he did not condemn his father. Ethan pursues my throne, my family's legacy, still. I will not have him scar it.

I look at Kane. "I am ready."

Chapter 9

I WAKE WITH THE SUNRISE to Alfreda opening the drapes. She asks where I would like breakfast, indicating that the generals and advisors usually meet for a meal before a big event such as today's. While glad for her counsel, I take my food in my room. Peering over the garden, orchard, and village beyond, I watch the garden fae tending to the flowers, picking fruit from the trees. Further out I eye the carts, filled with their goods, strolling into town. *Those people are who you fight for.* My stomach tightens. Anxious, I force down small bites of the cheese and bread. For as much as I want these tests over, the trials finished, I dread the day.

You are doing this for your people. Remember your core. This is your destiny. I recite these phrases in my head as I clean my face and dress. Not knowing if there is etiquette for such occasions, I wear my riding pants and skirt along with a blouse and vest, as has become my habit the past few days. *When you are not locked in a dungeon. By Ethan's father.* Looking at my ceiling, I realize I have not heard whether they found my crystals among Gunther's things. My mind spins. *Did Ethan know of his father's plot?* So many questions left unanswered, but there is no other course of action now. I acted rashly, as Kane said. *Could I have pushed for an investigation into Ethan's role in his father's dealings?* I have not even inquired as to anything in the kingdom. I am failing as a Queen already.

Lacing my boots, I circle back to my truth. This monarchy is my destiny. I *will* be a good Queen for my people, can defend our realm, and will fulfill our duty to protect Upper Earth. Once I best Ethan, no one will question whether I am fit to reign.

I swing open my doors and discover my four day guards standing in the hall at attention. I jump into the air, and they trail me to the study where I find Kane, Milo, and the advisors waiting. Not seeing Foster, my mood drops. *Did he leave for the border already? He would say goodbye, right?* He had not last time. I reel in my feelings and focus on those in front of me.

"Good morning. I trust you slept well. Please, sit." I motion them to the table.

I inquire as to the kobold. Kane reports no signs of them and that all is quiet in the kingdom.

"And the realm? Is there anything I should be aware of in the other kingdoms?"

He clears his throat. His eyes pan to the others.

I insist he apprise me of the situation although he says it can wait.

He reports that the other kingdoms wait for the result of the trial. Several have written expressing support for my reign, but Ethan spread rumors of equal letters of support for him.

"We cannot know whether these claims are true or false." Kane rises and crosses to the fireplace.

I stand. "This does not change anything. Is there news on the investigation into Gunther's role in sabotaging my reputation?"

Bran slides his chair back. "We have asked the judges for a warrant to search his property, but they will not answer until the trials are finished. The knowledge test will begin soon. We should focus on that."

"Yes, I agree. I will greet Father and Mother and meet you in the hall."

Although I wish to ask Kane about Foster, there is no opportunity. *You are Queen*, I remind myself. *You can request anything you like.* Still, I stay my course, finding Mother and Father eating breakfast. I kiss each of their cheeks and ask Father of his health. Reporting feeling stronger every day, he says he will see me in the hall.

I summon my courage to make my entrance into the great hall where the knowledge test will be held. Kane, Milo, and my advisors wait for me outside the entrance, and I am happy to have an entourage even if it does not include Foster. I alight on the ground, and we get in line, Kane beside me, Milo and Bran behind us, Terrence and Jesper following, and two guards flanking each side. Chin high, I stride into the hall. A hush falls over the crowd, and my skin crawls with the knowledge that all eyes are on me. I smile and greet those that offer well wishes, eyes darting between their faces and the front of the space where Ethan stands with his supporters, all dressed in military whites.

My outfit, while nice, is more of a functional suit, and while queenly enough I guess, it is not military whites' caliber. Those uniforms are usually reserved for weddings, funerals, and coronations. I take a deep breath as we approach Ethan's party, march straight to him, and offer my hand.

"Best to you on this fair day."

"And to you as well." He dips his chin and smiles.

I am surprised to realize I do find him handsome with his broad chin and the pleasant dimples gracing his face. I had not ever been this close to him. My thoughts jump to Kane's words. *Do I think Ethan handsome because Kane suggested I might? Is Kane really on my side? Your senses are sending you into paranoia.* I picture Ethan's purple wings spread out behind him and my impression turns.

He is the enemy.

Following Kane to the other side of the room, I greet well-wishers.

Aleem calls the room to order, and I take my seat behind a table they have prepared with a water urn and a glass. As I scan the crowd, I catch a glimpse of a light-complexioned face over the heads and wings of the others. My eyes stop on the soldier I did not expect to see: Foster. He stands at attention, wings high and folded, in full uniform, with his shield up and spear held ready. As I stare, I think I catch a slight smile. It could be my imagination, but just to behold his face, bright eyes, and stray red curls under his helmet buoys my spirit.

I refocus on Aleem's words as he describes the rules. We are posed questions. If answered correctly, the other receives another question until one of us fails to reply with a correct answer. If the opposing side can supply the appropriate answer, then that party becomes the winner, and the other is the loser. Sudden death without the dramatics, for there are still two more tests, and no one is dying, just being banished from the kingdom.

The judges begin the queries with facts a primary school child would know: Name the kingdoms of Middle Earth, name the rings, name the rings' locations. Then those we learned in secondary school: List all the current monarchs, recite the types of crystals. We stand in front of the tables, answering questions until a midday break for a meal.

Even though I am anxious to have the test complete, I am glad we are given a short period. I eat, take a flying lap around the castle, and return to the hall. The next questions have longer answers: Name all the monarchs of Aubren, name those serving on the High Council, name the anchor stones for the rings, name the Keepers of Aubren's Daintree Ring in chronological order beginning with the first. I listen as Ethan recites the names, thinking what the next name should be. Oriander, Jesup. Knowing he has made a mistake, that Jesup was trained but never served as Keeper because he passed away days before the transition, I stay my features. Protocol states that the judges let the person finish their answer before calling it wrong so as not to clue the other contestant in to the source of the mistake.

"I am sorry, but that is incorrect," First Judge announces after Ethan takes his seat. "Titania, please, rise to try your answer."

Rounding in front of the table, I recall the names from my memory, the last ones being Oriander, Brighten, Constant, and Aleem. I hold my breath, thinking I should have the correct answer.

"Correct. Titania wins the knowledge test." First Judge dips his chin in my direction.

Cheers and claps ring out from in front of me. Across the hall, Ethan lowers his head a smidge and, straightening his jacket, strides towards the exit. I try to find Foster above the heads, but with fae milling about and wings held high, I cannot. Kane reaches me first, commending my performance, and Alfreda wheels Father's chair to me.

He pats my back as I lean down to kiss him. "Very well done, my daughter."

"Thank you, Father." I turn to Kane. "I need to start training for the combat test now. Let us meet in the courtyard. Gather Foster if he can be spared, as well as Grant, Nicholas, Adam, and Timothy."

I wish to be with the soldiers, learning as much as I can about wrestling, but many fae linger to offer congratulations and well wishes for the next day. It is an hour before I reach the courtyard where the men gather. Being in the space reminds me of my brothers, how they used to come here to socialize with their friends. Inevitably, there would be some contest of skill I would be entertained by. Now, it is my turn to learn to fight.

Kane and Milo greet me, advising that a more private location for training might be smart. We do not know who could be on Ethan's side, and knowledge of my strategies would be advantageous. Seeing their logic, we weave with

Foster and my guards to Father's inner garden. They debate weapons first, and lost, I ask them to teach me the terms. Their top picks are the Morningstar, a shaft with a chain and a spiked iron ball at the end; an iron-flanged mace, a staff with flanged head; and a spear. Kane sends Foster to bring examples of each for me to try.

The Morningstar would be most damaging, but it weighs the most, and because we are to use non-lethal force, I choose the mace. Being heavier than a spear, it will give me more leverage and can be used for choking as well. *Choking.* I picture me holding the rod to Ethan's neck. *Could I inflict that amount of force? Attempt to harm another fae to their near-death?* Fighting an enemy kobold is one thing, a countryman another. Of course, I have no doubt Ethan will do everything in his power to best me. He is a warrior, much better trained for this than I.

They review the rules for the test. Each contestant is allowed one weapon, and he or she is to fight until unable to fight anymore and either surrenders or passes out. No flying is allowed. The advisors join us as the guards describe various wrestling moves. They interject, suggesting that focusing on my skills for the next day's tests may be most advantageous.

I shake my head. "Assemble the top people in each field. Tonight, I will listen to their best advice, but I do not believe my skills in any of the areas can be increased significantly in one day. What will be, will be tomorrow. If it does not end favorably for me, Ethan holds the advantage in the combat test. Do you argue that point?"

They concede that I speak with wisdom and leave me to practice with the guards. Foster and I spar first, but I best him with ease.

"You did not even try." I offer my hand as he spins over.

"Perfect practice makes perfect. If you can do the technique correctly, you can best anyone."

"Ethan is huge. And he is not going to hold back." Looking into Foster's eyes, I realize I could never hurt him either, not really. He cannot help me in this.

I study Kane and the others gathered. "Ethan is big and strong. I need someone who will actually fight me. Can anyone here do that?"

Adam raises his hand. "It is not going to be easy or pretty though."

"Do you want me to win or not? Holding back does not do me any good. If I cannot hurt you, I will not be able to hurt Ethan either."

As Adam circles me, I see Foster turn and walk away. His absence pains me, but he cannot be what I need right now. I realize he may be more than a friend and certainly is not like a brother, not one who would be willing to risk hurting me to make me stronger.

Out of the corner of my eye, I catch a blur of motion, and Adam's staff contacts my calves, sending me to my back in one swift motion. "Where is your head, Queen? Watching your lover wimp out?"

Pain shoots through my torso. I draw in a breath and push up on my hands. Face flaming, I stand. "He is not my—suitor. I am too young for such things."

As I jab the mace at Adam, he catches the end of it with his weapon and flings it from my hands. "Fifteen? I had a daughter on the way at fifteen."

Out of the corner of my eye, I catch Kane and Milo exiting the courtyard. Today, I will have more than a lesson in fighting. I will know what it would be like to have my brothers here with me, have them speak openly and freely about many subjects, those that dare not come up with Father, my instructors, or Alfreda, who seems bent on protecting me from such things forever.

Adam and I spar until after dark, me gaining small victories and learning balance, pressure points, and counter maneuvers. As he rolls from an attack, I jump on his back and swing the mace around his front to his neck. He pries at my fingers, but I hold them tightly. He throws himself backwards so I land hard on the dirt, him atop me. I wind my legs around his middle as he tries to spin from my grip. The other guards count down and declare me the victor when I am able to hold him there ten seconds.

"You did not let me win, did you?" I balance his weight as he grips my forearm.

"I would never *let* anyone beat me. I was exhausted. If you can wear Ethan out, you can best him. That is how you win, Queen."

"Thank you for this." I spin to face the others. "Thank you all."

"Heavens, child, there you are. I have been hunting for you everywhere." Alfreda trots towards me, stopping short ten feet out. "Heavens, you are a mess. Come, dinner is soon. The others will be waiting."

Inviting my trainers to the meal, I follow Alfreda to my chamber, bathe, and dress in record time before winding to the dining room. Generals Kane and Milo, the advisors, several instructors, and Foster are gathered around the fire, speaking in small groups.

Sliding into the head chair, I feel every bruise, and my muscles sear with exhaustion. Still, I force a smile and welcome congratulations as they are offered. After dinner, I request a pen and paper, knowing I am too tired to take in all their advice for the next day's tests and hope writing the information down will help commit it to memory.

Order of the skills tests were drawn by the judges: archery, fencing, riding, hunting, and potions last. It is not ideal with the four energy intensive challenges in a row, but at least we will break for the midday meal before hunting. Riding and hunting will be my weakest skills, and I pen notes from each teacher on these. I am grateful the pharmacist has created a study sheet for me.

With my head filled with knowledge for tomorrow, I bid everyone a good night, planning to visit Father and Mother then get a good night's rest. Kane and Foster are the last in the room.

Kane reports the guards were impressed with my progress. "But I believe you can best Ethan tomorrow. He will be anxious about the potions section after today, and you are the best archer in the kingdom. If you can win one of the other sections, the victory will be yours."

"Let us believe it shall be." I look between them.

Cutting his eyes to Foster, and back to me, Kane says goodnight. Exiting, he leaves the door wide open.

My pulse races, and I wonder why I am anxious all of a sudden. *This is Foster*, I remind myself. But I cannot deny there has been a shift. More of a gradual evolution of my feelings, but they are there none the less. His full lips draw me in.

I fold my hands at my waist. "Did you have something to discuss?"

"I am sorry about today. I just could not. I cannot even fathom causing you pain."

Looking at my hands then back up at him, I whisper, "I do not believe I could have hurt you either. Will you be at the tests tomorrow?"

He smiles. "Yes. Kane is posting me as a guard for the event, so I will have a good view."

"For better or worse."

"It will be for better. I know it. But you should rest. It is late already."

We stroll out together and part in the hall. I watch him walk away. Reaching the corner, he glances back. My face warms, and I smile and wave. *It would be okay if I lost, and Foster and I could fly to wherever we decided we loved most, right?* I laugh at myself. As if he would leave his family, as if I even know if he may feel that way for me. I have never been in love before. *How am I to know if he is even right for me?*

My stomach turns at the thought of leaving Aubren. Taking a deep breath, I harken my resolve. This kingdom needs me, and I need this kingdom. This reign is in my blood. I can feel it. To be banished from this land, holding all the memories I hold dear, may be too much to bear. I take to the air and weave to Father's chamber. I find him reading to Mother.

He smiles as I approach. Alfreda apprised him of my progress, so I have little to share. Wishing me well, he bids me goodnight. I kiss each of my parents' cheeks and wind to my room. Alfreda has a hot bath waiting, and I study the potion manual as I soak. I wrap in my towel, change to my night clothes, and slide into bed. Exhausted and sore, I fall into a deep sleep, dreaming of fording streams, jumping fences, and rounding corners on my horse.

❦

I DRESS IN THE SAME WAY: riding pants and skirt with blouse and vest. When we meet in the orchard, Ethan wears his captain's uniform as if heading to battle. I scan the space, searching for Foster, but with the guards at such a distance, I cannot be sure which is him. As we hoped, I win the archery competition with ease and prepare for the fencing match. I win the first set, but he bests me by one point each of the second two. Frustrated, I prepare for the riding competition in the meadow beyond the orchard.

Kane urges me to clear my mind of the loss, and I picture fording the stream, jumping the fence, and rounding a curve as I had the night before. We draw grasses to assign ride order, and Ethan takes the first slot. I am tempted not to watch but realize I may gain insight into the course. Milo, being the cavalry general, talks me through the route as Ethan makes his run. Riders are scored on missed jumps or straying from the boundaries, and he scores well, only losing two points, with a finishing time of one minute forty-six seconds.

As Ethan leaves the course, I approach my steed, letting him smell my hand. I take the reins and swing my leg over the saddle. He takes a few prancing steps then settles. Nudging him forward, I approach the start and wait for the flag. When the white fabric drops, I squeeze my legs into the horse's center and shake the reins. He charges forward, and I hold tight with my thighs, lowering my torso to his back. Racing through the meadow, he takes the first jump easily and circles the rock as I steer him around the obstacle. Approaching a copse of trees, I slow him for the turn around the thicket. On the other side, I nudge him to speed up and lean into his back.

We clear the branches, and he stops short, rearing up. I am not prepared and am thrown off, landing hard on the ground, breath forced from my windpipes. Sucking in a lungful of air, I lift my head to find the steed cantering towards the stable and a deer staring right at me. Milo runs towards me, and I push up on my hands then stand, brushing off my skirt.

"Do I get to repeat that?" I fall in step with Milo as he reaches me.

They send guards to make sure the trees are clear and bring me a fresh horse. Back aching, I take care in swinging my leg over the saddle. When the flag drops, I nudge him forward, across the meadow, and over the first jump. Our swerve around the rock is wide, and I steer him back to the trees. He comes out the other side, and I push him to full speed to clear the fence. His back leg hits the top rail, and the horse slows, but I nudge him over the finish line and circle back to the time keeper. My time is one minute fifty seconds with two points docked. I lose the riding section and now am down an event. I must win both the hunting and potions sections, or I will face Ethan in the combat test.

Sliding from the saddle, I am met by Kane and Milo. I do not like losing and wish I could retreat to my chamber and hide. But much more is at stake than just my pride. Crossing the grass, I congratulate Ethan and make my way towards the orchard. I dread the hunting competition most. *What could be worse than dooming an innocent animal to certain death for mere sport?*

Perhaps I will insist we eat the catch for dinner. But I am not sure my stomach or psyche would allow it. Perhaps I could donate the meat for another's meal.

Alfreda sets a table under the trees. I ignore the sausage, opting for the cheese and fruit. My back hurts, and I sit at the front of the seat as the hunting instructor gives me final advice. I dread getting on a horse again and ask if the rules allow flying as opposed to using the horse for hunting. I guess I could sneak up on an animal more readily on foot or in the air than with a huge horse. We have two hours to complete the test, and the winner is chosen by total weight of animals brought in. Kane notes that I would not be able to carry much when flying.

I hate all of this. I am exhausted, and every part of me hurts. *How much can a girl withstand? This is part of it. Resolve. If you want to be a leader and help your fae through hard times, and your mother sees them coming, then you must stay the course, be the leader they need. If you are banished, your family will be ripped from this kingdom, the ground they have lived on since the beginning of time. Who knows what more your mother will predict, how she could help, or how you could benefit your fae?*

We make our way back to the meadow. Each contestant is given the same instruments, weapons, and a horse. I slide the quiver and bow on my back and tie the other tools to the saddle. Mounting my horse, I wait for the flag to drop then take off for the woods. I guess it may be an advantage that I know the terrain so head straight for the stream. Slowing as I near it, I slide from my horse and tether him to a tree. Being as silent as possible, I move through the brush, trying to stay hidden. I follow the brook, hoping animals will be drawn to it. With the high sun it is not as likely as at dawn or dusk, but I figure it is the best place to start.

In half an hour, I happen upon a doe with two fawns. Even with my determination to win, I cannot bring myself to kill them. Besides, hunting laws forbid killing a mother with young. I have no clue if these are meant to be ignored, but I plan to follow them and head deeper into the forest. I spot a flock of turkey with two large males. Loading an arrow, I release it, and the point lands in his neck. He drops, and the rest of the flock scatters.

I need a large buck or boar, and with the deepening forest, I cut through the large bushes. Spending half an hour and spotting nothing, I realize I have got to use a different strategy. Flying back to my horse, I tie the turkey to the back and head south to the savannah. Middle Earth mirrors the Upper Earth, and I hope to find a kangaroo or emu—for my turkey is but twenty pounds, if that. Stopping at the edge of the forest, I leave my horse tied to a tree. I check the time, figuring there to be a half hour before I must head back.

I spot a group of emu not far out and hunching down, inch closer. I pick out a large male and let my arrow fly. It lands in his breast, and he starts to run. I jump into the air, launching another arrow at the bird. It lands in his neck, and I descend to him. He is still breathing, and pulling my knife from my boot, I jab it through his eye. His body goes limp. I estimate his weight at 80 pounds and quickly realize the quandary ahead. If I leave him here, another predator is likely to get him. I rope his feet together and start to drag him towards my horse. With the grasses and rocks, the resistance is high, and I wonder if I can get back in time.

The sun beats down on me, and my arms and legs ache with the struggle. My skirt catches on a branch, and I tug it free. An idea sparks in my brain. Dropping the bird's legs, I rip my leather skirt from the waistband and lay it on the ground. Then I roll the emu atop it. The smooth leather slides over the ground much easier, and when I am within twenty feet of my horse, I dart into the air, retrieve the steed, and gallop to the bird. I wrap my skirt around the emu and secure it with a rope. I heave the bird onto my shoulder and then onto the saddle. I slide into the space in front of the bird and nudge the horse, directing it back north.

For speed, I skirt the woods. As I enter the meadow where we started, I spot Ethan already on his podium and note the time. One minute left.

Chapter 10

I press my knees into the horse's side and lean forward as we speed across the grass. I cross the line and the timer sounds. Pulling my steed to a stop, I slide to the ground. Kane and Milo approach as I heave the emu from the horse. I transfer it to the podium and return for the turkey, which seems much lighter after the giant emu. Spinning to assess Ethan's catch, my heart sinks. Two huge red does sit atop the scales.

I approach Milo. "Is doe hunting allowed during fawn season?"

Milo shakes his head. "Not generally, unless there is overpopulation."

"Those deer are easily a hundred pounds each. My emu and turkey together may only weigh that much. I think I have lost this."

"Not so fast," Kane whispers. "I overheard the judges. They are not happy about him killing two does."

Ethan's deer weigh two-hundred eighteen pounds, and my emu and turkey come to one-hundred three. Ethan's brothers and aides start to offer congratulations, but the judges call for silence. They announce a recess to determine whether Ethan broke a rule of the game by hunting doe during fawn season.

"If you win this one then you have a chance of finishing this today, and you will be queen." Kane wraps his arm around me and squeezes my shoulder.

I shake my head. "Let us not jump to conclusions. They could rule for Ethan, or they could call for a rematch."

My stomach turns at the thought of having to kill another animal. I instruct the staff to take the birds to the castle kitchen. Alfreda brings me water and bread, and I sip the water, but with butterflies churning my stomach, forego eating.

Ethan's entourage takes to the air, and discerning bright purple wings, I study the figure. *Gunther? Could it be? They released him?* I turn to Kane. "Is that Gunther with them?"

"Without a warrant to gather evidence, there was not any credible basis to hold him save your supposition."

Unable to control my churning thoughts and the what-ifs stewing in my head, I excuse myself to change into more suitable attire and ask that I am advised when the judges have a decision. I scan the space for Foster, but with the distance, cannot pick him out from the others. Grant, Nicholas, Adam, and Timothy flank me as I fly to my chambers, discussing how they felt Ethan cheated and how he should have known better than to hunt doe in fawn season. I try to block them out and focus on the next test, potions.

In my room, I discover blood and mud coat my clothes and skin. I heat water for a bath and strip my outer layers. The water feels soothing, but I have little time. I change and sit at my table, reading the notes on various medicinal ingredients. The pharmacist was smart and broke them down into different categories for their active properties and in order of potency. I review each section and am on the last when there is a knock at my door.

We are called to the hall where Ethan and I are directed to tables at the front. Aleem announces that the hunting portion of today's tests will be scratched, leaving me with one win and Ethan with two. If I win the next test, the day will be called a draw, and the combat test will decide who wins the trial. If Ethan wins the potions section, he wins the day, but it still leaves us in a dead heat with the fate of the monarch decided by combat.

Gunther stands. "So, there is no reason for the potions section, am I right? Why not give the contestants time to train?"

My anger flares. *Why is this man even walking around free when I was detained in the dungeon for two days?* Of course, he does have a point. I would rather be sparring with guards, learning skills to best Ethan. The judges retreat to discuss the proposal and we are left sitting at our tables. I note Ethan wears his military white uniform again. *Who does he think he is impressing?* But, if you listen to enough Upper Earth television, you would hear the phrases dress for success, dress the part, and dress to impress. Well, I do not need to dazzle anyone. Even if I lose this contest, I will be remembered as the princess—for a short time, the queen—who saved her kingdom from a kobold army and fought a brute almost twice her size to retain her reign as the first female ruler of Aubren and the whole of Middle Earth.

I search the far walls for Foster, and finding him, I smile. I do not let my eyes linger on him long or fear my affection will be discovered. *If I become Queen, can I continue to have him as a friend? What are the protocols for queens and friends?* I wish I could ask Mother. She was raised a princess in Bedham, met Father when she visited our kingdom. She used to tell me the story of how she knew she loved him the second she saw his face.

The back doors open, scraping the stone floor, and I rise as Aleem and the other judges make their way to us. Aleem bows in front of me, and I motion for him to address the group. He announces the potion section of the skills test will proceed as planned in order to maintain consistency of the trial. I cut my eyes to Ethan, and he shakes his head, appearing frustrated. Unlike the knowledge test earlier in the day, the potions section is a written exam, with the person scoring highest considered the winner. I smile, thinking I can shore up my reputation with a win in this section if nothing else. If I lose, perhaps I will move to Elita. I hear their rain forest holds some of the world's most exotic plants, and locals favor concoctions, especially tranquilizers, like ours.

Ethan and I are handed a stack of paper each and a writing instrument. Aleem turns over an hourglass, and we are instructed to begin. My fingers fly across the pages, including as much detail as I can about each query. I do not look up from the sheets until the bell sounds. The judges take the tests to assess them, and we are left to wait yet again. I feel I might go mad but realize no matter the outcome of this portion, I still have to face Ethan in combat tomorrow. I instruct Alfreda to bring drinks and snacks to those gathered in the hall and take my leave to the inner courtyard to spar with Grant, Nicholas, Adam, and Timothy.

Part of me hopes Ethan stays behind to eat and drink his fill. I would love nothing more than for him to be over-confident about our fight. Just thinking this is really happening feels surreal, but I focus on my stance, balance, form for jabs and kicks, and handling the mace. It is two hours before Kane calls us to the hall to hear the results. I notice Ethan drinking with his soldiers and smile. *Yes, drink up, dear friend. For tomorrow, I will best you.*

I come out on top of the potions section with a formidable ten-point lead. I wonder if the judges are accruing as many scores as possible in the event tomorrow's combat test ends in a draw. *How could it with the rules stipulating that you fight until one can fight no more?*

Accepting congratulations from my supporters, we move to the dining hall for dinner. As Father joins us, I change the topic of conversation whenever it moves to the next day's event. Thinking about the last two days and my failures makes me anxious. I hate that perhaps I am disappointing Mother and Father, letting my brothers down. I stare at my half-eaten emu portion and clutch my armrests. *What if I cannot win? Nobody would bet on me, right?*

I stand. "Thank you all for your support these past days and weeks. You may stay and finish your meal and visit as you like. I will retire for the evening."

They stand and offer congratulations, and I avoid eye contact as I dip my chin and move from the table. There are no last words of advice or inspiring phrases that will help me now. I must best Ethan on my own. Two guards trail me to my room. As I am about to shut my door, Foster lands on the other side.

"May I have a word with you?" His eyes grow as round saucers.

If I wanted to talk to someone, it would be him, and because I could not ever be rude, especially to Foster, I follow him down the hall, out of earshot of the guards.

"Are you okay?" He reaches out.

Forcing a smile, I take a step back. "Of course, I am tired and want to be rested for tomorrow."

He bends down so we are eye to eye. "You are lying."

I stare into his beautiful green eyes. "No, I am not. I am fine."

"If it were me fighting Ethan tomorrow, I would be terrified."

"Well, that does not help anything. I am not scared. The only thing he can hurt is my pride. I want to win, for myself, for my father and brothers, for my kingdom."

Lifting his hand, he tucks a stray lock behind my ear. "And so you will."

My skin tingles as he pulls his fingers away. His face is so close to mine, I can smell the wine from his breath. Green eyes hold my gaze. I cannot have him looking at me this way. Especially tonight, when I must focus on besting Ethan.

I take his hand and press it to his chest. "You cannot touch me that way."

He grips my fingers. "I miss you."

My heart pounds at his words. No matter the outcome of tomorrow, I see no clear path for us to pursue what may be between us. There is nothing I would like more tonight than to fall asleep with him beside me. Feeling tears threatening, I tug my hand from his. "Thank you for coming. I should get my rest."

His eyes widen, then jaw sets. He takes a step back. "I did not mean to intrude. Of course, Queen."

Stomach clenching, I glance at the guards and spin so my back is to them. "Please do not be mad. I would like nothing more than to pass the evening with you. But things are more complicated now than they were before."

"It is not complicated when you care for someone." He jumps into the air and flies away.

It takes every ounce of resolve not to rush after him. I bite my lip as my eyes fill with tears. *How can I be so mean after he asked to be reassigned for me, spent two days in a dungeon because of me?* But if I lose tomorrow, I will be banished and may never lay eyes on him again. It is better to let him go.

Straightening my shoulders, I return to my chamber and close the door behind me. Within a few minutes, Alfreda arrives with hot water. She brushes my hair, and I fight crying. *How had things gone so wrong?*

"Talk to me child." She squeezes my shoulders.

"There is nothing to say."

"You know you can beat him, right? If you want to, you can best him."

I place my hand on hers. "How can you be sure?"

"Because I know you. You have never backed down from a challenge, and there is something inside you, innate in your blood, that this kingdom must have you at the helm. Do not forget that."

"Thank you, Alfreda. I needed to hear that."

She hands me the brush and kisses my forehead. "Rest well, and by tomorrow night, there will be no one who questions who is ruler of this land."

I hug her tightly. "You are right, Alfreda. Thank you. No one could ask for a better friend than you."

When she leaves, I soak in the tub until the water cools. Then I wrap in my warmest night clothes, open my window, and pile all my blankets atop me in bed, forming a warm cocoon. I spread my fingers again and again, trying to illicit a reaction, a tingle, a spark, *anything* that would confirm I possessed some type of latent power. Giving up, I picture all the moves Grant and the others showed me, replay them in my head until I drift to sleep.

My dreams feature swarms of kobold, dark bodied and purple winged, descending from the air, surrounding me as I stand alone in a field. The sky darkens, and a speck in the distance grows more detail as it approaches. It hovers over me—a huge dragon, black as night with wings spanning some fifty feet on each side. Fire spews from its nostrils. Giant talons reach down, ready to pluck me from the ground. I hold up my hand, nothing. The beast cackles and lifts it wings. Above it I see a host of blue orbs rising towards the Ring's portal.

I sit up with a start and throw my covers off. *Hot. I just got too warm, right?* I fly to the window to let the breeze cool my skin, shiver in the cold air, and pull the panes closed. Looking out over the bright night sky, I count the days in my head. It is a full moon. The magnetic pull must be triggering my psyche. Letting my eyes adjust, I linger on the garden, the orchard beyond, praying this will not be the last night in my home, the only home I have ever known. My survey stops at the horizon. A small blue orb floats up towards the ring.

My heart thuds in my chest. *What being passes through our realm?* Sounding the alarm, I dart to my closet, change into my warmest leather, and grab my quiver. As I swing open the door, I find Grant, Nicholas, Adam, and Timothy already there and spot Foster approaching. We fly through the corridors and exit the castle. Seeing more orbs rising towards the portal, I head straight for Aleem's home. Blue balls dot the whole sky as we alight in his front garden.

"What are those?" Foster trails me to the door.

"Souls. Someone is harvesting the souls of the fallen witches."

"What?"

Bam, bam, bam. I pound Aleem's door, yelling for him. When the door creaks open, he stands before us in his nightrobe, candle in one hand, cane in the other.

"Titania, what are you doing here?" After a crackle, his voice deepens.

"Look." I point at the sky. "I need a set of anchors, and I need you to close the ring once I am through."

"Good heavens." His face goes blue. "I cannot believe he would allow it."

"Aleem, we do not have time to figure this out. I need the extra set of anchors to get back through the portal."

Foster grabs my arm. "You are going to Upper Earth?"

Grant interjects. "Queen, you should not—"

"We have to figure out what is going on." Hardening my resolve, I spin back to Aleem. "You need to close the ring, and not just this one, all of them. You must signal to all the ring keepers and keep the rings closed until all the souls retreat to Lower Earth. I am going up to figure out who is doing this. If someone is amassing that much power, it cannot be good."

Aleem waves us in and shuffles across his wood floor. He moves a stone in the hearth and retrieves a bag from a nook within. "Do not lose these."

"Do not worry, I will not." Tucking the bag in my quiver, I zip outside to the others. "How many of you have been to Upper Earth?"

They all raise their hands save Foster.

I study each face, trying to gauge their mood, but they are soldiers, and I only find hardened jaws and eyes locked on mine. I wish my innards felt as sure. The times I have passed to the upper realm I can count on one hand. It has been over three years. My brothers would take me, but we never strayed from the Daintree forest our ring calls home. *Where are the souls going? How far will we have to travel to get the answers I desire? What will be waiting for us? How long will we be in the upper realm?*

I grip my quiver. I have placed the stones before from the inside. Aleem taught me after we lost my brothers. I know the order because I recited them two days prior for the judges.

Refocusing on those before me, I apprise them of the risks. If I fail to place the stones in the correct manner, and I only get one try, then we will be stuck in Upper Earth until Aleem opens the portal from below. I wait for each to voice consent. None falter in their commitment to follow me. Looking at the sky, I find it is overrun with blue orbs, crowding around the ring and slipping into the portal. I reiterate that Aleem should close the ring as soon as we cross the threshold. We leap into the air, heading straight for the opening.

As we approach the entrance, orbs surround us. My wings beat against the soft, apple-sized spheres, and they pelt my body. I shudder, knowing they house beings, that souls slide over me. Our progress slows the closer we get to the ring, and I fear we may be crushed. My heart thuds in my chest. *What have I led us into?* Gasping for breath, and with one last hard beat of my wings, I slide through the portal. I land on the soft grass outside the ring and wait for the others, anxious to know they made it through without harm. The warm, humid air surrounds me, and tall trees of the Daintree forest, besting the height of any tree in our realm, tower over me.

The stream of orbs rises in the sky and floats northeast. I shiver despite the climate, wondering what kind of magick controls them. If Lucifer allowed them to be released, it cannot be good. *And what if, whoever is orchestrating this, their aim for me is as Mother foresees? Are we flying into a trap?*

Leaning over the portal, I make out Grant approaching, followed fast by the other guards and Foster bringing up the rear. I grab their arms as they fight the waves of souls rushing out of the ring. As soon as Foster is beside me, one anchor disappears, followed by the second and third, until all twelve sit dark and the earth seals in front of me, stopping the influx of souls but leaving us trapped in Upper Earth.

"I have never seen the likes of this." Grant shakes his wings to release a sphere trapped between them.

I swallow and nod in agreement. "I do not think anyone ever has. Does everyone have their weapons? We need to stay together and invisible. Are you good with that, Foster?"

The air ripples, and he disappears. Reforming, he studies his limbs. "Whoa, that was freaky."

Noting that we will follow the souls and reassess when we reach their destination, I jump into the air. From cloud level, I spot souls entering Upper Earth from other rings of the realm and pray those ring keepers can close the portals soon. We follow the glowing balls, what must be tens of thousands of them, over southeast Asia, China, India, across the Middle East, the Mediterranean Sea, and Italy to an island on the western side, Sardinia.

My heart races in my chest as we follow the river of souls. This is much larger than my kingdom or our realm. Lower Earth allowed them to escape. *Witch souls?* I pray they are witch souls. For if they are dark souls, damned to Hell for eternity, we have a much bigger problem than I assumed. I tick through the knowledge in my head. *Blue, witch souls, I am sure of it.* Sheol holds them for eternity.

Souls from every direction coalesce above to an island off the coast of Italy. As we close in, I realize they seem to be absorbing into a castle structure on the south tip of the island. We land beyond a stone wall ringing the compound. The stone façade of a castle glows blue with the reflection of the glowing souls descending from the sky. As soon as my feet touch the grass, I sense it: magick. Powerful magick vibrates through the ground, pricking at my nerves. My wings stand up taut on my back.

"Something wicked this way comes." Grant steps in front of me. "I am not sure we should investigate further. There are witches and lots of them."

"Witches, cool." Foster steps to my side.

My side ticks. The Upper Earth word sounds odd coming from him. *Does he use the phrase to mask anxiety?* I have plenty. "Witches doing evil magick is the opposite of cool."

"I think the word is gnarly." Adam steps in line with the three of us.

"Okay, be serious. Let us vote. I say we go in. But maybe only some of us." I take stock of the faces before me.

"I am in." Foster and Grant raise their hands.

My mind pings with warning. *This could be dangerous. What of your mother's warning? Perhaps you should stay behind.* But I will not ask my soldiers to do anything I would not, and I want to know what is happening to these souls. I instruct Adam, Nicholas, and Timothy to wait under the trees and to leave if we are not back in an hour. I figure the souls will not linger long in Middle Earth, and Aleem will reopen the ring. *How long do souls last in our realm, or in Upper Earth, outside a host?* I have no clue, but I cannot imagine Lucifer, or whoever allowed this, would leave them free. They would be too valuable to him.

Adopting our invisible forms, we enter through an open window in the top of a turret. I assume the space is used by a potion maker because bottles, bowls, and mortars and pestles litter long tables. Weaving to the door, I press my ear to the wood. Not sensing anyone about, I test the knob. It turns, and we slip out onto a landing. Breath held, I listen for noise and peer down the tower. Seeing no one, we descend the staircase. As we near the bottom level, the hum of magick vibrates through my nerves. My ears detect a low hum I recognize to be chanting. We alight on the last landing on a cold, stone floor. I wish the door had a window and, finding it bears no lock, figure at least we will have an exit should we need one.

I press my ear to the door, and electricity hums through my body. Whatever, or whoever, draws the souls must be here. *Strong magick smolders behind this door.* I push the thought to Grant and Foster.

We have come this far. Grant's opinion rings in my head.

Peeking out the door, I find it leads to a large cavern, the top of which glows blue with spirit orbs. We slip through the door, backs to the cave wall. Witches, hundreds of witches, line stone benches.

"Ancestors, we call on you to deliver Sonia's spirit to her body," they chant.

The souls swirl down in a funnel to a to a body lying on a stone slab and enter her chest. I guess the body to be that of Sonia. My shoulders shudder. *Do these witches not know that more than her soul is being delivered into her vessel? How can a physical vessel contain that much power? Even if she is a powerful witch?* My brain twitches with the idea that perhaps it is the opposite way around, and the souls will give her power. *Immortality.* The word pops into my head. *It cannot be! An immortal witch?* Even faeries, who are closer to the angel species than any, do not possess immortality.

She would be more powerful than any being in all the realms, perhaps even more so than a seraph. I lean on the stone behind me, watching in stunned amazement, bordering on hysteria, and horror as thousands of souls enter her chest, wondering why Lucifer would allow a witch to become so powerful. *What does he hope to gain? An ally in Upper Earth?* My mind jumps to the next question. *What of the curse?* Witch souls are damned to Sheol for all eternity. *What magick is circumventing the absolute?*

The stream of glowing orbs flowing from the cavern ceiling lessens to a trickle. Realizing I had been holding my breath, I exhale. The Keepers must have gotten all the portals closed. The last soul enters her chest. I wait and watch, wondering if now is the time we should make our exit. Sonia's eyes flutter. She lifts her hands to her chest, and a wound I guess is the result of a sword, closes.

Standing, she motions to one wall and raises her crown in the air. "Do you wish to join us dear? Is this what you seek?"

I follow her gaze to the opposite wall where a blonde girl stands on a ledge.

"Or perhaps it is the blade." Sonia points to a dagger in a young man's hand.

The girl darts into the crevice behind her, disappearing.

"Get her! Now," Sonia yells.

Chaos erupts in the hall. Every nerve in my body tenses with fear. Pushing Foster and Grant towards the exit, we rush into the stairwell. We speed up the turret, through the potion room, and out into the night sky, not stopping until we descend on the other side of the wall where our comrades wait.

Breathing hard, I lean against a tree trunk. I do not dare risk dropping my invisibility cloak and signal the others to follow as I jump into the sky. My mind reels with worry for the decisions that lay ahead. *Should we wait until the portals open again? Can we risk staying in the forest, not knowing how long that will be? And what did I learn?* I pray information from my rash decision to travel to this realm is worth the price. Retracing our prior route over the Mediterranean, Middle East, India, and China, we make our way back to northeast Australia and the Daintree forest. I land on the grass next to our home ring, the others close on my heels.

"What was that?" Grant doubles over, panting.

"What happened back there?" Foster steps to my side.

"She absorbed all of those souls, thousands of them." I pace away and back to them. "That basically makes her immortal. What are the witches doing?"

"That is not hard to guess. They are gearing up to end the vampires." Adam rests on a stump.

"The vampires and witches have been at peace for decades." I counter.

Grant stands upright, folding his wings. "That does not erase centuries of bad blood. Behaving peacefully does not mean you want peace. We need to find out who Sonia is and what is special about that dagger."

Adam jumps up. "The ring keepers and judges watch for such activity. Hopefully, they have been following her, have some information. Someone must know something."

"Do you think it is safe to go back now?" Foster motions to the ring of toadstools.

I suggest we wait for Aleem to open the ring, and the others confirm my opinion. It looked as if the witches finished their spell, but I do not want more souls to escape. Who knows what would happen if they traveled free in Upper Earth. I am surprised one of the archangels did not intervene and wonder why not. *Is this witch more powerful than they are? Such an imbalance would not be allowed, would it? Is Sonia aided by Lucifer? Or is Sonia helping Lucifer? Or perhaps it is a mutual arrangement.* Lucifer has been reaping souls of fallen witches for centuries. Those that turn to the darkness join him and his dark angels. *Why would he let all these souls go?*

There is no use in guessing at motives or repercussions, so we hike to a nearby stream. Catching fish, we build a fire and roast them. We decide that I will place the anchors for the ring before sunup if Aleem does not open it by then. I cannot imagine that he would not but do not want to risk exposure with the unknown threats that lurk in Upper Earth. I guess that Sonia could snuff us out with the flick of a finger. If she aligns with Lucifer, that may be their plan—to eliminate Middle Earth so Lucifer would have free reign in Upper Earth.

I look at my comrades and wonder at how trusting they are. They did not hesitate to follow. *Me*, a fifteen-year-old girl, who may be dethroned and banished within a day's time, into the unknown. My heart swells with warmth, thinking they want to support me, believe in me. I listen to their banter as they swap battle stories and watch Foster's face as his eyes fix on each orator.

"You look deep in thought, Queen." Grant pokes me with his spearhead.

"I am surprised that you would follow me, trust that I could get you back home."

"Our families have served as guards to your family for generations. It is in our blood. I have watched you these past weeks. There is not one in our land I would rather travel to this realm with."

My face flushes at the commendation. "I pray you all still have jobs tomorrow."

"Aye, we will. You have the best wrestling coaches in the kingdom." Adam stands and kicks dirt onto the fire. "But what say you? I am ready to be back in my own bed."

Making our way back to the ring, we wait for the portal to open. I fight sleep as the wee hours of the morning come. The forest falls silent, and my skin tingles. *The witching hour.* Senses piqued, I jump when a beam of light shoots from one of the anchor toadstools. We hover above the ring, waiting, as each of the twelve nodes light up and the portal opens. Speeding through the barrier, I head straight for Aleem's cabin. He reports the souls stayed pressed against the gateway until an hour ago when they traveled back to Lower Earth, flowing like a river into the ground and disappearing.

"And all else? The kingdom?"

"Few awoke. Those that did gathered here. They wait in the meadow behind the cabin for your return."

I realize I should have left someone notice besides Aleem, alerted the First Advisor, but that would be Gunther, or Second Advisor, but he would be Angus, who sided with Gunther. Perhaps Kane would have been a wise choice. But there seemed to be no time. I make a mental note to shore up protocols.

I wind around Aleem's home to the grass field with Foster, my four guards, and Aleem following. The first rays of sunlight grace the meadow as I call for attention. Some hundred fae have gathered, a mere ten percent of the population of Capitolshire and the surrounding farms. Generals Kane and Milo huddle beside Terrence and Jesper. I do not see Gunther, Ethan, or anyone from their family and pray they have not cooked up another elaborate charge of treason with a plan to present it here for all to witness.

Climbing on a rock, I address my people, describing what we witnessed. Many pose questions we have no answers for. I request each of them ask their elders whether they have experienced such things and pledge to research our histories and investigate for additional meanings or implications. Bidding the gathered fae well, I hop from the rock to Kane and the advisors.

As we speak, a herald approaches. "Queen, Ethan awaits you at the arena. A crowd gathers to behold the combat test today."

"Tell Ethan we will be right behind you."

The herald takes his leave, and I approach Aleem. "What of the combat test? Ethan waits in the arena."

"You have not slept, nor have I, nor have several of the other judges. None of us are prepared. I will conference with the judges to consider postponement."

"Thank you. I will go to the arena and await your decision."

Flying to the coliseum, I try to prepare myself to address Ethan and those gathered, but there are no more eloquent words than I have already used to relay the past night's events. Nearing the stadium, I spy throngs gathered for our combat test, twice the number present in the meadow behind Aleem's cabin. I alight in the center of the space and call for attention. I describe the events of the past evening and apprise them that the judges will rule on a postponement of the trial. The arena descends to chaos as questions arise from the group. I answer as many as possible in an attempt to ease their fears.

Out of the corner of my eye, I catch movement and spin to find Ethan approaching. He lands beside me, wings at attention.

"So, this is yet another attempt to delay, cheat in the trial? Look at what this *girl* is doing! She says she cannot do her job. This is what it means to rule. There will be tests and trials, and a monarch cannot take rests. A ruler must attend to the people, the kingdom. If you, Titania, cannot do the work, I say you concede the trial to me right now."

The blood rushes to my wings, and they fan out. *How* dare *he.* "Aleem requested a postponement because the judges are tired from the long night. Where were *you* when our kingdom needed you? Sleeping in your warm bed? I was gathering information to help keep our kingdom secure. But the rules of the combat test are quite simple. If we can amass appropriate judges, I will proceed with the test."

Ethan raises his arm. "I call the advisors and generals to judge. Surely they are up to the task. What say you?"

With eyes cutting between Ethan and I, each of the advisors and generals agree to the terms.

Hands on hips, I raise my chin. "So be it."

Chapter 11

I TRUDGE TO THE SIDE WHERE my guards and Foster stand.

"Are you mad?" Grant takes my quiver as I slide it from my back. "You slept, not even two hours, and flew halfway around the world. You are not in any shape to fight Ethan."

"Get me something to eat. If I back down today and win tomorrow, there would always be someone to question my reign. I win today, and no one will ever question me again."

The judges inspect our armor and weapons.

Ethan chooses a mace, and I picture methods for making him unhand it. That should be my first goal, to disarm him. I have a far better chance at winning in hand-to-hand combat. If I can get in a few good blows before I lose my weapon, that will give me an advantage as well.

As I scarf down a roll, Foster approaches. "I cannot watch this. I cannot bear it. Please, do not be rash. Use your head. That is how you will beat him. Disarm him quickly, get in some good blows, and then tire him out. Use your speed."

I hold his stare. "I will. Thank you for everything, coming last night, being my friend. You have made these past two weeks bearable. I am sorry I could not show you that last night. Will you do one last thing for me?"

"You know I will do anything."

"See to my father and mother. Make sure they are distracted or entertained, and Alfreda as well. Make sure no one brings them news. I will come to you when this is over. If things do not go well for me, make sure they are protected." Looking at his full lips, I find I want to kiss him. He became more to me than just a friend. Every cell of his body, his mind and soul, attracts me. How he values my thoughts, trusts my instincts, and that face. It draws me like no other. I blink. I will not have my first kiss in front of half the kingdom when I have just mashed a pastry into my mouth. Face warming from the thought of his soft lips on mine, I waver. I hold his gaze, not knowing what to do.

He wraps his arms around me and whispers in my ear, "I will still call you Queen when this is finished. I know it."

"Thank you." I melt into him, wishing it were just he and I, surrounded by trees and forest. Releasing him, I kiss his cheek.

Face flushed, he backs away, spins, and flies off.

"Well, that was sweet." Grant's voice sounds behind me. "I am glad he will not be here to distract you."

My cheeks flame with embarrassment, but I straighten my back. "I will not be distracted. Any final advice?"

"Everything Foster said."

"How long were you listening?"

"You know I will do anything." He mimics Foster's voice.

"Stop." I slap his arm. "You should go home as well. Take the rest of the guards with you. They need to see their families."

"We are not leaving you."

"Only I can decide my fate now."

"Still, you are my queen."

My heart swells with gratitude. "I appreciate your support. Stay if you wish."

Locking arms with each of my guards, one after the other, I march to the center of the field to receive my armor. As I do, I observe Aleem and the other judges entering the coliseum and am glad they will be present to witness the test. I want as many witnesses to this fight as possible. If I best Ethan, goddesses willing, I want every fae in Aubren to know it was a fair contest.

The armor weighs more than I guessed, and the helmet is too big. I tie the chain mail vest around my torso. It reaches from the top of my neck down to my hips. Then, I slide on the arm covers and chaps. I leave the helmet doubting he will aim for my head *Right? Or will he?* A blow to the head would risk a fatal wound. If he kills me, he will be banished, nonetheless. A trumpet blares, and my heart thuds.

Pulse racing, I look at Ethan and see him spreading his wings. I fight the urge to laugh. *Pompous, arrogant, peacock struts for show.* His father put him here. I, on the other hand, have trained for this job for three years. I will not be bested by a stage animal.

Another blast signals the beginning of the test. He grabs the mace laying in front of him and swings it towards my legs. I jump back, and he snatches my weapon as well. *Weasel. But smart. All spirits, now I have no weapon.* I guess as they say, all is fair in war. I must get at least one weapon from him.

Ethan swings the maces at me, first with one arm then the other, forcing me backwards.

If he corners me, this will not last long.

When his next blow comes, I swing my leg up, and it intersects his forearm. He drops the weapon. Kicking my other leg out, I get enough space to snatch the mace from the dirt. His staff intersects mine, but I hold it fast with two hands. I use his momentum and swivel sideways so the club end of my mace hits his leg. He hops back, and I jab at him again.

This time, he blocks, and our weapons clank together.

Swing, block, swing, block.

We move forwards and backwards in the center of the arena. My arms begin to wear, and I know I need to switch tactics. Gripping my mace with two hands, I turn it over and over in a rowing motion. He retreats but slings his weapon out low, almost catching my ankles. I hop away, and he pivots so his back is to me with the mace aimed at my face. I drop to the dirt and whip my weapon forward, knocking him to the ground. Bounding up, I bring my weapon down hard. He rotates his weapon over his chest. It impacts mine, and I lose my grip. My mace goes flying away.

I spin away, but he is quick and whips his mace at me, catching my foot. I land hard on my hip. Grabbing my leg, he drags me towards him. Stomach clenching in fear, my brain searches for a way out. I clutch my fists together and bring them down on his helmet.

Ethan's eyes go wide. He grunts, tightens his grip on my ankle, and twists.

My bones crack in his grip, and pain blasts through my leg up to my spine. Fear shoots through me as I imagine him getting hold of my other leg. I jerk them into my body and look up to find him looming over me, purple wings spread. For a second, the kobold looms over me. *Think. He means to intimidate you. Be smarter. Use your speed and wear him out. Disarm the brute.* I roll right and jump up on my one good foot.

Even with my ankle, my only advantage is my speed. He wears full armor, and it makes him slower.

I whip my leg around and get a hit to his side.

His breastplate pops open.

I dodge another blow and jab my arm at the same spot. I need all that metal off him if I hope to use any of the wrestling tactics Grant and the others taught me.

Ethan lands a blow on my back, and that side sears with pain.

Focusing on the gap in his armor, I try for the same spot over and over with my injured foot. Blinding pain blazes through my leg each time. Charging him, I thrust my elbow into his side. It lands between the front and back plates, and the pieces clunk to the ground.

Ethan raises his mace over his head, coming down towards me again and again. Pivoting one way then the other, I dodge his blows and focus on the lower armor with jabs to his hip with my knee. Using only one leg to support my weight puts me off balance, and I chance putting weight on both. Sharp pain, like my bones have been hit with a hammer, shoots up my injured leg, and Ethan's club lands on my thigh. I swivel my torso and fling my arms out, fending off further attack. My wings pop out, and I realize I can use them for balance and extra force. Raising them together and popping them out gives me increased thrust, and my fist lands square in his chest.

He steps back, and I advance, jabbing with my fist. His lower armor falls to the ground, and I lunge at his thigh.

His staff sideswipes my leg, and I land hard on my side. Gasping for air, I fold my arms over my middle.

Clutching my good foot, he yanks me towards him. He straddles my stomach and mashes the mace against my arms.

His hot breath drenches my cheek. "You know you cannot win. Give up now."

"I will not." I jerk my knees up into his back.

The rod presses against my biceps, and I fear he may break both the bones underneath. I beat his back with my knees. He rolls off me, and I spin quickly. He jumps and lands, spread eagle, on top of me.

Air whooshes from my lungs, and I struggle to inhale. My arms ache under the weight of his chest, and my feet press into the dirt. *Think. Think.* I squirm my hips, trying to get him off.

His fingers wrap around my neck, pushing my head to the sand.

I know the grip. If I cannot get his hand off, I will pass out soon. Disoriented as to my location, I scan for my guards. *Goddesses save me.*

Grant's teeth reflect the light as he screams something I cannot hear over the yells of the crowd. He gyrates his hips.

I clench my stomach muscles and push my hips against Ethan's huge form.

One arm holds my arms to the ground, and the other compresses my neck.

"I did not want it to come to this. I do not like hurting anyone, especially a woman. But you wanted to be like any other fae. I cannot treat you as a girl in this instance. Concede."

"I shall not until I cannot draw another breath."

"Then forgive me."

Ringing sounds replace the shouts from the crowd, the bright sun fades, and a haze descends across my vision. The scene morphs to a cottage nestled under tall trees. Mother sits in the garden watching Father chop wood. I look into the forest. Tree trunks become thick kobold legs, hundreds of thousands of them, marching from the mountain, across the meadow, towards the castle... My castle.

Blinding light shatters the scene, and an electric shock shoots through my body. I open my eyes to see Ethan's sweating face above. Using all the might I can muster, I draw in my legs and push out with my arms. Ethan topples off me to the ground. I roll over, straddle his hips, and pin his arms. Using his legs, he pivots, leaving me pinned under him again. I knee his groin. He curls up, and I wrap my legs around his thighs and one arm over his bulging biceps and chest. I hook my other elbow around his neck and squeeze.

His eyes grow wide. He wriggles in my grip, but power like I have never felt before ripples through my muscles, and I hold him taut. Constricting his neck, I watch as his face turns red, grey, then blue. His limbs fall slack, and I release his neck then legs and torso. *I won.* I scoot out from under him, supporting his head and lowering it to the dirt. Kneeling beside him, a chill washes over me. Scanning the crowd, I realize all eyes are on me. Not a whisper rises from the arena.

I press my palms to the sand and take a deep breath. *What have I done?* This magick or whatever courses through my veins overtook me. *What if he is dead?* I lift my hand and press two fingers to his neck. I feel his blood pulsing under my skin. *He is alive.* Body trembling, I lean over and feel his hot breath on my cheek. I stare into his face as his skin regains its rosy color. His eyelids flutter and eyes open.

Lifting his head, he looks at me and then pans the arena. "What happened?"

I push to a stand on my one good leg and balance on my toes. I offer my hand. "Will you do me the honor of being my advisor?"

Gripping my forearm, he sits up then spins and jumps to his feet. "I passed out? I lost? You were stronger than me?"

My heart beats wildly in my chest. *Will he know that I had been aided by magick or whatever power manifests within me?* "It was a hard fight. And only barely. What say you? I do not wish you to be banished. Our families have a long history of serving this kingdom together."

His eyes cut to the crowd and back to me. "First Advisor?"

Is he mad? "No."

"Second Advisor?"

I shake my head. I do not wish him banished but will never trust him. But like Father, I plan to keep my enemies close. "Advisor. One of the six."

He dips his chin and, gripping my arm, raises it above my head. "All hail Queen Titania, true monarch of Aubren!"

My heart and mind soar. *I won. The power within me ensured my victory. I did it. I am queen.*

A roar of clapping, cheers, and whistles erupt around me. The sound deafens me, and I draw in a deep breath. Heart beating wildly and leg trembling under my weight, I lift my chin and spread my wings out wide. Sweat and dirt cake my body, and I imagine I must look like a monster. I care not. My kingdom will know I would do anything for them, that I am worthy of being their ruler.

A cannon sounds, and all the fae take to the air. Grant, followed by Nicholas, Adam, and Timothy, are the first to my side. Bowing, they form a circle around me.

I tug at Grant's cloak, edging him closer. "I do not think I am under attack."

He winks at me and spins to stand behind me. "You have a point. I have no idea how you did that, but I would guess no one will ever try to cross you."

My leg sears as I greet my subjects, smiling and accepting their congratulations. All the while, I keep an eye on Ethan. He swerves through the crowd to the side of the arena where his father waits. I hold my breath as I watch them speaking. *Could Ethan realize I was aided by magick?* With my next thought, I refute the idea. *You have no idea where that power came from.* Panic can fuel chemical spikes, nervous system reactions. Smiling at the fae in front of me, I watch as Gunther pats his son's back, and they walk to the exit.

Seeing Kane approach, I refocus on my fae. Kane, the advisors, Aleem, and his judges, followed by more fae than I ever remembered, one by one and group by group, approach and take a knee, congratulating me on my victory. Legs shaking with fatigue, I use my mace Grant retrieved for balance. As the numbers draw thin, Angus and Cedric approach. Eyes to the ground, the advisors that sided with Gunther kneel and address me as Queen. I realize there are so many things to think about: the advisory council, my generals… *Who do I trust?* With the occurrences of last night, these are not matters that can be put off.

"Rise, gentlemen. I will call you to the castle to discuss your places in our kingdom in due time." I take a deep breath and force a smile.

Heads down, they rise and back away. Grant inches to my side, whispering that I have greeted enough people and can take my leave. Noting Generals Raymond and Walter, who also sided with Gunther, are not present, I call to Kane, instructing him to tell them both to be ready to speak with me in the afternoon and that we should counsel before the meetings. If there is one I do trust, it is Kane. Milo also seems to be loyal. Advisors Bran, Jesper, and Terrence huddle close by as well, and I ask they gather Aleem and the judges to speak with me.

A wave of nausea passes over me, and my skin chills. My right ankle throbs, and I know I must attend to it. Gathering Grant and my other guards, I take to the air. It would have been my preference to march to the castle, my castle. I let the idea sink it. *I won. It is over.*

I look out over the land, green meadows, mountains in the distance, as I make my way towards the home I have always known, grateful the gods, goddesses, spirits, or whatever have aided me, granted me the strength to continue to serve my people.

I dare not let anyone notice me hobbling. Laughing, I think how stupid that is. Everyone saw Ethan break my ankle, heard the crack. I should bear the wound like a battle scar, proud of my bravery. *Would any warrior not do the same?* Still, I will not be helped, and I land in front of the castle doors, club mace next to my bad ankle to use as a crutch. Father sits in his chair just inside the doors flanked by Mother, Alfreda, and Foster.

"Look who returns from battle the victor. I am so proud of you. I knew you would be victorious." Father rolls his chair towards me.

Leaning over to hug him, I glance at Mother. Her gaze does not stray from the sky. Alfreda flits to me, tears streaming from her face. I hug her and look up as Foster approaches.

"My Queen." He drops to one knee.

My face flames. "Rise, Foster. And please, call me Titania. Thank you for seeing to my family."

Refocusing on the hall in front of me, I realize a crowd gathers. "Tonight, we celebrate a unified Aubren. Please, join us, all who wish for a feast with dancing and merriment."

Shouts ring out. "All hail, Queen Titania."

Smiling, I hobble down the passageway and whisper to Alfreda to call for the physician. My body feels as if it is made of gel, but I press through the main passage. At the fork that leads to my chamber, I announce again our plans for the feast and bid those trailing us goodbye. I turn to Father and say I will speak with him once I am cleaned up. A guard takes his chair and wheels him away, Mother following.

Alfreda wraps her arm around my waist, and I lay one arm over her shoulder as we weave through the corridors to my room. "You will have to get a chamber closer to court. I am sorry I did not come. I could not watch you fighting that huge man."

"It was not so bad." I stumble forward and clutch the latch as we reach my door. "I believe I shall take a bath now. Have the physician wait till I am done."

"I will get the hot water for your bath." Alfreda slips past me.

"Thank you." I look at Grant, Adam, Timothy, and Nicholas. "I do not believe I could have done this without you. Please, go rest, and we shall have the most wonderful party tonight."

Congratulating me again, they leave orders with those posted at my door. Looking at Foster, I lean my head against the wood.

He takes a step towards me and cups his hand on my cheek. "My Queen. I cannot believe you beat Ethan. If I did not know you, I would be a bit scared."

Moving his fingers from my face and planting them on his chest, I smile. *If he were just a boy and I just a girl…* Smiling, I am reminded of the dirt crusting my face. *I must look like a troll.* I take a deep breath and straighten my shoulders. "That is the point. No one will question my rule again. Now go. I need to clean up."

"Your wish is my command." Dropping my hand, he bows, takes a few steps back, then jumps into the air.

Gripping the door handle, I force a smile at the guards and slide into my room. As soon as the doors click closed, my good leg buckles under me.

"Good heavens, are you okay?" Alfreda flies to my side.

"I just bested a two-hundred-pound soldier. I need you to bring me every energy drink known in the fae realm. I have to be recovered enough to figure out advisors and generals and make it through the feast tonight."

I wrap an arm around her waist, and she supports me as we cross to the bath. Sending her away, I undress and lower myself into the tub. Every cell of my body aches, and my ankle appears the size of a melon. I rest my head back and think about the last time I felt this way, not even two weeks ago, the day we defeated the kobold and Father passed me his crown. *Today, you earned it.*

Stretching my fingers, I focus on my center, trying to recreate the magick that emanated from my core. But nothing comes—no twinkling of light, no tingling of my skin. *Does it matter? Something must want you to be queen. You were saved from the kobold for a reason. Do not question it. But what if someone discovered my secret? What then?* I would be called a cheater, and my crown would be stripped away as fast as I won it. *How could anyone know though?* Adrenaline. That is what humans call the chemical that surges through the body, giving one superior speed and strength. It would be my alibi.

I scrub my skin and soak until the water cools. Alfreda bring pastries and fruit juice and, flitting away, declares she will fetch the physician. Drying off, I slip on my robe, sit on my bed, broken ankle now purple and propped in a pillow, holding the plate in my lap. I look at the ceiling where my hundred or so crosses still hang in random places and think of my brothers, praying they look down on me with favor. I picture Rigel's body bleeding from his middle, face placid and white.

"I am sorry," I whisper to the heavens. Swiping a tear from my cheek, I rise and dress in the white blouse, green corset jacket, and brown leather riding skirt Alfreda set out for me.

Picking up my mace and thinking I shall never be without this weapon again, I hobble to the door. The physician enters with his bag, setting and wrapping my ankle. He begs me to elevate it and let it rest for the remainder of the day, but there is too much to be done, and grabbing my mace, I take to the air and fly towards Father's chamber.

"Father?" I crack open the door and see him and Mother sitting in front of the fire.

"Here she is. The hero of the day."

"I would not say hero." I cross to them, kissing Mother then him on the cheek. Sitting on the hearth, I relish the warmth from the flames. Looking from her to him, I dare to ask, "Has she? Does she know?"

"I cannot tell. There is no difference. I do not know why I keep hoping."

"She bears a heavy burden."

Father lifts an eyebrow. "As you do now."

"Yes." I look at my hands.

"I still cannot believe you bested Ethan." He leans forward and lays his hand on mine. "I am so proud of you. Your strength, your speed. I do not believe the fae of the kingdom will forget it very soon."

"Nor will my muscles." Sliding my fingers from his grasp, I run my hands up and down my biceps.

"I thought surely he would best you. They said he had his hand to your neck."

"Yes. He nearly bested me." I keep my eyes trained on his. I want to tell him. *But should I share this with anyone?*

"There is more?"

I lean forward and whisper, "I… I have many questions. I need to decide on advisors and generals."

"Titania, I see it in your face. What weighs on you?"

My chest feels like it might burst, and tears form in my eyes. "It was the same as the day I slay the kobold."

"What do you mean slay? In the skirmish last week?"

I shake my head. "No, three years ago."

"Slay? You said you played dead and the kobold left you."

"No. I lied." I blot my tears. "I killed that kobold with some power. I never exhibited it before, or since, until today."

"You killed it?" His words are but a whisper on his lips. "You lied?"

I collapse on the floor in front of Father, chin to my chest. "I am so sorry. Had I known what I could do, I could have saved Rigel. But I did not know. I swear, I did not. Please, forgive me."

"How did you do it?"

Water streaming down my face, I look into his eyes. "I shocked it, killed the kobold with this power like a wave of energy that flowed through me when his sword hit my arm. The second the blade touched my skin, it was as if a forcefield flowed over me then up into the kobold's metal sword and through its whole body. It fell dead before me. Forgive me. I did not know I carried this power, and I have never been able to repeat it until today. I do not even know where it came from. But I feel the guilt of not saving my brother every day."

"Heavens be, you are the one."

My skin tingles, and bumps form on my arms. *The one? The one who what?* "The one? I do not understand."

"Your mother said it, but I did not believe. She told me you survived because you were the one."

"Have you been lying to me this whole time? You said she saw my death. That a kobold killed me. That I was still in danger. What is the one?"

"The one that will end all evil."

Chapter 12

"The one that will end all evil? I have never heard of such a thing. Why have you never mentioned this?"

"It is folklore, old wives' tales"—he chuckles—"or more like old ring keepers' tales. The legend says there will be a fae who will end all evil, herald peace in Upper Earth."

"All evil? As in Lucifer? Because I think someone may have just trumped him."

"What do you mean?"

"Last night—"

"Yes, about last night. You are a monarch. You cannot go shooting through portals, chasing spirits. You have to send someone else."

"There was no one else. There was not time. May I tell you what happened?" I proceed to explain how the spirits entered the witch they called Sonia and about the dagger.

Father rubs his beard. "So, either the magick from the dagger supplanted Lucifer's, or he allowed the spirits to leave Lower Earth. But to what end?"

Pointing to a high shelf, Father asks me to retrieve a book titled "Saints." I flit up to retrieve the text. He flips through the pages to a description of St. Maurice, who was believed to have carried the Holy Lance into battle. Any that possessed the sword are prophesied to be bequeathed power beyond compare and life everlasting. Father lifts the book, and I examine a picture of the sword. It matches the dagger I saw in the witch's castle.

"So, the sword is granting Sonia the power to gather the witch souls?"

"It seems that would be the case. I believe the sword was lost after Hitler's demise, but perhaps the witches found it."

"Hitler? The Hitler? Of Germany? The man who ordered the slaughter of an entire race? What does he have to do with the sword?"

"Legend says Hitler gathered his power because he possessed the sword."

"So, he used magick to compel armies?" My side ticks. *If a human who wielded that sword commanded so much power, what can an immortal witch do with such a weapon?*

Father wheels towards me. "The witches prepare for something big."

"What would they need that much power for?"

"To end the vampires. She means to end the vampires."

"But vampires and witches are at peace." I repeat the words I said to Grant and recall his answer. I cannot fathom how a whole people could harbor such grudges for thousands of years. "I am not sure how much of this I can process right now. I must choose advisors and generals. I need counsel on that first. Then we will deal with prophesies and legends."

Vowing to do more research on the dagger and Sonia, Father lends me advice on generals and advisors. He confirms my thinking on general choices and urges me to do more research before advisors are chosen. With Ethan's acceptance, I have two slots left and wonder where I should even start. I decide my first action will be to speak with Kane about generals. I exit Father's chamber, instructing a guard to call Kane to the study. Flying towards the meeting room, my ankle throbs, and I wonder how I will get through the afternoon, much less an evening of festivities.

Ethan waits in the passage outside the study, and my guards close in. Waving them back, I land in front of my opponent, mace tight in hand for support.

He dips his chin. "May I have a word with you?"

"Of course. Come in." I wave to the doors.

The guards follow us, and I ask them to wait at the far wall. We cross to the table, and I sit at the head.

Taking the seat to my left, he leans forward. "My sincerest apologies for your injury."

I hold my back straight. "It should heal quickly."

"Yes, but still, I did not enjoy hurting you. I appreciate you allowing me to stay in the kingdom and the position you offered me. Do not mistake my next request. Being monarch would have been a high honor, one I would have served with all my might, but being an advisor is not something I wish for. I enjoy my place in the army and would rather serve there. I hope you are not offended."

I am surprised by his words, thought his family would want to maintain their influence. "I am not offended in the least. This job is new to me, and I would not wish to have someone advising that does not wish to be in that role. As for your role in the army, I will leave that to Kane. He is head general, and those decisions shall be his."

He clears his throat. "Being an advisor is something my father loved. He wishes to be reinstated. He would be most honored to serve you. Our family has long served as advisors to the monarchy of Aubren, as you noted before."

My pulse races, and I feel as if my head may explode. *How dare he ask for his father to be restored to the council? After staging a coup against my throne, accusing me of plotting to kill Father?* There remains the lingering suspicion that he was behind the loss of my faerie crosses. I realize that accusation may have been made in haste, based only on his stench, and there is no way to take it back now. I add that issue to the growing list I must attend to.

Taking a deep breath, I refocus on Ethan. "I have a lot of research to do regarding the council positions. It will take time for me to assess the knowledge base of each advisor and decide who may best be suited to round out the group. You can tell your father that a decision will be forthcoming."

Laying his palms on the table, he smiles. "You are most gracious. I appreciate your time."

I rise and he does as well. I wait for him to round the table and follow. "I will let Kane know of your wishes as to the army position."

"Thank you." He bows and backs from the room as the doors are opened behind him.

Eyebrows peaked, Kane stands in the doorway. He steps back to let Ethan pass and shuffles inside. "What was he doing here? I thought the advisors were meeting later."

"They are. He does not want to be an advisor. He wants to keep his position in the military. Also"—I hobble to my seat—"his father wants to be reinstated to the council."

"That"—Kane clears his throat as he sits to my right—"excuse me… How dare he! What did you say?"

"I told him you would make decisions about the armed services positions, and I would be investigating who I needed as advisors."

"Well spoken."

"Thank you." I tell him about my decision to let him choose replacements for Raymond and Walter, the Archer and Militia Generals.

He thanks me for trusting him with the task. I assure him that I hold him in the highest esteem and inquire about the advisors Bran, Terrence, and Jesper. He recommends each for being loyal and knowledgeable. I realize I must meet with each of them to decide their strengths and how to proceed in filling the three remaining seats. Our conversation circles back to events of the past night.

"You should not have left the kingdom. As monarch—"

Lifting my hand, I stop his direction of discussion. "Father already scolded me, but I will not sit back and let others put themselves in harm's way when I am not willing to do the same. Plus, there was no time. We had to get the portal closed and needed to know what was going on."

"How were you the first to alert Aleem? My soldiers on watch did not even notice the orbs until after you sounded the alarm. Were you awake?"

I wonder if I should admit to my dream and realize I need to trust those closest to me for the good of the realm. I pray he will not jump to some prediction of a savior fae destined to defeat all evil. "I dreamt of a dragon, and the blue orbs rising behind it, and woke to see them in the sky."

"A premonition. I did not realize you possessed that gift."

Feeling exposed and judged, I stand and cross to the fire. "And neither did I. It appears to be my lucky day."

"Yes, besting Ethan was quite a feat."

I spin to face him. "I have Grant and my other trainers to thank for my win. I could not have done it without everyone."

"And what of Foster? Where would you like him to be posted?"

Thinking of Foster, a smile crosses my face before I can stop it. I focus on looking serious. "He should have the position he is trained to do if he wants it. He is free to direct his own path."

"Would you like to speak with him before he decides?"

Would I like to talk to him? Yes, of many things, but I would not sway him one way or the other. "I do not need to meet with him. But will if he desires."

"You are well trained in your speech." Kane winks at me.

"I watched my Father for years. There are pressing issues. Are Aleem and the other judges gathered?"

"I would like to talk to you about the kobold. We have not seen the last of them. They are getting smarter. Cutting off our access to Upper Earth was an intelligent move."

"I know, and I would like to explore this issue further. We need better safeguards in place. But that is a longer discussion for another day. I think we should get Aleem's counsel as well. Let us talk about that tomorrow."

"As you wish."

Kane calls in the Ring Keeper and his judges. I take my seat and welcome them, asking each for an introduction. Following, Aleem reiterates how fortunate we were to close the portal quickly but reports many souls were transferred to Upper Earth through portals all over the world. He affirms my quick action in following the souls to the castle in Italy as there has been no information gathered through normal channels.

"Whoever is behind this is keeping things under layers of security." Aleem reclines in his seat.

"Sonia." I rise and cross to the fire. "The witch's name was Sonia. I trust my father included you in his discovery of the origin of the dagger and what this could mean."

"Yes, a war between witches and vampires. It is a good theory. But that would be none of our concern. What matters is the imbalance of power. Who is she siding with? Will she transfer power to Lucifer? Or will the souls be released to find their final resting place?"

"But if humans are harmed as a result of this war, that *is* our concern. And perhaps she plans on keeping the souls to sustain her own immortality?" I offer.

204

Aleem consents. "Again, a shift in the balance of power. We cannot foresee what this will mean for humans or our kind."

"So, we watch and wait? As will the rest of the kingdoms, I assume?"

He confirms our communication with the other kingdoms, and I add a new item, introductions to other monarchs, to my list of priorities. Retaking my seat, I address my next concern: Gunther and the investigation into my missing faerie crosses. With the monarchy trial, they halted their investigation, but they inform me they plan to restart on the 'morrow. Aleem reports he kept the crosses exhumed from Mt. Kosciuszko, and that I may inspect them. I instruct them to question the guards on duty outside my chamber the night my crosses were stolen. Further, I ask them to gather a list of names of all who sided with Gunther.

"You wish all of them to be charged with treason?" Aleem's eyes grow wide.

"That is for you to decide. I believe it is appropriate. The line of succession was clear."

Looking down and back up to me, Aleem clears his throat. "I believe it was a valid question as to whether you were the best person to be monarch. You were not yet of age."

My heart races, and I grip my armrests to keep from jumping out of my seat and calling him a traitor as well. Swallowing, I meet his gaze. "I understand your point of view. Still, I would like you to investigate Gunther and any who may have aided him in stealing the faerie crosses from my chamber."

"I believe *that* to be a valid line of questioning. It does seem unlikely that a kobold stole them from your room. And with his other allegations towards you, it makes sense there would have been motive to induce you to be off kilter."

I cannot let the question burning in my brain sit. "And Aleem, tell me, what do you think now? Do you think me worthy to serve as your monarch?"

His eyes do not leave mine. "Without a doubt."

Releasing my hold on the chair, I smile. "Thank you, sir."

I thank each of them and end our meeting. As the judges exit, I welcome Bran, Terrence, and Jesper into the study. My ideas around the advisors feel less well formed, and I invite each to summarize their roles and background on the council. They ask for a recap of the prior night's events, and I share the information we have gathered and theories as to Sonia's motivations. Each offers to help Father research her background, and I affirm my gratitude for the aid. They reiterate Kane and Father's opinion on me traveling through the portal, and I begin to feel lectured to. Waiting for someone else to do a job never worked for me, but I also realize I will not be able to do everything.

As the sun passes below the horizon and darkness falls, I ask that they brainstorm who else may serve as advisor and have a list by tomorrow. We end our session, and I retreat to my room, foot throbbing and swollen. I wish there was some magick potion that would heal my bones and, unwrapping the bandages, lay my hands on the broken ankle. Feeling no tingling or warmth pass through my palms, I give up and hobble to my dressing table. Even more than for a fixed leg, I wish I could sleep.

Picking up the gown Alfreda left out for me, I dread the night—not only because of my exhaustion and aching foot, but because I fear what may come. *What other calamity could be waiting around the bend?* The past two weeks have been nothing but a whirlwind of tragedies. *Will another attempt to usurp my rule? Not after my show this morning, right? Do more kobold or other enemies lurk beneath, waiting to pounce? Will Sonia unleash Hell on Earth? And what will happen to our realm if she does?*

An hour's worth of elevating my leg produces superb results, and I pull a dark green pair of riding pants on. Attaching a matching skirt over the tight britches, I pair them with a white lace-collared shirt and light-green velvet vest. I know Alfreda will not approve, but I am tired of following fancy celebration etiquette. I wish I could dictate every detail of the celebration to control every interaction, every guest. At least I gave strict seating chart orders. Exhausted, I plan to stay for the meal, watch a couple of dances, and take my leave early. I am glad not to have to worry about who I will and will not dance with. That is one plus in having a broken ankle.

The morning, and my brawl with Ethan, seems like a passing nightmare in my brain. So many issues weigh on me, and I almost laugh at myself for worrying about party etiquette. I am the guest of honor, after all. I should do as I please. What I desire is to have those dearest to me close at hand: Father, Mother, Alfreda, Foster, Kane, and my guard friends. They will sup with me at the head table. All will be welcomed at the castle tonight, for I am holding the tenet of having my friends near and enemies nearer. Kane doubles the guards on duty, and I shore up my optimism, knowing I will be with my security detail.

The ladies come to curl my hair, and I eye the faerie cross on my dresser. No matter that it is not one I found with my brothers, it reminds me of them. I slip it around my neck. This is their victory as well, and I want to honor them. Once my hair is finished, they place my crown on top of the curls. My entourage of family and friends waits for me outside my door, and we parade through the passageways lined with fae to the grand hall.

All inside rise as I enter, and the national anthem starts. Mace sure at my side, I stride to the front of the room to cheers of "All Hail Queen Titania" and "Long Live Queen Titania, Ruler of Aubren." I hold my chin high and spin to face the crowd as I reach our table. Waiting for the last note to sound, I raise my hand to call for attention. I recited, over and over, what I would say as I rested earlier, but now, looking at all the waiting faces, I freeze. These are my people, I am responsible for them, and they are looking to me to ensure their safety, prosperity. My chest tightens with stress. Panning the crowd, I stop at Foster. He smiles and blushes. I release a breath. This is my home, my family.

"Brethren of Aubren, I stand before you humbled that you have bestowed upon me the great honor and duty of serving as your leader. Be assured, you will not be let down. I will bear our burdens as my family has for generations, and we will know prosperity and happiness.

There hath been much strife the past weeks. Let us come together as one to celebrate."

Turning to the table behind me, I pour wine in a goblet and lift it high. "To Aubren."

"To Aubren." Cheers ring out, and the band begins a traditional jig.

Servers stream in with plates of meat, breads, cheese, and fruits. I weave around the table and sit at the head, Father and Mother, Alfreda, Foster, and Grant to my left, and Kane, Adam, Timothy, Nicholas, and Milo to my left. I find I am quite hungry and enjoy the meal, the light conversation, and the warmth of the room after the past days of strife. Seeing Ethan smiling with his men, my disdain for his father flames anew. I must get to the bottom of his treachery and confirm if any still hold ill will towards me.

When the dancing begins, I say my goodbyes and make a quiet exit out the back of the hall. Followed by my four night guards, I feel safe—even with Foster, Grant and the others still taking part in the celebration. In a week, perhaps even less, my leg will be healed, and I will be able to enjoy such an event. *Perhaps I will plan the coronation for a month's time.* January would be a good month for such an occasion. By then, my generals and advisors should be chosen, and I will feel more settled and ready to present my kingdom to the rest of our realm.

Changing into night clothes, I am asleep as soon as my head hits the pillow. I rest in a deep slumber, not even dreaming, and wake to bright sun streaming through my window. Lifting my legs, I remember my cast and sigh. *A week.* With our fae healing speed, I should only need a week at most to heal the fracture. I lift the mace from beside my bed and hobble to the window. Sun warms my body, and it seems as if the last two weeks were but a dream, a passing nightmare. I spin to find only a couple of reflections of light from the few faerie crosses left. *No, it was real.* Someone was in my room and took my crosses, the kobold nearly cut us off from the Upper Earth, and Gunther tried to take my crown.

I cross to my dressing table and fit the crown atop my hair. *Things will be better now.* I can help protect this kingdom from whatever is coming. Sitting at my table, I nibble my bread and look at my crosses. I am not sure how it went unnoticed before, but their disarray feels unbearable. I fly to the ceiling and spin around, brainstorming how they should be arranged. I decide on a plan and start moving them a few at a time, lining them in front of each opening in my room. If it is true that they are to bring good luck and ward off evil, then having them around my door and windows makes sense.

Seeing the sun reflect my crosses and form a line of light dots on the other wall warms my heart, and I feel as if my brothers are looking over me, protecting me.

"What are you doing?"

I spin to find Foster hovering outside my window. "Rearranging my crosses."

"You are wasting a beautiful day inside." His eyes sparkle as he smiles.

"I just woke, and should you not be working?" I fly to the window.

"It is Saturday."

"Oh, right." I tighten my robe sash.

"Come, walk with me in the wood. We could find more faerie crosses for your collection."

Eyes cutting to the guard standing below my window, I wonder if I can go with Foster. *Of course you can. You are Queen.* Then I realize I am wearing my crown and nightrobe.

"But of course, maybe you have many better things to do now, more important things, probably."

I look at Foster's face and know there is nowhere I would rather be than with him. "Give me half an hour to eat breakfast and change. Come through the castle and to my room to be welcomed officially, and then we can walk in the woods. Okay?"

Biting my lip, I pray he will want to go through all these formalities. Further, I hope that it is allowed. I will go crazy if not allowed to walk in the wood, but I will not have people whispering about a girl queen who runs off with boys, shirking her duties. Further, I do not want any gossip or slander associated with Foster. Or, spirits forbid, him be implicated in another plot, as Gunther charged.

"Where did you go?" Foster squeezes my hand.

My face warms. *He must think me rude or crazy.* "There is so much to think about now. If you do not want to come, I understand."

"Oh, no. I am honored. I will meet you in half an hour at your door."

Watching his face as he talks and smiles, I want to reach out and touch it, but that would not be right. I must remember who I am. Wriggling my fingers from his grip, I dip my chin and flit back. "I will see you then."

Closing the windowpanes, I draw my curtains. There are still a few stones to move, but those can wait. Flinging my robe off, I stuff a pastry in my mouth, lay my crown atop the dresser, and wrangle my curls into a bun. I dress in the same type of outfit I have worn every day since Father handed me his kingdom. Today, I choose tan pants and skirt and a brilliant green leather vest. I grab a coat and, lifting my quiver, remember that an extra set of anchors still sit in the bottom.

Thinking there can be no safer place than in my quarters, I tuck them in the back of my closet. I make a mental note to inform Aleem as to their location after my walk with Foster. Checking my look in the mirror, I grab my bow and fly to the door, swinging it wide. I am met with a crowd of Fae, including Foster, Kane, Alfreda, Aleem, several workers stacking brick behind Alfreda, and a herd of guards behind Kane.

My heart races in my chest, and I land in front of Kane. "Good morning. I did not know I would have guests."

"You are awake, good dear." Alfreda's eyes switch from me to Kane and Aleem. "The workers are blocking up the end of the hall to make a sitting room for you to entertain guests."

"Oh, that will be nice, thank you." I squeeze Alfreda's hand as she scoots around me.

Kane steps forward. "Good morning. Sorry that it is so early, and on a Saturday, but we brought you the faerie crosses recovered from the kobold caves. We hoped you could tell us if they are the ones from your chamber."

Stepping aside, he motions to the fae gathered and they haul two larges chests to me. Opening the chests, I lift several crystals from the pile. Caked with mud and littered with chips, I find most of them at odd angles. Picking up several more handfuls, I find they are the same. Few possess the right angles like the ones I collected with my brothers.

"I do not believe these are mine." I jump into the air and retrieve several of my stones from the ceiling.

Comparing the crystals from my collection, the men agree. Aleem confirms they will question the guards posted at my room those nights. Kane intends to widen the scope to all who sided with Gunther to make sure we are not missing any rogue entity who may still be against my rule. I am glad to hear I am not the only one worried about lingering allegiance issues. Kane launches into a discussion of my coronation, and I stop him.

"General Kane, apologies. Is it possible for us to discuss this over lunch or later this afternoon? I was hoping to take a walk in the woods to clear my mind." I hold my breath, hoping that I have not overstepped or offended.

He bows. "Of course, Madam. Enjoy your walk."

I confirm a time to meet with Aleem later in the day as well. I want no one to know where we are hiding the second set of anchors and feel his home will be more secure than the castle. Making a mental note to have all the peepholes I have discovered over the years sealed, I move towards Foster. Smiling, he motions down the hall, and we start to the exit. My four guards trail us, and I feel like every eye stares at us. I cannot wait to be outside where we can take to the sky.

Once clear of the garden, I shoot into the air. We fly over the orchard, past the meadows, and to the forest. Alighting on the soft grass, I savor the feel of the cool air, sound of the light wind through the leaves, and tinkling of the brook. Even with my leg and having to use the mace as a crutch, being in the wood feels like heaven.

"This is just what I needed. Thank you." I smile at Foster.

"We were in dire need of some fun."

"I can hardly believe everything that happened in the past two weeks."

"You should not focus on that. It is good that they are investigating Gunther. I want him and his whole family gone. Everyone that sided with him should be banished."

"That is a little extreme. They do have a point. I am only fifteen."

"Fae in Westshire get married at fourteen even."

"Really? Like, most fae or just some?" I look at him sideways.

"Most are married by sixteen at the latest."

"Why are you not married?"

"I always wanted to join the army, be a warrior. I was too focused on that. I mean, between school and my chores."

I ask him what school was like and what they did for fun. His descriptions harken memories of my childhood. Even though most I think of with fondness, I would rather not remember my loss just now. I change the subject, asking him to describe more of his farm and family.

"You should come to dinner tonight. My mother is making a big feast to celebrate the solstice. I mean, I know we are a bit late, but she put it off until we could celebrate together."

"The solstice. What day is it?"

"It is the twenty-third."

I grab his arm. "You mean the night Sonia harvested those souls was the winter solstice? No wonder she was able to harness such power."

"I bet that is what had the kobolds on edge as well. They usually strike around such events."

"Really? How do you know this?"

"We learned it in the army. If you look at the history of kobold attacks, there is a definite pattern."

"There is so much I do not know." My mind starts to swim with the enormous task of ruling a kingdom I have in front of me.

"This walk should not cause you more stress. Let us not talk about the kobold or politics. Unless that is what you want to talk about. Shall we look for crosses in the brook?" He folds his hand over mine.

Loving the feel of his hand on mine, I smile. "No, you are right. I would rather pass the time with you doing something fun."

Hobbling into the stream, I dip down and pull up a big handful of mud and rocks. We sift through the silt, looking for crosses. He asks again if I will come to his home for dinner, and not knowing if it is even possible or sure of whether his family would want me, I skirt the question. *Why would they want to meet a girl who led their son into a tunnel filled with kobold, got him imprisoned, and risked getting him stuck in Upper Earth?*

He assures me they want to meet me and feel nothing but respect. "You are the Queen, so you can do whatever you like, right? Unless, perhaps, you do not want to come."

"Of course I want to come, silly. Why would I not?" Raking my hand across the water, I soak his shirt.

He counters, spraying droplets across my front. "Maybe you are scared of being seen with a lowly farm fae."

"But you are a decorated warrior. How many from Westshire can say that?" Wetting my hand, I flick droplets at his face.

He catches my wrist. Our faces are inches apart, and he smiles. "I have been in the army four months, I am hardly decorated. But please come. I want my family to meet you."

I hold his gaze. "Do they know you were going to ask me?"

"No, Mother would be nervous." Staring into my eyes, he releases my arm.

I take a step back, telling him I will inquire as to protocol for a visit. The idea that there are so many things that I do not know sends my brain into another swirl of anxiety. Pointing to the stream, I insist we continue our hunt for crosses. The sound of the water bobbing over the rocks, the slight wind in the trees, and the cold mud in my hands calms me. I take deep breaths, telling myself I can only do one thing at a time. We find one cross, and even though it lies on a diagonal, I count it a victory for the day and suggest we head back to the castle.

The flight dries my clothes, and I am happy for this as the sight of the building reminds me again of all I must attend to. We alight in the courtyard, and I tell Foster I will find him later to answer about dinner.

He gives a tight-lipped smile, dips his chin, and bows. "Of course."

My heart thumps in my chest. *Is he angry? Does he think I do not want to come?*

Chapter 13

"I do want to meet your family. You know that, right? Thank you for the walk. You should keep the cross." I slide it from my pocket. "For luck. It is even the color of your wings."

He bows low. Standing, he slides the gem in a leather bag tied to a string on his chest. "I will keep it to remember today. Thank you."

"Until later." Not able to look into his eyes for fear tears will come, I dip my chin, spin, and jump into the air.

Can I have supper with his family? Should we even be friends? My heart tinges with the idea the answer is no. My kingdom must come first. *How does me falling in love with a farm-boy-turned-soldier benefit my people? Would it hurt?* Perhaps not, but maybe I will need an alliance, one that will ensure we have other kingdoms to come to our aid. *But do fae not always help each other?* Even I know that is a perfect ideal for a perfect world. Even fae help their own first. The threat of the kobold to my family has driven Mother's sisters away. *How many else believe us to be cursed?*

Landing in front of my parent's chambers, I knock on the door.

Father opens it. "Titania, glad to see you."

"And you as well. On your feet. You look stronger."

"Another week, and I will not even need this cane." He shakes the wooden staff.

"We are a pair, are we not?" I hold up my mace.

Father joins Mother and I on our walk through the garden and orchard. He reports he testified to the judges that he shared his plan with Gunther to groom me to reign several times. Gunther never expressed objections to me taking the monarchy. I ask if any others spoke of concerns, and Father reports none. Then he moves to the topic of my coronation, indicating we should plan it sooner than later. As early as two weeks, he suggests.

My side ticks, and I counter that I would prefer a month or more. He relays his belief that I need to squash any question as to my fitness for the position. I agree to discuss it with Kane and the advisors. Which brings me to question Father about who else may serve as advisor. Thinking of Foster and Westshire, I wonder aloud if we should have a representative from each region rather than relying on family lineage.

Father's eyebrow shoots up. "Like governments of Upper Earth? It may not be a bad idea. You should not let it be a stand in for visiting those regions though. It is important to stay connected with all the fae of the kingdom."

I bite my lip, wondering if I should ask him about visiting Foster's home. I thought first of asking Kane, Grant, or Alfreda, but I am not sure I want to breach the subject with any of them. I have not missed a dinner with Mother and Father in years. *Will he be offended?* Sucking in a breath, I say the words before I chicken out. "Foster invited me to his home for their Solstice celebration tonight."

Father's face shows no reaction.

I know he is good at this and make a note to myself to remember to practice such.

The edges of his lips turn up. "You mean the soldier assigned to guard you? The one who helped you sneak away from the castle and steal the arrows?"

I smile. "The soldier you awarded a metal to for aiding in fighting the kobold."

"Well spoken, daughter." He walks ahead then turns to look at me. "I think it may be appropriate if we go together."

My hopes of spending an evening with Foster vanish. But Father makes good company, and I appreciate the value in having him present. I wonder if he means to include Mother. That could be awkward. But I will not ask in her presence. The evening could be viewed as a king and queen thanking a valuable warrior for his service. Otherwise, it would look like what I am sure Foster intended, what in Upper Earth they would call a *date*, but what is known as courting in our realm. Courting sounds so formal and laborious, and I hate the word—no romance at all to it—but that may be my fate.

"We have not talked about courting yet or who may make a suitable mate for you. With the coronation coming, we should."

It is as if Father read my mind, and my stomach twists. I do not want to discuss my love life with him. But I guess he may not be talking of love, and his thoughts would answer some questions swirling in my head. I brace myself for the worst.

He repeats that he does not wish me to marry until seventeen. That in the end, the decision as to who I marry will be mine. But as I already knew and did not want to hear again, a marriage for purposes of alliance tended to be advantageous.

I ball my fists. The insolent teen inside me wants to stomp my foot and throw in his face that his alliance with Mother's family caused the opposite. No one from her family dares enter our kingdom.

I wonder how it will affect my chances of an alliance. *Will others think I am cursed as well? That any friendship with my monarchy dooms them to death by kobold?* Surely that information had not been shared outside these castle walls. But that is reality. Mother saw my brothers' deaths and mine. Except I am not dead. *Because of what or who I am? Does that negate the curse? Or worse yet, will they think me a brute that can best a huge warrior?* The idea of setting a coronation date sooner than later grows more appealing with that thought. I want the whole realm to see that I can be elegant as well as strong.

I wind my arm around Mother and kiss her cheek. "What say you, Mother? Shall I marry for love or alliance?"

Father hobbles towards me. "That is not fair. Perhaps you will meet someone with whom to make a good alliance, and you will become smitten with them. It happened for me and your mother. Please, tell me you have not already fallen in love with this Foster boy."

"He is not a boy, and of course not. I have only known him for two weeks, not even." *But I could*, I think, *quite easily.* I picture his strawberry lashes, white cheeks peppered with red freckles, and golden wings, and know I would if I were given the chance. *Golden wings? You already embellish his looks.*

"So, we will go to dinner tonight then." Father takes to the air, leaving me with Mother.

I walk her through the orchard, but my mind is on too many things to speak. Part of me wishes to call the advisors to meet today, review my idea with them. But I am sure their lives have been as upended as mine. I should let them rest, enjoy their families. We can start work on Monday. Until then, I intend to start making plans, outlining districts of representation, and brainstorming ideas for the coronation so we can set everything into motion first thing Monday.

Looping back, Mother and I eat lunch with Father and Alfreda. We set the date for the coronation for January sixth and make a list of invited guests, including monarchs and their families from each of the other eight kingdoms. Father suggests referencing the family trees to invite every known relative, and I wonder how big the event will be. Alfreda sets out a timeline of guests' arrivals, starting the morning before coronation day, as it is customary for each royal guest to meet with the new monarch individually. I take deep breaths, reminding myself that before I lost my brothers, we attended these events all the time. *But now, you are the center of attention, a new ruler with a tenuous crown on her head.*

Out of the corner of my eye, I catch Kane and Aleem striding towards us. I excuse myself from the table and meet them near the fountain. One of the guards posted at my chamber the nights my crosses were stolen has confessed to robbing me upon orders from Gunther. They have detained him and the other guard in the dungeon.

"What of Gunther? Is this enough evidence to arrest him as well?"

Aleem shakes his head. "They were instructed to throw the crosses in the river, so there is no physical evidence. It is the guard's word against Gunther's."

"Can you not force him to be read as I was? What if his sons were also involved? That is four of your soldiers whose allegiance may not be pure. And what of the others that sided with Gunther? How do we know they are with us now? I do not want to go each day, wondering if there are those who still plot against me. I cannot live like that."

Aleem's eyes cut to Kane and back to me. "Forcing someone to be read sets a very bad precedent."

Kane nods. "No ruler can ever have one-hundred-percent approval, no matter if they are the most loved in the realm. And do not fear, Titania. You are much loved and will win the hearts of this entire kingdom. After your victory in the trial, there is no question as to who should be ruling Aubren. You need to get out and greet your people. Let them see you, get to know you. I feel you will be more loved than any monarch ever: a girl princess turned Queen, carrying the torch for her brothers. Who will not love you?"

"Father and I are to have supper with Foster's family tonight. Perhaps we will stay overnight in an inn and tour the kingdom from there. My journey could lead up to the coronation we have set for two weeks from today. Would that be appropriate? Can you arrange it?" I look at Kane.

He agrees accommodations can be made ready, and we instruct Aleem to continue the investigation. Aleem feels finding three credible witnesses to testify against Gunther would sway the judges to hold trial. Realizing I have much to do before the trip, I leave them to their work and update Father and Alfreda. Next, I call for the advisors to meet and then fly to the soldiers' quarters to find Foster.

Seeing him sparring with another warrior, I stand behind the circle of soldiers surrounding them. I study their moves, thinking I could do with regular military-style training myself. Plus, there is the education Foster spoke of. I would like to learn military strategy and history as well. Perhaps I could take some books to read while travelling. Foster brings his sword around, and the other soldier's flies out of his hand. Picking up the fallen weapon, Foster raises both above his head. Because my first instinct is to clap or cheer, I hold my hands tightly at my side.

I hang back as others congratulate Foster, but I am impatient and, realizing he means to duel the next contender, weave through the crowd. As I pass, soldiers take a knee, and when I reach the center, all gathered drop as well.

My face grows hot. What I want to say is "no need" or "do not do that," but what I know I need to say comes quick to mind. "Thank you. Please, as you were."

Foster's eyes hold mine. Every head turns towards us. My face burns anew.

"Congratulations on your win." I recover.

"You are blushing," Foster whispers.

"Can we speak?" I motion to the side yard. We weave through the crowd and huddle near the wall.

"I hope you have good news."

"I hope you think it is good. My father wishes to come as well."

"My family is going to host not only a queen but also a king?"

"Did you ask your mother yet?"

"I did not have time to fly there and back."

"My father cannot fly that far. We will need to take a carriage." I explain how the trip has become a kingdom tour.

He asks if he is to be an escort during my travel.

I explain Kane is to handle the guards. As we speak, I cannot help but feel eyes on us. Scanning the area, I catch quite a few of the soldiers glancing our way. *Perhaps I should not have come but sent word or note via page. You will learn,* I tell myself. I keep my hands by my sides and complete plans for riding to his family's farm.

Finished with our conversation, he takes a step back and dips his chin.

I smile and bid him farewell.

"Queen!" I hear someone call from the center of the court. "Will you spar with your friend Foster, the victor of the day thus far?"

"I believe Foster may have an advantage." I point to my ankle.

"Foster will duel with one hand behind his back."

Even with my task list a mile long, I will not be rude. "Of course. What are the rules?"

I hobble to the middle of the circle and am given a sword. The metal weapon is heavy, and I swish it back and forth, getting a feel for its weight.

The game is simple: The first person to drop their weapon loses.

Foster stands before me, smiling, and I wonder if I can be serious. *And should I try to win, or should I throw the match?* I guess Foster to be stronger than I, but I do not want to be viewed as weak, either.

Everything about being Queen seems to be about walking a fine line.

We touch swords to begin the match. I focus on his face, which gives the direction of his aim away, and swing my sword to intersect his. Our swords clank together, blow after blow, no one getting the upper hand. My arm starts to tire, and I pray his is as well.

He draws his sword up high, and I grab the end of mine with my left hand and force my arms up to block his blow. He is caught off guard, and his sword bounces off mine, flying over his head into the crowd.

Looking into my eyes, he takes my arm and lifts it into the air. "The victor. Long live Queen Titania."

"Long live Queen Titania!" The cheers from the crowd echo in my ears. I spin around, realizing the soldiers are ten deep and the windows above are lined with fae.

I raise my sword and bow low. Standing upright, I offer Foster my weapon. "Let the matches resume."

A warrior hands me my mace, and I make my way through the fae, accepting congratulations.

Kane stands, arms crossed over his chest, as I emerge from the crowd.

I follow him inside the hall.

"What was that? You should not be mingling with the soldiers."

"I went to see Foster, and they asked if I would spar. I could not say no."

"You cannot just go talk to Foster whenever you want. You are a queen and have a reputation to think about. You are not a girl anymore."

My blood boils. It is not like I have been *just a girl* since birth. And the day my brothers died, I became what Upper Earth people would know as a china doll. "It is Saturday, and we walked in the wood earlier. I told him I would answer his dinner invitation."

"Dinner invitation? You are *not* going to dinner with Foster."

"Father is coming with me."

"Fine, but you need to use a page to send messages."

Like I need a second father. I admit to realizing his concerns as well and apologize. I get the sinking feeling Foster will not be joining us on my Kingdom tour, but I take heart in knowing I will see him tonight.

Leaving Kane to arrange the tour, I go to the study for the texts. I find the family tree and the military books and, leaving the family information with Alfreda, head to my room to pack. I select my standard pant and skirt outfits for travelling and dresses for dinners. I realize I have nothing for the coronation and make a note to find Alfreda before we leave.

Advisors Bran, Terrence, and Jesper wait outside my room, and I invite them into my half-constructed study. I apprise them of my idea for the advisors, noting they would be retained as advisors but suggesting we create three spots from regional representatives. They like the idea, and we discuss the best way to define the areas. I task them with creating a suggested list of capable representatives for me to approach when visiting. Reviewing the plan for the coronation, I leave them with direction that Kane will be serving as First Advisor until one can be decided on.

I review my packing list and roll my chest to the carriage.

Alfreda hurries towards me. "Dear child, what are you doing?"

"Putting my bag and chest in the carriage."

"Oh no, you are far too busy for such things. We must discuss the coronation." Instructing a guard to finish my tasks, she drags me back to the half-finished sitting room.

I pick a dress style and fabric and leave her to finish the guest list, invitations, and managing schedule and ceremonies. She offers last minute instructions on greetings and appropriate topics of conversation. Tucking her hand in a pocket, she produces a small journal.

"This is from your parents' last tour of the kingdom. Your mother kept good notes. I thought it may help you to read it, memorize names of families and land they own."

Recognizing Mother's script, I open the book to the first page. I remember the trip. Being eight, I grew bored riding in the carriage for so long. The driver let me sit with him so I could see the countryside. Every night, there were parties with wonderful desserts. Although I hated dressing up, shaking hands, and smiling at everyone, the sugary treats made it well worth it. Plus, I did not have to compete for Father's attention since my brothers were left at the castle to focus on their studies. *Such a childish thing to enjoy.* I wrap my arms around Alfreda. One thing I know I crave is a mother's affection.

Checking my room a final time, I realize I should alert Aleem as to the location of the anchors. If something were to happen, he would need to know. I find Father, Mother, and Kane at the carriage. Father and I kiss Mother's cheek, and I leave last-minute instructions for Kane. I inform him of my decision as to his position as First Advisor.

His face flushes, and I am surprised to find him looking uncomfortable. "Are you sure? There has never been a general to serve as First Advisor."

"I am sure. Judges cannot serve in politics, and I trust you above all others. I gave the advisors notice today as well. When other advisors are selected, they will vote as to who should serve as First Advisor. Until then, I will entrust you with the appointment."

He bows low. "I will not let you down."

⋙◆⋘

WE STOP AT ALEEM'S CABIN, and I inform him as to the hiding place of the anchors, instructing him to share the location only with the First Judge and during direct conversation, and we speed out of the capital.

Westshire lies southwest and is the only major city in the region. I review Mother's notes on the land and families. Consisting mostly of farmland, the area supplies much of the capital's vegetable products because it is hard to farm the hilly wooded terrain near the castle.

Father updates me on his most recent visit to the shire. There is a judge who is well respected Father suggests we visit the following day.

Our carriage rambles through the forest to the open meadows, and we reach the village at sunset. I wash my face, arms, and legs and dress in a red frock with laces of silk ribbon crisscrossing over the bodice. I think of how Mother would say I could wear red, green, white, or tan, that those were the only colors that looked right with my mahogany hair and light green wings. Checking my look in the mirror, I realize the red brings out the markings on my face.

With a huff, I release the front ties. The last thing I need is to look like some type of painted warrior for Foster's family. There is a knock on my door and, holding the ends of the ribbons, I inch it open.

"You are not dressed? We are going to be late." Father hikes his hands to his hips.

"I have to change. I will be right there." Shutting the door, I slip out of the red dress, opting for a tan one with white trim. I exit my room to find Father leaning against the wall.

"Where is your crown?"

I pass him. "I am not wearing my crown to visit Foster's family. They know who I am."

"This is an official state visit. You should wear your crown."

Hiking my skirt up, I proceed down the stairs. "Well, if it is an official visit, then I am in charge, and I say that I am not wearing my crown."

"You sound like an obstinate teen."

I stop and turn to face him. "No, I am your obstinate queen."

"At least you know your faults." He chuckles and shoos me down the stairs.

Does he not realize I am nervous enough without his opinions? I look out the window of the carriage as we pass farm after farm. My leg bounces. *What shall I say to his mother? His sister? And Father? What will we talk of during dinner?* I know little of farming and animals. *What will Father talk to them about?*

The driver turns off the main road onto a lane, and my heart races. *What will we say to each other? Will they like me?* I look out over the fields as the last light leaves the sky, wishing we had come when it was light and wondering if there would be an excuse to return tomorrow. I so wanted to see the farm, but the darkness hides everything save a small cabin of stone with a wood-shingled roof at the end of the rutted path. Light shines through each window, and I smile, thinking it is exactly how Foster described it.

Father exits the carriage ahead of me, and before I am even out, Foster's family is lined up in front of us. All with coloring similar to his, red hair in various shades, light eyes, and brown wings, they bow. An older male fae, I guess him to be Foster's father, offers his arm to Father in the traditional fae greeting.

"I am Matthew. These are my wife and daughter, Jasmine and Nissa. Welcome to our home."

Foster steps towards me and offers his hand. I lay mine in his, and he kisses my fingers. Even though the gesture is a traditional fae greeting, my face flames. He introduces me then Father to the family. I pull the basket Alfreda made from the carriage and present it.

Pulling the gift for Nissa from my pocket, I hold it out. "This is for you. For good luck."

She steps forward and lifts the stone from my palm. "It is beautiful. Thank you. Is it true that you had a thousand hanging from your ceiling?"

My eyes cut to Foster and back to Nissa. "Almost. This one is yours now. You can hang it above your door to keep away the harmful spirits."

"Like the kobold? Foster says they are magick and can come steal our things in the night without us even seeing them."

Resisting giving Foster another hard stare, I shake my head. "You need not worry about the kobold. We will make sure you are safe. They were far from here, and our soldiers watch for them around the clock."

Jasmine invites us inside, and we enter through a wood-paneled door. As with most Fae structures, the ceilings reach high above my head. The cottage consists of one large room, a cooking hearth on one end and fireplace on the other, with dining table and rocking chairs between them. I look up to find a loft portioned off by curtains—which I guess are their sleeping areas. I realize the whole house is about the same size as my chamber. *How spoiled had I been to think being sequestered to a castle was such a horrid fate?*

I flit up to the ceiling above the door with Nissa and help her hang the faerie cross. Father sits in front of the fire with Matthew. I wonder at how normal it all feels when, in reality, it is anything but. It has been over three years since I visited another fae's home. Alighting on the floor, I cross to the kitchen to aid Jasmine. She shoos me away, and Foster and Nissa grab candles to escort me to the barn where we meet their horses and barn cat.

Jasmine serves lamb, vegetables, fresh bread, and berry pie for dessert. As stories and laughter are traded around the table, I remember dinners with my brothers and how loud the castle used to be with their constant antics. After the meal, Foster's father brings out his fiddle and starts a tune perfect for a jig. Father claps to the beat while we fly in a circle above their heads, weaving past each other to the cadence of the music. As the song ends, I settle on the floor next to Foster. His mother insists I take the stool, but I convince her that it is most comfortable with my legs straight in front of me.

"This queen"—Foster points at me—"is not like queens in your story books, Nissa. She is just like one of us, except more fearless than even I."

Foster proceeds to tell the story of how we found the kobold. I watch his face and Father's, wondering if he will admonish me for the, until now, undisclosed antics of the days preceding the battle. Still, had I not been so obstinate, we may not have been so lucky as to find the creatures and our missing anchors.

With Nissa yawning, we say our goodnights. As Foster walks me to the carriage, I ask whether he will be accompanying us on the kingdom tour. Learning he will not, I am saddened. Still, there will be much to learn on the trip, and I should be focused on my work, as should he, I guess.

Chapter 14

Morning brings bright sunshine and chirping birds.

Father coached me in wearing more traditional garb, so I dress in a skirt and military-style, double-breasted jacket of green velvet. We eat breakfast at the inn and walk into the village.

Vendors sit on carts, selling goods and fresh fruits, vegetables, and breads. Fae bow and curtsey as we pass. Children bring picked flowers, and I grant each a faerie cross, the extras I had not hung in my room.

Father finds Judge Kerith's home and, walking his farm, we converse with him. He reports Westshire to be quiet and prosperous. "It seems there is only drama in Capitolshire. I wonder why that could be?" His eyes cut to me.

"Advisor Gunther challenged my reign and charged me with treason, and I have more than shown my worthiness to serve as monarch."

"By letter of the law, yes. But you are quite young."

Father clears his throat. "What would you have me do? Hold a post I am too tired to serve properly? I am forty-eight years old. Many fae only live to forty-five."

"Oberon, your line have enjoyed longevity for centuries. You could live to be sixty."

"I feel I will serve my kingdom better as advisor to my daughter."

I fold my hands in front of my torso. "Do not most fae in this area marry and have farms by sixteen?"

"It is true. But farming is quite different than ruling a kingdom."

"It may be. But I intend to prove my worth. May I share some ideas with you?"

I detail how I intend to learn all there is of our kingdom and the history of the threats, especially the kobold, with haste. Then, I lay out my ideas for the advisors and inquire as to whether he would be interested in serving or could suggest others who may be.

One of his eyebrows perks up. "Would these representatives have to live in the capital permanently?"

"I do not see why they would. We could schedule meetings, laying out agendas ahead of time so all the issues could be addressed. I would like a vote by the people, an election, as are held in Upper Earth."

"Is that not a slippery slope for a monarch? Holding a vote? What seat will people ask to elect next? Yours."

"I believe the gods have spoken in this case." Father walks ahead of us.

Kerith details issues in his region, giving us information on population, births, deaths, and trends in farming and crafts. We eat lunch with him and his wife.

She leads me on a tour of her flower garden following the meal.

I learn of their children and their grandchildren, who are already school age. Circling back to the men and their conversation, I review that we will formalize and announce the representatives' positions after my coronation and invite them to be a part of the celebration.

Wishing them well, Father and I load into the carriage. As soon as we travel beyond the last farm, I ask Father if I may fly a bit. It is only midafternoon, but I feel drained from talking to so many fae. I hope some fresh air and activity will recharge my mind. Changing into my riding clothes, I jump into the air, wishing I were closer to the castle for a walk through my woods. Further, hearing wings of my guards following me, I crave my prior life of solitude. If I were alone, I could go see Foster, his farm. I realize it still does not hurt to fly over the property.

I rise in elevation. The last thing I want is to be caught stalking him. But I am too high, and the most I can make out is fields of golden wheat with paths and trenches for water. His home and barn appear as mere chips on the land. Cutting west, I fly to the border and overlook the vast desert land that lies in the middle of the continent.

I circle back to the inn to bathe for dinner. Father and I sup with the other guests, learning of their travels and homes, and we walk the garden afterwards. He asks of my opinion of Kerith and how I felt about the day. Cautioning me that I may encounter more with negative attitudes on my reign, he encourages me not to be disheartened.

"Everyone will come to love and admire you, just as Kane and the other generals and advisors do."

"I do not need them to love me. I need them to be honest and aid me. This is the only thing I will ask of those serving our kingdom. I will not stand for someone like Gunther, who agrees to your face and plots against you in secret."

"You are wise to hold such opinions. Gunther craved approval. I did not realize how much until he turned on us."

Seeing a group of guards approaching, I walk ahead to meet them. Kane and Aleem are in the group, and my heart skips a beat. I brace myself for their news. They greet me then Father, dipping their chins.

"Excuse the interruption, but there is news from the investigation of Gunther." Kane's eyes cut between me and Father.

"Urgent news is never an interruption. Please, tell us." Fearing for Aleem's aging form, I motion for us to sit on nearby benches.

Looking at the ground, Kane relays he is embarrassed a second guard admitted to aiding Gunther as well. The stones were not thrown in the river as the first reported, but found hidden in Gunther's wellhouse. Both guards have been relieved of their duties, and Gunther is detained in the dungeon. Aleem apprises me of my choices of pressing charges and requesting punishment.

"Shall you return to witness the trial? We can hold it tomorrow or wait until you return," he asks.

I stand and pace in front of them. Rage burns in my chest for Gunther. "I have little to offer as to testimony, save they were there when I went to sleep and gone when I woke. The guards could have been in and out of my chambers in minutes. Have all of the family members and others who supported him been cleared of any charges?"

Kane stands. "It seems Gunther plotted against you on his own. No others are implicated."

I stop in front of Aleem. "What punishment would you recommend for Gunther and the guards?"

"The guards have been relieved of their posts. They will never work as soldiers again. This would normally be sufficient. For Gunther, I am unsure. To plot against a member of the royal family, against an innocent child, is treason."

My wings pop out, and I raise my chin. "This was but two weeks ago."

"Sorry, Highness. I mean no disrespect."

I drop my wings. "No, you are right, but I do not want to be involved in this. This matter is for the judges. Do as you decide is right."

"Then, it is settled?" Kane looks at Aleem.

Aleem rises and, noting he is without his cane, I lend him my mace. We hobble back to the inn and have drinks. Afterwards, they board their carriage to return to the capital with directions to send the faerie crosses to me before the morning. I bid the men well and latch the door. Their coach disappears into the night.

Out of the side of my vision, I see Father open his mouth and raise my palm. "Tomorrow, please."

"You should have ordered Aleem to banish Gunther."

"Perhaps he will do that anyway, but I will not be judge and jury in a case where I am the accuser. That is not my job. The decision is too much for me."

"Your compassion is a weakness. Be wary of it."

I ball my fists. I want to yell at him. *Do not be obstinate, do not be hasty, do not be angry, do not be compassionate. Which is it?* I take a deep breath. "Tomorrow, Father."

I leave him standing in front of the inn. Exhausted, I climb the stairs to my room and draw a hot bath. *Should I not be compassionate?* I know how I felt when it seemed I may be banished from the only home I have known. I would not wish that fate on another, even someone like Gunther. I search for areas of my psyche that I may need to guard. Empathy is not my problem. But if I am honest, my feelings for Foster could be. Soaking in the tub, I allow myself to envision what spending time with him may look like. There would be those who knew. We could not keep it a secret. *Does it matter? Would it be okay for me to marry someone like him?* I would hope so. Maybe Foster would not be my true love but another like him could be.

I wish he were here. *But would I talk about this with him?* Perhaps Mother or Alfreda. Wrapping in a robe, I draw a note page from my chest. I pen Foster a letter, telling him of Kerith and news of Gunther's trial. I tiptoe out of my room and downstairs. Father sits playing cards with one of the guards. Handing him the envelope addressed to Foster, I bid them goodnight.

Upstairs, I lie on my bed, staring at the ceiling. Anyone I married within our kingdom would hold a lesser title than I. Again, my brain questions, *does it matter?* My answer is the same. *Tomorrow, please.*

—◆◆◆—

OVER THE NEXT TEN DAYS, we crisscross the kingdom, stopping in every major shire, greeting as many fae as we can. I gift my crosses to every child I meet, and we spend time with all the judges. Many older judges, like Kerith, express hesitation in trusting I am suitable to rule, but younger ones are more open, save those that wish I were male. We end our tour at the southern end at the second, and only other, Faerie Ring in our kingdom.

This ring holds the name Nariel, given for the land it connects to in Upper Earth. The Keeper, Regin, greets us as we exit our carriage and welcomes us into his home with his wife, Fiona, at his side. He looks much younger than Aleem. When she excuses herself so we may talk, Regin slides to the front of his chair.

"I hope you have come with news of how we may fortify our ring. I do not want to be put in the situation we were before. Many fae could have died."

"It *was* dire almost losing our rings. I will be reviewing all the protocols and will make adjustments with General Kane's input."

He grabs my arm. "Almost? Our ring failed. The kobold took all the anchors from our ring as well as the second set. Were you not aware?"

I want to fire daggers at Father. *Why was I not briefed?* "I am sorry. There has not been time for me to be made aware of all the details of the attack. I assure you, this will happen soon. I would like to review policies and make sure both you and Aleem follow the same procedures."

"Who is Aleem?"

"The Keeper of the Daintree ring. Do you not know him? I assumed you would conference." I look between Regin and Father.

Each shakes his head, and I fight huffing. Thinking Aleem will not handle travel as well as Regin, we plan a summit for two days later in the capital. I invite Regin's wife to be our guest at the castle and for them to stay for the coronation as well.

We tour the ring, and I meet the First and Second Keepers. At the end of the visit, I meet with Regin alone, alerting him to the change we have made in securing the second set of anchor stones. Taking me to his basement, he shows me where he keeps them hidden under a loose board in the floor. I assure him that he will be given more guards for protection.

We bid Regin and his wife farewell and climb into the carriage. As it speeds over the lane, I lay my head against the wall. Regin is our last stop in the tour, and I look forward to being home.

Father squeezes my hand. "I was not keeping information from you intentionally."

I open my eyes. "I know, Father. I should not have appeared frustrated. I still have a lot to be briefed on when we return to the castle. Speaking of, would you mind if I flew home tonight? I am anxious to be in my own bed."

"What of your leg? I would not think it to be comfortable to fly so far with the brace."

"The doctor said it would be healed in two weeks. And it has been ten days. I can put a cloth bandage around it until you return tomorrow."

He lays a hand on my knee. "I envy you. If I could fly that far, I would be doing the same."

Closing my eyes, I picture the one face I miss most: Foster. Others, yes... Mother, Alfreda... The list is short. But Foster occupies my mind. Our friendship came so easily, and being with him calms me, makes me happy like no other can. I wrote him each night and am anxious to see him as I have not received any correspondence back. I imagine him to be quite challenged in his training and look forward to hearing every detail.

At the inn, I alert the guards of my plans. Four stay behind to accompany Father home the next day, and four take to the air with me. We fly straight north over the farmlands of the south; over the central, dry-desert, herding regions; and to Capitolshire. Alighting in the main castle courtyard, I head straight to Mother's chamber. Her eyes shift to my face as I kneel before her. I think I catch her mouth twitch just a smidge.

Could that have been the start of a smile?

I gather her hands in mine. "I have missed you, Mother. How have you been?"

Waiting for her answer, my heart breaks when her eyes cut back to the fireplace.

"Father will be back tomorrow. I will come in the morning to walk with you in the woods. I have wanted for our talks."

With no reaction, I lean up and kiss her cheek. Sitting on the hearth, I lay my hands atop hers, enjoying the sight of her face after being away for so long.

"Still danger." The words sound as a whisper above the crackle of the fire.

"Danger?" I squeeze her fingers, waiting for acknowledgement, but none comes, so I tug at her hands. "From where? Who? To the Kingdom? My reign? Gunther or others like him?"

Her eyes cut to me then back to the flames. I place my hands on her shoulders, beseeching her to tell me more, something, anything. I want to yell, shake her, but I force myself to use soft tones.

Still, she says nothing.

I lay my head on her shoulder and wrap my arms around her. "I love you, Mother. I wish you would come back to us. It is not your fault. I know you think it is, but it is not."

Arms limp at her sides, she does not move.

I release her and back away. A tear escapes my eyelid, and I swipe it away.

"Goodnight, Mother, I will walk with you in the morning."

Her stare does not leave the hearth, and I cross to the doors and go out into the hall. I find Alfreda in the kitchen and fix a plate of supper, eating at the chef's table beside the stove as I did when I was little. I could watch them cook for hours. They would teach me how to measure, mix, and knead the bread. Tonight, puff cookies bake in the oven, and pan after pan, the chefs cool the treats and roll them in sugar for the coronation dinner.

"You look as spent as the dishwater, dear." Alfreda pulls me out of my stupor. "I should fix a bath for you."

I kiss her forehead. "You look as tired as I. I can do it."

Flying through the passageways, I find I am happy to be home. Inside these walls, I have no need for guards trailing me. At a turn, I swerve to miss a fae entering the stairwell with blankets and an urn of water. I realize the girl started down the stairs and circle back.

I catch up to her halfway to the first landing. "Where are you taking these?"

"To the prisoner in the dungeon."

Taking to the air, I shoot down to the bottom. Ignoring the two guards, I snatch the torch from the wall and enter the small chamber holding the prisoners' cells. A large, dark-headed fae with purple wings sits with his back to the wall.

Gunther.

"What are you doing here? Your trial should not be taking this long."

"Ha." He stands. "They cannot figure out what to do with me. I believe they are too scared to pass judgment. Perhaps they are waiting for your return."

"You have been here for ten days? This is unacceptable."

"Believe me, I agree, Queen." Gunther grips the bars.

How cruel. Even for a traitor like Gunther. Plus, I want him nowhere near my castle. *Why have the judges not sent him away?*

Shoving the torch at a guard, I speed up the stairs, out of the castle, and to Aleem's cabin. I bang on the door and wait. It feels like forever before I hear shuffling across the wood floor.

The door opens and Aleem slumps. "You are home."

"What is Gunther doing in the dungeon? Why have the judges not given him his sentence?"

"They cannot, or will not, decide."

"There are five of them. First Judge should break the tie."

Aleem lowers himself to a chair. "I believe he is scared of Gunther, afraid of what he or his sons may do if they banish him."

"You cannot leave him in the dungeon forever. You must decide."

"It is not my job."

"Are you not in charge of them?"

"First Judge wants to banish him, as do two of the others. I believe he may be more dangerous if we do not know what he is doing. I asked the First Judge to await your return."

"What about a jury like they have in Upper Earth? A jury of peers, I believe it is called. Surely there are those who witnessed the trial, could be asked to serve on such a committee?"

Aleem rubs his chin. "We would have to redo the trial."

"I will not have him in the dungeon for my coronation. This needs to be decided. What about Kane? What does he say? Did you ask the advisors? They are his peers, and there are three of them."

"Believe me, we have counseled with all. None can decide what his fate should be. This is unprecedented. No fae has ever targeted a princess in this way. Believe me, we have searched the records."

"Summon the judges, and meet me at the castle at once."

Spinning on my heel, and making for the door, I catch sight of a cane leaning against the wall. I remember to reel in my temper and treat Aleem with respect. I turn back as I open the latch. "I am sorry. I did not mean to be short with you. I hoped this would be settled before my return. Please, ask the judges to meet me at the castle. I will call for Kane and the advisors."

My heart races and my head spins. If they all are afraid of Gunther, I should be, too. *But what power does he have now?* I won the trial. Still, I cannot forget the others, prominent people, advisors, generals, who sided with him. I round to Kane's home, then Bran's, Jesper's, and Terrence's, and we fly to the castle.

In the study, each lays out his argument. Banishment may be appropriate, but there are those who favor Gunther that would think it too harsh a punishment for robbery. But the fact that he intended to discredit me makes him a traitor, in which case banishment would be appropriate. My mind spins with the conundrum. *Why do none of them have the guts to send him away?*

For fae, home means everything. No one moves or leaves, except maybe to become a soldier, and they always return. They are born in their homes, and they die in their homes. We marry from within our shires. Families live on and work the land their forefathers have for generations, since the beginning of time. Banishment may be one of the worst fates, second only to loss of our wings. Still, I had been willing to give up my home if I lost the trial. It would have ripped out my heart to do so, but I was willing to do it. I guessed that to be a lesser punishment than having another in my castle, on my throne.

My leg bounces with fury. *Can they not do what needs to be done?* I stand. "Call for Gunther."

I limp towards the dungeon stairwell, Kane and the others on my heels. As I reach the entrance, the guards exit with Gunther.

My head spins. I am not sure what I mean to do. *Should I send him so far away we will never see him again or keep him here where he could cause additional trouble?*

"I will not have you rotting in my dungeon. That is a fate worse than death. *You* will decide your fate, Gunther. Either accept banishment to Willhelm, where you will be a ward of that kingdom, watched till your dying day, or accept a position as hunter at this castle. You and your wife, if she chooses, may live in the hunter's quarters and serve this court, your peers and the people of this shire will serve as your keepers, watching for any sign of deceit or unlawful actions. Seeing any, you will be sent to Willhelm."

The words come as I think them, same as when I offered Ethan an advisor's position. Giving Gunther a role as hunter keeps him close but away from my sight. Even though a humiliating life it may be for someone as proud as Gunther, it was a just offer. If he chose banishment, then that would be his choice.

Kane sidesteps to me and whispers, "Willhelm? That may be worse than the dungeon."

I keep my stare focused on Gunther. "It is cold there, I hear."

"That is an understatement," Kane mutters.

Gunther's gaze drops to the floor, to those gathered, and back to me. "Would my wife be allowed to come to Willhelm?"

"And any other family members who wish to go with you."

"May I have time to council with her?"

"No. Say now, and it shall be." Father was wrong. It is not my compassion I should be worried about—it is my temper. I prayed the others would judge me to be fair in this matter and hoped I could live with whatever decision Gunther made.

Gunther drops to one knee. "Then I shall serve as your hunter until my dying breath."

"Thank you." I look at Kane then the advisors and judges. "You are all witness. Gunther and his wife shall be given quarters on the castle grounds. He will work as a hunter, serving the members of this household, hunting for game in the woods and bringing food for our tables to the kitchens. If there is another offense, he will be banished to Willhelm."

Chapter 15

I GIVE ALFREDA ONE DAY TO fit my dresses and coach me on etiquette. Mother sits in the corner watching, and I try not to let her disengagement dishearten me. Still, by the end of the day, it is all I can do to sit and eat with her and Father and not scream.

Father requests I play the harp, but I ask to be excused, saying I am exhausted. Changing into riding clothes, I do a loop through the castle courtyards and grounds, hoping to see Foster. Not finding him, I take to the air. The cool air on my face, the dark, night sky calms my nerves. Still, I dread the days of ceremony and pomp to come. Even more, my stomach turns, wondering what I will say to Mother's family. *Will they rebuke us for not making her well?* I console myself with the fact that they have done little save write letters.

The next day I spend time with Kane, Father, the advisors, and Aleem, being briefed on the total of our recent skirmish with the kobold, High Council news, and all events for each kingdom within the realm. Much of the time, our only interactions tend to be with Bedham to the north, where Mother's family lives, and Hilbron, the kingdom that shares our western border. I take notes on each of the monarchs, their wives and families, and which guests we will be hosting from the High Council.

At the end of the day, I pull Kane aside. "I want you to have extra eyes and ears everywhere this weekend. Especially watch Gunther and those that sided with him."

"I believe you are being paranoid. Your reign is secure. You won the trial. No one should question it now."

"I am not just worried about threats from within. Several judges from the shires expressed discontent with a female monarch. There are those on the High Council, perhaps even other monarchs, who do not support female rulers. We have no idea who they are, what they may do. I want you to have guards posing as normal fae, servers, attendants, pages… Have them everywhere to be our eyes and ears."

"I think this is unnecessary. It is not the way of the fae to undermine a monarch." He raises his eyebrows. "Further, it is not the way of the fae to spy on friends."

"The fae are, first and foremost, traditional. My reign represents a break with that culture. There are those who may not believe me fit to help protect our realm. With the problems with the witches, I want to make sure that the leaders of Middle Earth are in solidarity. Not just in what they may say to me, but in what they may tell each other, or speak of to their wives and family." I do not wish to go so far as to tell Kane of Mother's gifts and her predictions, but if he is not willing to place spies, I believe there may be no other choice.

"I understand your point as to this. I will do as you say. I pray your apprehensions are for naught and hope we will learn that over the next days."

"I pray that is the case as well. But given the events of the past month, I feel warranted in my position on this matter."

I sup with Father and Mother and, excusing myself after the meal, stroll through the castle, trying to spot Foster. Not finding him, I take to the air with Grant, Adam, Timothy, and Nicholas. Two of these soldiers will be at my side every moment of the next four days. Sitting on my bed, I study the names of those visiting from each kingdom and fall asleep reading the history of battles against the kobold.

There have been other creatures to attempt invasion of our land over the centuries, trolls and elves, who desire a realm of their own, but none more formidable than the kobold. And now, with the seeming aid of magick, they pose a large threat.

Morning of the eve of my coronation, I wait with Father, Mother, and Alfreda in front of the castle to greet Mother's family from Bedham. Their carriage stops in front of the bricked walk, and King Herman, my mother's brother, and Queen Natasha; along with Prince Jakub, next in line to the throne; and his wife, Annabelle, step out. I note how their coloring matches Mother's. With light skin and fair hair and wings, one may not even see them crossing the sky. Since no other carriages follow, I wonder where Mother's sisters are. We were told all three would attend with their families.

I approach King Herman, curtsey, and kiss each of his cheeks. "King Herman, Uncle, I am happy to see you. Thank you for coming."

He steps back and bows. "Titania. My, you have grown since I last saw you."

"Herman, you forget your manners. Titania is a queen now, and you should address her as such." Natasha kisses my cheek.

Taking a step to the right, I dip my chin. "Welcome, Prince Jakub. It has been too long."

"Yes, Queen." He bows. "Allow me to introduce my wife, Annabelle."

Annabelle curtsies and kisses each side of my face. "It is wonderful to meet you. We have heard so much about you."

I force a smile, hoping the news is not negative. "I am sorry to have missed your wedding."

"It was a small affair." Jakub supplies.

I guess his words are meant to ease my guilt at my inability to attend the event. For a year following my brothers' deaths, being in crowds triggered crippling fits. My heart raced out of control and breathing became labored. Jakub's wedding represents one of many state events I missed that year. Jakub holds the honor of being the first-born son, and therefore, he will succeed his father. Four years my elder, I remember playing with Jakub as a child. He took cues from my brothers, treating me as one of them—which I appreciated because most boys tended not to. I am happy he joins us as it may not be long before he succeeds his father, and we will rule neighboring kingdoms.

Watching King Herman and Natasha greet Father then my stoic mother makes my side tick. It saddens me that none of Mother's sisters have come as they said they would. I thought they might aid in pulling Mother from her shell. But after three years, I should accept that hope on this front may be misplaced.

Alfreda calls for attendants to help with the bags, and we show the four to their chambers, informing them there will be lunch in the garden and lawn games following. I leave our guests to unpack and rest from their journey. Hearing a bugle sound, alerting a guest's arrival, I weave through the passages to the front entrance.

Father joins me, squinting as the occupants step from the carriage. "I cannot believe they came."

"Who is it?"

"My distant cousin, Victor, and his son—"

"Quinn." I swallow. "I did not realize we invited them."

"I told Alfreda to be all inclusive. But we did not receive a reply to the invitation. I have not seen Victor since we were children."

I lift my skirt and walk towards the pair as they approach. "Cousins Victor and Quinn, welcome."

With coloring, warm mahogany hair and dark green wings, matching that of Father's family, the two stop before me and bow.

Kissing my cheek, Victor steps before Father and wraps both arms around him. "It has been too long, Oberon. Please, meet my son, Quinn."

Quinn tips his chin and bows to Father. "I am happy to make your acquaintance." His eyes cut to me and back to Father. "Both of you."

With broad shoulders and muscled arms, Quinn looks nothing like I pictured him. Especially for one whose family holds no trade. Most royals without title serve as advisors or judges, and Victor holds a judge's position in a small shire on the western isle of Bedham. I would expect Quinn to hold the same, but he appears to use his muscles often.

Refocusing on Victor, I remember Alfreda's instructions on welcoming guests. "Please, come this way. We did not expect you, but I believe there are available chambers near your King, Herman. We will be having lunch with them at noon, and it would be nice for you to join us."

Quinn flanks me as we proceed to the castle entrance. "I have heard much about you, cousin. It is an honor to meet you. You are a legend in Bedham, and I am guessing all through the realm."

My face flushes. "Legends are not always complimentary. What do they say of me to the north?"

"That you are strong and brave, smart, tactful, thoughtful, just, and above all—and to this I can now attest—most beautiful."

Cheeks flaming, I fold my hands in front of my waist. "Thank you. You are very kind. I expected there to be rumors of me being some sort of female brute of a giant with arms the size of tree trunks."

"Rumors are that you hooked your opponent into a neck grip. You do not have to be large to be good at wrestling. Do you remember meeting when we were young?" His large eyes do not leave my face.

I turn my chin in the direction of the guest quarters. "I do not."

"You were only four and I six. You hit me because I tried to help you up after you tripped."

Taking a deep breath, I search for a response. "Well, I am still just as stubborn and obstinate as I was then, ask anyone. Especially Father. Right, Father?"

I look around Quinn at Father, hoping to draw him and Victor into the conversation. There is nothing I hate more than talking about myself. Finding Father deep in conversation, I force a smile.

"Tell me, what do you do in Bedham?"

"I joined the army this year. I have been training in the cavalry. It keeps me away from my annoying siblings. They have a new girl to set me up with every week because they think one is not complete without a mate."

Water forms in my eyes as I picture my brothers' faces and think how I would give anything to have them aggravating me. "You have three older sisters, correct?"

"Yes, they all married at seventeen, and now that I am almost eighteen, they think me an old hermit already."

We reach the door to their room, and I spin to face him. I look at the ceiling and bite the inside of my cheek to keep more tears from forming. Perhaps if I remind him of my loss, he will stop this line of conversation. "I would guess that they do such because they care for you. There are worse things that siblings could do."

His face drains of color. "Queen, excuse me. How thoughtless of me, rambling on about… Forgive me."

His eyes are so golden, and his face so warm and sympathetic, my anger wanes. I swing open the double doors. "Of course. We look forward to enjoying your company at midday for a meal in the garden."

The attendants follow Quinn and Victor into the suite, and Father and I leave them to rest. He hooks his arm in mine as we walk towards the center of the castle.

"Quinn is a good-looking fellow. Victor says he is well on his way to becoming an officer in their army."

I fight the urge to lash out. *Was it not just two weeks ago that he said he would not suggest a suitor for me until I am at least seventeen?* "I am sure he will serve Bedham well."

"He is in the cavalry. Perhaps we should invite them riding this afternoon."

"Whatever you wish, Father."

He cuts his eyes toward me. "I cannot decide if I like you better when you are being agreeable or when you are yelling at me."

Patting his hand, I lay my head on his shoulder. "Enjoy it while it lasts, Father, for this weekend, I shall be agreeable to everyone. After that, I will go back to being my normal, obstinate self."

We join Mother and Alfreda in the courtyard and wait for our guests to arrive for lunch. Unable to sit still,

I toss rings at a stake and hit a lawn ball through metal hoops. Our guests arrive in a big group, and I review my goals for speaking with King Herman in my head. I want to know if the kobold have attacked there, what he thinks of Sonia, and his feelings on my reign. But I must tread with ease.

Father believes I should be social, get to know these rulers first, but the amount of knowledge I feel I need in a short time weighs on me. Perhaps I will find what King Herman likes to do and plan an outing with him.

Tea sandwiches, fruits, meats, and cheeses are brought out with wine. We sit at a big, round table with King Herman and his family to my right, Father and Mother to my left, and Victor and Quinn opposite.

Father mentions the tour we finished, and I summarize our trip. Then he launches into memories of past celebrations, and I grow frustrated to be left out of the discussion. At a break in the conversation, I ask King Herman about his hobbies.

"I favor fishing and sailing. Did you know our kingdom is the only in the realm with a navy? It is a vestige arm of defense, really, a holdover from when we were attacked by the merfolk."

I almost chuckle but stop myself. "The merfolk attacked Middle Earth?"

"Five centuries ago, when the humans decided the world indeed was not flat and took to the sea. The merfolk were scared of being discovered and thought they may take our realm for their own."

"Indeed. Who has not tried to take our realm?" Father chuckles.

I think through the enemies in my head: the kobold, the elves, the trolls. "I was not aware mermaids would want to live here."

"Have you ever been on a boat? Most fae have not." Herman points at me.

My heart drops. Finding something I have in common with this fae may be challenging. "I have to say, I have not. I enjoy swimming, and I have fished in our stream in the wood."

"Swimming." Herman pops a grape in his mouth. "That is odd for a fae. What else do you enjoy?"

"Riding and archery, hiking in the forest."

"Do not forget your crystal collection," Father says.

I want to throw daggers at him. *Does he mean to bring attention to my weaknesses?* Hopefully, none outside Capitolshire know of my obsession with counting them. Still, I take the opportunity to highlight our recent victory in the kobold skirmish.

"Have you had any incidences with the kobold of late?" I push a bite around my plate.

"Oh, hideous creatures. Who wants to talk of such things during a meal?" Natasha lifts her wine. "I am glad fortune took your side."

"I remember you were magickal with a harp. Do you play anymore, Grace?" Herman looks straight at Mother.

Seconds and more seconds pass. Mother's stare stays glued to her plate.

"Titania plays very well." Father pats my back.

Herman turns towards me. "Yes, such a good skill for a woman."

Father squeezes my shoulder, and I grip my fork.

"I tried to play, but my fingers were too big," Quinn says. "I have heard you are a master at archery, Titania. Should we?" He lays his napkin on the table.

"You must play often. I see the harp just there. I would love to hear you play," Natasha adds.

I scan the table and their faces. I cannot refuse King Herman's wife. Rising, I cross to a harp, which is new to the garden. I never play for anyone but my music teacher and parents. *Alfreda?* Of course, she would have every possible prop laid out. I take requests and select a short tune suggested by Jakub's wife, Annabelle. Plucking one string to make sure the instrument is tuned, I run my fingers across the strings, picking at them to create the melody. The song is a traditional fae love story of a boy who meets a girl at a festival, falls in love, and searches the kingdom over to find her.

All gathered, including the attendants standing at the edges of the courtyard, clap. I cannot be sure how well I played, and I know the tempo was quick. If there is one thing I hate more than being labeled or etched in a canvas, it is being the center of attention. Which, of course, is what this weekend is all about. Everyone wants to see Titania, the woman who brought down a two-hundred-pound soldier. I guess playing a harp goes far in reducing that image of me.

I motion to the yard games, and the others join me in successive rounds of croquet and ring toss. The elders grow tired and leave Annabelle, Jakub, Quinn, and I to socialize. Quinn suggests again that we could shoot, and when Annabelle and Jakub express a desire to walk through the gardens, I am left to entertain Quinn. Gathering my quiver and two bows from the line of props, I lead him to the meadow.

"The elders are just set in their ways. They will get used to you." Quinn takes an arrow from the bag and aims at the target.

"I do not want them to get used to me. I need them to respect me as they would any other monarch."

Shooting the arrow, he turns to me. "But you are not just any other ruler, are you?"

If the comment had come from someone from Mother's family, I would have been more worried about his meaning. "Yes, I am."

Lifting an arrow to my bow, I release it. The point lands in the exact center of the circle. We shoot several more arrows each.

"No, you are not." Quinn lifts his hand, pointing to his arrows at various locations on the target and mine at dead center.

"Skill grown from pure boredom."

We shoot several rounds and set out on a tour of the castle grounds. As we cross from the orchard into the garden, a trumpet sounds. Excusing myself to meet my next guests, I jump into the air. As I fly, I study the figures below, looking for Foster. *Where could he be?* I long to see him. I do not want to go through this whole weekend without my only friend.

I land at Father's side just as the party from Hilbron exits their carriage. King Luther steps to the walk and his bride, Raven, follows. With hair and wings as dark as night, I appreciate why she bears her name. The next fae out stands half a head taller than Luther and bears a pleasingly chiseled square chin and muscled chest. With light-blue eyes, fair hair, and bronze wings resembling Luther's, I guess them to be family.

"King Luther." I dip my chin in welcome.

"Queen Titania." He bows. "Please, meet my Queen, Raven."

"It is a pleasure." I kiss her cheeks as she kisses mine.

"And my youngest brother, Prince Holden." Luther motions to the man beside him.

"You may call me Holden. It is a pleasure to meet you, Queen Titania." He bows before me and offers his hand.

When I place my hand atop his, he raises my fingers to his lips. Holding my gaze, he releases his grip. Face flaming, I take a step back and introduce Father and a stoic Mother.

"Welcome. Let us show you to your chambers so you may rest from your journey."

Luther and his wife fall in beside Father, and Holden takes a few long strides to my side.

"We were not expecting anyone else from your family," I say to Holden.

"I hope it is not an imposition. I heard of your recent problems with the kobold and wish to know more."

"Are you in the military?"

"Yes. I am a captain and hope to serve as a general one day. It was lucky you were able to sight the souls so quickly. We may never have known why they were released from Sheol."

Finally, someone who takes me seriously and speaks of important things, not music and sports. "I will be happy to share all I know. I believe we could use some problem solving and brainstorming to find answers to all our queries. I have done some research but not had time to completely dedicate myself to it. I am thinking to form a committee of researchers to help me comb the history texts. Perhaps there is precedent of magickal kobold existing as well as a record of a witch harnessing the power of souls from Sheol."

"I could do the same in Hilbron, and perhaps we could enlist some from each kingdom to search their histories."

"That is an excellent idea."

Nearing Luther and Raven's quarters, I leave information as to when and where we will meet for dinner and bid them well.

Father excuses himself to spend time with his family.

I weave through the halls with Holden to find Alfreda so we may secure a room for him. It turns out the only room left is Rigel's, which lies next to mine. Steeling my emotions, I uncover the furniture and leave Holden to unpack. I take a few minutes to freshen up in my room and rejoin our guests in the courtyard. Out of the corner of my eye, I catch sight of General Kane. He tips his head towards the hall, and I excuse myself.

"Please do not tell me something bad occurred. I need to be able to get through one day without a catastrophe."

"No, nothing bad. Just news from above. You said you wanted to be alerted when there was any intelligence on the witches. Aleem has discovered a male witch named Jude who escaped Sonia's castle. He is in Los Angeles, California, in the United States, searching for two witches, Alena and Hunter, believed to be two of the trinity. Apparently, Sonia is holding the third of the trinity, Camille, on Sardinia. Jude thinks Alena and Hunter can help him rescue Camille from Sonia's grasp."

"The trinity? The witches have found the trinity? How did Aleem get all this information?" My skin tingles at the implications. I pace away. "They only get this chance once every century. The three witches of the trinity have never been united. Correct?"

"True. They must wield the Lance of Longinus to break the curse that damns witch souls to purgatory for eternity."

"Releasing the curse means fallen witches may find peace in Heaven with The Creator. How did Aleem find Jude? And what stake does he have in this?"

"Jude participated in some ritual. I am not clear on that part. I believe Aleem has been at that looking glass day and night. He believes Jude to be a herald of the trinity, one who aids them."

"Does Aleem know where these witches, Alena and Hunter, are? Can we aid Jude in any way?"

"Getting involved in witch business is not advised. And even if we wanted to, Aleem cannot find the two of the trinity Jude searches for."

"Someone is hiding them, protecting them. I wonder if Camille is the girl we saw in the castle's cavern, the one Sonia was after, and if the dagger was the Lance of Longinus."

Hearing footsteps behind me, I spin to discover Holden approaching. I introduce him to General Kane, telling the General of Holden's interest in the kobold and the councils we may create to research the anomalous events of late.

"Are you joining us in the courtyard?" Holden points to the others.

"I will be there in a few minutes. Go. There is some lovely wine." I point out where his brother and sister-in-law have gathered outside.

"Is everything okay?" Holden looks between Kane and I.

"Of course. We were just wrapping up the General's report for the week."

Watching Holden walk outside, I wonder what all this means. *Why would Sonia hold Camille? To prevent the curse from being broken? Why would she want that?* If the curse is broken, Lucifer and the other evil spirits of Lower Earth have fewer souls to attempt to gain for their armies. Perhaps Sonia is in league with the evil spirits. I guess her craving for power, perhaps immortality, trumps her desire to free her kind from an eternity in a spiritual purgatory.

I spin to face Kane. "Is there anything we can do to get Camille away from Sonia?"

"You want to anger an immortal witch?"

"No, you are right. If she suspects our involvement, it would be bad for every fae."

A bell rings, signaling the time for the evening meal.

"You should join your guests." Kane points to the group in the courtyard. "The rest can wait until after the coronation."

"There is more? No, you will tell me now."

Kane rolls his eyes to the ceiling and looks back to me. "Is that an order? I would rather wait till after the weekend is over."

"Why?"

"Because you are already like a hound with a bone, you will not sleep. You need your rest for the festivities."

"Now you *must* tell me."

"The two witches, Alena and Hunter, were last seen with the vampire chancellor over three months ago. There have been no sightings of them since."

"THE VAMPIRE CHANCELLOR? The vampires kidnapped them?"

"We do not know."

"Go back to Aleem, and make sure he is using all his resources to get to the bottom of this. And tell him to watch Sonia. I do not like how much power she possesses."

"Believe me, Aleem is watching Sonia. She remains in the castle."

"Have Aleem learn all he can about her coven and those closest to her, especially the male witch we saw with the dagger. There was something off about him. Ask Grant if he sensed it as well."

"You should not worry about this. The witches and vampires will do as they have for generations, leave us alone. Plus, we are more powerful than they are. There is no threat from them."

"Maybe not to us, but to humans. And Sonia… She is something entirely different now, and we have no idea how much power she controls or what she means to do with it. Our realm served as a portal for those souls. What if whoever she is dealing with in Lower Earth is aiding the kobold as well, controlling them, or worse yet, hath bred a new species capable of magick? With magick, they could be more powerful than we are."

"We beat them before."

I shake my head. "Because we outnumbered them. What if they come back with tens of thousands?"

Kane places his hands on my shoulders. "This is not today's problem. Tonight's problem is who you shall dance with."

I lift his hands and step away. "Then I shall dance with everyone. Join us and bring your wife."

Kane refuses to attend the meal, saying he does not attend royal family affairs. I wonder how bad it could be and realize it could be horrible indeed. Walking to the small dining hall, I wonder if the vampires have really taken two of the trinity. *Why would they care if the witches broke the curse?* My head spins as I dread what the kobold are up to and when they will attack next. *If they develop more magickal powers, how will we stop them?*

As I enter the dining room, I force myself to focus on those gathered. Alfreda sits with Mother, and I greet them first, followed by Father; King Herman, Luther, and their wives; Victor, Jakub, and Annabelle; and Quinn and Holden, who seem deep in conversation.

"What are you two talking about?"

"The magick kobold. They are a curiosity."

"That is one word for them. I have not been able to find any history of the kobold yielding magick—not in our realm at least."

"Perhaps there was a witch with them," Holden says. "A spirit to cloak them."

"That is a good theory."

"Young ones, always so serious!" Victor approaches. "It is a celebration. Please, let us speak of something a bit happier."

He inquires about Holden's service with the archers of Hilbron, and Quinn admits the cavalry are a small force in Bedham. Victor notes them both to be up and coming soldiers, serving their countries well.

Our food arrives, and I sit at the head of the table, Father and Mother to my left, followed by Victor and Quinn. King Herman and Natasha hold the places to my right with King Luther, Raven, and Holden beyond. I describe my recent tour of Aubren and speak about my ideas on representatives to serve on my council of advisors.

"Elected fae? How strange. What of the family lines that have held those positions? Surely they would be offended." Herman sips his wine.

"There were two other advisors that sided with Gunther when he challenged my succession. I do not believe these families should be reassigned their positions. I feel the elections will increase diversity and help bring all ideas to the council. We have such varied fae, from the mountains to the grasslands to the desert. All these should be represented."

"Yes, because elections have worked so well in Upper Earth." Herman rolls his eyes.

"Well, it is somewhere to start." I raise my glass. "To new beginnings and new friendships."

The others lift their glasses and echo my sentiments. Once the dinner ends, we take our drinks and move to the sitting room. Holden and Quinn huddle around me, applauding my ideas for new forms of communication between fae and rulers. I ask about their interests in government, and they indicate they are more in favor of action. I think of Ethan and his unwillingness to take an advisor's position and then I wonder if, like my guard friends and Kane, Foster will make a career of military service. I guess I, too, fall into that category as commander of all the forces.

THE NEXT MORNING, I RISE EARLY, ready to greet all our guests. They file in, party after party: the Kings, Queens, and High Council members from Chastam, lying under China and the middle east; Willhelm, below Siberia; Lindleton, beneath Europe; Rotuga, with fae of red, green, blue, and purple skin, beneath Africa; Elita, underneath South America, also holds fae of bright colors; and finally, the Borean group, from underneath the North American continent. I am most interested in speaking with this group, along with the Lindleton royals, because I believe they may have the most information about Sonia and the supposed trinity of young witches.

Father warned me about hounding them too soon, and I decide to leave questions for the next day, hoping they will stay long enough for me to find out what they know.

The welcomes last well into the afternoon. As we leave the Borean King and Queen to their rooms, Alfreda steers me to my chamber, insisting I must rest, bathe, and dress. I soak in my tub and wrap in my robe.

Looking out over the garden and orchard, I think of Foster. *Where is he?*

Father and Alfreda convinced me it would not be proper for him to sit at the head table. Only Father, Mother, the generals, and the advisors would hold that honor.

Still, I feel the celebration will not be complete without seeing him. But I have not heard from him since our dinner at his family's home. No letters came in response to the ones I wrote each night.

Maybe he does not want to be my friend anymore. Maybe his family did not like me. Perhaps he means to focus on his career. Blinking my tears away, I look at my crosses, think of my brothers. *At least your spirits are here with me.*

Alfreda flits in and darts to me, wrapping her arms around my shoulders. "Why the tears, love?"

"I was just thinking of my brothers." I wriggle from her embrace.

"Should I bring your mother?"

"No, it will only make it worse. I will meet her and Father in their study to start the progression to the hall."

Two ladies curl and pin my hair atop my head. Then I slip on my gown and lace up my heeled boots. I slide a knife between the leather and my skin and look in the mirror. Even with all these people, some uncles, aunts, a cousin even... *How can I feel so alone?*

I bolster my mood. This is a good night. I am where I want to be, in charge of my own destiny. I suck in a deep breath, spin, and exit my room.

Seeing Grant, Timothy, Nicholas, and Adam, I smile. The only person needed to complete my night is Foster.

We wind through the back halls to my parents' chambers. Dressed in military whites, Father greets me with a kiss. Beside him, Mother looks radiant in her golden gown. Kissing her cheek, I study her face. Still, it holds no recognition.

I straighten my back and squeeze Alfreda's hand. "Thank you for everything."

Exiting their study, I enter the main hall.

Torches light the walls, and every candle on the chandeliers is lit. I cannot ever remember the castle looking so bright. Fae, four and five deep, line the passage, and I make my way down the hall, greeting as many as I can. Children throw flower petals in my path, and women pass me flowers and ribbons. By the time I reach the coronation hall, my arms overflow with fragrant gifts.

Huge urns of flowers line the aisle, and trumpets blare as I enter. I pass Generals Kane and Milo; Advisors Bran, Jesper, and Terrence; Aleem; Victor and Quinn; Holden, who winks at me; King Luther and Raven; King Herman, Natasha, Jakub, and Annabelle; and dignitaries from every kingdom. I search for the face I long to see but do not find him. Determined not to let his absence mar my experience, I bow to the High Judge as I reach the end of the aisle. Dipping to one knee, I lower my head.

"Rise, for you have been called to serve your kingdom." The judge recites the age-old words. "What say you? Do you promise to uphold the laws of the land, work for the fae of this kingdom, nae, the realm, do your best to protect Upper Earth as is the solemn duty of all fae?"

"I promise to uphold the laws of the land, work for the fae of this kingdom, nae, the realm, do my best to protect Upper Earth as is the solemn duty of all fae." I repeat his words, my vow to those gathered, the kingdom, and all the realm with a loud voice.

"By the power vested in me by the High Council, and as you have proven to all your worth to rise to this position, I crown you, Titania Alpheaus, sovereign monarch and ruler of the Kingdom of Aubren. Long live Queen Titania." He places the crown, once Father's, on my head.

Warmth spreads from my head to my toes, and my skin tingles. Trumpets blare, and the chorus of chanting, "Long live Queen Titania," is deafening as I spin to face the crowd. I look at Father, whose face shines with tears; Mother, her eyes fixed on mine; and then Alfreda, weeping into her tissue.

Smiling, I raise my arms, and the crowd goes silent. "Thank you for entrusting me with your safety and prosperity. I will not fail you. Long live the fae! Please, let us celebrate."

I make my way outside where huge tents are lined with tables. Fae after fae offer congratulations, kissing my cheeks and squeezing my hands. I search the faces beyond the first row but catch no glimpse of Foster. I tuck my disappointment away and focus on those before me. Trays of meats, cheeses, and fruits are brought out for any who wish to celebrate, and I pick at my meal as lines of fae wish me well. Alfreda keeps water at my hand, and just as I believe I cannot smile for a second longer, the music shifts.

A jig begins, and the masses move in a wave towards the courtyard lit with hundreds of torches. The clapping begins with a few, and by the time I reach the center, the sound is like thunder in my ears. Offering my hand to Father, I begin the traditional dance, pulling King Herman, Luther, and their wives into the open space. Victor, Quinn, Holden, Kane, the advisors, and Alfreda join us, and a huge circle forms, a chain of people weaving in and out. A circle of dancers assembles around us, followed by another, and another, until the whole space is filled with concentric circles.

Blasts from above stop me in my path, and I look up to catch sight of fireworks shooting into the air and exploding overheard. Cheers ring out as we stare at the light show.

Father wraps his arm around me and squeezes my shoulder. Kissing my cheek, he hugs me tightly. Tears form in my eyes as I realize, it sinks into my psyche, my bones, my soul, that I am here, and all will be well.

I dance two more tunes and, finding Alfreda, leave the revelers and weave back to my chamber. My heart still races as I part with my crown and gown. She leaves me to soak in the tub. The music from the party reaches my windows, and I hum along with the tune. The dancing and drinking will last until early in the morning, but my festivities are not over. Tomorrow, we will have brunch in the garden and games in the meadow with the other dignitaries. I need to be rested for another day of entertaining and conversation.

Huddling under my covers, I am too tired to worry about Foster or be disappointed, or whatever I should be. If something happened to him, I would know. *Kane, someone, would tell me, right?* I bolt up. That is it. A pit grows in my stomach. They would not tell me. Not this weekend. He was attacked by a kobold, drowned in the sea, killed by a stray arrow… Wrapping my covers around me, I run into the hall.

"What is wrong, madam?" Grant is before me in an instant, blocking my path.

"Something is wrong with Foster. I have not heard from him in two weeks, and he was not there tonight. He should have been at my coronation. I asked him to come. What do you know?"

"Nothing. I have heard nothing of Foster." Grant looks at Timothy and the other guards, asking them if they have heard anything.

When they answer no, I spin to face Grant. "Let me by. I want to talk to Alfreda right now."

"It is very late. I am sure Foster is sleeping in his quarters. Alfreda turned in as well. This can wait until the morning. If something happened to him, we would know it."

"Not if you all are hiding it from me."

"Why would we do such a thing?"

"So my coronation would not be ruined. That is the only explanation." *Or that his family hated me, and he decided I was a brutish fae queen who was not appealing after all,* my mind pings.

Grant tells Timothy to fetch Alfreda with some tea and to summon Kane for information and corrals me into my new study. Alfreda appears in her robe, tea in hand; sits beside me; and pats my shoulder, reassuring me that Foster is fine and I am just tired. I sip the mixture, sure it is chamomile meant to calm me. I do not even care right now. I just want to know that Foster is safe.

Hearing a knock on the door, I tighten my grip on the blankets around me and cross to it. Kane stands on the other side, and I welcome him in.

Kane looks between Alfreda and I. "Grant said you had questions about Foster?"

I lift my chin. "Yes. I expected him to be at the celebration tonight. Where is he?"

Kane's eyes cut to the floor, to Alfreda, and back to my face. "I put Foster on the special team you wanted. I thought he would be a good person for the job, since he is one we trust."

"So, he has been in the castle this whole time?"

"Yes. He may still be among the revelers. If you must see him, I am sure we can find him."

"No, of course. That is fine. Thank you. I am sorry to bother you. I just got this bad feeling."

"With the many festivities anyone would be frayed. You should try to sleep. Tomorrow brings more hosting requirements."

"Yes." I hug my blankets to my chest. "I will retire for the evening, thank you."

Kane dips his chin and backs out the door.

Alfreda approaches and wraps her arms around me. "What is bothering you, dear? Did you have a premonition?"

"No, I am tired, like Kane said. And I just thought"—I pry her hands from my torso—"never mind. The tea was wonderful, thank you. We should both sleep."

I say goodnight at my door and click it shut. Looking at the lights from the torches, tears form in my eyes. *Two weeks of unanswered letters, what more of a sign do I need?* Foster does not want to be my friend anymore. *So, I will make other friends.* Quinn is quite nice as well as Holden. I am sure there will be others who I may befriend. Raven and Luther, as well as Annabelle and Jakub, may also become companions. I vow to connect further with these comrades the next day, perhaps to even invite Raven and Annabelle on a vacation with me. I roll my eyes. *When are you to take a vacation?* Or at the very least be writing friends. Mother wrote to her sisters often, and perhaps these women will, in time, feel like sisters to me.

⸏⸎

WAKING WITH THE SUN, I am dressed in my finest riding pants, skirt, boots, lacey white blouse, and favorite green-velvet vest when Alfreda knocks on my door. I love having brunch in the garden, and with my renewed energy and plan to forge friendships, I look forward to the day.

I take my place at the entrance to the formal garden, greeting each of the dignitaries. Once everyone arrives, I sit at the head table and welcome them. After brunch, we play croquet in rounds, and I ask Raven and Annabelle to join my team. I wonder if they would rather partner with their husbands, but they agree. We do not win but have laughs at how bad our shots are. Next up is the ring toss, and the two opt to sit with the women and sip tea. I join with Quinn and Holden, who bring forth new ideas on the makeshift kobold-fighting group we have formed.

After lunch, Quinn asks me to shoot with him, and we make our way to the meadow for archery practice. I catch his errors straight away but keep to my bow and arrow.

He watches as I hit the bull's-eye, time after time. "Please, save me from my torture, and show me how you do that."

"You have to find the right stance for you."

"I am standing wrong?"

"Not wrong, just not right for *you*. You are standing with your feet straight. Try opening up a bit more."

"I have no idea what you are saying."

I illustrate with my feet, showing him how I angle the foot closer to the target towards the target a bit. Noting his shoulders are scrunched, I instruct him to relax his back.

"So basically, you are telling me I am doing everything wrong?"

I stand behind him. "Just breathe. Close your eyes. Position your feet. Let your shoulders drop back. Now, raise your bow and point it at the target."

His eyes cut to me. "Like this?"

"I said eyes closed."

"How can I see where I am shooting?"

"Do you want to learn or not?"

He does as I instruct, and his arrow lands closer to the center. With more practice, he is hitting the inner circle more often than not.

"Kane said I would find you here." Holden's voice breaks my concentration, and I turn to find him approaching. "The hunt is starting, Quinn."

"The hunt?" I shield my eyes from the sun to gauge their expressions.

Holden clears his throat. "I believe your father organized a hunt."

"I was not invited. Who is to take part?" I look between them.

Quinn looks at the ground. "I believe most of us."

"Most of you? As in the males? As in all the male royals?"

"Well, Quinn, Jakub, and I were included," Holden says.

"So, again, all the male royals?"

"I guess." Quinn starts for the target.

"I think your Father said you did not like to hunt." Holden squints in the sunlight as he looks back at the castle.

"I am a superb archer. I can bring down a goose or duck quicker than anyone."

Holden looks at the ground. "I believe it is to be a traditional hunt with hounds."

I steel my jaw. He is right, I do not favor that type of hunting, but I hate even more being excluded from an event meant for bonding. "Is there room for another rider?"

"I am sure whatever pleases you can be accommodated. You are the host, after all."

"And look! I already have my riding clothes on." I motion to my leather pants.

Grabbing my quiver, I realize Quinn holds my arrows. I take them from him, shoulder my bag, and start to the meadow. Both of them flank me, throwing out additional ideas for the kobold council. I am sure they mean to divert me from the awkward topic of the hunt, and I oblige them.

Quinn holds out his palm, offering to carry my quiver. "I was thinking I could stay here for a few extra days. That would give us time for intense research."

"What a brilliant idea, Quinn," Holden says. "I believe I could ask my brother for a leave as well."

Out of the corner of my eye, I catch Quinn rolling his eyes. Something dings in my head. *While I thought I would been passing time, making a friend, had Quinn actually been courting me? My fourth cousin once removed?* I fight a shiver. He is not a bad-looking fae. And closer cousins marry all the time. He does seem to respect my position.

Holden stops in front of me. "Join my team. You and I will make an excellent pair."

Quinn shakes his head. "There are not really teams. Everyone goes after the fox. Let me talk to your father, Titania. I mean, he is my uncle."

I look between them. "I do not wish to offend anyone."

Holden lays his hand on my arm, and his blue eyes hold mine. "Queen, I believe it is you who are offended. And rightly so. I do not think—"

"I will go find Uncle Oberon at once." Quinn spins and walks away.

Chapter 17

REALIZING I SHOULD PROBABLY speak to Father, I bid fare-well to Holden and jump into the air. Flying over Quinn, I reach Father as he is bringing out his favorite horse. My first instinct is to plant my fists on my hips and demand to know why I was not invited. I decide a softer approach may serve me better.

"Hi, Father. I did not realize you were riding."

"Yes, it is the"—he stops mid-sentence, mouth agape—"the traditional host hunt."

I stare into his eyes, waiting.

"And I guess you would be the host." He looks to the ground. "I did not even think to invite you, I am sorry."

I had been ready to yell, but his apology stops me. "Thank you, Father. Would it be inappropriate for me to join in? I want to be one of these people, not an outsider. But I also do not want to overstep a boundary."

Father chuckles. "You have erased many boundaries, daughter. You should be included."

"Thank you." I kiss his cheek. "I will get my horse."

By the time I exit the barn with Ginger saddled, I find Quinn and Holden, as well as the rest of the male royals, beside their horses. Father approaches and holds Ginger's reins while I climb on.

Leaning in, he whispers that I should not win.

Winking, I whisper that I know the etiquette.

The huntsman blows a horn and releases the hounds. They charge across the meadow and into the woods. Signaling for Quinn and Holden to ride ahead of me, I canter through the field behind them. I hold back, waiting for the kings to ride ahead, noting which way each one goes in case someone is lost. Between the fourteen of us, four foxes come back tied to the saddles of Herman, Luther, and the kings of Lindleton and Elita.

As we return to the stable, Holden steers to my side. "It is always good to let your older brother, the King, win."

"Do they teach that in prince school?"

"You would have stolen a win from your king? You remember, I have three other brothers to compete with."

I laugh, thinking I would let slip those small rules of interacting with a king. "No, I guess you are right."

He speaks of Hilbron and the dry expanse of desert spanning much of the kingdom. "It is a pleasure to see green and have cool, moist air surrounding you. I hope that all will agree that I can stay to do more research."

My face warms as he holds my gaze. "I believe we should ask for a representative from each kingdom to serve on the council. There may be knowledge in other kingdoms that would aid our cause."

He commends the idea, and as we approach the stable, I slide from my horse. I excuse myself to wash her down then return to my room to dress for dinner.

Dinner is a dull affair with only the dignitaries for entertainment. I make no inroads with befriending Annabelle or Raven because the two converse about decorating and dress designs the whole meal.

Dancing afterwards proves fun. I am careful to dance with everyone, not favoring one male over another. After all, my thoughts should be on my kingdom, not men. I do not want complications.

We dance until after midnight, and I traipse to my room, undress, and fall into bed, exhausted and mostly happy save missing Foster. My eyes slide closed.

—◦◦◦—

TICK, TICK, TICK. TICK, TICK, TICK. I wake to the sound of rocks pelting my window and, heart racing, fly to the glass. Throwing open the pane, I find Foster before me.

"I have something you need to hear. Come, quick." He takes my hand.

"What? No." I snatch my fingers from his grasp. "I have not heard from you, seen you, in two weeks. And you show up, unannounced, in the middle of the night. I am not going anywhere with you."

"Well, if you would answer my letters and had not stuck me on spy duty, maybe things would be different. That does not matter now. You need to hear this." He flits away.

I dart to him and catch his jacket. "See what? And what letters? I wrote to you every day and never got one acknowledgement back."

"What? I... It does not matter right now. There is something important you need to hear."

283

Flying towards the center of the castle, he ducks through a window leading to the slim passageway behind the royal study—the one he and I spied on Father from some four and half weeks ago. It reminds me I never had the holes in the bricks covered over. Foster alights on the ground in front of the crevice. Placing a finger to his lips, he points to the crack in the wall.

I land beside him and duck down to peer inside. Father and Kane stand in front of the fire, just six feet from the wall we stand behind, heads inches apart.

"I saw her laughing with Holden in the meadow. I believe she may favor him," Kane whispers to Father.

"She spent time shooting with Quinn. He would be a good match as well." Father strokes his beard.

"Should I approach both gentlemen or their kings? See who may be open to a union?"

"It is too risky with the spies lurking about this weekend. I heard Titania talking about Quinn and Holden staying on to research the kobold. Let us contact them once all the other guests leave."

"You are sure you want to push her in this way?" Kane raises his eyebrows.

"You said yourself she is becoming more paranoid. A union with another royal will secure her reign, stabilize the kingdom."

My breath catches in my lungs. I turn around, pressing my back to the cool stone. The tunnel spins around me. "I must get back to my room."

"Titania." Whispering, Foster lays his hands on my shoulders. "You are okay. Breathe."

Closing my eyes, I gasp for air. "No, I cannot. I need to get back to my room. No one can see me like this."

"Titania, look at me. When is the last time this happened?"

I open my eyes to find his inches from mine. "In the dungeon."

"When you were not in control of the situation. But you are in control now. You are the Queen. You get to decide what is best for you and this kingdom." He slides his palms to my hands, wrapping them around my fingers.

"How could Father and Kane betray me like this? Go behind my back?" I wriggle my hands from his grip.

"Titania?" Foster raises his palms. "Do not do anything rash."

I pace away then spin to face him. "Do you think they are right? Should I be worried about the stability of my reign? Kane said he would come to me if there was anything to be concerned about. Have you heard anything?"

"Not a peep. You have completely won over all the royals. Although young, they see you as the rightful ruler of Aubren and are impressed with your skill and knowledge. You have nothing to worry about."

"So, why is Father so concerned?" Stepping up to the wall, I lean down and look through the peep hole again.

The room is empty, and I turn back to Foster, trying to make sense of why Father would do this.

"It sounds like just for you and your worry."

"But if Kane came to me with this report, I would not worry anymore. I do not understand why they would do this to me. And how did you know they were meeting?"

"I saw Kane and your father enter the room, thought it odd, and then heard them discussing you."

"Were you seen?"

"I have gotten so good at blending in, no one notices me."

I narrow my eyes. "Speaking of... What about the letters?"

"We should go someplace else to talk." Taking off his jacket, he offers it to me.

I slide my arms in and button the front.

He holds out his hand, I take it, and we wind through the passageway to the exit and fly over the garden. The feel of his hand in mine warms my soul.

I stare at his face as we pass over the orchard, thinking he could take me anywhere and it would not matter. Speeding over the meadow, we descend into the wood. Alighting on a moss covered clearing beside the brook, I fling my arms around him.

He hugs me to him, and my insides melt. His warm chest, strong arms around me... I can think of no other place I want to be than with him.

"I missed you so much. Why would you not come to me?"

"And I you. These have been the worst two weeks of my life."

I breathe in his scent, and it brings back memories of our nights spent watching for the kobold and dinner at his home. With Father and Kane conspiring to marry me off, Foster may be the only one I can trust.

I lift my head from his shoulder and release him. "It is so good to see you, know that you are okay. I thought maybe you decided me to be ugly or rude. Or your family did not like me."

"No." He clutches my hands. "I wrote every day."

"I wrote you every day as well. Where were you?"

Foster reveals how Kane had them trailing our tour, collecting information on what all the fae in the kingdom thought of me. He describes listening in on conversations in the markets and taverns, and he learned that, for the most part, I won over the fae of our kingdom, was beloved and revered.

"I would never do anything to hurt you. You know that, right? For as long as you want me, I will stay with you."

Tears fill my eyes. "So, Father and Kane hid our letters so I would think you did not care?"

"I believe so. And he put me on spy duty so you would not see me. But I was there. I watched as you received your crown, danced, played croquet, shot arrows with Quinn, and rode with Holden."

"I was just making friends. It saddened me to think maybe you did not want to be my friend anymore. I cannot be alone in this. And now with Father and Kane? What am I going to do about them? And what if they are right?" I pull my hands from his. "You know I care about you, but I have to put my kingdom first. What if I need to marry a royal?"

"This is not new information. My thoughts went to that the first day we met."

He leads me to a rock, and we sit beside the brook, tossing out ideas for how to handle Father and Kane, whether marrying a royal from another kingdom would hurt my reign or help it. Who I may trust and how Foster and I may stay in touch if Kane and Father conspire against us is also a topic explored.

Standing, I square my shoulders. "I am the Queen, and I can take Kane's position. It is treason to conspire against a monarch. And that is what they have done—interfered with my personal affairs, tampered with my correspondence. How dare they?"

Foster stands before me. "It sounds like they are just looking out for you, want what is best for you *and* the kingdom."

"I will put you under Milo's lead. Kane will not have say over your position. I will lean on Grant, Timothy, Nicholas, and Adam. They shall report only to me."

"Perhaps you should have all the castle guards report to you directly, and no one else, create a Queen's Guard." He paces, brainstorming how I may make sure my affairs remain secure.

I insist he be the one in charge of the guard, at least be a part of it, but he declines.

"I have to make a name, a career, for myself. You understand, right?" He weaves his fingers in mine. "How did we become so complicated?"

We. I like the sound of that. He cares for me as much as I do him. I smile. "I am the complicated one. You are free to run away at any point."

"That is the problem." He rests his forehead on mine. "I cannot leave you."

My heart races. I bite my lip and close my eyes. His lips brush mine, and an electric buzz radiates though my body to my toes. I press my lips to his, and the warmth of his skin envelops me. Dropping my hands, he wraps his arms around my waist. Ending the kiss, he releases me.

His green eyes hold mine then widen. He lifts a strand of hair from my forehead and tucks it behind my ear. "That was improper. You are my queen."

"No." I stare into his eyes. "There is no queen here. Just a girl."

Wrapping his arms around my waist, he pulls me to him, kissing me again. His lips are warm and soft, and I want to kiss him forever. I know it is wrong for me to allow him to kiss me, for me to kiss him. But I cannot deny this is what I want, and he is who I want.

He ends the kiss with a quick peck and grasps my hands. "No matter what, I will remember this night for the rest of my life."

"And I as well." I kiss his lips and jump into the air.

We fly deeper into the wood, following owls and flitting with fireflies, until I note the first light of day. Knowing Alfreda will send out a search party if I am not in my room, I kiss him once more at the end of the meadow and head straight home. The night guard dips his chin as I alight in front of the window. I press my finger to my lips, and he winks at me. Heart soaring at the memory of my kiss with Foster, I slip inside. *He cares for me.*

"Oh, you are already up." Alfreda's voice startles me. "What are you doing wearing a guard's jacket?"

I hug the jacket to me and sniff the collar. "Oh, I wanted some fresh air and was standing at the window. It was chilly, so the guard lent me his jacket."

"Well, you better get dressed." The sound of Alfreda's voice drifts into the background as I remember the feel of Foster's lips on mine, his arms around my waist, his words, *I cannot leave you*, and know I will never be alone again.

"Titania!" She grips my shoulders. "Dear child, quit gawking out the window and start dressing. We still need to fix your hair. And what happened to it? It looks like a bird's nest."

Running my fingers through my locks, I hit a snarl in the first inch. "I guess I tossed in my sleep."

"Well, do not just stand there, get over here." Raising my brush, she points to the chair.

I jump into the air, and it feels as if my body floats like a feather. Rounding the room, I follow Alfreda's direction, all the while making mental lists. As soon as my guests are gone, I will have Grant help me create a Queen's Guard. I am still not sure what to do about Father and Kane, but I find I am not as mad as I could be.

Foster cares for me, perhaps as much as I do him.

This is a good day.

Before breakfast, I find Quinn and Holden. As I do not want to play favorites between them and do not know their skills in whole, I ask them to serve as co-chairs on the kobold task force. Further, I suggest they go to their countries to do research and return in a month's time.

Each seems disappointed but agree with the request. After greeting everyone and eating the meal, I announce the formation of the group. All the kingdoms pledge to attain all knowledge they can and meet again next month.

I watch Father closely and Kane as well. They shift in their chairs and look at each other. I take a mental score. *Titania, one. Father, zero. Let the games begin.* The guests have their luggage brought out and, one by one, load into carriages destined for the monarchs' home kingdoms. King Luther and Queen Raven approach, and not seeing Holden or his luggage, I inquire as to his location.

"Did your Father not tell you? He invited Holden to stay for your birthday celebration next weekend. I hope you are not offended we cannot stay as well, but we have been away four days already. Thank you for having us. It is nice to be acquainted with you, and I look forward to further collaboration." King Luther leans in and kisses my cheek.

"Of course. Thank you for coming." I kiss his cheek and hug Raven.

Drat Father. He is a fast thinker. Titania, one, Father, one.

As was with Holden, Quinn is not with his party, and I am informed he was invited to stay for my birthday as well. King Herman, Queen Natasha, Jakub, Annabelle, and Victor congratulate me again and say their goodbyes.

My next task is to find Grant and request a meeting with Kane to inform him of the formation of the Queen's Guard. As I wind back to my chamber, a server approaches.

"Bread, my Queen?"

"No, thank you." I flash him a smile.

"My Queen, I am sure that this bread would be most to your liking. It is warm, just pulled from the ovens." The fae holds it out, cornering me against the wall.

"Thank you. I just ate. Perhaps the guards will appreciate it." I force a smile and look both ways down the passage, realizing I am alone.

"Titania," the fae whispers.

I look at his face and recognize the green eyes peeking out from under his low cap. "Foster?"

He motions for me to follow, and we find our way to the secret passage behind the study.

"I realize I should stay in Kane's service, that you should let him direct me wherever he wants."

"But what if he sends you far away? Father invited Quinn and Holden to stay a week to celebrate my birthday."

"Drat! Your idea of sending them home to do research was such a good one."

"You heard that?"

"I told you. I hear everything."

"I cannot have Father and Kane making a marriage deal behind my back. If they do, and I refuse, it will be a diplomatic nightmare. And I cannot be mean to Quinn or Holden."

"Still, it is better for me to stay in Kane's service, be your eyes and ears as much as possible."

"What if part of my Queen's Guard is a spy network? I could enlist servants I trust behind Father's back." I bite my lip, thinking how low I have sunken, spying on my own family, on Kane, after he helped so much. But if they plot without me, this is their doing.

"You should go find Grant at once."

"I will." I turn to walk away.

Foster grabs my hand, and his face is suddenly inches away. He smiles and presses his lips to mine. "I will come to your window tonight."

"I will be waiting." As he drops my hand, I jump into the air.

At the main passage, I alight and walk to my chamber. My lips still tingle from the kiss, and I smile and trace my finger across them. Seeing Timothy, I remember my task and request he find Grant. I pace my study, waiting for him to arrive. I wish this were not necessary. *But really, is it?* I have always been open with Father, and I had assumed him with me. He *did* keep Mother's gift a secret. I can understand the reasoning behind this. But to steal my private mail and make an engagement arrangement, *without my knowledge?* His actions cross a line. But if I do this, I escalate the situation, perhaps make myself look even more unstable. Maybe I should confront him. Have all out in the open.

I decide on this course of action and ask my guard to tell Grant to wait for me when he arrives. Halfway to Father's chamber, I meet Grant. Not wanting to hold him up, we trace back to my study. Inside, I explain what happened. He counsels me to speak with Father but also suggests I have a group that will feed me information and answer only to me. Grant pledges his loyalty and service to my cause and says he will speak with Timothy, Adam, and

Nicholas as well. I indicated I will speak with them and request Grant give me names of others who may help me keep abreast of things within the castle and Capitolshire. After he leaves, I pace my study, thinking of how I shall approach Father.

Alfreda bursts into the room. Shuffling past me, she closes the shutters. "Heavens, dear, you are driving everyone mad. What is the matter?"

"Have you not heard of knocking? You need to be announced."

"Since when?" She props her hands on her hips.

"Since now."

"Oh." Her eyes drop to the floor. "Well, anyway, the noon meal is served in the courtyard. Your Father waits with Kane, Quinn, and Holden."

I fight rolling my eyes. *Of course.* Swinging open the door, I take to the air. In the courtyard, I greet each of the men. Leg bobbing, I smile and make polite conversation. Quinn invites me to shoot arrows in the meadow later, and after bidding goodbye to Kane, I snag Father's jacket as he rises to leave.

"Walk with me, Father. It has been too long since we have enjoyed the garden together."

"Should we get your mother?"

"I would like to talk to you. I promise to walk with her in the wood tomorrow morning."

I hook my arm in his, and we stroll in silence to the end of the garden. Patting my hand, he admits to noticing me pacing my study.

"You seem on edge. Does the schedule of entertaining wear on you?"

Sliding my arm from his, I step in front of him. "Why did you invite Holden and Quinn to stay for my birthday? You have no right to plan such an event without asking me first."

"Oh." He looks at the ground then back up at me. "That was to be a surprise. I thought you would like your friends here for the celebration."

"My friends? I have known them all of three days."

"But you appear to get along well."

I exhale a long, slow breath. "I heard you speaking with Kane last night."

His face flames red. "What did you hear?"

"That you were plotting with Kane to have me engaged to either Quinn or Holden. Did you also intercept my letters to Foster and his to me?" I ball my fists as anger burns inside my chest. "How could you? You had me thinking I needed my own militia. Of all people, I thought I could count on *you* to be honest with me. If you thought I needed a husband, then you should have come to me first. I am a queen. I am old enough to handle such things."

"You are right. I am sorry. Yes, I want you to be happily married. But it is not a husband so much as a successor that is needed right now. I know you. If there is a battle, you are going to want to be front and center. With no children of age, you need an heir presumptive so the kingdom will not fall into turmoil if you are lost. Having a husband as a successor, especially if he is from another kingdom, makes that easier. Because you love him, the people will accept him."

A successor? This is about a successor? "And you think Quinn or Holden would make good successors? They will not be accepted because they are outsiders. Quinn is family, but he has never lived in Aubren. And Holden is from a different line and different kingdom. Neither of them know much about our fae."

Even with this new information, going behind my back and intercepting my letters is crossing a line. I want to point a finger at his face and rebuke him as a parent would a naughty child.

"Father, this is something you should have brought to me. I will not tolerate you and Kane conspiring behind my back. Do you know what would have happened if you forced my hand? I would have rejected them, making a huge blunder in diplomacy, ruining our relationships with their kingdoms. If there is ever another instance of this, I will send you and Mother to a cottage in the woods, and you will never see me again. And tell your friend Kane the same."

Taking a step back, I turn on my heel and walk away. My heart races in my chest, and tears form in my eyes. I hate being angry, and being this mad at Father breaks my heart. Further, he has ruined the trust I had for him.

I am truly alone.

Chapter 18

"I AM SORRY. IT WILL NOT HAPPEN again. I thought I was helping you. I wanted to save you one hardship, know that you were happy and cared for, that your reign was secure." Father hurries after me.

I do not want him to see my tears. I stop, raise my chin, say thank you, and keep walking. I slip off my boots and enter the orchard, and the cool grass soothes my mood. The green trees calm my senses. The tears still flow, and I realize that beyond being angry, my soul feels crushed, injured because he betrayed me, and hurt because I feel he does not think I can handle the role I have ascended to. I lift my face to the sky and let the breeze flow over my skin.

I can figure this out. *An heir presumptive need not be a husband, right?* I will allow Quinn and Holden to stay and decide if either of them would be a good successor. Perhaps I will make a list of other potentials. One from Mother's family would also be a good choice, and I decide to research King Herman's children. Jakub will rule after Herman, but he may have a brother, *or sister*, who could fill the role.

Circling back to the courtyard, I find Quinn, and we shoot several rounds of arrows. I ride with Holden, asking both young men to meet me for research after dinner. We convene in the study after the meal and load the table with books on the kobold and witch histories. I send a note to Aleem, asking the Ring Keeper to meet us the next day so we may learn any information he possesses. Afterwards, I retire to my quarters and dress in warm pants and a jacket, waiting for Foster.

He arrives at ten, as promised, and we stroll through the woods, jumping toadstools and downed trees. We fly over the brook and decide to follow it up the mountain. At the top, we alight on a rock, lie back, and look at the dark sky.

Each night, we repeat this, finding a new forest or mountain to explore. Being with Foster helps me feel less alone. It feeds my soul. I wonder if I love him, if this is what being in love is. The sight of his face causes me joy. The tone of his voice calms me. With him, I am safe. My heart tells me *this* is love. Still, even with our kisses, I do not voice these feelings. We have come far, but there lies much ahead.

My birth day arrives. Capitolshire celebrates with a festival in the market, and I spend the day dancing in the square. In the evening, I gather with Foster, Quinn, Holden, Mother, Father, Kane, Alfreda, and my four guards. *Sixteen.* For a fae, sixteen is a third of his or her life. Most fae marry by sixteen, at the latest seventeen or eighteen, and some even before, at fourteen or fifteen. I am aware of Foster, Quinn, and Holden, sitting around the table, perhaps each expecting something from me. I let my mind wander into the future, down one path then another.

"You look way too serious to be at a birth day gala, especially your sixteenth." Holden tops off my glass with wine.

My initial assessment gives him points for strength, quick wit, confidence, and directness and minuses for stubbornness and arrogance. *Of course, who am I to slight someone for being hardheaded?* A good choice for a successor. Quinn ranks higher in the listening and thinking department, also a qualified choice. But I believe having a member of Mother's family would be of value. The magick running through her veins, through mine, could be in theirs as well. They could protect the kingdom.

I start my research the next morning in diligence, learning each of them have ties in their birthplace, either being married or engaged to be married. Father had been right. Quinn and Holden represent the best choices for a successor. I plan to keep them here until I can choose by keeping the kobold council's task list full.

We study and train in archery, weapons, fencing, duels, and riding and perform drills with the soldiers, flying farther and farther each day to increase stamina. By day, they are my constant companions. When Foster and I are in public, we pretend to be friends, little more than acquaintances. I watch him train in the yards with the soldiers, his arms, back, and torso muscles growing by the day.

Father catches me watching one day. "He comes from hearty stock, I will say that for him.

My face flames with embarrassment. "Father."

"What? Do you not favor him?"

"I am watching all my soldiers train. This is what a queen does."

Foster comes to my room each night, and we walk and talk. I tell him things I learn, and he helps me think through situations that arise. He keeps me abreast of the soldiers' moods and gossip in the castle that leans towards me falling in love with Holden. I worry that I will not be enough for Foster or will be too much. He assures me he likes the path we are on, wishes to make a name for himself, not be tied to being the lover of the Queen.

My cheeks warm with his words, for we have only exchanged kisses, not talked of love or the future, save for the path he may fashion for himself. "That sounds so tawdry. I hope you do not think of yourself that way."

"Yes and no. We do live a bit of a double life."

I want to say that someday it will be different. But this position is so new to me, and with Mother's premonitions, I do not want him thinking we may have a life together. I do not ask if he sees a future for us. I cannot think of it either. For if I do, I know my heart will break if I am unable to fulfill his desire. There are too many things that could go wrong for us. I could be killed in battle. He may be ended in the same way.

⋄⟐⋄

IN A MONTH'S TIME, WE HAVE learned all we can about the kobold and Sonia. The kobold have not ever exhibited magickal powers until the most recent attack. And we do not know whether they are spelled or have been bred with a magickal being. Sonia's history includes many incidences of violence against the vampires, and until the solstice, everyone thought she lay sealed in a crypt, kept in a coma by a sleeping spell, for her crimes.

All is quiet on both fronts. No evidence of kobold activity can be found. The witches and vampires seem to have gone underground. If it were not for the headway I make in having new advisors elected to the council, Kane naming new generals, learning systems and processes of operations, and becoming an expert on all military conflicts of Middle Earth, ever, I would be on edge every second, waiting for Mother's prophecy to come to fruition.

The kobold council convenes for Imbolc, with representatives arriving two days before. We meet on the eve of the holiday and learn all that others have gleaned from their archives. No information brings us any closer to where the magick kobold came from or how they may be stopped.

I fear my time may be running out on deciding who to name as successor. I cannot keep Quinn and Holden here indefinitely, especially if they hold no title. *And if they knew why I entertained them with rides and sport, then would they want to stay?* I commit to deciding soon.

The night of February second, we celebrate Imbolc with bonfires. From the castle roof, I look out over Capitolshire and watch all the fae light their fires, appearing as candles dotting the land. I scan the line of those gathered and pray our determination and might may help us be victorious over what may sit on the horizon. I dread the months to come, knowing the beasts of Lower Earth lie in wait and those above sit on the brink of war. All I can hope is that we are ready to do what is needed to keep balance.

"Queen." Grant's voice pulls me from my thoughts. "Aleem wishes to see you. There is news from Upper Earth."

My heart races as I take to the air, following him to Aleem's cabin. Inside, Aleem sits in his study with representatives from the kingdom of Lindleton. I take a seat beside the hunched Ring Keeper. He explains a disturbance has been detected, an incident with a great amount of magick being used, off the coast of Sardinia.

"Near Sonia's castle?" I inquire.

"Indeed, and there is more—evidence of a seraph."

"An angel?"

Aleem leans forward. "The signature is unmistakable. It was a powerful angel."

"An archangel? Is there history of angels interfering in witch affairs?" I stand and pace behind my chair. For an angel to intervene, it must be of utmost importance.

The First Judge hands Aleem a text. He opens it and holds it out to me. In the eighteen hundreds, an angel with the same signature saved a settlement of vampires from a witch attack, and there are several other entries of the same angel disrupting witch attacks on vampires.

"The angel is protecting the vampires, ensuring peace, balance of power?" I look at Aleem.

"It would seem."

"Or preventing a war between the witches and vampires that would not end well for humans." The First Judge takes the book.

"Is that all?"

"The fae in Lindleton will be sending spies to gain more information." Aleem props himself on his cane.

"Good. Keep me informed, and happy Imbolc to you all."

<hr>

THE LINDLETON SPIES FIND no more information on what happened the night of Imbolc. It remains a mystery as to what the witches were doing and why an angel stepped in. The incident, and a growing hunch that evil lurks on the horizon, fuel my commitment to choose a successor. I ask Father's council and watch both Quinn and Holden over the next days, and by week's end, I make a choice. After the noon meal, I invite Holden to walk with me in the garden.

As we enter the hedge maze, he clears his throat. "This must be serious. We have not been alone in over a month. Are you sending me away? I know you have not asked me here to profess your love. I see the way you look at Quinn."

I cannot stifle my laugh fast enough and cuff my hand to my mouth. "You think I am in love with Quinn?"

"Why, yes. I mean, you have not asked to talk to me alone in weeks."

"But neither have I asked Quinn."

"Oh." He latches his hands together behind his back.

I stop and turn to face him. I hate what I have to say and bite my lip.

Before I realize what is happening, he wraps his arms around me and presses his mouth to mine.

Shoving him away, I jump back. "What are you doing?"

"I thought you meant that you liked me."

"And you favor me?"

"Is it not obvious? And how could anyone not? You are strong, beautiful, smart. I thought my feelings were apparent."

"I am sorry if you misjudged. I believe my heart is spoken for."

"Whoever he is, you have hidden it well."

Motioning us to continue on our path, I admit wanting to talk about the successor to my throne. He guesses from my tone it is not favorable for him, and he hangs his head as my heart breaks. My attachment to him feels stronger than I guessed.

I clasp his hand. "I know you probably will not want to stay, but I like having you here, helping me, as a friend. I hope that you will. I am sure there are many fae here who would want to be your wife."

He lays his palm atop my hand. "I do not care to have a wife as much as I care to have purpose. This quest to stop the kobold and whatever evil the witches are brewing gives me that. I want to stay and fight with you."

"It is settled." Smiling, I squeeze his hand. "You shall be my Fae at Arms. We will fight the kobold together."

Dropping my hand, he continues to the end of the hedge. "I am starting to believe the kobold are just a myth."

"They are very real, believe me."

"Sorry. I know you lost your brothers to them. I am just so jealous that you have fought them twice, and I have never seen one. Why do they always come here?"

"Father thinks it is because this is the original birth-place of the faeries, the first kingdom of fae." I wonder if I should trust him with my secret, but if he is determined to fight alongside me, he should know what he is getting into. "You should know that my mother saw the kobold kill my brothers and me. I escaped the first time, but she still sees my death at the hands of a kobold."

"She is a seer?"

"Yes. This is not information I share with many."

"Your secret is safe with me. Maybe they are drawn to you for some reason. Not to the kingdom, but to you. Could you be the one?"

My face warms and breath catches in my lungs. *How had he been so quick to put those two together?*

He grabs my arms. "You *are* the one. That is why you kept glossing over that passage. Every time we brought it up, you dismissed it."

"It is only a premonition by a woman who may be crazy."

Rubbing his hands, he smiles. "This is even better than I thought. My brothers will be so jealous. My name will go down in fae history as the soldier who fought beside the great Queen Titania, ender of all evil."

I am frozen, stunned by his glee at finding he is bound for certain death. "You are mad!"

"Do you want my help or not?"

"Yes! I do. But I have just told you we face almost certain death."

He bows low and raises his head. "No matter. I shall be your Fae at Arms, and you, my queen. I must go write to my family at once."

His cadence borders on a skip as he walks away. I had not thought that would go so well, but it seems we have a mutual interest, and I am pleased. Save the incident of the kiss, I pat myself on the back for my diplomacy skills. I pray Quinn has not decided I favor him as a love interest as well because he needs to be my next conversation.

I stroll from the garden to the orchard wondering how to start the conversation. I do not want to elicit Holden's reaction. Thinking it best to start out with telling him I have been thinking of choosing a successor, I wind back to the courtyard. Father and Kane sit near the fountain, foreheads close, speaking. Approaching them, I inquire as to the topic of conversation.

Father clears his throat and looks at me. "Holden looked very happy just now. Have you decided on a successor?"

"I have."

"And you chose Holden? I thought you were favoring Quinn?"

"I am not divulging details of my talks with either of them until there is an acceptance. That is all I can say." I hate being secretive with Father but have not begun to trust him again.

Bidding them farewell, I wind through the castle to locate Quinn. I find him in the study in discussion with one of the new advisors and smile. He will be a good successor should something happen to me. I pray he thinks so as well. I let him finish the conversation and ask him to walk with me to the meadow.

He has been researching seraph activity surrounding Sonia's movements. "I just want to understand why this witch would gorge herself on souls of fallen witches."

"She has a history of hating the vampires. It is not a stretch to think she plans to try and exterminate them again."

"But why? They live in peace now. The Vampire Chancellor has made sure vampires do not harm humans, for the most part."

"You know the histories. The witches and vampires have been enemies since the beginning. Witches believe vampires to be soulless creatures, part demon. Not all have adopted the philosophy that all beings are equal. We should be worried about Sonia as well. If she goes after the vampires, who will be next? The werewolves? Elves? Pixies? Us?"

"But like witches, we are from The Creator, actually purer forms of The Creator."

"I am sure we will know more in the coming months. The spies in Lindleton work day and night to find any clue of what the witches could be doing. I have another matter to discuss if we could. I wish to name a successor and would like you to be that fae." Stopping, I spin to face him.

"A successor? Me?" His eyes grow wide.

"Yes, you are intelligent, smart, and obviously care about this realm. You have royal blood, the blood of my Father's family, my family, in your veins."

"So, I would be King when you die."

"If I die before naming another successor."

"What if you marry and have children? What then?"

"I do not have any plans to marry, and I may not marry one who would want to be King. If I live to marry and have children, when they are old enough, we can revisit the line of succession."

"Do you not plan on surviving?"

"We do not know what will happen. But I will fight with my army."

"A ruler does not have to go to battle. That is what armies are for." He inches closer.

Sensing the intense emotion flowing from him, I take a step back. "That is not the type of leader I am."

"But you are going to ask me not to fight?"

"Yes."

"May I think about this for a bit?" He steps back and motions ahead of us. "Walk with me?"

After moments of silence, he requests we get approval from the advisors and generals, a vote to approve the succession so any transition would be smooth. I realize this is a good idea and agree to write out my reasons for believing he will make a good ruler of Aubren in my stead.

Stopping, he turns in front of me. "And what of Holden? Is that why we were here? So you could choose a successor?"

"That and I needed the help. I am sorry if you do not wish to be here. Both of you have been great assistance and good company."

"I did want to be here, I still do. I assume Holden is leaving because he was not chosen."

"No, actually he—"

A page lands in front of us. "Queen Titania, Aleem says to come at once."

Jumping into the air, we follow the messenger to Aleem's cabin. The door is open, and I rush inside, thinking something has happened to the Ring Keeper. Weaving through the rooms, I find him in a back chamber surrounded by the judges. Seeing me enter, one waves me into an adjoining room, explaining they have detected witch activity in northern Sardinia and are tracking it back to the Italian coast.

"Do we know who it is or what is going on?"

"They are cloaking, so we are only getting bits and no images. Aleem wants to see if the seraph will return."

"What will that mean if it does?"

"We do not know. We just have to keep watching."

I pace the chamber until the judges shoo me to the garden to wait. It is an hour before they call me back into the cabin for a report. The seraph does show again, but they only get a signature, no images, and have no idea what happened.

"There is no use spending all this energy for getting nothing." I bring my hands to my hips.

"But we cannot be in the dark. Sooner or later we will get something that will tell us what Sonia's mission is and why she is trying to stop the curse from being broken," Aleem says.

"She is harboring the souls from Sheol. What happens to all those souls if they break the curse?"

"Anything we could guess would be just that: theory." He puts his chin on his cane.

———◦◦◦◦◦———

AT DINNER, I ENLIST FATHER AND Kane to aid me in convincing the advisors to elect Quinn as my successor. They agree to promote him. Looking around the table at Quinn, Holden, Kane, Father, Mother, and Alfreda, I realize that I indeed am doing a good job. Yes, there may be unknowns, the kobold, Sonia, but I have a good team assembled.

After the meal, I play my harp for Father and Mother, as has been our tradition. Anxious to be with Foster, I ask if one tune could be enough for tonight.

Father cuts his eyes to me. "Seeing Foster, are we?"

"I am tired. It has been a long day of high emotion."

"Yes, that kiss Holden planted on you has the whole castle talking. And with the way he almost skipped away from you. There were many rumors flying about as to an engagement announcement."

"And you are just telling me now?" My stomach lurches as I realize Foster must have heard as well.

"I assumed you heard."

Darn Grant, I think. I jump into the air and speed to my chamber. Grant stands in front of my door and swings it open as I approach.

"Why did you not tell me someone saw Holden kiss me?"

"I thought Nicholas had."

"Ahhhg!" Entering my study, I slam the door behind me.

Something must be done right away to stop the rumors. Foster was to go to his family's home for dinner. Perhaps he did not hear. But even if he had, I can explain. He will understand. I look at the clock—nine pm. I will see him in one hour. Tearing a piece of parchment from the scroll, I dip a quill in ink. *Formal announcement*, I write at the top. I outline that, because of Holden's service in researching and commitment to the cause of fighting the kobold, I have offered him a Fae at Arms position. Further, I announce my intent to name Quinn my successor upon approval of the advisors. Marching to the grand hall, I nail the announcement into the stone outside and instruct everyone I pass to spread the word—which, at this hour, amounts to a total of three fae. I stomp back to my room. Queen Titania is not marrying Prince Holden.

I try to relax. A bath does little to calm my nerves, and I sit on a windowsill to wait for Foster. I look at the sky and the clock a hundred times. Ten passes, ten-oh-five, ten-ten, ten-fifteen… He has never been late. *What if something happened with his family? What if he is hurt?* Speeding into the hall, I am halfway to the exit before Grant catches me.

"Where do you think you are going?"

"To find Foster. He is never late. I am afraid something is wrong."

"Go back." He points to my door. "I will go check."

Hand to my hip, I obey. I circle my room, counting my crosses to pass the time. Grant returns, telling me that

Foster is fine and with the other soldiers. My brain explodes. *What does that mean?*

"So, is he coming?"

"I do not think so, Highness."

"Why are you calling me Highness? You never call me that."

I want to yell at Grant, tell him to bring Foster to me at once, but that is not the way you treat friends. Jogging to my study, I pen a note.

Foster, I had hoped to see you tonight. I would still like to if you can come.

I do not know how to end the message and write an X, followed by *Titania.*

Handing the folded page to Grant, I ask that he wait for a reply.

Wondering what could be wrong, I slump into my chair. *If he had heard of the kiss, he would know I do not care for Holden, right?* Foster and I have spent so much time together over the past month. And he said last night he would come again tonight. *Why would he not?* The minutes on the clock tick by, and the knots in my stomach turn my insides to stabbing knives.

Grant enters the study. "He asks if his presence is required. If this is a direct order from his Queen."

"What? What is he talking about? Is there a letter from him?"

"No, that is what he told me to ask you."

I raise my chin. "Well, tell him yes then."

"Are you sure?"

"Either that, or I will go there myself and demand he speak to me. Which do you prefer?"

Huffing, he stomps out the door. I cross to the window and wait, wondering why Foster does not want to see me. *Have I done something to make him angry? He would know about the succession announcement and that I would never kiss another, right?* We had never talked about it, but I assumed we were a couple. Hearing a knock, I call for the person to enter.

Foster inches the door open. "You sent for me?"

Jumping from my chair, I cross to him. "Why did you not come? You said you would. If you heard of the kiss with Holden, that was not me. I would never—"

"It is not that. I know you do not favor him."

"Then why?" I tug at his hand.

"Please, just let me go. I am tired, and I need time to think."

"Think about what?"

"Please?" His eyes grow wide.

Tears fill mine. "Has something changed? Do you not care for me? I thought? You could at least send word you were tired. That is understandable."

He closes the door behind him. "You did not tell me you had made a decision about the succession."

"You knew I needed to."

"What is the rush?"

"I cannot just keep Quinn and Holden here indefinitely without them knowing my intent. Someone must be named."

"It has been three years since the last major kobold attack. It could be three more years."

"We do not know that. They could attack at any time with stronger forces and more magickal powers."

"I am not sure that I can be with you."

My stomach lurches and new tears form. "Why?"

He raises his chin. "This is why I did not want to see you. I need time to think."

I look into his eyes. "What is there to think about? Naming a successor is a good thing. And when the kobold come, we will fight them together, just like before."

"You say this like you know it is inevitable. You make plans for your death."

"You knew this. It is not fun to think about, but I must. What has changed?" My side ticks and breath catches in my lungs. *Has he found another?* I clutch his hands. "Do you not favor me anymore?"

"No, I just do not know if I can be with you. It is too hard."

Dropping his fingers, I take a step back. "How? What do you need from me? What has changed since yesterday?"

"When I heard of the succession announcement, it became too real. You will stand against the kobold when they come, and you may die."

"We will fight them together. We can win."

"I will not fight with you."

My heart skips a beat. *He does not want to be with me.* There are too many strings, hoops, *problems* with being the friend of a queen. I ball my fists and take a step back. "If you do not care for me anymore, then you should go."

He grasps my hands. "I could not watch you battle Ethan, Titania. I am falling in love with you. The thought of losing you hurts too much."

My heart thuds in my chest. *He loves me.* Water fills my eyes. "I believe I love you as well. I would do anything for you. You know that. I will not, I *cannot*, lose you."

Releasing me, he takes a step back. "Except you would march to your death."

"That is my job. You are a soldier as well, have pledged your life to defending this kingdom, the realm."

"But you do not have to fight. You could send others, but you will not." Tears fill his eyes.

I think about Mother's premonition and Father's belief that I am the one. It is not fair that I have not told Foster. The tale predicts the one who will defeat evil. A how is not given, nor is a promise the one will not be consumed in the process. But something in my gut says I can figure it out. Foster speaks true, though. I will face whatever monsters come for us. My stomach turns, thinking I could be leading him to harm as well.

Water streams down my cheeks. "If it were up to me, I would be with you every minute of every day. And once the succession is approved, I believe we can be as any other couple. But it would break my heart to cause you pain. So, for as much as I crave your friendship, your love, I want you to be happy. I will respect whatever decision you need to make."

Taking a step back, he nods. "Thank you."

I want to fall at his feet, beg him not to go. My chest tightens as he backs to the door, clicking it open and sliding through the space. My lungs seize, and it feels as if the air has been vacuumed from the room with his departure. My knees collapse, and I catch myself with my palms against the cold stone floor. Garrison, Bryce, Rigel, Mother, Father, and now Foster. *Am I destined to walk this realm alone?* Perhaps the one has been named such for a reason. Maybe the one fae must bear the burden companionless.

Tears dot the rock floor below me. Mother saw my death at the hand of a kobold. I am cursed. Foster speaks true. *No one should have to share in my misfortune.* I raise my head. It is better this way. I will surround myself with those I can endure the loss of. But thinking of my guards, Grant, Adam, Nicholas, Timothy, even Holden, my stomach turns at the notion of endangering their lives.

The door creaks open, and Grant's face appears above me. "Queen? Are you…?"

"I am fine." Getting my feet under me, I stand. I snatch my shawl from the chair. "I will turn in for the night."

Brushing past him, I exit the study and enter my room. I latch the door and slide to the floor, my back to the soft wood. Above me, my crosses sway in the breeze, and I am reminded anew of all I have lost. Hugging my legs to me, I pray Foster will not be another. This will pass. Quinn will be named successor, we will vanquish the kobold and whatever evil awaits, and Foster will return. I had known a relationship with anyone other than a royal would be complicated. I rock back and forth, counting my crystals, holding on to the one hope I have.

Foster loves me.

Chapter 19

The next morning, I wake to find a note beside me on the stone.

Titania, I hope you understand that I need time to sort out my path. - Foster

We had planned to spend the day on the coast, swimming. *How am I to pass the time with this void in my soul?* Crumpling the sheet, I throw it across the room. I gather my shawl and cross to the dressing table. My hair a mess and face looking like death, I study my crown. A queen does not wallow, certainly not because of a boy. Reconstructing my hair into a bun, I dress in riding clothes and head to the courtyard for breakfast. Quinn, Holden, Father, Mother, and Alfreda sit at the table, sipping orange juice. Kissing Mother and Father, I take my seat.

After the meal, I walk Mother through the garden and orchard, but the slow pace and silence gives me too much time to think. Two weekend guards trail me, and when I drop Mother off, I request they take a flight with me. Finishing a circle to the western border and back, I take to the meadow, launching arrows at haybale targets. I break for lunch and find Father with Kane in the courtyard. Their talk of hunting itches my nerves, so I make for the soldiers' yard for fighting practice with my guards.

I find it exactly as I had hoped, empty for the weekend. I spar against one guard then the next. The two switch out for the others on the weekend team as they tire. These guards hold back, do not give it their all, and let me win each match. Still, I push them because any training increases my strength. As all my challengers grow weary, I request that a page find Grant and Adam, knowing they will not rein in their strength.

We battle long into the evening, missing the supper meal. My muscles sear, and with the dropping temperature and energy depletion, my body begins to tremble. Still, I power through, requesting that they come at me one after another.

"Queen, it is late, and I have my family to attend to." Adam wipes the sweat from his brow.

Eyeing Grant, I catch sight of Alfreda behind him. *Sent to reel me in, I guess.* Huffing, I lower my sword. "Fine. I will see you Monday."

In the back of my mind, I figure I may be able to use Nicholas and Timothy tomorrow. As Grant and Adam lumber from the yard, Alfreda approaches.

"What are you doing? It is late, and you are covered in mud. They said you have been out here since midday."

"Yes, well, those kobold are not going to dagger themselves, are they?" I slam my sword into the dirt. I head towards my room, telling Alfreda to have dinner brought to me.

Bathing, I dress in my favorite nightwear and robe and eat my venison and broth-dipped bread while I read a text on the history of the rings. Our kingdom contains the two oldest rings, one here in Capitolshire, the Daintree Ring, and one to the south, the Nariel Ring. Hilbron to our west keeps two rings, while Bedham, to the north, only one. I study the diagrams. I know the rings connect us to Upper Earth and Lower Earth and make a note to find history of fae traveling to Lower Earth.

The portal with Lower Earth allows not only freed witch souls to find peace in Heaven but also other spirits to pass through our realm. Dark spirits do not linger in Middle Earth. Either they are consumed by Lower Earth, or they ascend to the above. The dark spirits target the beings of Upper Earth, for fae souls, being of The Creator, cannot be tarnished by evil. Save in the rare case such as Gunther. My mind wanders to whether he believed himself to be doing the just thing by attempting to end my reign. The powerful, evil spirit Lucifer holds free reign in any realm, as do the angels, but angels seldom cross into Middle Earth and even less often to Lower Earth. Their charge lies with the humans.

Weaker evil spirit sometimes attempt to pass to Upper Earth, but those are rare and are stopped by closing the rings, forcing them back into Lower Earth. I wonder if a lesser evil spirit aids the kobold and add to have both keepers check for such signatures to my list. Although the kobold attack occurred two months ago, their imprint may remain.

—◦◦◦—

319

I WAKE WITH LIGHT STREAMING IN through my windows, my head resting on the book. Seeing Foster's crumpled note on the floor, I snatch it up and toss it into the hearth. Striking the stone with a metal rod, I alight the balled sheet. I dread the day, wish it could be skipped. The Ring Keeper nor my advisors favor working on weekends. *Drat them.* I have already taxed Grant and Adam, so I plan to call on Timothy and Nicholas after exhausting the other soldiers.

Looking up at my crosses, I remember my counting routine and realize the itch of my nerves feels the same. My psyche craves respite from all that ails it. Chest tightening, I exhale. A queen cannot be besieged by anxiety fits. The memory of my last near case causes me to think of Foster and how he thought my episodes to be triggered when I did not feel in control. Ironic that he be the one I wish to sway to my way of thinking.

I dress and grab the text and my list. I can at least pen notes to the Ring Keepers, Regin and Aleem, to ask them to search for spirit signatures. Plus, I want to find instances of fae crossing into Lower Earth. Perhaps the librarian will help with that. Quinn also seems to be knowledgeable, and I think I may ask him and Holden to help in this task as well. They at least appear to be eager to learn all about the kobold that we can. Like me, they do not adhere to the weekend policies of relaxing with family. Because, like me, they remain partnerless.

These thoughts swirl in my head as I make my way to the courtyard for breakfast. *Have I kept Quinn and Holden from finding love?* If I am guilty of this, I hope my decision of the succession and Fae of Arms appointment frees them to such pursuits. Both would be catches for any fae. I think to tell Alfreda to plan more social gatherings in the coming weeks.

We eat on the patio, and I walk with Mother and Father through the garden and orchard.

Afterwards, I find Quinn in the library and share my latest research quest with him. We gather texts that may be of use and begin searching the pages for instances of evil spirits in Middle Earth. Although curious about fae travelling to Lower Earth, I keep this topic to myself. Quinn favors conservative courses with most things, I have noticed, and I do not want him clued into any plans that may be forming in my brain.

I last in this pursuit till midday when I can sit no more. Gathering two guards, I fly south into the interior of Aubren, over the dry desert land. I steer clear of the coast and circle back west to the castle where I snack on sausage and cheese and make for the soldiers' yard. Two hours in, I call for Nicholas and Timothy. More aware of their time and sacrifice, I break at dusk. I sup with Mother, Father, Quinn, Holden, Kane, and Alfreda, shoring up our arguments for the advisors the next day.

When I meet Mother and Father in their study, Father inquires about my extra training. I lie and tell him I have had a gut feeling about an impending attack. He lifts an eyebrow and shifts his gaze to Mother, saying she has mentioned nothing. Still, he moves on, discussing Quinn's succession and Holden's position. I tell Father of my plan to host more social gatherings for them, and he commends the idea.

"It will be good for you to socialize as well. You do not have much opportunity to meet fae your own age. I think inviting some officers would be a good idea. And perhaps families of the new representatives."

I shake my head. "You know I do not favor such gatherings, but I will make sure Alfreda invites many different fae for these events. I want Quinn and Holden to be happy here."

"And what of your happiness? I am surprised not to see Foster this weekend."

Thinking of an excuse, I say he needed to help his father on the farm. I hate that Father uttered Foster's name. I had been doing so well all day. I roll the harp to my side and play a tune for my parents then wish them goodnight. Circling to the library, I find it empty and search for texts on Lower Earth. I fly to the top shelves and scan the titles. Wiping dust from a ragged volume, I open it to find a map of the underneath. I slide the tome in my jacket and wind to my chamber.

There, I pen notes for Aleem and Regin, and begin reading the texts. At some point, I fall asleep. Images of kobold, fae soldiers, witches, vampires, angels, and demons fill my dreams. I wake with a start when a huge dragon rises from a bubbling pit of lava and looms over me, inhaling then releasing a torrent of fire. Sweat beading on my face, I throw my blanket to the floor.

I rush to the window, thinking the dragon to be another premonition, but observe nothing amiss. Throwing on riding pants, I summon my guards, and we fly through the castle, the grounds, and then to Aleem's cabin and the nearby Daintree Ring. All is quiet. Still, the feeling remains, and I fly south, all the way to the Nariel Ring. I check Mt. Kosciuszko, and with no evidence of disturbance at either location, head back north to the castle.

Alighting at the front entrance, we are exhausted and starving. I leave the guards in the dining room and head to the kitchen for sustenance. Finding some sausage and cheeses in the cellar, I load them on a tray and add a couple of bread loaves to the top. I grab a canter of wine and return to find the guards warming by the fire. Circling back for chargers, I pile on five chalices.

I apologize for the midnight mission as we eat. Because they all know of my prior dream and Sonia gathering the souls, they do not begrudge me for the decision. With our energy restored, we head to the barracks to find guard replacements and make for my chamber. Inside, I wash and dress. My mind and body tingle with left over adrenaline, so I continue my search for Lower Earth visits by fae. The book consists of journal-like entries. Thus far, none tell of a fae entering Lower Earth. I scan the pages, reading of seraph, dark angels, and demons. The last entry starts with a date I recognize as the day before the kobold attack three years ago.

The record tells of the signature of a witch detected entering the lower Nariel portal and then exiting some hours later. There was no sighting of the being. Jumping into the air, I rush to the library to check the records for the upper portals. No witch signature passed through either of our upper portals that day. I examine records about travel for the days leading up to when we detected the witch's signature, but there were none reported. So, the witch must have entered through a different portal. Those records would be housed in each kingdom. I will have to weigh whether to ask for a search of each portal's entries.

"Preparing for today? I am nervous as well." Quinn's voice startles me.

"Yes." I slam the text shut. "Just making some notes."

I look at the window to see the first light of the day. Realizing I have not outlined Quinn's defense for the advisors, I set to that task. I write down his lineage, military training and record, knowledge of the realm, and budding familiarity with our kingdom. I hope it will be enough. Father and Kane will testify on Quinn's behalf as well. With their votes, I do not expect Quinn to be rejected.

Finished with my notes, I inquire if Quinn will join us for breakfast. He agrees, so we make our way to the courtyard. I assure him there is no reason for apprehension. Still, he echoes my sentiment of wishing the day to pass with ease and speed.

After the meal with Father and Kane, we join the advisors in one of the small halls. I outline my reasoning for wishing Quinn to be named successor and his qualifications. Father and Kane testify next, followed by Quinn.

The panel requests to speak with Quinn alone.

I pace the hall while Father and Kane sip wine brought from the kitchen. I do not understand how they can be so calm. At least worry about Quinn trumps my distress over what to do about Foster for the moment. *How can I convince him all will be well?*

Quinn exits the chamber, and the advisors relay that we should wait for a decision.

"Is this bad or good?" he asks.

"It is a new council, so I have no way of knowing. Bran, Jesper, and Terrence served Father as well, so I would guess they will take his blessing as assurance."

"And what if there is a stalemate?"

"Aleem, the Daintree Ring Keeper would break the tie, I think."

Bran slips through the door and ushers us inside. The council asks for a break for lunch and then the afternoon to deliberate. Thinking this more than fair, I order the kitchen to bring a meal, and we take to the courtyard for ours. Afterwards, Quinn asks to be excused for fencing practice, and I head to my chamber for a change in outfit then make my way towards the meadow.

As we pass the soldiers' yard, I see Foster's battalion gathering around their captain. I slow to scan the faces. Not finding him, I stop and repeat my search, looking at each eating table, to the well, and to the pile of weapons. *Why is he not there?*

"Queen, come away. Everyone is staring at you." Grant pulls at my arm.

Realizing he is right, I flash a smile, wave, and ask the soldiers to continue their meeting. My stomach lurches as we skirt the garden to the meadow. As soon as we are out of earshot of those few walking the grounds, I ask Grant to join me.

"I need you to find out where Foster is. Why he is not with his battalion," I whisper to him.

"He asked to be reassigned to the southern keep."

I fight the bile rising in my throat. Still, my mind refuses to accept what I know to be true: Foster does not want to be with me. "How do you know this? And why would he?"

"Kane briefed me this morning."

"Kane, of course." Clutching my middle, I pace away. "What time? Did you speak with Foster before he left?"

"Queen, you should let him go."

"Did you talk to him?"

"No, but he left a note."

I stop and spin to face Grant. "Where is it? Give it to me now."

Pulling my arm, he drags me farther from Adam. "It was not for you. What are you planning with the kobold?"

"What do you mean? There is no way to plan. We have no idea when they are coming, how many of them there are, or what powers they will have."

"He is convinced you have some suicidal, save-the-realm strategy."

"He is crazy. I told him I will do what all monarchs do, fight with their soldiers. My father has fought in every battle of his reign. Foster wanted me to sit in the castle, protected, while all of you risked your lives. That simply cannot be. That is why I am naming Quinn successor. Foster said he cannot bear the thought of me in battle. Which I do not understand because he knew this all along. I mean, we fought the kobold together before so—"

"Okay, I get the picture. I do not need the whole story." Grant rubs his beard.

He cuts his eyes to Adam and back to me. "If it were my love, I would want her safe as well."

Rolling my eyes, I fight tears. "I know. Why do you think I am worried that he has requested to go to the south keep?"

"Aye, you love him as well. That is why you are in such a state and forcing us to push you to your limits."

I square my shoulders. "I am not in a state. Foster has made his choice. Now, come shoot arrows with me."

"I will not. Nor will any of your other guards. We are not your distraction. Go find another for that."

"Fine."

I snatch up my bow and dump my arrows on the grass. One by one, I shoot them at the target. Breathing in and out, I let my grief settle in.

Foster does not wish to be near me. He has sent himself as far away from me as he can get. Part of me wonders if he chose Nariel to punish me, show me how it feels to have the one you love in harm's way. But he does not know how strong I am. I have lived with this fear all my life. It is a way of life for royals and soldiers. If he decides he is happy without me, I will let him go.

Reaching for another arrow, I find the space empty. I detect motion and rub my water-filled eyes to find Grant approaching.

"Feel better, Highness?"

"Yes, thank you. Is there news?"

"The advisors wish to see you."

Heading to my chamber, I splash my face with cold water and change to a dress.

Quinn, Kane, and Father wait outside the hall. I enter the room and sit at the head of the table. As First Advisor,

Bran leads with their appreciation for the thought I have put into choosing a successor. I hold my breath, waiting for the *but*.

Bran rises, circles to the other end of the table, and faces me. "We feel we need assurance that you think this man to be the most qualified, honorable, and even loved for the position of monarch of this realm. Your people need to know that in your heart you believe there is no other. To that end, we ask that you marry Quinn, make him King, and only then will we accept him as successor to your throne."

My heart thuds in my chest. *How dare they?* Looking at my fingers, I tap them on the soft wood of the table-top. Of course, royals marry for diplomacy all the time. Father and Kane wanted me to. I have no idea whether Quinn would want this, but I certainly do not. If there is one thing my reign will be known for it will be breaking the mold, staying true to my soul. *But how to get around their decision?*

"Perhaps there is another you wish to marry that may serve as successor?" Bran raises an eyebrow.

Rising, I take a deep breath. "I can assure you, one-hundred percent, that I believe in my soul Quinn is the best person to succeed me at this time, but I do not wish to marry him. I am but a month older than sixteen and just beginning to know my heart."

Bran raises his chin. "But that is our requirement."

"May I have the night to think about this? And can you swear to me this decision will not leave this room?"

"I believe that is fair." Bran looks at his colleagues, who nod.

I dip my chin to each gathered. "Thank you, gentlemen, for your time and dedication to this kingdom. I will have your answer in the morning."

Back straight, I exit the chamber and pull the door to, glad we chose the small hall for the meeting because no peepholes line the walls. Father and Kane stand, and a wide-eyed Quinn holds my gaze. I ask him to walk with me to the orchard, and he matches my step as I exit the passageway. Mind spinning with ways to get around their request, I wait until he and I are past the orchard in the wood before stopping.

"I am guessing it is not good news?" Quinn asks.

I stop and face him. "They want us to marry if you are to be named successor."

Quinn's face turns five shades of red. He looks down at his feet. "I guess that would be the traditional path."

I do not want him thinking I find him ugly or ill-mannered and do not know how to put my thoughts into words. "My Father suggested it before as well."

"But you must not want that."

"I do not know who I wish to marry yet."

"But I am guessing it is not me or Holden. Otherwise, we would not be in this situation."

"I am sorry. This is the worst scenario. I would never want to hurt you. I like you, even love you, as family, but I do not know that I could love you as I should. Are you greatly offended?" I cover my cheeks as I feel them warm.

Quinn wraps his hands around my wrists and pulls down gently. "I am not offended. I went into the army because I did not want to follow a traditional path either. I love you as a cousin, nay, even a sister, and would do anything for you and this family. If you wish me to be your successor and wish me to marry you to achieve that goal, I will."

"But do you want that? To be married to me?"

His silence tells all I need to know.

"I do not either. I want us to both to be free to find happiness to the full extent we can. Being royal weighs heavily enough without giving up the hope of finding true love."

We walk through the woods, brainstorming ideas, and by the time we circle back to the castle, we have one I pray will be acceptable to the advisors. He will undergo the first two parts of the trials as I did against Ethan, but Quinn will be tested on how many questions he answers and tasks he performs correctly with a score of eighty percent being a win in each category. At dinner, I catch Father and Kane exchanging glances and wiggling in their seats, likely wondering what the advisors have decided. Still, I will not announce their decision until after I have made my plea.

I go to my parents' chamber and play the harp for them. Father asks about the decision, and I tell him they will continue discussion on the 'morrow—which in most ways is true. In my chamber, I soak in a hot bath, thinking of all that has passed this day. Foster's admission to Grant, and Grant's obvious concern over my plans, could be a problem. He cares for me too much. I made a mistake in befriending him. I need comrades who will put the mission above all.

Holden, I think. He kissed me but seemed even happier to get a chance to stay and fight the kobold. I think of Ethan and the others who sided with Gunther. They were willing to do anything for this kingdom, even bring down their prior king's family. I begin to plan out what I will say to Holden and the others, what test I will present to know I can trust them to do what needs to be done.

Chapter 20

Father and Kane wait outside the advisors' hall as I approach with Quinn. Saying good morning, I enter the room. I stayed up half the night and hold my arguments etched on a page in my hand. To loosen the advisors up, I greet them and ask of their families and recent Imbolc holiday festivities. I hope to remind the men how important such things are and wonder if I might even resort to begging or tears. Neither would benefit me as Queen.

When Bran asks that we attend to the matter at hand, I lay out my wishes. I contend that the trials will reveal what Quinn knows of this kingdom and the realm and reveal his skillset and dedication to the post. I watch their faces, and seeing nods and smiles, pray it means I will be successful in swaying them. When I finish my arguments, Bran asks they be given time to discuss my proposal in private, and thanking them for their consideration, I exit.

I force a smile as Father and Kane jump from their chairs. "I believe they will be finished deliberating soon."

Praying that I am right, I pace the passageway. I would love to speak to Quinn, tell him it seemed they will decide our way, but do not want to risk tipping off Father or Kane as to what has passed. We wait twenty, thirty, fifty minutes before Bran exits the hall. Quinn and I follow Bran inside and stand in front of the council. He explains they will accept Quinn if he completes the trials successfully under the stipulation that they may interview his father and the officer Quinn served in the Bedham army.

He agrees to the terms. I release my breath, wanting to jump and clap for joy. My shoulders relax as I realize this means they will never require me to marry for this kingdom. Not that I would not, but the consequences need to be graver than my choice of successor being approved. I hold my hand out to Quinn, offering him congratulations, and he grips my hand as a warrior would. *Yes, my friend, we have been victorious.*

I thank the advisors for their deliberations. They give Quinn one day to study for the trials. We exit the room, and clicking the door shut, I fling my arms around him. He lifts me up and swirls me around.

When he sets me down, Father's face hangs inches from mine. "And what are we celebrating?"

"They will name Quinn my successor when he successfully finishes the knowledge and skills portion of the trials."

"And after an interview with Father and my captain." Quinn adds.

"How is this a success? He still needs to pass the tests, and the interviews could go badly."

I hook my arm in Father's. "I have chosen a smart and worthy replacement. He will be named. Do not fear."

Quinn and I study late into the night and the next day, focusing on Aubren's history. The day of the trial, I cannot bear to watch, fearing it will drive me mad to sit in the room waiting. I ask Holden to ride with me. We venture deep into the woods, and as we stray well out of earshot of my guards, I question him.

"What say you? In battle, would it be more important to defeat the enemy or protect the monarch?"

He narrows his eyes. "Do not be coy with me. You have already shared your secret. Do you speak of the prophecy and whether I would let you fulfill your destiny?"

I roll my eyes. "Yes, I do."

"Then I say I would defeat the enemy at all costs."

"You answer so quickly. Are you quite sure?"

"Why do you question me? I agreed to be your Fae at Arms for a reason."

I tell him of my concern for how Grant and Kane may side. He agrees that I should have a small battalion pledged to act as I instruct to defeat whatever evil we may face. I give him the list of names, describing how I selected them. He agrees to send word that we will meet the next night beside the bend in the river. I know Nicholas and Timothy will be on guard and pray they, too, will follow me in the endeavor.

As I have had the least interaction with Timothy, I single him out the next night, asking how he believes one should proceed when faced with the question of defeating the enemy or saving a monarch.

Timothy answers in a second. "Why do you ask this? I am pledged to follow your command. If you wish that I protect you, then I will do so. If you send me to fight, I will fight, no matter the foe. I promise, I am true to you."

"That is what I hoped, thank you."

I ask Nicholas in the same manner, and he answers as Timothy did.

After I play the harp for Mother and Father, I dress in riding clothes and wait till I hear no sound from the castle or surrounding grounds. Then, with Nicholas and Timothy at my side, take flight to the wood to meet up with Holden and those I instructed him to invite. I am surprised to see only three: Ethan, former General Raymond, and former Advisor Cedric. Still, six fae will be a good start. Perhaps they may enlist others.

———◆———

THE ADVISORS CONFIRM QUINN as my heir presumptive. Days, weeks, and a month pass. Holden and I create a battalion of ten who pledge to honor my direction in fighting the evil to come. It sounds biblical, even to me, and with no sign of the kobold or movement from Sonia, I start believing it will never come. Still, I stack my days and nights with fencing, dueling, and weapons training to prepare for what comes and to fill the void of Foster. I will not call him back. He must decide on his own. After weeks of no word from him, I guess he may have forgotten me, perhaps found another.

On weekends, I host party after party, entertaining different groups to make castle life as social as possible for Quinn, Holden, and all others who serve under me. Father, Kane, Grant, even Alfreda introduce soldier after soldier, sons of friends, to me, hoping that one will catch my eye, I am sure. Most seem nice, some look quite handsome, but none are Foster. *And how is one to really know someone just through dancing and party chat?* As my acquaintances tend to be aging men, the chances of finding love may be slim. But it does not bother me greatly, for as Foster surely knew, I am a fated girl. Still, weekend after weekend, I dream of spying his face in the crowded hall.

The Vernal Equinox comes, and there is still no word from Foster. But the holiday has always been my favorite, and Alfreda and I plan a weekend celebration, rivaling those Mother and Father hosted, with egg hunts for children, games, duels, jousting, dinner, and dancing. Part of me braces for the worst because the Spring Equinox tends to be the largest witch celebration of the year, but the night passes with only one odd occurrence: A witch's, or witch-like being's, signature traces across Mexico and disappears.

⋙⋘

APRIL BRINGS NEWS THAT VAMPIRES all over the globe are missing. Even those blood bonded to them have no success in finding their mates. Theories and guesses fly like birds around the fae community, but none can figure how the vampires vanished. Then there comes news that a witch of the trinity, the male they call Hunter, sought out the fae in Rotuga. Several soldiers spoke with him, and his request includes warriors to help capture Sonia. He reports that she is casting fallen witch spirits into the soulless vampires.

My mind reels at the implications of a powerful vampire body housing a witch spirit, especially one that may be controlled by Sonia, or worse yet, a servant of Lucifer. The monarchs of each kingdom and the High Council assemble in a conclave to discuss pros and cons of aiding the trinity. Five kingdoms vote to remain neutral as we have for centuries. I, along with King Herman of Bedham, King Luther of Hilbron, and the monarch of Willhelm, favor helping the trinity before Sonia gains enough power to move against us.

If she means to destroy ethereal beings, will she stop with soulless creatures like the vampires and werewolves? Or does she mean to dominate every descendant of The Creator? What could be more evil than controlling another being for your own gain? And what is her plan for these vampire-witch hybrids?

All the worries remain in my head along with the question of how and when the kobold will strike. I question Father every night as to whether Mother has spoken, but no words have crossed her lips since the last premonition in January. I walk and talk with Mother in the mornings, as is our habit, but she never utters a word. By day, I train, and at night, I read every history text of kobold and witches I can find.

Holden and Quinn travel to their kingdoms, borrowing volumes from the royal libraries.

—◈◈◈—

THE NEXT WEEK, I AM SPARRING with Holden when a page approaches, alerting me that Aleem requests my presence in haste. We speed through the air to his cabin, alighting on the front lawn. We are ushered inside where Aleem and the other judges use their looking glass to view the world above the ring's portal. A group of teens traipse through the Daintree forest not far from our Faerie Ring. I recognize their signatures. *Two male witches; a female witch, the one they call Camille I recognize from Italy; and two witch-vampire hybrids, one female and one male?*

I grab Holden's arm. "Are *two* of them hybrids? Are they two of the vampires witch souls have been cast into?"

Aleem shakes his head. "No, these are the witches of the trinity and their heralds. One of the trinity females is a vampire-witch hybrid. I am guessing this is why they have been hiding themselves."

"How did the fae of Rotuga not pick up on this?"

"I would think they cloak their true nature. The signature was quite faint when we first detected it."

I pace away from the group. "How is this possible? Why were these beings allowed to survive? Both vampire and witch law forbid it."

"They must have powerful beings protecting them."

"I want all the information we can get on these beings. Every time their signatures show up, I want to know, and I want every detail of where they are from, their lineage, everything."

All the judges, save Aleem, exit the room to scan for information.

Quinn, Holden, and I watch as the group of teens hike deeper into the jungle, closer and closer to our Daintree Ring. They speak of finding faeries to help displace Sonia from power over Michael's coven and the souls she has transported into the vampire bodies.

I cannot make sense of these witch-vampire hybrids. "The fae of Rotuga may not have realized they were witch-vampire hybrids but would have known they were vampires. I can smell them from here. Why would the Rotuga fae even approach a being who associates with vampires?"

Holden shrugs. "Maybe they were trying to scare him away. They did tranquillize him."

"So, the fae of Rotuga hid this information?"

"The High Council would not look favorably on fae conversing with those in league with vampires."

I huff. "Such an antiquated idea. Vampires have evolved into peaceful beings."

Aleem clears his throat. "For the most part."

The judges find no other traces of the witch-vampire hybrids. It is as if they materialized from nowhere.

Quinn, Holden, and I set to researching the history of Michael's coven, family trees, anything that would point to who created these beings. Aleem recounts finding witch-vampire hybrid signatures from time to time. All those he has found remain unaware they are part vampire or part witch.

"Like the being we spotted on the Vernal Equinox. The one who disappeared. Is that the same signature?"

Aleem compares them, and they do not represent the same being. The quandary plagues my brain. *How were these beings kept secret? And what are we to do with this information?* If we tell anyone, there will be no way we can aid their cause. Our laws forbid us to fraternize with soulless creatures, and I swear all present to secrecy.

That evening, I crawl into bed with a book on the legend of the trinity. It describes how they are to break the curse on the witch lines that damns their souls to purgatory. A sword holds the key, and I guess it to be the one I saw in the castle on the winter solstice. The text traces the location and holders of the sword through time. I fall asleep, head on a page. I dream of thousands of kobold streaming out of Mt. Kosciuszko. Foster stands in their path, and they trample him into the mud. I run towards them, dagger held high, my army behind me. Screaming, I slay every one my sword touches. I reach Foster's body and fall on my knees beside him. Holding his head, my tears splatter his face.

"This is your fault. All your fault. You could have stopped it." I look up to find Sonia hovering over me.

Sucking in a breath, I bolt upright and zip to the window. The night looks darker than I have ever experienced before. Glancing at my clock, I realize it is the witching hour. I know sleep will not come again now. I dress in my warmest riding pants and vest and, hopping to the windowsill, gather Grant and Adam, and we jump into the air, bound for southern Aubren. With a view clear of the Nariel ring and Mt. Kosciuszko, I note nothing amiss. We circle back north to the Daintree portal.

Looking through the opening, I see what, or who, drew me: Hunter.

"Is it the male witch of the trinity?" Grant asks.

"It is. I had a dream. A witch, I think it was Sonia, told me I could have stopped it. I believe she and the kobold are connected somehow. I am going to talk to him."

Grant catches my arm. "You could have stopped what? You are not supposed to just go through the portal. Remember the protocol? And the vote by the High Council? Did they not clearly state to stay out of the affairs of this trinity group?"

"What if my dream is right? What if we can help stop her? What if ending her means the destruction of the kobold? Plus, if the witches start a war with the vampires, many humans will die. That *is* our concern. What if Sonia means to come for us next?"

Not wanting to waste time arguing, I shoot through the exit and land in the soft grass.

Grant and Adam flank me.

Grant cusses. "Why do you never listen to me?"

The male witch spins to face me.

Raising my wings, I point my arrow at him. "Why are you here?"

Slower than honey on a cold day, he lifts his palms. "Don't shoot. I'm alone and mean you no harm."

"Why do you think you could do me harm?"

He straightens his back, and twisting his wrist over, lifts his sleeve to reveal the mark of archangel Michael. "I'm Hunter Michaels."

"I have heard of you." Approaching him, I circle the witch. "You contacted my brethren in Africa."

"Then you know what I need. Who are you? Will you aid us in defeating Sonia?"

"I am Queen Titania, ruler of Aubren, the Kingdom below this realm."

He pleads his case, explaining in length why they need faeries to help. I fight yawning in his face. *As if I had not plucked every thought from his brain the second I landed in this realm.* Faeries have no magick in Middle Earth, but in Upper Earth, we receive our full gifts: mind reading, magick, a life span of a thousand years, much like those of the being who stands before me. I lift my hand.

He stops and dips his chin. "Sorry, Queen. I just wish you to understand. We have to stop her."

"We have experienced the powers of the creatures of deep earth. They try to invade our realm also. Our primary goal is to keep the human realm safe from evil beings. This Sonia appears to be an evil soul that must be stopped."

"You'll help us then?"

I consider his offer. A couple hundred soldiers is a fraction of our full force. "I can only lend you two hundred soldiers, but there are other kingdoms that may give their support as well. I could go to them on your behalf. You must give me a day to speak with them. Come tomorrow, and I will have an answer for you."

"Can't you go now? My time is limited. We must move fast. Coming here took a lot of effort."

"I saw you in the forest earlier. You were right to come alone. We are forbidden to commune with soulless creatures. The hybrids pose a problem. If the other kingdoms know you are with them, they will not aid you."

"So, you believe Alena is soulless?"

Reading how deep his love is for the hybrid girl saddens me. *Is he, like Foster, doomed by her presence?* I envy the pair in that they are as close to equals as two beings can be. They fight together. Only she cannot help in his current endeavor. "There is not a question of beliefs. She is until she is made full witch."

He holds out his hand. "I will wait here until you return then."

Ignoring the gesture, I raise an eyebrow. "You will wait here a whole day?"

"Can I enter your realm, plea the case myself?"

"No, it shall not be."

Grant touches my arm, making himself visible to the male witch. "Titania, we should go."

"You *won't* take me, or *can't*?" Hunter's mind cries out in desperation.

"You would not be able to re-enter Earth's plane." I listen as his brain swims with questions. He thought you must eat of fae food to be trapped in our realm. I love human fae fiction.

His brow furrows. "I'll come tomorrow night. We can discuss our plan of attack."

I hear his mind. He has no idea if a return without being detected is possible. He wishes to shield his love, Alena, from knowing her nature hinders their cause. Being in his presence, reading the intensity of his emotion for this girl, overwhelms me. Grabbing Grant's and Adam's arms, I descend into our realm.

General Kane and two soldiers wait inside the portal. Kane folds his arms over his chest. "Perhaps we should review protocol on using the portal."

"I had a dream that Sonia and the kobold are connected. I believe we should aid this witch in defeating her."

"Are all your dreams premonitions now? I dreamed I had a queen who lived in the real world, not in a world of unicorns and rainbows. But that has not come true yet."

"How dare you speak to me this way. Remember who I am, who you are. If you wish to remain my general, you will respect my decisions."

His eyes drop. "Sorry, Highness. But it is the middle of the night, and Aleem is—"

A dark shadow passes over the portal. The air shifts, and ice crystals form around us. I place my finger over my lips, indicating they should be silent. Spinning to face the ring, I peer through the portal, but there is nothing but black. The smell of rot and mold invades my senses, and I back from the ring. Motioning for the others to stay behind me, I lift my bow. I drop straight to the ground. We land in Aleem's garden and run inside. He stands in front of the looking glass.

"What is that?" I bend over the glass, but all is black.

"A dark seraph."

"What is it doing? Why can we not see anything?"

"It must be very powerful."

"Hunter." I start to the door, intending to jet up to the ring and into the forest above.

Grant catches my arm. "What are you doing?"

"Hunter could be in danger."

Aleem taps the glass with his cane. "This dark seraph may be powerful, but Hunter is of Michael's line. His father is the leader of Michael's coven and of all the witches. He can defend himself."

"Against a dark seraph?"

"You should know more. Sonia is his grandmother."

"His grandmother?" I let my wings fall. "He wants to kill his grandmother?"

"She is pure evil. He knows it must be done."

Grant huffs. "Plus, he has to convince the witches to accept his love as well."

Kane looks between us. "What is he talking about?"

I nudge Grant's leg. "Nothing. He is in love with one of the other witches of the trinity. He will do anything to prevent her soul from being entombed in Sheol forever."

Aleem backs from the glass. "The dark seraph is blocking us from observing his interaction with Hunter. We will gather no further information. If you will excuse me, I will retire to my bed."

"Of course. Thank you for your service." I dip my chin to Aleem.

He hobbles from the room. I leave instructions that what has been witnessed tonight should not leave the confidence of those gathered. I will not have the fae of my kingdom worried about dark seraphs. Winding back to the castle, I find Holden exiting his room.

"You are up early."

"I could not sleep."

I cock my head to the exit. "Take a flight with me."

On our journey, I tell him everything from the night: my dream, conversation with Hunter, and of the dark seraph. I convey I wish to aid him and ask Holden's opinion. He is of the same mind, and we brainstorm a proposal for the generals. In addition, he offers to travel to Hilbron to ask his brother, King Luther, for troops. As we circle back, I think to ask Quinn to speak with King Herman of Bedham on our behalf. Four, perhaps five, hundred fae soldiers should be enough to subdue the witches of Sonia's coven. Even if they are as powerful, use of magick will weaken their bodies.

Witches are humans with the ability to gather energy and transform it, but they are still human. Their physical form cannot withstand the pressure of harnessing power for long. Fairies, however, are true beings of The Creator, not a race bred by an angel and human pairing. In the realm of Upper Earth, our powers become almost limitless. We will know their plan of action before they carry it out. We need not be in their realm long to defeat them. By the time we reach the far border and come round for our return to the castle, I am sure of my path.

I will lead an army against Sonia with Hunter.

Chapter 21

I WAIT UNDER THE RING THE NEXT evening for Hunter to show, but he never does. It is no use to guess why. We search for his signature and find no trace of him or the others in his party. As these beings seem to have a history of disappearing, I have faith they wait in hiding for a chance to stop Sonia.

This leaves me with the question of how Sonia and the kobold may be connected. She reaped souls from Lower Earth. *Can she also control the souls left there? Could her powers extend to that realm? Is she the one aiding the kobold? Is it her magick that flows through them?*

There is nothing that can be done but train and wait. And that we do through April.

As Beltane approaches, I dread the holiday. For on Beltane, the ruler of the land, being me, blesses the union of each fae couple who wish to be married. As a child, I loved the celebration, young fae coming from far and near, wearing their best suits and gowns to be joined in marriage. As younglings, my friends and I would sit and watch the couples stream into the castle grounds and pick which dresses we loved best.

The day arrives, and from dawn to dusk, I stand in the main courtyard and offer blessings and congratulations to each beaming couple. By nightfall, I am beat and drag myself to my room, shed my dress, and crawl under the covers. I let my tears flow freely. *Foster is not coming back. We will never be together again.*

Bang. Bang. Bang.

Thudding on my door wakes me. Sliding on my robe, I inch the door open. A page stands on the other side. Face white as a sheet, he explains I am to follow him to Aleem's cabin at once. Taking to the air, I arrive at the cabin in seconds. Foregoing a formal entry, I speed through the doorway and find Aleem in front of the looking glass.

"What is going on?"

"Strong signatures in Los Angeles."

"L.A.? Did the trinity lure Sonia there?"

"No, it is the boy." Aleem points to figure on a high-rise rooftop.

I recognize Hunter and the boy from Sonia's castle. I pick up the name. They call him Theron. Odd… A boy named "a hunter" battling a boy named Hunter. A girl is with them, Alena, I assume. But Alena and Theron bear similar signatures. They both carry the burden of being a witch-vampire hybrid. *So, Sonia entertained, even lauded, a hybrid in front of her own coven, hundreds of witches, and they did nothing?* The witches are scared of her. *If even the witches of her own coven fear her, how much more should we fear what she has become?*

We watch as Theron pulls a dagger from his coat. He hurls it at Alena, but Hunter deflects the path with his magick, and it leaves but a small scrape on the girl's cheek. The next second, Theron darts away, and Alena and Hunter run into the building. It is impossible to glean information from the encounter, and I wonder if I will drive myself mad by continuing to pay attention. *Perhaps this is why fae take a stand of neutrality.* It seems impossible to discern the good from the bad. Every character looks grey to me. Even Hunter's signature weaves strands of black therethrough.

Exhausted and perplexed, I leave them to investigate further.

The next day, I walk with Mother through the gardens and orchard, into the wood, like we used to. I reveal all our new information and describe my dream.

Spinning to face her, I clutch her hands. "Mother, I have to know. Am I ruining my life preparing for some prophecy that may never occur? My days are consumed by thoughts of danger lurking under each rock. Am I to know no happiness?"

For a second, I think I see it: a glimmer of understanding, reaction. The gloss of nothingness returns, and I drop her hands. Weaving her arm in mine, I continue on the path.

"It is okay, Mother. One day, this will all make sense." I pat her arm as tears fall from my cheeks.

Winding back to the castle, I contemplate if it will. *Would I have been happier to let another take this position? Should I marry Quinn and hand him my monarchy? Or Holden. He is nice enough and good looking. At some point, I should produce an heir.* My shoulders quiver. *Ugh!*

The things I must think of as a queen. Kane's words play through my memory.

I dreamed I had a queen who lived in the real world, not in a world of unicorns and rainbows. But that has not come true yet.

Well, your Queen is in the real world now, I think. No unicorns, no rainbows, no prince to love, not even a kobold to kill anywhere in sight.

Leaving Mother in her chamber, I wind to the library. I fill my arms with books on the dark angels and lug the tomes to my room. Bathing, I change into dress clothes and squat on my bed with the texts. Lists of dark, or fallen, angels are long with two being the most notable: Abaddon and Lucifer. Having heard stories of Lucifer and his envy of humans and their domain over Upper Earth, I research Abaddon. He was hailed as the fallen angel of death, and his name literally translates as "to destroy." He commands an army of winged creatures with long hair; human-like eyes, nose, and jaws; lion-like teeth; and a tail like that of a scorpion. Goosebumps rise on my skin, and I slam the book shut. Kobold. This describes the kobold. *Could this Abaddon be the evil one who controls the kobold?*

"Heavens." I flinch at the sound of Alfreda's voice.

Wrapping my blanket around me, I jump to my feet. "What is it?"

"Where have you been, child? It is nearly dusk, and I have been looking for you for an hour."

"I have been here since before noon." I look at the window, in awe of how much time I spent researching the dark angels.

"What are these?" She lifts a text from my bed.

"Research. I wanted to know more about the dark angels."

"I swear… And look at you. You are not even dressed for dinner. All this study of these evil beings is truly sending you into a state. You need to get out of this room."

"Alfreda." I snatch the book from her hand. "I have spent half a day of the past six months lounging after marrying over fifty couples yesterday. I think I deserve a day of rest."

"Yes, you deserve a day of rest to lie in the sun, not to have your nose in these histories. Most of which may not even be real. You are squandering your life away worrying so much." She rounds the bed, piling the texts in her arms and smoothing the quilts.

"What else am I supposed to do? This is my destiny, or fate, or birthright… Whatever you want to call it, it is mine."

Lowering the volumes to the table, she crosses to me. She cups her hand on my cheek. "I only say this because I love you. I want you to be happy."

I place my fingers atop hers. "I will be happy, one day. But for tonight, I wish to take my dinner in my room with a large glass of wine."

Her eyebrows shoot up, but she agrees. Within an hour, I have a loaf of bread, fruit, cheeses, and a cake of dense chocolate laid out on a blanket on my floor. I light candles to brighten the space and pretend I am on a picnic. It reminds me of the time Foster and I spent together in the days before finding the kobold. I push the memory away and, pouring a glass of wine, open the next book in my stack.

Hearing a rap on my door, I flit over to answer it. Holden stands outside with a decanter of wine in hand. "I intercepted this. Someone stole all of the books on dark angels from the library, and I am guessing that is you."

"Thank you." I take the wine from his hands. "Yes, guilty as charged."

He stands on his toes to peek over my shoulder. "A picnic? May I join you?"

Mouth open ready to answer yes, I ponder his request. It is not proper to be sure. But I crave someone to share my new information with, and I trust Holden above almost all.

"Are you going to answer?"

"Yes, come in. I believe they have provided enough food for an army." Looking between Nicholas and Timothy, I invite them in as well.

They rest their swords against the wall, and I tug more blankets from the bed and spread them on the stone. It is odd to see such large men sitting in the center of my room, but I decide I quite like it. Nicholas and Timothy chat and eat with us. They share all the castle gossip, entertaining me with the drama of who has fallen in love and who is in trouble with the head cook this week. Finishing their meals, they excuse themselves to reclaim their positions in the hall, leaving the door wide open.

Holden fills my wine glass. "So, are you going to tell me what you learned?"

I hop up and grab the text describing Abaddon and the kobold like creatures and lay it in front of him. Finding the page, I point to the passage of interest. Shoulder to shoulder, we read through the description of the beasts and how their poison is said to torment those not marked with the seal of God for five months.

"These sound more like warriors for God. It would scare non-believers into believing, or at least pretending to believe by getting the mark? I have never heard of anyone branding a forehead with a seal, have you?" He flips to the next page.

"No, but it is the closest we have come to an answer of who may be controlling or aiding the kobold."

"What if the kobold evolved, bred with something, or are organizing themselves?"

"Argh! I throw my hands up. I cannot think of this any longer. We keep running around with the same questions."

"Then, let us drink and dance and not think of any foe for the rest of the night."

"I love that idea." I down the last of my wine. "But we have no music. If only we had the devices of Upper Earth."

"But you are Queen. You may request music to be played for your enjoyment."

"But then there would be others here. I do not wish to be around others. I want to just *be*."

He rises and starts to hum a jig. He offers his hand, and I place mine in it. Piling the blankets in the center, we dance around them. The feel of his skin, his strong arms around my waist, the spinning and twirling, his smile and laugh, intoxicate me. Soon, we are dancing to nothing. He pulls me to him, and our faces are inches apart. I note his deep blue eyes and full red lips. Leaning in, he smiles. His eyes close, and I freeze.

His lids pop open. "You are not ready for this, are you?"

My face burns. "I am sorry, no. I—"

"You still care for Foster."

"I do not know. I do not want to deceive you. I do like you, find you attractive."

His mouth forms a smile again. "That is a step in the right direction."

He loosens his grip, and I step back. "Perhaps we should say goodnight."

Bowing, he holds my gaze. "Until morning then. Do not forget, if you have a bad dream, I am right next door."

My cheeks heat again. "I will keep that in mind."

"Goodnight." He backs through the doorway and closes the panels.

Pouring another glass of wine, I choose a new book from my table and crawl into bed.

⸻◆⸻

"THEY ARE COMING." MOTHER's eyes burn red, and I wake with a start.

Sitting up, I yell into the darkness. "I am not falling for the stupid fears of my psyche. I am going back to sleep."

Tugging the blankets over my shoulders, I cover my head with a pillow. Perhaps it is exhaustion or maybe the wine, but I fall to sleep again within minutes. I wake to bright sun streaming in my windows and smile. Sitting up, I find Alfreda putting a breakfast tray on my table.

"Just like old times. You do not know how happy I am to see a smile grace your face. Should I bring you the pastries?" She holds up the plate of food. "Am I to guess that your picnic with Prince Holden had something to do with this mood?"

"I think it was more the wine." I flit over and grab a strawberry from her tray.

"Well, your father is happy."

"What?"

"Dearie, do you think anything happens in this castle without everyone knowing? He just wants you to be happy."

"I will be as soon as I kill all of the kobold."

"Nasty creatures." She shudders and returns the tray to the table.

I stare at my crosses while eating. Memory of my dream plays through my head. *You will not rule me today,* I tell it. Standing, I cross to my closet, dress, and exit my chamber.

Holden's door opens as I pass. A huge smile crosses his face, and I wonder if he was listening for my door.

"Good morning, Highness." He dips his chin.

"Do not look so smug. It is not attractive."

"No bad dreams?"

I ignore the question and his flirting. "I would like to train all day. Are you up for it?"

"Whatever my Queen desires." The sides of his mouth turn up, and he looks like a cat that just caught a canary.

I peer at him, but I cannot be mad. We round to the fighting yard and spar with Quinn then shoot arrows in the meadow. After the noon meal, Holden and I ride then practice fencing in the gym. The afternoon ends with weapons training. As evening comes, I sup with Mother, Father, Kane, Alfreda, Quinn, and Holden, thinking these people could be all I need to be happy.

Out of the corner of my eye, I catch movement. A page hangs near the doors, summoning me with a wave. I excuse myself and flit to him. He hands me a message from Aleem.

Hunter and his factions are moving against Sonia at her compound on Sardinia.

My heart stops. Swallowing, I call for Kane, Holden, and Quinn. I instruct Quinn to stay safe, request Kane assemble the two hundred troops destined for Italy, and ask Holden to follow me. We meet the troops at the portal. Grant, Adam, Nicholas, and Timothy flank Holden and I as we dash through the portal, bound for Sardinia. Leaving Nicholas with another soldier at the portal entrance, we speed to the castle. Descending to the compound lawn, we find vampires and witches flooding from the doors. I abhor harming any being save a kobold but steel my psyche, remembering these vampires have been possessed by witch souls. I pray they return to their prior state once the toxin wears off. We tranquilize the vampires and witches alike with our poison darts until none remain upright.

Surveying the field, I see Alena and Hunter approach.

"What are you doing here?" Hunter asks.

"Hunter, I told you the faeries—" Alena supports Hunter's torso.

"You aided our troops?" Hunter asks.

He relinquished his magic, is human again, and is hurt badly. My mind swirls with questions, and I listen to his thoughts. They are so jumbled I cannot make out a clear stream. "Yes."

"Why would you come help us?"

"I have a soft spot for teens on a suicide mission." I use jargon of Upper Earth.

"Teens? How old are you?"

"Let us just say I have a couple hundred years on you. I heard the witches were scared. I have not ever known the witches to fear anything. I figured if they felt threatened, we could be next."

A vampire motions to the soldiers behind me. "Titania's soldiers captured a good number of Sonia's troops with their poison darts."

Hunter places a hand on his chest. "Thank you. We're in your debt."

"There is no debt when we fight for each other." I hold my hand out to him.

He locks his palm around my forearm. "Until we meet again."

"Until we meet again. You know where to find me."

"Can't I get your cell number or something?"

I straighten my jacket as a voice sounds in my chest. Nicholas. *Queen Titania, the kobold. They are here.*

I force a smile. "It will be light soon. You will excuse us to take our leave?"

"Of course." He dips his chin.

Jumping into the air, I send a thought to Nicholas. *Where are the kobold?*

Attacking in the south.

"What happened back there? Hunter is human now? I could not glean anything from their minds. Is Sonia defeated? Why would you tell him you are so old?" Grant pelts me with questions.

"I do not know. But we must get home. The kobold are attacking." *Of course. Of course, they would choose today.* It cannot be a coincidence. How stupid I was to leave Aubren. But Kane can hold them off until we get there.

My mind jumps to thoughts of Foster. I berate my psyche. *He proved he does not care for you. Why hang on?* But if it were not for me, he would be at the castle, not in the south. No, he made that choice. I beat my wings as hard as I can. Looking ahead at the sun low over the horizon I see glowing blue orbs rising from every portal. *Souls? Released souls? What does that mean?*

"What are these?" Grant asks. "Thousands of souls? Does that mean the curse is broken or Sonia was victorious? Perhaps she stripped Hunter of his powers and the trinity could not best her."

"That is not our problem now." My mind ticks with worry. Or it is, and we cannot fathom the implications.

Approaching our ring, I realize the orbs block our path in. They flow through the opening like a swift current.

Nicholas hovers beside the portal, batting the spheres away.

An army will not get through that any time soon.

To the southern ring. I message to Holden, Nicholas, and the guards closest. We shoot south, the troops trailing us. Only minutes pass, and by the time we reach the southern portal, few souls rise from the opening. We race through and head straight for Mt. Kosciuszko. A line of dark, purple-bodied kobold ooze from several fissures like a stream of melted tar. In the meadow below, our soldiers battle the beasts one on one.

Locating Kane at the far side of the field, I direct my troops to aid the others and speed to him. Landing at his side, I ask for an update on troop positions. More are in route from the north. Still, with the number of kobold, many of our soldiers will die.

"I know what I must do. Signal for all the kingdoms to close their rings to the underworld. The kobold want me. I can lead them through our portal and into Lower Earth. Once they are all through the opening, you will close the ring. The kobold will be trapped in that realm and perish."

"That is a ludicrous plan. How do you even know they will follow you? And if so, how are you to return?" Kane scoffs. "I will not allow it. We may lose many, but we will fight to the end."

I signal to Holden, and he, Nicholas, and Timothy close ranks. "This is not a debate. This is an order. Holden, you are Fae at Arms. Signal the ring keepers."

Kane steps forward and reaches for Holden.

Nicholas and Timothy block the path.

Holden blows into his trumpet, calling for the ring keepers to alert the other kingdoms to close their lower portals.

Grant crosses to stand beside Kane. "We will not let you do this. You have no idea if it will work, and we will not let you sacrifice yourself in this suicidal endeavor."

Grant looks at Adam, and I suspect some sort of unspoken communication happens. Raising a bugle, Kane plays two short notes, a longer one, and another shorter one.

F? What is F for? A group of soldiers, about ten, run from the woods, joining Kane, Grant, and Adam. One weaves through the pack to the front.

Foster.

"Please, Titania. Whatever you are planning, do not do it." His eyes cut to the others and back to my face. "This kingdom needs you. I need you. I only left because I could not bear to think that you may die. I love you. I want to be married to you. I want us to have a long life together."

His sweet face, green eyes, and red lips draw me. My side ticks.

He loves me? After three months of hearing nothing, he thinks I will swoon at the sight of his face? This was Kane and Grant's big move? I smile. *Well played.* If there had been one I would die for above all others, it would have been be him. Before. He is but one of the many fae I plan to save today. I place both my hands on my jacket collar, indicating my special battalion is needed.

Seconds later, Ethan, Cedric, and eight others land behind me.

Kane and his fae raise their swords.

We are wasting time, and I will not lose one more soldier. I lower my hand, a gesture meant to initiate step two of our plan.

Holden and those beside me release a huge net, throwing it over the top of Kane and his men, ensnaring them together. I look at Holden, wink, and mouth thank you. Feeling for the bag of anchors in my quiver, I jump into the air.

I hover above Kane and the others bound by the net. "As I said, this is not a debate. Prince Holden is now the general in charge of all my troops. Obey him or become a traitor to this realm."

Flitting to Foster, I place my hand on his shoulder. "This is bigger than you or me. If what you said is true, I am sorry."

I blast up above the meadow. Surveying the field, I realize I have no idea how to get the kobold's attention. This is a hail Mary plan based on my mother's premonition and a hunch that if I am the one fabled to end all evil, the kobold will desire to hunt me. I go in low, swooping over the heads of the fighting kobold, sweeping my wings against them. The first one I make eye contact with stares, wide eyed, and my soldier lands a club on its jaw. The second jumps up, grabbing for my leg.

That is it, my scent. With small, dark eyes; small ear canals; and no ears, they use smell as their primary means of recognition. I beat my wings in wide swoops above their heads, and scads of them look up as I pass over. I rise a bit higher, and one takes to the air after me. I smile. *I have got them.*

As more and more of them take flight, I rise in a spiral above the field. Pack driven, they tend to follow others of their kind, and this holds true now. As the field is cleared of kobold, the ones streaming from the mountain take wing, and soon, they form a river of purple ribbon behind me. Their heavy forms and small wings make them slower, and I keep a couple of body lengths between me and the first kobold. Heading for the ring, I wait until it is directly underneath to descend so the beasts do not happen upon one of my fae.

I fly straight down towards the ring and through the portal. Cold air like ice crystals hits my face. Ahead, I see nothing but blackness. Praying there will be a way out for me, I venture on, the line of kobold following behind. As I descend farther, light from the opening fades and the darkness, cold, silence, nothingness surrounds me. Stopping to look back, the portal looks like a pinhole in an unlit box. *The cellar*, I think, *like the dungeon*. I make out faint silhouettes of kobold that float, more ghostlike than real. But they no longer follow me. They appear to have scattered into the abyss of this realm.

The light from the opening dims, and realizing they are closing the portal, I propel myself towards it. My heart soars, thinking the plan worked. But If I do not get there before they close it, I may never find my way back. My breath freezes in my lungs. *What if I cannot locate it? What if I have no powers here, not even that special one that does not want me to die? What if I have achieved my destiny, and this is my fate?* To die alone in this darkness. Knowing something may happen and having it occur are two very different experiences. My chest aches like never before, and I realize a living being cannot process death until it becomes imminent.

Fight. The thought comes from deep within me.

Chapter 22

Charging towards the last snippet of light, I slam full force into the portal door. I bounce off and spin, kicking my feet to inch back to it, palm out, until I touch the boundary. Smooth and soft, the barrier feels more like a field. Pressing my fingers into the surface, I detect a slight vibration. I press my ear to it and hear a faint hum.

Okay, think. You have the anchors. You just have to figure out where they go and put them in in the right order. But which way is up?

Breathe, Titania. Use your bearings. Let the Earth's magnetism guide you.

With a small push, I float away from the portal. Weightless, I am weightless. I close my eyes and imagine myself as a compass. Spinning a quarter turn, my body stops. Weightless except for a direction spell. My powers work here. I wave my arms and move to the ring. Laying my palms on the surface, I climb to the upper edge and run my hand up past the portal opening, feeling for the anchor cask. My fingers detect the crevice. *Twelve,* I think. I inch in an arc down to the next cask. *One, the first anchor should be placed here.* I search in my quiver for the bag of stones. Pulling it from the bottom, I realize my next challenge. *Light. How am I to see which stone to put in? Once the first is in, it will make some light, but the first one must be placed correctly, or I will be trapped.*

I hold the bag tightly with my left hand and focus on the right. My palm glows, and I hold it above the stones. Identifying the first, I slide it out and check the orientation. I hold my breath and slip it into the cask. It glows green, and my spirit soars. Creeping to the second cask, I place the next anchor, then the third, fourth, and fifth. Moving to the sixth position, I hear the faintest rush of air, feel a breeze sweep over my skin, and spin around, keeping my back on the portal. I peer into the nothingness, thinking a kobold may have been attracted by the light, and draw my sword.

"You think a sword will hurt me?"

Sucking in a breath, I listen, watch, but sense nothing.

"You must know who I am."

I reach out with my mind to read the being's thoughts. *Void.*

"Do you faeries not know you cannot read a higher being? Surely someone has not been studying. Oh, but you have." Hot air washes over my face.

Gripping my sword, I swing as hard as I can. Hitting a surface, the sword bounces back and out of my hand. I watch as it spins into oblivion.

The being cackles. "One down. I know you have got more."

My mind races. *Abaddon? Or Lucifer? Or Sonia? Does it matter? Too bad I did not find how to kill a dark angel.*

"Oh, I cannot be killed in this realm, dear."

I smell and feel its hot breath on my face, and the being materializes inches from me. Face as dark as night, the eyes glow red in their sockets. The light reflects off gold metal on its head, illuminating a crown. *Abaddon?*

Vapor clouds my vision, and blinking, I wave the smoke away. I open my eyes to flaring nostrils; long, sharp fangs; huge, bulging eyes; and a long, reptilian body with wings. The dragon of my dreams. The beast sucks in a breath, and I realize it is about to incinerate me. Magick. I need tons of magick. *The portal is pure fae magick.* Resting my palm on the surface, I suck the magick into me.

As a stream of fire emerges from the beast's mouth, I wave my hand in front of me, creating a barrier spell. The flames bounce off and singe the hairs hanging from the dragon's chin.

"I thought you could not be harmed?" I smile.

The beast ignites with a poof, and the embers scatter. I do not care why it is gone, but I am not going to waste time. Holding the anchor bag up to the light, I move to the sixth position and fix the stone inside.

"You think they want you back?" Hot, steamy air cascades down my neck.

I spin to see a man… An angel, a dark angel, I assume, by the black feathers of his wings. *Lucifer?*

"Perhaps I am Lucifer. You think if you know who I am you can kill me. But I have another question. Even if you could get back, why would they want you? You have caused nothing but problems. And not just in the past six months, really for the past three years. A girl plagued by anxiety fits who must be guarded twenty-four hours a day.

And now by four guards at a time. Even the boy you love does not care for you anymore. You know those were just lines Kane made him repeat."

I bite my lip. He is right. Foster does not love me. It was obvious he acted as a puppet. *And why would you want him back anyway? He left you. Everyone leaves you, your brothers, your mother, your father, Kane, Foster... Because you are broken. Look at the chaos your reign caused. What have you been living for? To slay the kobold? You did that. So now, you have no purpose. Anyone could fill your shoes.*

No. You are smarter than this. "You are playing on my insecurities."

The being shrugs and floats away then back. "It usually works. What you want is real power. You would never have to fear anything again, never have to be alone, never die. Join us, and you will have all that and more."

"Join you? Stay here? This is literal hell."

"We have full reign to go anywhere we want. Do you have that?"

I post my hand on my hip. "Actually, yes. I guess I do now."

"No, you are bound to your people, your kingdom, your family. You have no real freedom."

"This is still a mind game. I will find a way to get out of here. And when I do, I will find a way to end all of you."

"No, you will go crazy trying. You will be that insane fae queen who thinks of nothing else but how to kill us. And what is the worst for you is that it is not possible. We have been here since the beginning of time, so you will spend your whole life searching in vain, alone."

"Why are you trying to stop me from leaving then? If you really have nothing to fear from me, why even bother?" I raise an eyebrow.

"I was just offering you an option. You have a strong spirit just like Sonia. Hers was as pure as yours in the beginning."

I hold his stare. "I will never be Sonia."

"Well, dear, then you will die." He raises his hand and balls it into a fist.

As it tightens, my chest constricts, lungs gasp for air, diaphragm refuses to move, heart struggles to pump. *Think, Titania. Your magick, the magick of the ring. You are going to have to do better than a barrier spell.*

"And I do not think you will be needing those anymore." He flicks his wrist.

The hand holding the bag jerks sideways, cracking my wrist. Pain shoots up my arm. My fingers flail out and the bag floats from my grip. I reach out to grab it with my other hand, but he is faster, locking his fingers around my forearm.

"Did I mention it will be a long, slow death?"

I rest my body against the portal.

"That is right. You know there is no escape. Why fight? Better to die quickly." He morphs back into Abaddon's form. "I believe I have some friends who would be happy to see you die."

The sound of beating wings alerts me to the presence of others, and by the time they are before me, deafening clacking noises fill my brain. *Kobold, thousands of them.*

"Was it not these minions that killed your brothers? Your mother saw it. You know there is no escape."

"They are not real. They cannot hurt me." I press my back and palms to the portal, siphoning its magick.

"Are you sure? I do thank you for returning them. You think you know so much. You know nothing of our reach." He leans towards me, his hot, dank breath spewing into my face.

My body pulses with the power coursing through it. "Evil villain mistake, long monologue."

I throw out my arms, shooting the magick from my palms. The blast hurls me backwards and out of the portal into Middle Earth. Body tingling from the burst of electricity, I soar through the air. A branch slows my descent, and I land with a thud on the forest floor. Ears ringing from the blast, I push up on my palms, my wrist still stinging but not broken, and look around. My vision clouded, I lay my head back on the soft earth. The hum in my ears subsides, and I sit up. I note the sound of running water and squint to find the creek some dozen feet away. I crawl to it, cupping my hands and dipping them in the water. I sip the liquid, quenching my parched throat.

Catching my broken reflection in the stream, I feel my hair. Long, matted strands stick out from my head. That is fine. I am alive and home. I douse my face with cool water. As my fingers rake across my forehead, I feel smooth knobs protruding from my skin. Shimmying to a quiet pool, I check my reflection. The markings on my face have been transformed into shiny, hard nodes. My mind reels. *Did the evil being transform me? Am I a monster now?* No, I would sense the evil inside. *Unless you are pure evil.*

Shifting to a patch of moss, my muscles tremble with wear. I look at the sky, realizing the sun is about to set. I do not favor being alone in the wood after dark. I laugh at the thought. *You just blasted yourself out of literal hell. I do not think anything could harm you.* Even though my body craves rest, I push to a stand. I unfold my wings to find them singed. They are not getting me anywhere. Spinning to get my bearings and seeing less dense forest to my right, I head northeast. I stumble and trip over grasses, roots, and logs on the forest floor.

The trees grow thinner, and I exit into a clearing. Peering ahead, I make out funeral pyres in the distance. My heart sinks. *How many did we lose? Were we not able to trap enough of the kobold? What if Sonia came with her witches?* My stomach turns. I should have told them to close the upper portals as well.

Hobbling forward, I make out hazy forms descending from the sky. I squint, trying to form a clear picture. Three beings land on the ground in front of me.

"Titania." Arms encircle me.

I would know that voice anywhere. *Holden.* "I am sorry. I tried."

"No, you saved us." Releasing me, he inches back. "All but a few kobold followed you into the portal. We only lost six soldiers. We were waiting for you to exit the ring and saw the—I guess you—shoot out."

"I am a little…" My legs buckle under me.

"Let me." He fits his arm around my waist, supporting my weight.

"Queen." The other two fae drop to their knees.

As we get closer, I realize they are Nicholas and Timothy. "All of you are heroes as well today. What of Kane and his contingency?"

Holden explains they were not happy but acquiesced to his leadership once they saw my plan working. He relays that the others wait at the ring for word on what the supposed shooting-star object is. We limp across the field, and Holden offers to carry me. My pride overrides my fatigue, and I power through. We reach the pyres, and Nicholas and Timothy pick flowers for me to lay on the bodies. As I honor the last fae, a group exits the trees.

I whisper to Holden that I cannot focus well, and he stands beside me, naming each. The line of fae close in and bow before me. At the closer distance, I recognize Kane at the front, Grant and Adam close behind, and Foster, Aleem, Regin, and the advisors and judges bringing up the rear.

Kane stands. "Queen, your army awaits your safe return in the next clearing. I believe they would like to see their leader."

I turn to Holden and swallow to soothe my throat. "The army should gather here. Have the families been summoned for the rites?"

"They have. I will bring them and the army."

As soon as he steps away, I regret his absence. Nicholas steps to my side and offers me his spear. Leaning on it, I make my way to the center of the pyres.

Kane, Grant, and Adam trail me.

With my ears still ringing, I catch but half of their words which I glean to be praise for my safe return and apologies for not following my lead. I suck in a breath to speak, and my lungs resist, sending me into a coughing fit.

As it passes, I stand upright. "Grant and Adam, I do not blame you for trying to protect your queen. That is your job. Kane, you have loved my family for a long time, and we have loved you. Your loss would have been a hard one. I can understand how thinking of mine would have spurred you to act as you did, but the kingdom and realm must come before any affections we may carry for one another. Please, let us talk of this later. We have soldiers to honor."

The soldiers file into the field, surrounding the pyres. I greet the families and offer my condolences. Tears streaming down my face, we light each pyre together. I stand in the center, watching the flowers burn around each soldier and flames consume them, sending their bodies back into the earth and their souls to Heaven. I stay in the meadow with the families until the last ember dies out.

"Titania." Holden wraps his jacket around my shoulders. "You are shivering. We should get you somewhere warm. There is an inn nearby."

I shake my head. "I want to go home. Can you take me home?"

He slides his arm around my back and lifts my legs. Jumping into the air, Nicholas and Timothy follow us as we rise into the sky. I lay my head on Holden's shoulder and, encircled by his warm arms, slink into slumber. Feeling us descend, I lift my face to see the castle. My eyesight improving, I find Alfreda, Mother, Father, and Quinn standing in the courtyard below us. We alight on the ground before them and Holden sets me on my feet.

Alfreda's face contorts, and she lifts her hands to her cheeks. "My stars. What happened to you, dear love?"

"It was nothing, really." I stumble forward, and Holden catches me. "Just a short trip to Lower Earth. I am quite tired and would rather tell you all about it tomorrow."

Palm raised, Mother approaches. She runs her fingers along the stones on my forehead. Dipping her chin, she lowers her hand. Her eyes cut to mine. I hold my breath. She stands there stoic, staring at me. *What does that mean?* I am too tired to process. I wrap my arms around her and hug her tightly. Tears threaten to form, and I look at the sky. Releasing her, I step back.

Father wraps his arms around me and hugs me to him. Kissing my cheek, he whispers, "I knew you would be victorious."

I raise my eyes to Quinn. He presses his fingers to his lips and salutes me. I mouth thank you to him.

Stepping out of Father's embrace, I falter again. Holden's arm wraps around my waist. We hobble through the passageways lined with all the fae of the castle, flanked by Nicholas and Timothy and followed by Mother, Father, and Alfreda. I smile and nod as the sea of faces pass by.

By the time we reach my small hallway, it is only Alfreda, Nicholas, Timothy, Holden, and me. Thanking them for their brilliant service, I give leave to Nicholas and Timothy. Alfreda enters my room, runs to the bath, and starts filling the tub. Wanting to have a few moments with Holden, I motion to the study. Once inside, he shuts the door and lowers me into a soft chair. He kneels before me.

I look into his eyes, clear on who I care for. It is the man before me. "Thank you for believing in me."

"I did not think you were coming back." Tears fill his eyes. He stands and backs away. "I am sorry. I know you do not feel—"

"No, I should be apologizing. I thought I still cared for Foster. And he probably thought he loved me. But if you love someone, you stand by them even when it is hard. I saw that in Alena and Hunter, and you did that for me today. I do not know what it means, but yours was the first face I wanted to see when I got out."

Stepping to me, he leans down. I raise my chin, and he presses his lips to mine. My lips warm, and a zing of magick emits from my skin.

Backing away, he smiles. "What was that?"

"I believe I am a bit charged still. I absorbed a lot of magick from the portal."

He blinks. "You absorbed the magick? How?"

I press my finger to his lips. "Tomorrow."

"Tomorrow." Wrapping his hand around my finger, he kisses me again.

Chapter 23

Holden helps me to my door, and apologizing to Alfreda, I stumble to my bed and crawl under the covers. I care not how dirty or singed I am, a bath can wait. I need sleep.

"Do you need something to eat? Drink?" Alfreda tucks a blanket under my chin.

"Water, yes," I nod.

My eyes close before she returns, and I fall into a deep slumber. Images of angels, pixies, unicorns, and rainbows flit through my dreams. Holden and I sit in a flower-covered meadow, having a picnic in the sun. I lay back on the blanket and bask in the warmth of the light. Clouds form overhead. *Clouds?* My mind tries to comprehend. There are no clouds in Middle Earth. They transform from white puffy cotton, to grey, to purple, then to dark, rolling seas of moisture. Descending, the clouds surround me until there is nothing but black.

"We are waiting for you." Swirls of grey vapor morph from an image of Abaddon, to the dragon, to Lucifer, and back to Abaddon.

I draw in a breath and open my eyes to a bright room. Aubren, Capitolshire, *my* room. Sitting up, I note my crystals, windows, curtains, table, Alfreda.

"Oh, heavens, you are awake. I was so worried." She jumps from her seat.

"What time is it?" I squint in the light.

"Nearly midmorning. I did not want to wake you." She holds out a glass of water. "How are you feeling?"

"Okay, I think." I try to recall what needs to be done. "Are there preparations for a celebration? I would like to thank the soldiers properly."

"Yes, and Holden and Foster wanted to speak with you as soon as you woke."

"Foster?" I grab my robe. "What is he doing here?"

"I have no idea what happened yesterday, but I assume from your face and your hair, a lot. Bath, now."

I cross to the tub, instructing her to find a dress for me for tonight; to ask Father if Mother said anything else; to tell Foster I will speak with him this afternoon, *or never, preferably*, I think; and to assemble my advisors, Aleem, Regin, the judges, generals, Holden, Quinn, and Father.

She plants her hands on her hips. "I am not your page."

"Alfreda, please, arrange a lunch with all those people."

I scrub from head to toe and soap my hair twice. I dress in my riding pants and skirt, as always, and bundle my hair atop my head. I exit my room to find a bulging group waiting.

I look from Quinn, to Father, to Holden. Seeing his beaming face warms my heart. I tamper my smile. "Did Alfreda not tell you about lunch?"

Each of them steps forward with requests to meet with me sooner than later. Wanting to have Foster out of my sight, I figure better to get him out of the way first. I invite him into my study. Puffing his chest and eyeing Holden, Foster follows me in.

"Are you okay?"

"As you can see, I am fine."

"I was so worried."

My anger flames. "What was that stunt yesterday?"

"It was not a stunt. I meant what I said. My heart broke thinking you would never come out of that portal." He grasps my hand.

I tug my fingers from his grip. "You do not love me, Foster. Or maybe you did, or thought you did, but you left. You would not have left if you felt half of what I thought I felt for you."

"*Thought* you felt for me?"

"Yes, before you left. And even when you were gone, maybe."

"But I *do* love you. I thought you had some suicidal martyr plan, and they suspected it as well. We had no idea what it was. I would have done anything to stop you."

"Do you not understand? You do not realize you love someone, want them back, only when you think you may lose them. And if you love someone, you support them, believe in them, stand by them."

"Like Holden, I am guessing." The edges of his mouth turn down.

"This has nothing to do with Holden." I think back to when I marched through the halls, proclaiming that Queen Titania was not marrying, nor would ever marry, Prince Holden. *How immature.* I chuckle.

"What is funny?"

"Nothing, sorry." I straighten my smile. "You were the first boy I loved. I hope we can call each other friend. There will be another who will hold an even dearer place in your heart. I know you will find her."

"So that is it? What if I came back? We started over?"

I shake my head. "I have feelings for another."

"Holden." He slams his fist on the desk.

"It matters not. I have no idea where these feelings will lead. But I want to find out. I hope you will be happy as well."

"But?"

"Foster, leave."

Taking a deep breath, he bows and backs from the room.

I hate I had to be firm with him but am glad to get the task over with. As I exit the study, Holden steps forward. I smile before I can check my reaction.

Father clears his throat.

"Holden, Quinn, Father, I will describe all that happened yesterday at my lunch with you and all the generals, advisors, and judges. Now, I would like to walk with Mother. Father, will you join us?"

Holden and Quinn dip their chins and excuse themselves. I take Father's arm and walk with him towards his chamber. He insists I am killing him by not sharing what happened. I counter that I would rather not relive my ordeal numerous times.

We retrieve Mother, and as we stroll the garden, I wonder how much I should share. I have no idea whether the magick I used came partially from me. *Did I wield it as any fae would in the Lower Earth, or was it the power that manifested as before when the kobold attacked and when I fought Ethan?*

Getting this wrong could have disastrous effects. I may recount my experience for Mother, hoping that she can shed some light on the beings I encountered, but not yet. Perhaps the events of yesterday will be my secret. Maybe I will tell Holden, but I do not think it wise to go blabbing to all the realm. Plus, I have no indication that these dark angels pose a danger. If they have been around for millennia, they represent no more threat to us now than before. They have been trying to absorb our realm since the beginning. That is the legend of fae beings, created to protect The Creator's children from the dark ones.

These thoughts play in my mind as I think about all the histories we have read, those written by various beings. *Had some, like me, altered the truth? Kept details to protect those that came after?* As we enter the orchard and cross to the far side, I spin to face Mother and Father. I recount luring the kobold into the ring and them floating into the abyss, encountering what I think to be dark beings, that they tried to trap me in Lower Earth, and how I escaped when they flung me against the portal barrier.

"Evil beings? And you passed through the closed portal?" Father's eyebrows shoot up.

"I have no idea how it happened. But it did, and I am here." I squeeze their hands.

Seeing no reaction from Mother, I release their palms. I stare into her face, waiting, hoping, praying. *The kobold are gone!* My mind screams. *Come back to me.* Her eyes twitch and widen. She raises her finger to my forehead and touches the middle stone. *Mother?* My heart races as I wait for more. She lowers her hand and folds it across her middle. I wrap my arms around her shoulders, squeezing her tightly.

Her body remains rigid as it always does. Her eyes… There was recognition. I will hold to that. Releasing her, I think I will tell her about Foster and Holden when we are alone. We pass back through the orchard, and Father takes Mother to her chamber. I wind around the hedges and, spying Quinn, catch up to him.

As I fall in step, he dips his chin. "Are you alright? You looked pretty beat up last night. They kept me apprised the whole day. We were all so worried about you."

"I am feeling better. I am glad you were informed the whole time. Our arrangement worked as it should."

"It was good strategy to have the small battalion at your command."

"Thank you." I smile, thinking how wonderfully perfect that plan had gone.

"It is hard to believe that, after all these months, all these years, the kobold are gone."

"I agree. Even though I was there, it still feels like a dream." I hook my arm in his. "I cannot thank you enough for taking care of my kingdom, cousin. I hope you will continue to stay and be happy here."

"For as long as I am wanted." He pats my hand.

Smiling, I kiss him on the cheek. "I think we shall all be very happy from now on, now that the darkest days are behind us."

We walk to the courtyard to find all the leaders streaming in. I greet each and receive thanks and commendations on our victory. Sitting, we eat. Only after all are finished do I start the meeting. I inquire to Aleem, Regin, and the other judges what they have heard from Italy and the trinity. They report the witches of the trinity disappeared again as they always do.

"And what of Sonia?"

Aleem stares as me, and I wonder if his looking glass could extend into Lower Earth even with the portal closed. His eyes cut to the others. "There is no trace of her."

"So, she is gone?"

"Or in hiding," the First Judge says.

I stand and pace behind them. *Where did she go? Does she lurk below us? Are all those evil spirits waiting for a chance to overtake our realm?* I cannot go down the rabbit hole. I will go mad just as the demon proposed. Winding back to my seat, I grip the chair back and recount what I told Father and Mother. The kobold descended into oblivion and a dark being, trying to kill me, blasted me against the portal barrier with such force I burned through it.

Wide-eyed, Aleem, Regin, and the judges shake their heads and mutter between themselves.

I raise my chin. "I know it seems disconcerting that a being could cross through our closed ring. But I am a fae, a queen. I can only guess that the magick of the ring recognized me as such. I do not believe the ring failed. We are safe from the kobold. They will die in that space. There is nothing there, no sustenance for them. Their physical forms will cease to be."

Clutching his cane, Aleem stands. "I believe Titania to be right. We have tested the ring, and the barrier stands. The magick of the ring saved her, and we need not fear the kobold ever again. They are no more."

Aleem's wisdom stands without question. He, above all, would know the ring's magick best, as well as details of Lower Earth.

It is true. We are free of the threat from the kobold.

I raise my glass. "To all those who fought valiantly on behalf of our realm. Godspeed to the fallen. May they rest in peace. For Aubren. For the Realm."

"For Aubren. For the Realm," the others repeat.

Beside me, Holden rises. "To Queen Titania. For without her bravery and dedication to this realm, we would have lost many more. To Queen Titania."

"To Queen Titania," they echo.

Sipping from my glass, I hold it up high. "To Kane; General Holden; and Heir Presumptive, Quinn: thank you for training and leading our armies in victory. And to all of you for entrusting me with the security of this kingdom. I will always give all for you and this realm."

"Here, here!" Those gathered toast one another.

"I hope to see you all at the celebration tonight. Thank you for coming."

As they part, I greet each, accepting congratulations. Kane waits with Father, and I realize I have more to deal with this afternoon. I doubt either of them are happy about me usurping Kane's power, especially since I used Ethan and those that sided with Gunther to do it. Plus, I handed Holden the highest position in the army. *Should I return Kane to his position or keep Holden in place?* As Kane and Father approach, I cut my eyes to Holden.

He cocks his head, and requesting Kane and Father wait, I cross to Holden. "What should I do about Kane? I made you General."

"You did." He smiles wide.

"Is this what you want? To be General of my entire army?"

"No, I want to be your Fae at Arms, in charge of your guards, spies, and special battalion. This way, you will know you are safe and your plans secure. I think I may desire to be at your side always."

My cheeks warm as he stares into my eyes. "I believe I may want that as well."

Hearing Father clear his throat behind me, I straighten my back. "Thank you, Prince Holden. If you could gather our battalion, I would like to thank them personally."

Father, Kane, and I take seats around a small table. Father admonishes me for creating the secret army, saying I should have gone to Kane to discuss my concern.

Taking a calming breath, I admit my actions may have been rash. I counterpoint that Father and Kane plotted without my knowledge before. Neither of them has proven to be truly in my service.

Father shifts in his seat.

Holding my gaze, Kane stands.

My heart races, thinking he will berate me as well. Under the table, I ball my fists, waiting for a chance to match his defiance.

Kane drops to one knee. "I failed you, Queen. For that, I am heartily sorry. You did the best thing for this kingdom and the realm. Even if we lost you, it still would have been the right choice. You trusted Quinn and Holden, and they have proved worthy to serve this kingdom. If you must relieve me of my post, I understand."

Inside, my smile is as wide as the ocean, but I keep a straight face. "Kane, can you promise to serve and obey me, as your Queen and rightful monarch? To be obedient and true from this point forward?"

"I can, yes. I will not fail you again."

"Then you shall remain General of all my armies. Thank you for your service."

He rises and I stand as well. I offer my arm, and he wraps his hand around it in the traditional warrior greeting. Seeing Holden at the door, I take my leave.

We weave through the castle and out to the stables. Taking two horses, we charge across the meadow and into the wood. When I spy the others gathered ahead, I slow my pace, stop, and slide from my saddle. Nicholas,

Timothy, Ethan, Cedric, and eight others stand in a large circle in a clearing.

Approaching, I smile and lift my chin. "Though they may not know all of your faces, this kingdom and this realm are in your debt. Because of your willingness to do the right thing by me and your kingdom, we are victorious today. I salute each one of you."

I step in front of each soldier, greeting them with the traditional handshake of a warrior as I had Kane. Afterwards, I invite them to stay in my service, so that we may help secure the kingdom and realm together.

They lift their weapons in the air. "To Aubren. To the Realm."

Drawing my sword, I repeat their words. "To Aubren. To the Realm."

Ho, ho, ho, ho. Their chants echo through the forest. My heart races and spirit soars. *We are victorious.* Someone starts a tune on a harmonica, and we clap along. Holden offers his arm, and we dance a jig. The others join in and weave in and out of each other, forming a Fae circle. When I tire, I sit on a stump and clap to the tune.

Holden lowers himself to my side. "Should we go prepare for the feast?"

"We should."

Bidding farewell to the others, we return our horses to the stable and wind through the castle, receiving commendation from all we pass. He walks me to my room and leans towards me. I take a step back. He bows and, returning his smile, I back into my room.

"Oh, dear, thank goodness you are here. I have several dresses for you to look at." Alfreda holds up a gold dress as well as a burgundy one.

"Alfreda, I always wear green."

"But this victory is like no other. You need a distinctive color. I mean you literally went through Hell and back."

I study the gold and red fabrics. I think of Abaddon, Lucifer, and the dragon. *Could that beast really have been Sonia?* I may always be at war with them. "I shall choose the burgundy, then."

After bathing, I slide on my robe and sit in front of a mirror while two girls curl my hair and pile it in ringlets atop my head. Attending to my face, I note their eyes widen as they examine the jewels, there is no other way to describe them, embedded in my skin.

"It is okay. They do not hurt." I press my fingers to the stones. The small ones form a line in the middle of my forehead. A large oval one hangs below them. Two other ovals flank the center, forming the shape of an arrow. Four small stones sit atop my cheeks, four jewels, one for each of my brothers. I like the idea and decide these are pieces of my siblings, forever etched in my skin.

They brush powder on my face and blush on my cheeks. I slip on my dress, and while Alfreda left some slim dancing shoes beside my bed, I opt for my boots. I lace them up above my knees and slide a dagger in each one. A queen can never be too careful. I think of my last battle celebration and how it ended in turmoil. Odd how things come full circle. *I believed I could count on Father,*

Kane, and Foster. I felt so sure of those closest to me. Each chose different paths, though, and I felt so alone the past months save for Quinn and *Holden.*

Holden. *Had he really thought he could kiss me in the hall in front of everyone?* I touch my fingers to my lips and remember the spark of magick that passed between us. I smile when I think about him wanting to kiss me again. He said he thought he would always desire to be at my side. Me, the damaged, broken Queen. I extend my hand and focus on producing energy, but nothing happens. Still, I know it is inside me, and I will be able to best any problem we face. Even the dilemma of falling in love with a prince from a foreign land, one I said I would never marry.

Hearing a knock on the door, I cross the room and swing it open. Holden stands in front of me holding a bundle of red roses. He is wearing a gray jacket with a burgundy rose on the collar, white kerchief in the pocket, and starch white shirt. I look to his feet, and find... *Boots?*

Smiling, I raise my skirt and hold up a boot. "It looks like we think the same."

He holds out the roses. "And I picked the right color."

Taking the flowers, I tuck them in my arm. He holds out his elbow, and I fit my hand in it. *I wonder if this is how I should be parading through the halls after such a victory, on the arm of my Fae at Arms.* As much as I enjoy being near him, I kiss his cheek and slide my hand from his elbow.

I am Queen, and this is *my* victory.

We walk down the hall to the main passage with my four guards following. Holden opens the doors and

Quinn, Kane, Mother, Father, and Alfreda stand just on the other side. I kiss Mother's and Father's cheeks. I nod to Quinn and Kane and motion for them to fall into the procession.

Fae fill the passageways, and I greet countryman after countryman and hug women and children, who fill my arms with flowers. Reaching the grand hall, I hear soldiers in the courtyard start a chant, calling my name. I exit the castle to find the space packed with troops.

Tears fill my eyes.

I turn to Holden. "Help me get to the middle."

"It is not going to be pretty." Bending down, he lifts me onto his shoulder.

I perch there, greeting each soldier we pass with the traditional warrior grip, until we reach the fountain in the middle. He sets me on the wall.

I lift my crown into the air. "Today, this is everyone's crown. We fought for each other and for this realm, and we were victorious. Long live Aubren."

The answering shouts fill my ears, and I throw my roses into the fountain. *This is for you, brothers.*

Making a path for my return to the hall, the soldiers chant my name. I enter the passageway and greet the advisors, generals, ring keepers, and judges. I usher them into the Grand Hall, and they sit at the front tables. The officers march in, filling the benches. I wind around the head table and take my seat, Quinn to my left and Holden on my right.

I lift my chalice. "Blessed be the Fae."

"Blessed be." The crowd replies.

The music starts, and servers pour in with bread, fruit, and meats. I watch everyone and their merriment and wonder if I could ever be happier. After the meal, the tables are cleared, and the players start a jig. I offer a hand to Quinn and then Holden. We round to the dance floor and begin the traditional fae jig. Everyone joins in, and we twist from arm to arm. Grabbing Quinn and Holden, I dance to the back of the room and out into the courtyard. We form a long line and twist through the castle, adding dancers on our way.

It is almost dawn when I say farewell to the last guests, soldiers drunk on wine who Kane corrals towards the barracks. Quinn on one arm and Holden on the other, I walk through the empty corridors, our footfalls echoing through the passageways. Holden and I say goodbye to Quinn at his room and proceed to the west wing.

Holden stops in front of his door, and I spin to face him as my guards proceed to my room. "I cannot believe it is almost dawn."

"Tonight was a most magnificent celebration. I do not think anyone shall soon forget it."

"It was perfect. I loved every minute. I cannot thank you enough for staying and supporting this cause, and me."

"I knew the second I saw you I would never leave this kingdom. You have a fire, a light within. And now everyone can see it." He touches the middle stone on my forehead.

My cheeks warm. "They are quite odd are they not?"

"They are perfect, just like you." He stares into my eyes.

I laugh. "No one has ever called me that before—stubborn or hot-headed, yes, but never perfect."

"I happen to think those are perfect qualities." He leans in, and before I know it, his lips press into mine.

They feel soft and warm and taste of wine. The pressure of his skin on mine is not too light or too hard, but just right, perfect. I feel I could be lost in his kiss forever. As he starts to pull away, I answer his kiss with another. His arms wrap around my waist, and I hook mine around his neck. My lips tingle as he ends the kiss. I smile, and his perfect, red lips form a smile as well.

How had I not noticed this perfect man right in front of me for months?

"I cannot tell what you are thinking."

I look into his blue eyes and bite my lip praying he loved the kiss as much as I. "I was thinking I enjoyed kissing you."

"It was quite a perfect kiss."

My heart sings with joy. "A perfect end to a perfect night, then?"

"It does not have to end. We could go see the sunrise from one of the peaks." Releasing me, he takes my hands.

"I think I will already sleep half the day."

"Then, I will let you sleep. Sweet dreams."

"Sweet dreams." I stand on my toes and kiss his cheek.

He holds my fingers till our arms can reach no farther. Dropping them, he blows a kiss.

"You are being silly."

"It is romantic, but I will blame it on the wine if any-one asks."

"I am sure there will be much talk tomorrow." I cut my eyes to my guards.

"Those are *our* guards." He winks.

I slip into my room and close the door. I rest my back on the soft wood. *Holden.*

It is a nice name. *Queen Titania could marry Holden.* I touch my lips where they still tingle from our kiss, trace my finger over the arrow on my forehead, and then move to the four jewels along my cheeks. Light catches my eye, and I look up to find sparkles on my western wall. Tracing the path, I realize the sun's first rays reflect off my crosses.

Yes, dear brothers, the perfect ending to the perfect celebration of your souls. You may rest in peace, for your sister has completed your quest, and she knows happiness.

<del>THE END</del>

UNTIL WE MEET AGAIN – READ ON FOR THE EXCITING EPILOGUE

Friend,

You've experienced a bit of the Fae Realm. Do you crave to know more? Join me as I share the story of the Fae.

Visit: http://bit.ly/DiscoveringFae to begin this exclusive journey of discovering the Fae.

I look forward to our first council.

Until we meet again,
Titania

P.S. Wondering what you will experience in our gatherings? Through a series of five electronic correspondences, i.e. e-mail only available on Upper Earth, we will explore Fae characters in fiction, Fae lore, and you will learn the whole story of our creation, purpose, abilities, and realm. This knowledge will only be shared with this assembly of truth seekers. Visit the website above to join us today.

Epilogue

I WAKE TO ALFREDA FLITTING around the room and smile. "Good morning."

"Good morning? You have slept until midafternoon. Quinn and Holden thought you might be dead."

I sit up. "Surely you are being theatrical."

"No, they wait in your sitting room." Her hands go to her cheeks. "Good grief, child! Your hair looks like a bird's nest."

"Yes, I will need some help with this I believe." I pat my head.

Even two ladies cannot release the tangles from my hair with combs, so I soak in the tub as the women spread oil through the locks.

With the knots finally released, I weave my hair into a braid.

Exiting my room, I wonder what we shall do now that the kobold stay trapped in Lower Earth. I berate myself for thinking how boring it will be to return to subjects such as crops and taxes. I open the door to the study and Quinn and Holden jump to their feet.

"We thought you may sleep forever. Are you hungry?" Holden slides a chair from under the table.

"I guess I will be eventually." I peer at Holden and Quinn, enjoying the sight of their creaseless faces. "What shall we do today? I am saddened that our celebration has ended."

Quinn lifts one eyebrow and cuts his eyes to Holden. "It does not have to be."

Holden rests his hands on the tabletop. "What if we go on a tour, a victory tour? Quinn and I have not seen all of Aubren. With nothing to fear of the kobold, there is no reason for us to not enjoy days of celebration with our people."

My heart beams at hearing Holden say *our* people. "I love this idea. Let us plan the tour at once."

Lifting a sheet of parchment, a pot of ink, and a quill from my side table, I write out our itinerary. I suggest we start with Westshire, thinking I would rather have Foster's home village out of the way sooner than later. We map out the journey and pen our proclamation. An hour later, we stride from my study, eager to have the notice copied and posted in every shire, village, and town of Aubren. I instruct Alfreda to prepare my luggage, and we gather my council for a dinner in the garden.

The advisors have much that I left unhandled with my occupation with the kobold of late, and we work late into the night. Still, I flit to my chamber full of energy to finish preparation for the trip. I remember the anchors in my closet and how another set needs to be secured after I lost one in Lower Earth. I set pen to paper and have a page deliver the note to Aleem. I am sure the Ring Keeper has already thought of such, but I will leave nothing to chance. I plan to procure the primary set from him before we leave the next morning. There would be nowhere safer for them to be than with Quinn, Holden, and me.

I work past midnight, finishing the chores, and climb exhausted, yet happy, into my bed.

WAKING, I ZIP OUT OF BED, dressing in my travelling clothes and nibbling on the pastry Alfreda left for me. I slide my blades in my boots and slide my bow and quiver on my back. I plan for there to be much time to shoot, ride horses across the countryside, fly over fields and mountains, celebrate, and dance with my fae. I check every corner of my room, ensuring everything is packed. Walking to my door, the light reflecting off one of my crystals catches my eye. They remind me of Mother, whom I have not seen since dinner last night.

Thinking I should visit her before we depart, I wind to her chamber. I find her sitting by the fire, take her hand, and lead her to the garden. I think to tell the whole story of what happened in Lower Earth, but the sun shines so brightly and the birds and butterflies flit here and there. *Why ruin such a beautiful day?* I have spent far too long focusing on what ifs. I must remember to enjoy the good. Meandering back to the castle, I leave her with Alfreda and Father, bidding them all farewell with hugs and kisses.

Quinn and Holden meet me at the carriage, and we make for the Ring Keeper's cabin. Aleem requires more persuasion than anticipated, but in the end allows me to travel with the anchors. I fit them in the inside pocket of my riding skirt, vowing to never be without them. We exit his cabin and load into our travelling coach.

Quinn slides in beside me with Holden opposite us. Gazing out the window at the forests as we ramble over the countryside, my mind drifts to thoughts of the future. For even though I had vowed not to think of the many questions, sitting with men, I cannot help but wonder. *Is Quinn happy? Will he be happy if I marry another? Would he stay? Am I wasting his life away here if he is to be replaced? Am I falling in love with Holden?*

Turning to Quinn, I place my hand on his leg. "Tell me, Quinn, are you happy here?"

"In this carriage with my best comrades? Of course." He sets his palm atop mine and squeezes my fingers. The smile spreading across his face looks nothing but genuine.

"No, I mean as heir presumptive. You were in the military before. Do you miss it?"

He chuckles. "You know how bad I am at archery. What do you think?"

I bump my shoulder to his. "Your skills improve every week. I am serious."

"Yes, I am. I liked my place in the military in Bedham but mostly because it kept me around young people. Tutors and council members tend to be older fae."

"Good." I squeeze and release his hand.

"Are you not going to ask Holden the same? You have kept him here, serving as your Fae at Arms, when he could be marrying a princess from another kingdom." Quinn's eyes cut to Holden. "Or perhaps he has fallen in love with this kingdom as well."

My cheeks warm. But worries ping my brain. Neither of us are truly free. I raise my chin. "I spoke with Holden yesterday. He made his choice, but he is free to do as he wishes."

Holden leans forward. "The Queen knows my desires."

Face flaming, I wave my hands in the air. "I promised myself not to worry with thoughts of the future on our victory holiday. Let us talk of Westshire and the celebration tonight."

I review our itinerary as well as meetings with judges and representatives. Before we know it, our carriage arrives on the outskirts of the shire. Farms dot the rolling hills, and we stop at each, gifting the young fae with small cakes from the castle. In the town, we are greeted with cheers. The square has been transformed to a festival, and after changing at the inn, we join the shire fae for dinner and dancing.

"Titania," a high pitch voice squeals my name, and I turn to find Nissa running towards me. She flings her arms around my legs.

I bend down and pick her up. "How have you been? You have grown since I last visited."

"Mother says I will be tall as her soon."

"I bet you will."

"Oh, my heavens! I am so sorry." Jasmine approaches, Matthew behind her. "Nissa, this is your Queen. You cannot be carried in her arms."

"I rather like it. Should we dance?" I set her down and lead her into the crowd.

I would much rather dance with this dear child than stay and try to find something to say to Foster's mother and father. But the song ends, and I must return Nissa to her parents. Plucking a flower from an arrangement on a table, I bend over and tuck it in her hair.

"It was good to see you. If you ever come to Capitolshire, you must visit me."

"Are you sure? Foster said you were not his friend anymore."

"Of course we are friends. All my soldiers are my friends." I stand and smooth my skirt.

Jasmine wraps her arms around me. "Thank you for keeping Foster safe. For all you have done for the kingdom."

"I am happy to be protector of this kingdom." Squeezing her shoulders, I slide out of the embrace.

The three bow, and I wish them well. And so the night goes, as does the next, as we make our way south, greeting judges, farmers, and all the fae along our route. I enjoy being on holiday with Quinn and Holden. I dance with each of them every evening, but after we retire to our rooms, Holden comes to mine. We talk deep into the night about everything: our childhoods, siblings, parents. He tells me of Hilbron and places he has visited and the army. Each night, he places a single kiss on my lips before we part. Every time, my lips tingle and heart flutters, and I fall asleep dreaming of traveling the world with Holden, seeing all the sights together.

As we make our way south, the celebrations grow larger and Narielshire, beside the south Faerie Ring, proves to be the biggest yet, complete with fireworks. As we are watching the lights explode overhead, Grant taps my arm and pulls me to the edge of the crowd where Regin waits. My breath catches in my throat, and my stomach turns at the sight of Nariel's Ring Keeper's pale face.

I swallow and spread my shoulders back. "Regin, are you well? Is there news?"

His eyes cut around us. "Not here. In my cabin."

Signaling for Quinn and Holden to join, our entourage walks away from the crowd and jumps into the air, following Regin to his home. Inside, he explains that the High Council set a schedule of opening the upper rings an hour a day to allow observation while limiting exposure.

"Regin, I know the strategy. Please, explain why you appear so ashen."

Wringing his hands, he divulges that the witches of the trinity are attempting to send Hunter's spirit into Lower Earth. "The Council ordered all the rings closed. I thought you would want to be briefed."

"Yes, thank you. Is there any more information? Do we know why?" My mind reels with worry. *Could we not just have one week of peace?*

"No, the council ordered the rings shut before Borean could learn more."

Why would they send Hunter's spirit to Lower Earth? There can only be one answer: He wants to end one of the evil spirits presiding there. But who and why? Images of Lucifer, Abaddon, and the dragon dart through my mind. There could be others. If the rings are not opened, the witches will never succeed in getting Hunter's soul into

Lower Earth. *Why would he risk it? For the same reason you would. His people.*

"Queen?" Holden's touch brings me out of my thoughts.

"We must help them. We must open the rings."

Regin shakes his head. "We cannot go against the High Council's decree. Opening the rings to Lower Earth puts this kingdom and Realm at risk. What if the kobold return? What if one of the evil spirits gains power here?"

"The spirits do not have power here unless we grant it. We can post the army at both the upper and lower rings to ensure the safety of our fae."

"What if this Hunter is evil himself? He has aligned himself with vampires. How much do we know of these witches? They could be helping the spirits of the deep. You have already put our kingdom in jeopardy once by aiding them." The Ring Keeper leans over his looking glass.

I straighten my back. "By assisting them in defeating Sonia? We have no idea what she is capable of. Helping them stop her was the right thing for this Realm."

"But you left, and the kobold attacked. You were not here when this kingdom most needed you."

"I came minutes later. And it was I who ended the kobold."

"You do not know whether Hunter and the others were successful in defeating Sonia. What if she is possessing him?"

"She is not. I saw him. His soul was made human. We cannot waste more time arguing. Open the rings to enable Hunter's spirit to pass to Lower Earth."

Regin raises his chin. "I will not have my rings opened."

I ball my fists. *I am Queen. He will follow my orders.* I have the anchors to the north ring. But I would require two sets, one for the upper ring and one for the lower. One set does me no good.

Quinn steps between us. "This is not helping anyone. We should summon Aleem, your Father, and the advisors. Will that appease both of you?"

Holden steps forward. "The Queen has ordered the rings open."

"Regin is the Keeper of the Ring for a reason. If he has doubts, we should gather more counsel." Eyes wide, Quinn looks at Regin then me.

"Fine, we shall all fly to the Daintree ring at once. Quinn, take guards to request Father and the advisors meet us there. Regin, bring your judges. Holden and guards, come with me."

I speed through the sky as fast as my wings will fly. Time moves askew from Upper Earth—their minute equals three hours of our time. Still, the witches will wear themselves out quickly using enough magick to send Hunter's spirit to Lower Earth. Their human bodies cannot withstand channeling that much power for long.

As I alight in Aleem's front garden, his door opens, and he steps outside. "I assume you have heard of the witches trying to cross to Lower Earth?"

"I have, and I want the rings opened to let them pass, but Regin refused, and Quinn suggested we seek counsel. Father and the advisors are on their way."

Regin and his judges arrive, and we follow Aleem inside, gathering around the glass viewer with Regin's First and Second Judge. With nothing to view, my leg bounces as we wait for the others to arrive. Under the table, Holden squeezes my hand. Wriggling my fingers from his grip, I smooth my hand down my skirt. I would much rather be wearing my riding pants and vest than this green frock with lace lining the collar. At least I have my blades and the anchors tucked in my boots.

Father, Quinn, and the six advisors squeeze into Aleem's study with us. I inform the newcomers what we have learned and state my position on helping Hunter and the trinity. I state Regin's concerns and, while admitting to their validity, outline how the dangers can be minimized. I address each of Regin's arguments, ending with the supposition that I sensed no evil within Hunter when we conversed in Italy.

Beside me, Holden straightens his back. "I side with the Queen. I also found Hunter and his comrades to be of true hearts and minds. I believe we should aid them. Our goals align with theirs. We all want to minimize the power of the evil spirits lurking in Lower Earth. And if Hunter thinks he can do that, we have a duty to help him. Who knows? He could be the one."

My skin tingles and goosebumps form. The ambience of the room shifts, as if someone has vacuumed all sensory information from the space. I have never heard the one mentioned aloud in a group of people. Yes, Father suggested I was that being, and I had spoken of it to Holden. But to have a fae utter the words in this venue somehow alters my perception. Before, the legend was just that, myth, rumor, folklore, stories told by mothers to soothe their children's fears. Now, the one feels tangible, real.

Quinn clears his throat. "You would side with Titania no matter what she said."

"That is not true. I believe Hunter fights to protect his people and that by doing so will help defend all the realms from evil."

"But if not for your love for her, you would not even be here. You are not an advisor. You serve at the mercy of your Queen."

As Father stands on my right and Holden on my left, my face flames with embarrassment. A pit forms in my stomach. *Could Quinn be jealous?* This is the first time I have heard him speak ill of Holden. "We should call other witnesses to attest to Hunter's nature. Grant and Timothy met Hunter."

Aleem has his page call for Grant and Timothy. Both testify they detected no hint of deceit or evil from his human form. Father questions how a human may be able to best an ethereal being. I counter, pointing out that he is of the archangel Michael's line. While Hunter seemed to be stripped of his connection to the divine, Michael's blood runs through Hunter's veins, and that perhaps he has regained his witch status. I review again how the rings need only be open for seconds.

Giving the men a few moments to reflect, I ask each to voice their thoughts.

Quinn favors adherence to the High Council's policy, and Regin reasserts the same.

The advisors each admit to being overwhelmed by the choice and so defer to the High Council ruling.

Aleem's eyes meet mine. At sixty-five, he is older than any fae in the kingdom's history.

I pray he sides with me.

He rubs his beard, and his eyes pan the room. "If it were any fae other than Titania requesting this, I would also side with the High Council. But I have witnessed her premonitions and dreams. Her instincts have not failed our kingdom, even when they have been contrary to traditional thinking. I will allow my ring to be opened for these beings."

I look at the First and Second Judge, and they assent to his opinion. Gripping the tabletop, I ask the last person in the room that may offer counsel. I hold his stare. "Father, what say you?"

"I have no authority here."

"If you were King?" I hold my breath, praying he sways to my side. With his approval, the advisors may also change their opinions.

"You have ascended to Queen for a reason, and I trust your judgment without question."

"Thank you, Father." I lay my hand atop his. "I would like to call for a vote. Are we in agreement that all around this table are worthy of this responsibility?"

I study Quinn, wondering if he will challenge Holden, a prince whose family has been burdened with ruling in our Realm for centuries. Except for being named heir presumptive, Holden outranks my cousin in the eyes of the Realm. I would rather not have to voice the fact.

Quinn's gaze locks on mine for a second.

Asking for a show of hands, I count Father, the six advisors, Aleem, his two judges, and Holden as in favor of aiding Hunter and the trinity. Quinn sides with Regin and his judges, but they are outnumbered eleven to four.

Pushing off the tabletop, I stand upright. I thank them for their time and consideration and ask Holden to assemble troops at the lower and upper Daintree rings. Our party walks outside to coordinate the portal openings. With soldiers at their stations within minutes, we open the top ring and bottom one seconds later. I hold my breath, praying I have been right about Hunter.

Hunter's ethereal form appears above the top portal and shoots straight down through the bottom portal into Lower Earth. We order the bottom ring closed and shuffle inside to use the glass to find the witches aiding him. Hunter's body lies in a circle of seven witches, linked by hand, in a penthouse room in Los Angeles. I recognize Alena and Camille, the other two witches of the trinity.

Alena's eyes dance behind her lids and pop open.

A second later, Camille's do as well.

"Send us. You have to send us as well. Hunter needs us," Alena pleads.

With the consent of the others, Alena and Camille lie on each side of Hunter. I dash outside, signaling to open the portals again.

Alena's and Camille's ethereal forms hover above the top opening and dart through to the lower portal and vanish. With heavy heart, I call for the soldiers to close the opening. The best we can do is pray the witches above have linked to the trinity and will know when to call them out. I dash inside to watch for signs the three wish to return to Upper Earth. I grip the glass top, remembering the vast darkness, the cold air, the nothingness of Lower Earth, praying Alena, Camille, and Hunter will achieve their goal and be returned to Upper Earth in safety. Images of the dragon, the feel of her fiery breath on my face. *Her? I wonder where that thought came from?*

A change in the witches' chant brings me out of my thoughts. I rush outside and order the bottom ring opened. Camille holds Alena tight to her chest as the female witches ascend through the portal to Upper Earth. My heart races. *Where is Hunter?* I rush to the lower ring and peer over the rim. I find a speck of light below. It floats one way then another. *Is he lost? Dead?* Kneeling, I lean as far over as I dare, trying to confirm the form to be Hunter.

Someone grips my arm. "Do not even think of entering Lower Earth."

Holden. "But what if he is hurt? He could be trapped there forever."

"The witches will find his lifelines or they will not. We cannot control this now."

"But what if he is the one prophesied to end all evil and the evil ones consume him?"

A smile forms on Holden's face. "What if there are many *ones* who fight to stop the evil before them?"

<del>THE END</del>
UNTIL WE MEET AGAIN

A Note From the Author

I'm thrilled you chose to embark on this journey into middle earth with Titania and her fae. If you loved this story and are ready to head topside, there is more to explore in the *Kingdom Journals Series*. Meet Alena, Camille, and Hunter, and learn their stories in *Kingdom of Embers*, *Kingdom of Darkness*, *Kingdom of Honor*, and *Kingdom of War*. As a bonus for you, here's a link to read *Kingdom of Embers*, the first book in the complete series, FREE.

Visit: https://BookHip.com/JTVZRH

Audiobook listener? Find the *Kingdom Journals* audiobooks at https://triciacopeland.com/audio/

If you're dying to know more about Sonia and her early life, *Of Witches and Vampires* finds her mother, Lilith, challenged to raise not one, but two sets of special beings alone. You can read this short story also FREE.

Visit: https://BookHip.com/NRNPXH

Want even more? The *Kingdom Journals* prequel, *Kingdom of the Damned*, traces Sonia's history from the sixteenth to twentieth centuries.

I believe in finding magick and aim to write stories that show what is possible when one commits to finding their own version of magick. Whether transforming hearts, lives, numbers, ideas, art, music, or simply enjoying nature, we emanate magick every day. To find a few more slices of magick fly to my website to browse all my titles including YA dystopian and NA and college romances at **www.triciacopeland.com**. Sign up for my newsletter, browse trailer videos, download playlists, and more on my website. Also find all my social media links so you'll know where to reach me when I'm not out enjoying sunny trails.

Happy reading & happy listening!
Tricia

More about Tricia…

Tricia lives with her family and four-legged friends in Colorado. She believes in finding magic in every aspect of our lives and world. Her stories ranging from romance, urban fantasy, and dystopian sci-fi, include characters with rich diverse backgrounds who strive to emulate goodness in their worlds. You can find all her books, including romances like *Deepest Scars* and the *Being Me Series*, at www.triciacopeland.com.